3 013

D0998121

June Ta[...]
years of [...]
to Soutl[...]
After le[...]
several years working on cruise [...] [...] Queen [...] [...] on the *Mauretania*, meeting many Hollywood film stars and VIPs on her travels. After her marriage to an airline pilot, she lived in Sussex and Hampshire before moving to Estoril in Portugal. June, who has two adult daughters, now lives in Sussex. For more fascinating information about June Tate and her novels, don't miss the additional material in the back of this book.

Praise for June Tate's well-loved novels:

'Tate has a marvellous grasp of the subtleties and complexities of human relationships. Her books are always guaranteed to touch the hearts of her readers'
Lancashire Evening Post

'High hopes and heartache share top billing in this compulsive read' *Northern Echo*

'A thoroughly enjoyable book' *Bournemouth Daily Echo*

'A heartrending tale' Gilda O'Neill

'Tate's romantic sagas are always uplifting so look no further for a good, old-fashioned read' *Wigan Evening Post*

'A cracking read with an urgent page-turning drive'
Coventry Evening Telegraph

'An engaging saga that recaptures its era with judicious use of telling details' *Historical Novels Review*

TALK OF THE TOWN

June Tate

headline

First published in 2007 by
HEADLINE PUBLISHING GROUP

First published in paperback in 2008 by
HEADLINE PUBLISHING GROUP

1

Cataloguing in Publication Data is available from the British Library

ISBN 978 0 7553 2968 7

Typeset in Sabon by Palimpsest Book Production,
Grangemouth, Stirlingshire

Printed and bound in Great Britain by
Clays Ltd, St Ives plc

Headline's policy is to use papers that are natural, renewable and
recyclable products and made from wood grown in
sustainable forests. The logging and manufacturing processes
are expected to conform to the environmental
regulations of the country of origin.

HEADLINE PUBLISHING GROUP
An Hachette Livre UK Company
338 Euston Road
London NW1 3BH

www.headline.co.uk
www.hachettelivre.co.uk

For my elder daughter, Beverley, who gives me
unconditional love and despite working long
hours and looking after a family home gives me
something even more precious – her time.
These are golden moments in my life!

With love to my skydiving younger daughter, Maxine, who is exploring South America on her own. I applaud and admire her adventurous spirit, but I am a mother . . . so I worry!

CHAPTER ONE

Spring 1920

Tilly Thompson was a wild child. At school she was always getting into scrapes when she couldn't refuse a dare from her friends. 'You go where angels fear to tread and one day it will get you into trouble,' her mother would warn her. But it didn't seem to stop her escapades. She had flashing green eyes and hair the colour of autumn leaves, and was typical of a redhead with her quick temper and fiery nature, but she didn't ever hold a grudge. Her outbursts would soon be over and life would go on as before.

Now that she was a young lady of nineteen, not much had changed. The spirit of adventure was just channelled into other things. She would ride her sit up and beg bicycle for miles, sometimes with a friend but often on her own. Although she loved the company of others, she also enjoyed the times when she was free, alone with her own thoughts.

The Thompsons were a working-class family. Her father, Joe, worked for a brewery in Southampton, delivering barrels of beer on a large horse-drawn cart pulled by Clarence, a big shire, who was always resplendent in glittering horse brasses. Joe was proud of his trusty steed and made sure he was turned out perfectly every day as they left the brewer's yard.

Ethel, her mother, worked as a maid in the household of a local solicitor. Tilly's two sisters were married and had moved away, which left her brother Jago, who was a butcher, living at home with Tilly and their parents. Jago was four years older than Tilly and watched over his youngest sister with a careful eye.

'You're not my keeper, our Jago!' she would exclaim if he ever took her to task over some misdemeanour.

'Someone has to keep you in check,' he would say. 'Dad and Mum are so busy, they don't have the time. I do.'

'It's time you found a wife and got your own home, then I would have some peace!'

He would just laugh at her suggestion. 'Why would I want to do that when there are so many young women anxious to be seen out with me?'

'You're too full of yourself. You think you're the answer to every woman's dreams. Well, to me you're just a nightmare!'

Jago was a good-looking lad and it was true,

he did have his pick of the local females, but Tilly wouldn't ever have told him that. The two siblings were good friends beneath their constant banter, and on occasion she would spend an evening with him when he would take her to the Palace of Variety to see a show. At other times, she would go to one of the local dance halls with her friends. She was a good dancer and she loved doing the Charleston. She was never without a partner.

She worked in Madam Leone's, a local gown shop, which satisfied her love of fashion. She was an excellent saleswoman with her ready charm, and regular clients would ask for her, knowing that if they asked her opinion, she would be honest.

'Well, Mrs Stanton, the cut is very flattering but the colour doesn't do anything for your lovely complexion. Why not try this one?' she would say, producing another dress.

She saved her money and bought a garment when she could afford to. She loved the dropped waistline and the handkerchief hems which were all the rage, worn with long necklaces and drop earrings. She even experimented with a cigarette in a long holder, but she didn't like the taste of tobacco much, and she found the holder awkward to handle. She had almost taken the eye out of one young man at a dance when she turned quickly. After that she decided to do without.

She had recently had her glorious hair cut short in the latest style, much to the consternation of her mother.

'Oh, Tilly! Why did you have your hair cut? Her hair is a woman's crowning glory and yours was so beautiful.'

'Oh, Mum, it was so old-fashioned. I haven't had it as short as an Eton crop, just a nice bob. Why don't you have yours done?'

'Your father would kill me. He loves my long hair,' said Ethel. 'Besides, it wouldn't do in my position.'

'I bet Mrs Bradbury has hers short.'

'Yes she does,' she admitted, 'but I can't look the same as my employer. It wouldn't do at all.'

'It wouldn't show under your maid's cap.'

'Then what would be the point? No thanks, love. Besides, it's for the young, not old married women like me.' And she wouldn't be persuaded.

However, Tilly's best friend, Beth Pearson, who worked in a store in the haberdashery department, was convinced. Tilly went with her to a local hairdresser one Wednesday afternoon, which was their half-day. She watched as the golden tresses fell to the floor and the assistant Marcel-waved Beth's hair with hot tongs. Tilly was impressed as she twisted the irons adroitly, shaping waves into the hair, and when she had

4

finished the girls were very pleased with the results.

'How on earth am I going to do it myself?' asked Beth.

'Just shampoo it, comb the waves into place and then hold them there with these.' The hairdresser showed her a metal wave grip. 'Look,' she said, squeezing the top of the clip, opening it into two halves with serrated edges. 'Place this over the crest of the wave until your hair dries. Don't forget to make a pin curl with the ends over your ears. Hold it in place with a kirby grip.'

The girls left the salon and went window-shopping.

'I heard our Jago talking about a new club that has recently opened. Why don't we get the others together and try it on Saturday evening?'

The others she referred to were a few friends, male and female, who used to meet together for either dancing or picnics, when they would cycle off to a nearby beach on a Sunday, when the weather was fine.

'What's this club called and where is it?'

'The Blue Pelican, in Bernard Street.'

Beth frowned. Bernard Street was near the docks, an area that could be a little suspect at night. 'Do you think that's a good idea?'

'Oh, come on, Beth. It isn't as if we were going

alone. The boys will be with us. Jago wouldn't go there if it was dodgy.'

In this assumption, Tilly was mistaken. Jago was very much a man about town. He had no compunction about visiting 'the fleshpots', wherever they were situated.

Beth eventually agreed and before the following Saturday they had spoken to their friends, Jack, Ted, Harry and Marie, who agreed to try out the club.

On Saturday evening at eight o'clock, the group all met outside Holy Rood Church and made their way to the Blue Pelican club, which was situated between two old Victorian houses. Outside were two small conifers in tubs on either side of the entrance.

Once inside they paid their entrance fee at a small reception desk. They signed their names in a book and walked in through the open glass doors. The room was large: to their right was a long bar, while to the left chairs and tables with small table lamps surrounded a dance floor. There was a small stage where a band of six musicians was playing 'Alexander's Ragtime Band'. Wall lights gave the place an intimate atmosphere.

'This looks all right,' Tilly remarked as the six of them sat down.

The friends all pooled their money on such outings and one of the boys was the treasurer, so when the waiter took their order it was Jack who paid for the drinks. The band struck up another number, and they all got up to dance.

Eddie Chapman, the owner of the club, was standing by the bar looking around for new faces when he spotted Tilly, who was dancing the Charleston with Jack.

'Hello,' he muttered to himself as he watched her. 'Where did she come from, I wonder?'

A little later that evening, he walked over to the table to greet the newcomers.

'Good evening. I'm Eddie Chapman. I just want to welcome you to my club. I do hope you are all having a good time.'

Tilly looked at him with interest. He was tall and well built, with broad shoulders and slender hips, smooth dark hair and brown eyes. There was something about him, a presence that seemed to fill the area around him, but his smile was sincere.

'Thank you,' said Jack. 'We're enjoying ourselves.'

'I like the band,' said Tilly. 'They're really very good.'

'I saw you dancing,' he said, gazing into her eyes. 'You're very good at the Charleston.'

'It's my favourite dance,' she said, beaming at him.

The band started to play. 'How are you at the tango?' he asked, as he recognised the music.

'Not bad.'

Holding out his hand he asked, 'May I have this dance?'

Before she realised what she was doing, Tilly rose from her seat as if mesmerised. Taking his hand, she walked on to the floor.

Eddie held her close, and they began. He was an excellent dancer. In his firm hold she was able to follow his steps. She felt the excitement mounting inside her as he interpreted the passion of the music with his body and his feet, making her do the same as he twisted her, turned her and dipped her backwards in time to the music. Never had she enjoyed dancing so much. When the music stopped, she was surprised to see the floor had cleared of other dancers; they were all standing watching the superb display.

Tilly felt her cheeks flush with embarrassment when she realised she had been the centre of attention. The colour deepened at the enthusiastic applause which was forthcoming.

'My goodness, I didn't realise we were alone on the dance floor,' she said.

Still holding her close, he said, 'You were stunning. You followed my every step.' Then he walked her back to the table, and held her chair for her to sit.

'Thank you, young lady. I don't know when I have enjoyed dancing the tango as much.' He looked at the others. 'Enjoy the rest of the evening.' To Tilly he said, 'I hope you will come here again.' And he walked away.

'Blimey!' Beth exclaimed. 'That was some exhibition. He's gorgeous.'

'He's dangerous,' said Jack.

'Whatever do you mean?' asked Tilly. 'He was a perfect gentleman.'

'I'm not saying he wasn't, but there's something about the man. I wouldn't like to get on the wrong side of him.'

Tilly glanced across the room and met the gaze of Eddie Chapman, who just stared at her. Then slowly he winked. She turned away quickly.

Jack was right. There was something about the man, but he was fascinating. She could still feel his strong arms round her. His touch had thrilled her, his dancing even more. He had a certain magnetism about him that she found irresistible. And she wanted to dance with him again.

Eddie didn't approach her for the rest of the night and when it was time for them to leave he was nowhere to be seen. She was disappointed.

*   *   *

The following day, over Sunday lunch, Jago asked her what she had done the night before.

'You all went dancing, I suppose,' he said, knowing her well.

'Yes, as a matter of fact we did. The six of us went to the Blue Pelican club.'

'You went where?'

'The Blue Pelican. I heard you talking about it so we decided to give it a try.'

'It's no place for you and your friends,' he said sharply.

'Why ever not? It seemed all right to me. We had a few drinks and danced. The band was excellent.'

'It's run by a man called Eddie Chapman. Not a man I would want my sister to know.'

'Why?'

'Just take my word for it. Did you see him there?'

'I have no idea who he is so how would I know?' she lied.

'Just keep clear, that's all. Don't let me catch you going there again.'

Tilly for once was silent. But she was very curious about the man who had held her in his arms so closely. She would have to find out about him somehow, because now she was intrigued.

CHAPTER TWO

Ethel Thompson arrived at the rear entrance of the Bradburys' house and, opening the door, stepped into the kitchen. It was seven o'clock in the morning and the cook was already there preparing the breakfast that was to be served at eight o'clock on the dot. Gerald Bradbury was a stickler for time. If his son, Simon, was late he went without. His wife always had hers served in bed on a tray.

'Good morning, Cook,' said Ethel. 'Everything all right?'

Cook grimaced. 'The old man is not in a good mood,' she said. 'Young Simon came home last night the worse for wear apparently, which didn't please his father. They had words this morning and Simon slammed out of the house just after I arrived.'

'Oh, dear. But, you know, the boy is just feeling his feet. At nineteen it's to be expected.'

'Not according to his father.'

Hanging up her coat, Ethel picked up the waiting cutlery from the side and went into the dining room to lay the table. She loved the elegance of the large room with its heavy flocked wallpaper, and the rich velvet drapes at the window. She dusted off the dark oak table before putting out the place mats and the cutlery. She moved the candelabra from the centre of the table and placed two large silver mats in readiness for the coffee pot. Then she took the three silver serving dishes from the sideboard to the kitchen, where Cook placed the bacon in one, the scrambled eggs in another and the devilled kidneys in the last one. Ethel returned the dishes to the dining room and replaced them alongside the two toast racks that were already there.

Taking a duster from the pocket of her dress, she quickly flicked it over the furniture and round the pot holding the aspidistra, resplendent on a tall plinth. On a side table stood a domed glass case containing a stuffed owl sitting on a branch with artificial leaves sprouting from it. Ethel always felt sad when she dusted this receptacle, knowing that the beautiful bird once flew free in the skies above.

She laid two places in case Simon returned in time for breakfast, then collected the mail from the mat at the front door, putting it beside the setting at the head of the table where Gerald Bradbury always sat.

Once everything was in readiness in the dining

room, Ethel returned to the kitchen and lifted the tray that Cook had prepared for the mistress of the house and took it upstairs. Knocking on the bedroom door, Ethel entered the room and, putting the tray down on a side table, opened the curtains.

'Good morning, madam,' she said. 'It's a nice day today.'

There was a murmuring from Dorothy Bradbury as she sat up in bed. 'Good morning,' she said and waited for Ethel to position the bed table in front of her. On this Ethel carefully placed the tray before leaving the room.

Ethel didn't have a lot of time for Mrs Bradbury. She thought she was lazy and arrogant. She looked down on the staff, which was obvious to them whenever she spoke to them. There was always a condescending note in her voice which made Ethel's hackles rise. She didn't ever show this, but carried on about her work as usual. Yet beneath this quiet exterior, she dearly wanted to slap the woman.

Whenever the Bradburys held a dinner, Ethel was in attendance, in a black dress, a small white frilly apron and a matching headpiece. It was on these occasions that she was privileged to hear the gossip exchanged between friends and business colleagues. It always amazed her that the folk sitting round the table could forget that a member of the staff was in the room. Servants were just part of the furnishings to them. She thought it was typical of moneyed people.

She knew which businesses in the town were doing well and which were in trouble. She had been surprised to hear gossip bandied around about unhappy marriages between prominent townsfolk, and the previous week, having heard Tilly and Jago mention it, she had listened intently to the discussion about the owner of the new Blue Pelican nightclub.

'He seems financially secure,' Gerald had remarked. 'The brewery and the wine merchants he deals with are all getting paid on time, but there is a whisper that he mixes with a few undesirables in the town.'

'Who do you mean?' asked someone.

'The Williams brothers,' said their host.

Ethel's ears pricked up at the name. The Williams brothers were identical twins, known in the town for dealing in prostitution and illegal gambling.

'What's Chapman's connection with them?' another man asked.

'Nobody seems to know. The police are happy with the way the club is being run. The chief inspector himself told me that only last week. They kept a strict eye on the place when it first opened, of course, but there seems to be no hanky panky going on.'

'It doesn't sound good though,' said the first man. 'Any association with the Williamses is bad news.'

Like all the information she gathered on such occasions, Ethel Thompson kept this to herself.

Simon Bradbury slipped into the kitchen by the back door when his father had left for the office. He put an arm round the cook's shoulder and asked, 'Any breakfast left, Cook, dear?'

Young Simon was a favourite of Cook's and she beamed at him. 'You're a bad lad upsetting your father like that, but go on, sit down. I'll warm something up for you from what's left. Can't waste good food.'

Simon sat at one end of the long kitchen table and said, 'I don't know what I'd do without you.'

'Now then, young man, none of that old flannel with me. I'm too old in the tooth to be taken in by such flattery.' But she smiled happily to herself nevertheless.

Both Cook and Ethel sat at the table to have their breakfast.

'So where did you go last night, you young monkey?' enquired Cook.

He took a long drink of his coffee before answering. 'I went to the Blue Pelican club with some friends.'

Ethel became very interested. 'What's it like?' she asked.

'It's really good. The band is fantastic, and they play all the latest jazz numbers that are great to dance to.'

'Did you meet the owner?' she asked.

'No, but one of my friends pointed him out to me. Seems like a nice bloke. Well dressed, efficient. He was watching everything closely, I did notice that.'

'Decent crowd, were they?' Ethel asked casually.

'Yes. I saw quite a lot of the young blood from the town – you know, from decent families – and a few older people too. The owner was talking to two men who looked like twins, but they didn't stay for very long.'

Again the connection, thought Ethel. How interesting. And she wondered what was going on between the three men.

Whilst this conversation was taking place in the Bradburys' kitchen, Eddie Chapman was in his office above the club, going over his books. He was very pleased with himself. The club was doing well. The bar was making good money and the club was full most evenings, except Mondays when it was closed. Monday was always a dead night so it would have cost more to keep it open. Chapman was too shrewd a businessman to lose money, and a night off was good for his staff and him too. It enabled him to take time off to do other things.

He liked watching horse racing, which he was able to do as the club was only open in the evenings, enabling him to go to race meetings within a reasonable distance of the town. He enjoyed a flutter and was a good judge of horse-flesh, and was usually a lucky gambler, making a lot of money most of the time. When he did lose, it was only an amount that he had budgeted for. He wasn't a fool like some who, when they lost, doubled up on the next bet. He had seen many a man leave a race meeting penniless. That wasn't for him. He calculated every move in his life.

He sat and thought about a business proposition put to him by the Williams brothers. They wanted to open a gambling club and wondered if he was interested in becoming a partner. He neither liked nor trusted the brothers, but he had told them he would think about it. But if he was to have anything to do with such a club, he mused, he could open one on his own. Why would he want to be in partnership with them? Of course, if he were to go it alone, he would meet with great animosity from the Williamses, which could be dangerous. For the time being, he decided, he would do nothing. He had a finger in a few pies other than his nightclub, which were bringing in a nice return, and for the moment he would be satisfied with that.

Tilly had been restless ever since her visit to the Blue Pelican. She kept thinking about the handsome owner, and the way they had danced together. It had been a thrilling experience, and one that for her was unforgettable. She had to keep reminding herself that for him it would have meant absolutely nothing and he had probably not given their meeting another thought.

On her half-day, she packed some sandwiches and a flask of tea and took off on her bicycle for Netley beach, wearing a woollen cardigan and a scarf around her head. When she arrived she found, to her great relief, that the beach was almost empty, except for a lone man sitting on a wooden groyne draped with seaweed, looking out to the horizon. He seemed lost in thought and she settled down to eat her lunch.

Whilst she ate, she amused herself by studying the stranger. He was very good-looking in a manly way: strong features, broad shoulders. His fair hair was neatly cut, and when he glanced her way she saw that his eyes were wide apart, which would please her grandmother, who never trusted a man whose eyes were too close together.

When she had eaten most of her sandwiches, she saw that the stranger on the shore had got to his feet and was throwing stones into the sea, making them skim across the water. Interested, she stood up and walked slowly towards him so she could watch.

He turned and saw her standing nearby. 'Good afternoon,' he said in a deep, melodic voice.

'Hello,' said Tilly, walking closer. 'I've always wanted to be able to do that and you make it look so easy.'

'It is,' he said. 'Look, I'll show you.' He demonstrated, explaining how to throw the stones, then held one out to her. 'You try.'

To her delight, after the first few dismal attempts she managed to skim one for quite a distance. She clapped her hands with glee. 'I can't wait to show my brother. He always said I was useless at this. Won't he be surprised.'

The stranger held out his hand. 'David Strickland,' he said.

Shaking his hand, she answered, 'Tilly Thompson, maiden of this parish.'

Laughing, he said, 'Originally I'm from Bournemouth, but I'm a seaman so I'm a traveller now.'

'How exciting. Which ship are you on?'

'The *Aquitania*. We sail to New York and back. A large ferry really.'

'Hardly! Do you meet many famous people?'

she asked, knowing that several film stars crossed the Atlantic on the liners.

'Good heavens no!' he said, laughing. 'I'm an engineer so most of the time I'm in the engine room in the bowels of the ship, or in my cabin.' Seeing the disappointment on her face he added, 'After dinner I do walk the decks to get some fresh air, and then sometimes I see some of the passengers. Last trip Douglas Fairbanks and his new wife, Mary Pickford, were walking around too. Mr Fairbanks actually said "Good evening" to me.'

She was thrilled. 'They were only married quite recently. What did they look like?'

'Just like everyone else, really. They are only ordinary people, after all.'

'Far from it!' she exclaimed. 'I am ordinary people, they are famous film stars.'

'Well yes, if you put it like that. He did look splendid in a dinner jacket and she was wearing some floaty kind of dress. She's very pretty.'

'Tell me about New York,' she asked eagerly.

'It's a big noisy city. Lots of people, lots of shops. Many different nationalities. It seems to me that nearly all the policemen are Irish. I don't think there can be many Irish folk left in Ireland. There are ghettos all over the city: German town, where the Germans mainly live; Little Italy; and of course Chinatown.'

'I read about prohibition. Is it strange not being able to drink there?'

'Believe me, you can drink. There are places called speakeasies where liquor is sold in teacups. Strange but true.'

'What about gangsters?' she asked, eyes wide with curiosity.

He hid a smile. 'I have never met Al Capone, of course. The Mafia are supposed to run these places, but as far as I know I've never seen any of them.'

For the next hour, she plied him with questions about his travels, New York fashions, and his life at sea, listening intently to his answers. Eventually she said, 'How lucky you are to have seen so much.'

'You forget about the many hours I spend below, covered in oil, perspiration dripping off me. It isn't all fun, you know.'

'No, I suppose not. When do you sail again?'

'Not for another ten days. I'm on leave right now.'

'But you're not spending it in Bournemouth?'

Shaking his head, he explained, 'No. My father is also away at sea, on the *Mauretania*, and Mum got lonely so she moved back to Liverpool to be with her family. Now tell me about you. I've been talking about myself for ages.'

She pulled a face. 'Who I am is very dull in comparison.' She told him about her family and her place of work. 'It's my half-day and I decided I wanted to be alone. I love coming here. I love the sea; it seems to be such a calm place. Well, here anyway.'

'You should be on board in a storm; calm is the last thing it is. The ship rolls from one side to the other. Sometimes I'm covered in bruises from being thrown against the bulkhead.'

'Oh, dear. I never thought of that. Isn't it frightening?'

'You get used to it.'

They sat quietly tossing pebbles, both lost in their own thoughts for a while.

'What do you like to do for relaxation, Tilly?'

'I cycle a lot but I really love to dance and I enjoy that more than anything else. My brother, Jago, sometimes takes me to the Palace to see a variety show. I like that too.'

'Some of the other engineers were talking about a new club called the Blue Pelican. Do you know anything about it?'

'I was there with some friends a couple of Saturdays ago,' she told him. 'It's very nice and the band is great. It has a dance floor, not really big, but big enough.'

'Would you like to go there with me this evening, Tilly?'

She gazed at the young man. There was something very likeable about him. The expressive blue eyes and his smile suggested both humour and kindness, and she felt she would be safe in his company.

'I'd love to,' she said.

'Perhaps we could meet and go for a meal earlier in the evening and end up at the club, what do you think?'

'That would be lovely, David.'

'Would you like me to call for you?'

Remembering that Jago had forbidden her to visit the club again, she said, 'No. I'll meet you outside Holy Rood Church about seven o'clock. Is that all right?'

'Yes, fine.' He rose to his feet and pulled her up as well. 'I have to go now, but I'll see you later.'

He picked up his jacket from the pebbles and a hat that was hidden from sight beneath it. Only then did Tilly realise he was wearing his uniform. How splendid he looked in it too, with its gold braid trimmings.

As she cycled home, Tilly thought how much she had enjoyed her time on the shore with David Strickland. What an interesting man he was. As they were going to the Blue Pelican, she hoped he was a good dancer too. How awful it would be if such a great-looking man had two left feet! She wondered also if she would see the club owner again. What a fascinating evening it would be!

CHAPTER THREE

Tilly dressed carefully for her assignation, choosing an emerald green dress which was a perfect foil for her auburn locks. She chose a long necklace of black and crystal beads with matching earrings, and twirled in front of the mirror, pleased with her reflection. She had cleaned her black shoes with the bar across her ankle. She still wondered how good a dancer David was, but thought no one could be as good as Eddie Chapman.

Placing a black-fringed shawl around her shoulders, she walked downstairs. Her mother was absent as the Bradburys were giving a dinner party. Joe was sitting in his favourite armchair smoking his pipe and reading the paper. Jago was fixing his tie in front of the mirror over the fireplace. When he saw Tilly's reflection behind him he turned to look at her.

'My word, you've pulled out all the stops tonight. Who's this in aid of, might I ask?'

Tossing her head, she said, 'No you may not,

so mind your own business! I won't be late, Dad,' she called as she sailed out of the house.

As she walked down the road towards Holy Rood, she was certain that if her brother knew she planned to go to the Blue Pelican this evening he would be furious. He hasn't the right to run my life, she thought as she stepped out.

She saw David Strickland waiting as she turned the corner into the high street. She thought he looked very smart in a dark grey suit and white shirt. She noticed the sheen on his shoes. He had obviously spent a lot of time cleaning them. This pleased her, as she liked men to care about their appearance. As he turned towards her and smiled, she thought how terrific he looked in civilian clothes as well as in uniform. How jealous her girlfriends would be if they could see her!

Stepping towards her, David said, 'Tilly! How lovely you look.'

'Thank you. You look very nice yourself.'

He took her arm. 'I thought we would go to the Tivoli restaurant, then we can get a taxi to the club later. Is that all right with you?'

'It sounds fine,' she said, and they started walking up the high street towards the archway in the centre of the Bargate, an old building which had once been the entrance to the city, beyond which was the area called Above Bar.

A little later they were seated at a table in the Tivoli, where they ordered from the menu and David asked for a bottle of wine. Whilst they waited, Tilly again plied him with questions about life at sea and the city of New York.

'There are women among the crew too, you know.'

'What do they do?'

'There are stewardesses who look after the cabins and the lady passengers and then there are girls who act as nursemaids and nannies looking after children.'

'How marvellous.' Then, frowning, she added, 'What would happen if they got seasick and couldn't work?'

'The doctor on board would give them something to settle their stomachs. You soon get used to the motion of the Atlantic.'

'Were you ever ill?'

Shaking his head, he said, 'Fortunately not. I found my sea legs right away.'

Tilly found David easy to talk to and liked his sense of humour. He amused her with tales of his travels until eventually it was time to leave. He paid the bill and ordered a taxi.

As the vehicle drew up outside the Blue Pelican, Tilly found that her heart was racing with excitement and anticipation. Would Eddie Chapman be there?

She didn't have long to wait for an answer because she saw him getting into a car as she stepped out on to the pavement. A feeling of disappointment engulfed her. But as David took her arm and led her into the club, she thought how very foolish she was being. Here she was being escorted by a charming and handsome man, who was a great companion, so what on earth was she thinking of?

The evening was very enjoyable. David was a good dancer after all, and knew all the latest steps, which he had learned in New York. He was able to teach her the Bunny Hop, the latest craze.

They sat back at their table, exhausted.

'That was such fun,' said Tilly. 'I'll be able to teach the Bunny Hop to my friends. They'll be thrilled.'

David made his excuses and left her to visit the gents. Tilly was sitting quietly alone watching the other dancers when she felt a light touch on her shoulder.

'How nice to see you again.' She immediately recognised the mellifluous voice of Eddie Chapman.

'Hello, Mr Chapman. How are you?'

'I'm fine, thank you. May I sit here until your escort returns?'

'Certainly.'

'I wondered if you would return to the club,' he said.

'Did you?' she asked with surprise and pleasure. 'You meet so many people, I'm amazed that you would remember me.'

'How could I forget the girl who danced the tango so well?'

She felt the colour flush her cheeks. 'You are too kind.'

At that moment David Strickland returned and Eddie relinquished his seat, introducing himself to the young man. 'Would you mind if I asked your young lady for a dance?' he said.

David looked at him, then at Tilly. 'I have no objection, but I think the decision must rest with the lady herself.' He raised his eyebrows at Tilly.

'If you really don't mind,' she said, feeling unable to miss the opportunity.

David stood up politely as she rose from her seat. The band was paying a slow foxtrot. Once more, Tilly felt Eddie's hand in the small of her back, pulling her close to him, then his fingers clasped hers as they began.

Again they drifted effortlessly across the floor in time to the music. Tilly felt as if her feet barely touched the floor as they traversed the room. It was like being in a different world and she lost herself to the melody.

As the music stopped, Eddie held her close for just a second longer and stared into her eyes. She was sure that had he not been holding her, her legs would have given way.

'You are an extraordinary young woman,' he said quietly. Then he released her, led her back to the table, thanked David, and walked away.

For a moment she was absolutely speechless. Then she saw that David Strickland was watching her closely.

'You two have met before,' he remarked.

'Only once, when my friends and I came here for the first time.'

'Did you dance with him then?'

'As a matter of fact I did. We danced the tango together. Why?'

'You dance together like a couple who have done so for a very long time.'

She didn't know what to say. 'He leads well and I just follow his steps, that's all.'

At that moment she saw a familiar figure walking towards their table. 'Jago!' she exclaimed.

He stopped and with a look of thunder asked, 'What are you doing here, Tilly?'

Ignoring his outburst, she said, 'David, I would like you to meet my brother, Jago.'

David stood up and asked, 'Is there something wrong?'

Jago looked at him and said, 'I told my sister to keep away from this place.'

David smiled. 'Why don't you join us and we can discuss it.' He called the waiter over and asked Jago what he would like to drink.

With little choice, Tilly's brother sat down and asked for a beer. He looked at David and said, 'I don't think this is a good place for my sister to visit, that's all.'

'I can assure you she is perfectly safe with me, you know. And to be absolutely honest, I've not seen any reason for your concern. The place is well run, and the clientele is all right. There are no rough people here; they all look very respectable.'

'It's the owner who's suspect,' said Jago. 'There's something about him that worries me. I don't want him near my sister.'

Tilly looked imploringly at David. Please don't tell him we danced, her look said.

'I'm sure you have nothing to worry about,' said David. 'And if you don't mind, I would like this dance with your sister?'

Jago just shrugged. David stood up and held out his hand to her, and she took it gratefully.

As he held her in his arms, Tilly said, 'Thank you for not telling my brother that I danced with the owner.'

'Maybe your brother knows something that you don't,' he said. 'Perhaps it would be wise to listen to him – he seems like a sound bloke.'

'He tries to run my life for me,' she complained, 'and I'm perfectly able to do that for myself.'

'He's only looking out for you. I would do the same if I had a sister.'

Over his shoulder she saw Eddie Chapman, quietly watching them dance.

Shortly afterwards, David suggested it was time he took her home. Jago was sitting with friends of his at the bar.

The evening wasn't cold so they decided to walk.

Holding her arm, David said, 'I would like to see you again, Tilly. I wondered if you might like to go to the cinema on Saturday evening? There's a new Charlie Chaplin film showing called *Sunnyside*. Have you seen it?'

'No, I haven't. Thank you – I would love to go.' Hesitantly she said, 'I do apologise for Jago's behaviour tonight.'

'No need, as I've already said. But you know, Tilly, I believe he has a valid point.'

'What do you mean?'

'This Chapman bloke. He's very smooth, well mannered and all that, but I've been around a bit and seen his type.'

'What on earth do you mean?'

Trying to make light of his concern, David smiled and said, 'He looks the type who in days gone by

31

would throw you over his shoulder and take you off to his pirate ship waiting nearby! And to be honest, watching you dance, I thought the way he held you looked possessive. To be perfectly frank . . . it's as if he's making love to you.'

'David!' She was shocked.

'I have met men of his calibre before. Believe me, Tilly, they can be dangerous.'

She was speechless. The blunt words shook her, all the more because when it was pointed out to her she knew precisely what he meant. Eddie did hold her close when they were dancing and she could feel the firm contours of his body, and at times he stared so intently at her, it was as if he could see into her very soul. And she knew she could not confess that it thrilled her.

'Here we are,' she said as they arrived at her door, thankful to be spared further conversation about the Blue Pelican's owner.

David kissed her cheek. 'Thank you for a wonderful evening. I'll pick you up on Saturday evening at a quarter to seven, if that's all right with you?'

'That'll be fine,' she said, 'and thank you for tonight. The meal was lovely, and the dancing. I can't wait to tell my friends I know how to do the Bunny Hop!'

He waited whilst she unlocked the door and

saw her safely inside before he walked away. Stopping to light a cigarette, he thought about the urbane owner of the club and decided that if he and Tilly continued to see one another, he would not be taking her there again. Although this had been their first date, he really liked Tilly and he had objected to the way Chapman had held her. The extreme closeness, in his opinion, had not been necessary. Still, he could understand the man's wanting to hold her. She was lovely and had character. And she was desirable . . . and that was what he had seen in Chapman's eyes. Desire! Chapman wanted her, David could tell, and he didn't like it. Not one bit.

CHAPTER FOUR

Ken and Charlie Williams were seated in their front room talking earnestly.

'We'll give Chapman another couple of days to make up his mind and we'll call round and see him if we don't hear anything by then,' said Charlie, the elder by five minutes.

Charlie was the fatter of the two, but in height, features, mid-brown hair, which was thinning on the crown of their heads, and narrow hazel eyes the two men were otherwise identical. Their voices too sounded the same, which sometimes served them well when they answered the telephone and the other brother was wanted. They would take on the identity of their sibling to save time.

These were not men to be messed with. They ran private gambling schools and an escort service, which was cleverly managed to keep the law off their backs. If accused of living off immoral earnings they would protest that their clients paid for the girl's company for the evening only, as far as they were concerned, and that was all. The girls were threatened with dire consequences if they ever let slip that their bosses knew they slept with the clients, and so far that had been enough to keep the Williamses in the clear.

The local police force was not fooled but had not as yet been able to prove their suspicions. The fact that the men had called on Eddie Chapman had made him a suspect too.

The two men pored over their appointment book, which was full for tonight. Some of their male clients used pseudonyms, which made them laugh, knowing who the men really were. As Charlie was fond of saying, 'Do they really think that fools anyone?'

Several of the clients were prominent townsfolk who banked on the discretion of the service, but in return the Williams brothers used their connections to their own advantage. One client was a builder so the twins were able to buy materials at cost price, another was a solicitor who gave them free advice, and a third a member of the local force with particular needs. To have such services provided cost him dearly, but he had no intention of giving them up and so would warn the twins if they were to be questioned or watched at any particular time. Such information was invaluable.

The girls were well trained. The brothers had

staked out various hotels to find those where women could enter without being stopped at a reception desk as they walked past to visit one of the rooms. Eventually they had a list of safe venues. Some were in the town itself, others on the outskirts, for those of the clients who were worried about being recognised locally. It was a lucrative trade, and of course not owning any premises to be used for prostitution helped keep the Williams brothers out of trouble with the law.

They themselves lived with their elderly mother in a terraced house in St Mary's. Old Hilda Williams had been on the game herself in her younger days, and later had been a madam, running her own brothel – until it was closed down, sending her to gaol for six months. She was a tough old bird who knew all about her sons' business and gave them many a tip on how to manage their girls.

'Don't get friendly with any of them,' she told them, 'and don't sleep with any yourselves, otherwise you'll cause trouble. Before you know where you are, the brass you've been fucking will get all possessive and you'll have trouble when you dump her. She'll grass you up to the filth.'

It was good advice, which they heeded. Charlie didn't need it anyway. He preferred the male sex. In this the brothers differed. Ken liked his women and he liked them big. He wasn't worried by his brother's deviation at all so it was never a bone of contention between them.

Charlie never had any trouble finding a man. Southampton was a seaport with ships coming and going all the time. All he did was visit a few pubs – when he felt the need – and take his pick. As for Ken, there were always women around the dock area who figured it was a feather in their cap to be bedded by a Williams.

One of Ken's favourites was Queenie, a plump, voluptuous barmaid who worked at the Horse and Groom on the corner of East Street and Canal Walk. It was one of the roughest and toughest pubs in Southampton and one favoured by seamen the world over who visited the port. In 1904, Harry Batten, the landlord, had two enormous stuffed brown bears placed in the huge bar to add to the atmosphere. The two animals each about seven feet tall, were standing on their hind legs with fearsome expressions, showing their teeth.

Queenie was very capable and as tough as any of her customers, and when the occasion warrented it she could snarl every bit as fiercely as the bears. She'd been known to floor a man with one punch if he got out of hand, and this was what Ken liked about her. She was the only woman he slept with who wasn't frightened by his reputation. Neither was she jealous of the other women he bedded. Why should she be? She took any other man she fancied to her bed too. They had a great understanding.

It was Saturday night, and after Ken had given the girls their appointments for the evening, he called in to the Horse and Groom for a drink. Walking to the bar he grinned at Queenie and asked for a pint of bitter.

'Hello, darlin'. How the devil are you?' she asked as she pulled the beer pump and filled his glass.

Taking it from her he looked at the head in the glass and said, 'Fine, love. Glad to see you haven't given me more froth than beer.'

'As if I would!' she protested.

'You got anything planned after closing?' he asked.

She gave him a provocative look and said, 'Why? You feeling a bit horny?'

'Yeah. I could do with a tumble with my best girl. How about you? Are you free?'

'As a bird,' she quipped. 'I'll be finished about eleven o'clock. Meet me at my place.'

Taking his beer to a table nearby, Ken sat down and watched the customers who filled the bar. There was a mishmash of seamen of all nationalities there. It was reasonably early and so none were the worse for drink, but he knew that by closing time it was odds on there would be a fight among some of them. It was almost a Saturday night ritual. The police would be called and somebody would spend a night in the cells. He was never around at closing time; he wanted no unnecessary truck with the coppers. He had enough trouble keeping them off his back as it was.

He watched Queenie dispensing drinks and bonhomie as she worked. His gaze moved to her voluptuous bosom, straining against the buttons of her blouse. He felt himself harden as he thought of each ripe breast being released into his waiting hands when at last they would lie together on the large comfortable bed at Queenie's place.

As Ken Williams sat contemplating the night of pleasure before him, Tilly Thompson was sitting in one of the local cinemas with David Strickland, enjoying the antics of Charlie Chaplin. The pianist, supplying suitable music to accompany the silent film, was especially good, adding to the humour and excitement of the film's content.

During the interval, David bought her an ice cream and they sat and discussed the film. The second feature was the Keystone Cops, charging around the country in a car with some of them being thrown out at regular intervals. It was hilarious, and when eventually they left the cinema they were still laughing.

'I'm amazed that they don't hurt themselves,' Tilly said.

'I'm sure they probably do,' he said. 'Harold Lloyd is the one for me, though. He takes so many chances in his films. He does the most dangerous stunts.'

As they were about to pass the Dolphin hotel, David asked, 'Would you like to pop in here for a nightcap? We have time before it closes.'

Tilly agreed and they walked into the lounge bar.

As she sat at a table and waited for David to bring their drinks, she saw Eddie Chapman sitting with a woman. She was slim, blonde, attractive and, Tilly guessed, in her late twenties. Eddie had his arm round the back of her chair, talking quietly, gazing into the woman's eyes, smiling as he did so. There was a definite feeling of intimacy between them as Tilly watched, and she wondered who the woman was. As far as she knew Chapman was single, so was this female his mistress? She was certainly more than a friend. She laughed at something Eddie said and caressed his cheek softly. He caught hold of her hand and kissed it.

Fascinated, Tilly found herself wondering what

sort of lover he would be, and was immediately shocked by such wanton thoughts. She made no mention of the couple as David returned with their drinks.

'The weather looks settled, so I wondered if you would like to go to the Isle of Wight tomorrow? We could catch a morning ferry and go over to Cowes for the day.'

'Isn't that a sort of busman's holiday for you?' she teased.

'Hardly. There's a great difference between a liner and a ferry. Besides, I wouldn't be taking to the sea to work and that makes another difference. What do you say? Shall we test your sea legs?'

'I'd love to. Shall I bring a picnic?'

'What a great idea. I'll bring a blanket and we can sit on the beach if the weather is warm enough.'

As they were finishing their drinks, Eddie Chapman and his lady rose from their seats and walked past them. Eddie looked over at them, smiled and nodded, and walked on. The woman glanced briefly at them in passing.

'That man seems to be everywhere,' David remarked sharply.

'You don't like him, do you?' said Tilly.

'I don't know him well enough to say, but I wouldn't trust him, that much I do know.'

They left the bar shortly after themselves and walked to Tilly's house.

'Shall I come and collect you tomorrow?' he asked. 'The ferry leaves about ten thirty so I suggest a quarter to, to give us enough time to walk there and buy the tickets.'

'Yes, that'll be fine. I'll be ready.'

He pulled her slowly into his arms and kissed her, gently at first, as if trying to gauge her response. When she didn't pull away, he slowly moved his lips over hers, and kissed her with great expertise. 'Good night, Tilly,' he said softly.

Taken by surprise by his kiss, and how much she enjoyed it, she murmured, 'Good night.'

As she walked into the living room, she saw Jago sitting drinking a cup of tea.

'You all right?' he asked.

'Yes, why?'

'You look a bit starry-eyed, that's all.' He grinned at her. 'Boyfriend kiss you good night, did he?'

She felt her cheeks redden. 'It's none of your business!'

Laughing aloud, he said, 'Obviously he did.'

'Where are Mum and Dad?' she enquired, trying to change the subject.

'They've gone to bed.' Getting to his feet, he said, 'That's where I'm going too. What are you doing tomorrow?'

'David is taking me to Cowes.'

As he walked towards the stairs he said, 'Nice bloke. I like him.'

'That's enough to make me nervous,' she said as she gathered her things together.

'Don't be cheeky,' he warned. 'Good night. Have a nice time tomorrow.'

As she undressed for bed, she thought what a strange evening it had been. She loved being with David – he was such fun – but when he had taken her in his arms and kissed her, now that was something quite different! It had completely thrown her. And she had enjoyed it. Then there was the enigmatic club owner. What had David likened him to . . . ? A marauding pirate? How exciting, and how fitting.

Eddie Chapman and his female companion walked into the Blue Pelican. He looked around, pleased that it was full. He walked over to the barman and asked, 'Everything all right?'

'Yes, guv, no trouble. We've been busy all night.'

'I'm off upstairs,' said Chapman. 'I'll be down to lock up later.'

He and his companion walked up the first flight of stairs to a locked door which led to Eddie's apartment. It was very spacious, with a large living room, a bathroom and a double bedroom. There was a small kitchen for his use should he want to prepare a meal.

The blonde took off her jacket, sat down and said, 'Tell me about the girl in the bar.'

Eddie Chapman looked startled. 'What girl?'

Greta gave a sardonic smile and said, 'Oh please, don't pretend with me. The attractive redhead you nodded to when we left the Dolphin.'

'Oh, her. She's just a customer. She's been in the club a couple of times.'

'Is she the one you danced the tango with by any chance?'

'When did you hear about that?'

Running her fingers though her hair she said, 'A friend of mine was there that night. It was quite an exhibition by all accounts.'

Shrugging, he said, 'She's a good dancer, that's all.'

'It was rather more than that, I think. I was told you were quite enamoured with her.'

'Just good public relations, my dear, that's all.'

She was not content to let the matter drop. 'I hope it remains no more than that, Eddie. I know you and I won't be messed about!'

'The only messing about I'm thinking of at this precise moment is with you in the bedroom.'

She started to argue further but he caught hold

of her hand and, pulling her up from her seat, took her into his arms.

'You talk too much,' he said as he smothered her with kisses, and lifting her up he carried her into the bedroom. As he removed her clothes, he nuzzled her neck and murmured, 'The only woman I want is you.' But even as he spoke, he knew he was lying.

CHAPTER FIVE

On Sunday morning, the Williams twins counted the money earned by the brasses the night before. It was a healthy amount, which normally would have pleased them, except that one of the girls had been badly bruised by one of their regular clients, and she was in the front room complaining loudly.

'I don't know what came over him,' she said. 'Normally he ain't no trouble. He likes his sex straight usually, but last night he wanted to experiment, so I went along with it, and then he was so stirred up he got violent and hit me across the face a couple of times. What's more, he enjoyed it and wanted more. I told him to fuck off!' With trembling fingers she lit a cigarette. 'Well, he was furious. I had to remind him we were in a hotel room and if he continued to make a ruckus we would be turfed out, and what would that do to his reputation. It was the only thing that brought him to his senses. Then I got dressed and buggered off.'

Ken was annoyed and said, 'Don't worry, I'll have a word.'

'Just don't book me with him again, that's all.'

'If he wants violence I'm sure we can accommodate him,' Charlie said, 'but I doubt he would like what I have in mind. Thanks, love – we'll take care of it. Here's an extra fiver for your trouble. You can't work for a few days with a face like that – it isn't good for business.' He pulled a wad of notes from his pocket and handed her a note.

The girl took the money. 'Ta. I'll be on my way.'

'Come and see us at the end of the week and we'll see what you look like then.'

When they were alone, Charlie looked at his brother and asked, 'Will you go and see him or will I?'

'You go. Book an appointment to see him in his office. That ought to scare the shit out of him when he sees you walk through the door.'

Laughing, Charlie said, 'No doubt! I'll do it in the morning.'

In another part of town, Jago answered the door when David Strickland called for Tilly.

'Come in,' he said.

'Do I get another third degree?' asked David with a grin.

'No, mate, I promise. I reckon you're all right. Come and meet the folks.'

He took David into the kitchen where Joe and Ethel were just finishing their breakfast. 'This is David, Tilly's friend,' he said.

David shook hands with them both.

'Off to Cowes I believe,' Joe said as Tilly emerged from the scullery carrying a basket.

'That's right, Dad,' she interrupted, 'and we can't stop and chat or we'll miss the ferry. Come on, David.' She walked purposefully towards the door.

'Nice to meet you,' David called over his shoulder as he followed her.

Once outside she turned to him and said, 'Sorry I rushed you, but once Dad got chatting we'd never get away. He'd end up telling you all about Clarence.'

'Who the devil is Clarence?'

'His shire horse. He dotes on the blooming animal. Dad works for Watneys brewery, delivering their beer on his cart—'

'Pulled by Clarence,' David ended her sentence.

'Exactly. My dad has a way with horses and he and Clarence are great friends. He talks to that horse like one of his mates!'

'When I was a little boy, we had a dog. I wouldn't go anywhere without him; we were inseparable. He was my best friend, so I can understand how your father feels.'

She looked bemused. 'My dad would love you!'

The sun was shining as they joined the queue for the Cowes ferry. Once on board they chose to sit up on the open deck. Tilly had brought a light jacket with her to shield her from the breeze.

'There will be a bit of a swell out in the Solent today,' David said knowledgeably. 'So it's better that we're up here instead of in a stuffy lounge, what with the smell of stale beer as well.' He covered their legs with a car rug he'd brought along.

'There speaks the voice of experience,' she teased.

'You have no idea,' he said. 'I've heard passengers say they feel seasick before the ship even leaves the dock.'

'Well, I feel fine!' Tilly said as the ropes were cast off and the ferry left the quay.

It was an enjoyable crossing, and when they arrived they walked to the beach and settled for the day. David laid out the rug whilst Tilly unpacked the sandwiches and flask of tea. The two of them sat gazing at the sea chatting about inconsequential things until she said, 'Let's go and paddle and see if I can still skim stones.'

'Come on then,' he said, taking his shoes off.

They ran down the beach like a couple of children. And to Tilly's delight, she was still adept at it.

'Mine went further than yours!' she called.

'Rubbish! That was just through a wave that came at the right time.'

Eventually they returned to their place and ate their sandwiches.

'I'm going to miss you, Tilly.'

She looked up in surprise. 'Miss me? Whatever do you mean?'

'I have to report back to my ship soon. We sail on Wednesday.'

Crestfallen, she said, 'Oh, David, I had almost forgotten you would be leaving. I'll miss you too.'

'Will you come out with me again when I return?'

'Of course I will.'

He hesitated, then said, 'Will you do me a favour?'

'If I can.'

'Promise me you won't go to the Blue Pelican whilst I'm away?'

Frowning, she said, 'What a strange thing to ask.'

He took her hand in his. 'Not really. That Chapman fellow is dangerous and I'm convinced he has a particular interest in you, and frankly that worries me.'

'David, you are being ridiculous. Good heavens, I've only been there twice and yes, I danced with the man, but that's all.'

'But if you persist in going, it will lead to more, I'd put money on it. You haven't seen how he looks at you!'

Tilly remembered very well the long insistent gaze of Eddie Chapman and the effect it had had on her as he held her, but she still protested.

'I really think you exaggerate.'

'Maybe, but I wouldn't like to see you get involved in a situation that perhaps you couldn't handle. Will you promise?'

'Of course, if it worries you so much.'

They spent the rest of the day reading the papers, paddling in the water and getting to know one another a little better. And when they eventually returned on the ferry, David arranged to take her out to dinner the following Tuesday evening.

On Monday morning, Charlie Williams was able to book an appointment with his client for the same afternoon. The man had a cancellation and his secretary was able to offer him the space.

'Can you tell me what it's about?' she enquired.

'It's about a compensation claim,' he told her.

'Fine, I'll just make a note of that. Mr Bradbury will be able to see you at three o'clock.'

'Thank you, miss. I'll be there.'

Gerald Bradbury pressed the intercom on his desk and asked for his next appointment to be sent in. He looked up with a welcoming smile as the door of his office opened, but when he saw Charlie Williams standing there the smile froze.

'What the devil are you doing here? When I saw a Mr Williams on my list I didn't think for one moment it would be you!'

Charlie sauntered over to the chair in front of the large desk, sat down and faced Bradbury. 'No, I don't suppose you did, Gerald.'

Bradbury puffed up with indignation at the familiarity.

'What do you want? My secretary said my client wanted to talk about a compensation claim, or was that just a ruse to get into my office?'

'No it bloody well wasn't! You beat one of my girls last Saturday night—'

'For God's sake keep your voice down,' the solicitor interrupted.

'As I was saying, Maisie's face is all bruised and she can't work looking like that, so I'm losing money, which means you'll have to compensate me for the loss. Fifty quid ought to cover it.'

'Fifty pounds? That's a ridiculous amount of money, and it sounds like blackmail to me!'

'So sue me!' Charlie sat back and, taking a cigar from his top pocket, he lit it, blowing the smoke across the desk. He glared at Bradbury. 'You can't go slapping women around. Not my women anyway. Do you beat your wife?'

'Leave my wife out of this!' The man was incandescent with rage.

'Now I'm a reasonable man, Gerald. If it's rough stuff you're after I can accommodate you. I can get a couple of my men to do the same to you.' He saw the man pale before him. 'But if you want to continue using my services, you treat my girls right.'

'Are you threatening me?'

'Yes, you could say that.'

Charlie watched the changing expressions on the face of his client as he quickly summed up the situation. Anger was followed by concern as Bradbury recognised that his reputation was in the hands of the miscreant in front of him, and finally resignation as he accepted that he would still want to use the services offered.

'Very well,' he said, taking a wallet out of the inside pocket of his jacket and removing ten white five-pound notes. 'Here you are. I'm sorry I hurt the young lady. It was an aberration on my part, one that won't be repeated. You have my word.'

Taking the money, Charlie pocketed it, rose to his feet and with a wide satisfied smile said, 'That's that all sorted then. No hard feelings, but as one businessman to another I know you will understand my position.' He walked to the door and left the room.

Bradbury took a handkerchief out of his pocket and wiped his sweating brow. He was very shaken by the meeting and he pressed the intercom on his desk.

'Cancel the rest of my appointments for today, Miss Brown, I'm going home.'

CHAPTER SIX

Ethel Thompson was very surprised when her employer arrived home early that afternoon. She was dusting the furniture in the hallway when the door opened.

'Good afternoon, sir,' she said. She thought he looked very drawn.

He ignored her. 'Bring me a tray of tea in my study and tell my wife not to disturb me,' he snapped.

A few minutes later, Ethel knocked on the door of the study and waited.

'Come!' called her employer.

Entering the room, she asked, 'Where would you like me to put the tea, Mr Bradbury?'

As he turned towards her she saw he was holding a glass with a fair-sized shot of alcohol in it. This surprised her, as she had only ever seen Gerald Bradbury drink liquor during the evening.

'Put it on the table over there,' he said gruffly and turned away.

Returning to the kitchen, she said to the cook, 'I don't know what's happened to the master but he doesn't look well.'

'Perhaps he's had some bad news,' suggested the woman.

'He looks very shaken,' she admitted.

'No doubt we will eventually hear about it,' said Cook as she continued with her preparations for the evening meal. 'Everything comes out in the wash eventually.'

That was precisely what was worrying Gerald Bradbury. Sitting in his chair, he fretted over the visit from Charlie Williams, earlier that day. He'd had a fit to think the man had actually come to his place of business. His association with the Williamses was one thing he did not want made public. He had been a client of theirs for some time now, and up until the other evening he'd had no worries about their keeping their promise of confidentiality. He blamed himself. What had got into him he didn't know. Normally he wasn't a violent man. He paid for the services of the prostitutes to liven up his sex life. He was a man with needs, which his wife was reluctant to supply. Sex for her was a duty, something to be ashamed of, never to be enjoyed. He doubted that she had ever had a wanton thought in her head. As for an orgasm, she wouldn't even know what it was. She certainly had never had one with him! He had never even seen her naked. How he hated those flannelette nightdresses she wore. By the time he'd rooted beneath them and found her bare flesh, he'd almost lost his erection.

With the girls the Williams brothers supplied there was never any problem. They would strip off at once. He would lie and watch them undress before feeling their naked flesh pressing against him, his hands exploring every inch of their voluptuous bodies. He could feel himself getting aroused now at the thought. But the other night he had been drinking with friends at a business meeting, and his few inhibitions had taken flight.

As he thought about it he realised his behaviour had been triggered by a conversation in which one of the men had told a story of a visit to a sex show in Paris where two women had flayed each other with birch twigs. That and the alcohol had brought forth an element of sadism he didn't know he had. It worried him that he had actually enjoyed hurting the girl. Good God! He was supposed to be civilised . . . yet he still remembered the thrill that had raced through him as she cried out in pain. He downed the last of his brandy and poured himself a cup of tea.

* * *

Tilly had arranged to meet her friend, Beth Pearson, after work on Monday. The two girls walked to the Lyons Corner House for coffee and a sandwich.

'What have you been doing with yourself?' asked Beth. 'I haven't seen you for days.'

'I've met a lovely man and he's been taking me out,' Tilly confessed.

'Oh, how exciting. Who is he and where did you meet?'

Tilly told her all about David. 'I can now skim stones like you wouldn't believe,' she chortled. 'He's taken me out to dinner, to the cinema, and one evening to the Blue Pelican.'

'Did you see that gorgeous man again? You know, the one you danced with.'

'I did, and I danced with him again.'

'Didn't David mind?'

'Well, not at the time, but afterwards he said he didn't really like it. He's made me promise not to go to the club when he's away.'

'Away, where?'

'At sea. He's an engineer on the *Aquitania*.'

'But my dear girl, how exciting. Does he go cruising?'

'At the moment the ship goes to New York, so he's not away too long. He's been on leave, that's how we met. He's lovely, really good-looking and a good dancer. He taught me the Bunny Hop. But what have you been up to?'

'Not very much. Went out for the day with the gang on our bikes last Sunday, that's about all.'

'David took me to Cowes on the ferry. It was lovely.'

'Life on an ocean liner, eh?'

Chuckling, Tilly told her friend, 'I said much the same to David, but he said it was very different.'

'So you won't be seeing the club owner again?'

With a note of disappointment Tilly said, 'No, I don't suppose so. Our Jago came in whilst we were at the club. He was furious when he saw me, and told me to keep away as well. Neither he nor David like Mr Chapman for some reason.'

'Ah, well,' said Beth knowingly, 'they aren't women. That Eddie Chapman is a lady's man, I would say. Let's face it, he has masses of sex appeal, and men don't like that in another man. It gets in the way of their ego!'

'I never thought of that. Do you know what David said to me?'

'No.'

'He said that when Eddie Chapman danced with me it looked as if he was making love to me!'

Beth thought for a moment and said, 'I have to be honest, I can see what he meant. I saw you dance the tango with him, remember? The way he held you and gazed into your eyes . . . well!'

'He's not interested in me. I saw him with an attractive blonde woman in the Dolphin hotel one evening when David and I called in for a nightcap. Now I swear he makes love to her – and not on a dance floor!'

Eddie Chapman was on his way home after spending the day at a race meeting, a large amount of money in his inside pocket. He had gone to that particular meeting because he owned a horse that was running and knew that the trainer had made certain the animal had an advantage by giving it a pill with its feed. It had paid off handsomely.

This was not the first time such an arrangement had been made. They had to be careful, of course, not to alert the Jockey Club to any shenanigans. Jeremy Frampton, the trainer, could lose his licence, but he was a canny man who had been in the business for years and knew every twist and turn of the art of winning races, albeit illegally. He had explained his motives to Eddie.

'I'm thinking ahead to my retirement and I want to get out of the game with a nice nest egg in the bank. Most of my life I've played by the rules, but recently the yard hasn't had many winners and that's a worry. Rufus is one way to tip the scales and I'm sure you wouldn't say no to a nice windfall?'

Eddie Chapman had never turned a good deal down in his life and, knowing the trainer well, he had always trusted him.

'Place your bets around the course and at the tote,' Jeremy advised. 'It won't cause a problem then, and with a bit of luck no one will realise what we're doing, which will keep the price up.'

And that was what he'd done, earning himself a nice little pile.

As he watched the countryside pass by the window of the train, he was mulling over the proposition the Williams brothers had put to him about a legal gambling club. He had no intention of entering any business arrangement with them at any time, but he was still considering opening one of his own. He wondered just how difficult it would be to get a licence. Perhaps he would have a word with the police about it. If he did so, the club would have to be on the up and up. The police would be watching closely and he wouldn't consider for a moment running anything dodgy. That was just looking for trouble, whereas the Williams twins had no compunction about such things. He would go through his finances and set up a business plan.

*   *   *

If Eddie's plans ever came to fruition, chances were that Jago Thompson would be one of his clients. Jago enjoyed a flutter at the tables and would take himself to London on occasion to visit a club where he could play roulette or chemin de fer or occasionally blackjack. At other times he joined in the odd card game run by the Williams brothers. He didn't like the twins but loved to pit his wits against the other players. He enjoyed most card games, but his favourite was poker.

Jago loved the psychology of poker. He would watch the other players' expressions, their body language when they held good or bad cards, and judge whether to fold or up the ante on his own hand. It always amazed him how bad a loser some players could be when their luck was out. He had seen such games turn to violence on occasion, which wasn't surprising given the collection of players that used to gather at the twins' evenings. There were some very unsavoury characters sitting round the tables sometimes. But Jago was no fool and could take care of himself if the need arose, and usually if he saw things shaping up for an ugly scene he would make his excuses and leave.

He was a clever player and often won at poker, which didn't always please the others involved in the game. He told them they didn't study the game enough, but certainly didn't explain that their own body language often gave them away.

He was content with his life at the moment, and eventually hoped to own his own business, but not yet. He liked being able to leave the butcher's shop on a Friday night, clutching his wages, and not have the financial worries of the owner. He wanted to enjoy life for a while before saddling himself with a business and perhaps a wife and children. At the moment he was playing the field and enjoying himself.

Tilly worried him. She was a vibrant, attractive young woman, feeling her feet. He didn't blame her for enjoying her youth, but when he saw her at the Blue Pelican club, he was concerned. He'd watched Eddie Chapman work on attractive young women who graced the club, and he didn't want him anywhere near his sister. He was well aware of the power of the man and knew that women were attracted to him. However, Tilly's new young man seemed a steady type who wouldn't stand for any nonsense with Chapman, and as he had himself told her not to go there again she should be fine.

Jago would have been very concerned if he had seen his sister at that particular moment, as she was talking to the nightclub owner himself.

After leaving Beth, Tilly had decided to walk

63

home and window-shop at the same time. She had been admiring an evening dress in one of the windows when a voice behind her made her jump.

'That gown is far too old for you.'

She turned and looked into the face of Eddie Chapman. Her cheeks flushed with embarrassment.

'Hello, Mr Chapman.'

'Eddie, please.' He took her arm and turned her back towards the window. 'Now that one over there has your name on it.' He indicated a mannequin wearing a beautiful diaphanous dress in shades of autumn, with the fashionable dropped waist and handkerchief hem. 'It would look wonderful with your colouring.'

'It is gorgeous,' she admitted, 'but I couldn't possible afford it.'

'A beautiful young woman should have a wealthy benefactor to treat her to these things.'

Laughing, Tilly said, 'That doesn't sound very nice. Are you saying I should have a sugar daddy?'

'Not at all!' he protested. 'Just someone who thinks you are a beautiful woman, which you are, and would want to buy you things to please you, that's all.'

'Like Aladdin's lamp?' she teased. 'A genie to grant all my wishes?'

'You know I don't mean that. If you were my

girl, I would want to do those things for you.'

She stared into his eyes and with a smile said, 'But you already have a girl.'

He denied the fact. 'She's not my girl, just a friend.'

'But a very close friend, I would imagine. I saw you together, don't forget.'

He burst out laughing. 'You, young miss, are a minx!'

'Maybe, but I'm not a fool.'

He looked thoughtfully at her. 'No, I can see that. Look, why don't we go to the Dolphin and have a drink together and then we can talk and I can find out what else goes on in that head of yours?'

'And would you tell me what goes on in yours as well?'

He looked bemused. 'If you would think that was interesting.'

'I am sure it would be quite an education!'

'Tilly, are you teasing me?' he asked, his lips twitching with amusement.

'Would I do such a thing?'

Taking her arm he said, 'I do believe you would. Come on, just for a while.'

Without a second thought she allowed him to lead her away from the window.

* * *

Once they had reached their destination and Eddie had gone to the bar to order their drinks, Tilly, seated in the visitors' lounge, thought to herself, what on earth am I doing here? Both Jago and David would be furious with her. But Eddie Chapman fascinated her and she wanted to learn more about him. What was the harm in that? But she knew she was flirting with danger. He was a man like no other she knew; maybe that was the fascination . . . and there was something akin to forbidden fruit about him, which made their assignation even more interesting.

He was not Southampton born and bred, she learned when she questioned him.

'No, I was born in London – Woolwich – but my parents left there when I was a child, and moved to the south coast.'

'Do they live locally?'

'No, they eventually moved back to London. I see them occasionally. And what work do you do, Tilly?'

'I work in Madam Leone's dress shop,' she told him. 'I enjoy being surrounded by beautiful gowns, and the clients are very nice.'

'But surely with your intelligence you would want more from life that that?'

'Of course I do! But I'm only nineteen. I can't afford to travel, but if I could I would like to sail to New York on an ocean liner, or go to Paris. I would even like to explore London.'

'I can't help you with New York or Paris,' he said, 'but I could certainly take you to London. I know the city well. What would you want to see there?'

'Buckingham Palace, the Changing of the Guard, the Tower of London – you know, all the things that tourists do. And I would like to go to Harrods!'

He was highly amused. 'Now why doesn't that surprise me?'

'I've seen pictures of the store in magazines and I know that people with money shop there. I would just like to walk around and look, that's all.'

'When is your half-day?'

'Wednesday,' she told him with some hesitation.

'If you could ask for the morning off so you would have a whole day, we could go to London and do all those things!'

She met his steady gaze but inside her stomach tightened with nervous tension. Was this man serious? And if he was, could she possibly accept his invitation?

Sensing her reticence, he smiled softly and said, 'You would come to no harm with me, lovely Tilly. I would take the greatest care of you and what's more it would give me the greatest pleasure. What do you say?'

She longed to say yes, but she suddenly felt shy and a little out of her depth. 'I couldn't possibly, but thank you anyway.'

Shrugging, he said, 'What a pity; we could have had such fun. Look,' he said, taking a card from his pocket, 'call me if you change your mind.' And he handed it to her. 'Think about it, promise me that?'

'I will,' she said.

They finished their drinks and rose to leave.

Kissing her very gently on the forehead he said, 'I hope to hear from you, Tilly.'

As he walked away she read the card. It gave his name and address and a telephone number. She placed it in her handbag and turned for home, wondering if she could pluck up the courage to accept his offer.

CHAPTER SEVEN

The Williams brothers were tired of waiting to hear from Eddie Chapman about their business proposition, so they decided to visit the Blue Pelican and find out what was happening. They entered the club and stood at the bar with their drinks, looking around, waiting for Eddie to appear.

Eventually he came down the stairs from his private apartment and, seeing the twins, walked towards them.

'Evening, gentlemen. What can I do for you?'

Ken spoke for them both. 'We haven't heard from you so we thought we would come and see if you have decided whether to come in with us on the gambling club?'

Eddie ordered a drink, then said, 'Yes, I have come to a decision and I'm afraid the answer is no, but thanks for asking.'

The brothers were not pleased. 'Why not?' Charlie demanded.

Candid as always, Eddie told them, 'For one

thing I don't think you will get a licence with your reputation, and secondly, I have other plans which will take my spare cash.'

Charlie demanded, 'What other plans do you have?'

With a confident smile Eddie said, 'That's my business, and at the moment I really don't want to discuss it. They're still in the early stages.'

Ken tried to calm his brother. 'That's all right, Eddie. I think you've missed a golden opportunity, but it's your choice after all. Come on, drink up,' he said to his twin, 'we have work to do.' He downed the contents of his glass and walked towards the door, followed by a disgruntled Charlie.

Outside, Charlie said, 'I bet that bugger is thinking of opening up on his own.'

Shrugging, Ken said, 'If he does there's not much we can do about it.'

'We'll see about that.'

At the bar, Eddie sipped his drink with a satisfied look on his face. Did those two really think he would do a deal with them, he wondered? So far he'd met all the legal requirements of the local police force and the last thing he wanted was to be tied up with the Williams twins who were always watched by the law. At the moment he hadn't any specific plans despite what he'd said to the two men, but he had played with the idea of opening his own gambling establishment and of buying another horse. He'd have a word with Jeremy Frampton before the next horse sale. He was far too late for the Newmarket sales but there were some more coming up at Ascot and Jeremy had a nose for horseflesh.

He'd like to take Tilly to a race meeting, he mused. He was sure she would enjoy herself. He had taken a shine to the girl and wondered if she would get in touch with him. If he didn't hear, he now knew where she worked and if necessary he would get in touch with her. She was definitely worth cultivating, but he would give her time. She had a certain way with her, which he found very appealing.

Tilly was out for the evening with David. He was sailing in the morning so he took her out for dinner to the Cowherds inn, in the Avenue.

As they ate he said, 'I really will miss you, Tilly. We've had such a good time these last few days. Will you meet me when we get back? We're only in port for a couple of days before we leave again.'

'That's not very long, is it?'

'Unfortunately that's how it is until my next leave. Seafarers are used to it, but it isn't easy on friendships, asking a girl to wait for you.' He gazed at her as if trying to gauge her reaction.

Smiling at him, she said, 'I dare say I can get used to it.'

With a look of relief he said, 'I'm so pleased to hear you say that. I'll write to you from New York.'

'I'd like that. You can tell me what you did in the big city.'

'I'll bring you something home with me. Then you'll have a souvenir from America.'

She was thrilled with the idea. 'Would you really? How exciting!'

'And what will you be doing whilst I'm away?' he asked.

'I'll probably go for a picnic at the weekend with my friends. We go on our bicycles somewhere in the country. Beth and I will probably go to the cinema too.' Please don't mention the Blue Pelican and Eddie Chapman, she thought, knowing that in her handbag was the card that the club owner had given her. She'd not even told Beth about it. It was like having a secret, a dangerous secret which was gnawing away at her all the time.

'That sounds like fun,' David said.

When at last he escorted her home, he took her into his arms. 'Thank you, Tilly, for making my leave such fun. I'm so glad we met on the beach that day.'

Nestling in his arms, she whispered, 'So am I. Just you take care during your trip.'

He kissed her until she was breathless. 'That's just something to remember me by when I'm gone,' he said as he caressed her face. 'You're a lovely girl and I'll miss you more than you know. You take care too.'

She watched him walk to the end of the street and waved as he looked back when he reached the corner.

Her mother was sitting in the kitchen, darning, when Tilly entered the house.

'Have a nice time with your young man?' she enquired.

'Yes thanks, Mum. He took me to the Cowherds for dinner.'

'My word, he must be doing well!' Ethel exclaimed.

'I suppose so. He's an engineer.'

'Oh, my. He'll be an officer then,' said her mother with some satisfaction. 'It's a lonely life being a wife to a seaman but it does have its compensations. You never get bored with having them under your feet all the time.'

Tilly looked at her mother with some surprise and asked, 'Are you bored with Dad then?'

'Gracious me, no, but then of course I work so we are not in each other's way all the time. My job gives me some other interest apart from everyday chores.' She paused, then asked, 'Do you think this is serious, you and David?'

'For goodness' sake! I've only just met him, and

it'll be a long time before I'll even think of settling down. I want to live a little first.'

Picking up her sewing, Ethel looked over her glasses at her daughter and said, 'I'm all for that, but you just make sure you don't live too much!'

'Whatever do you mean?'

'I'm just saying. As yet no one has brought trouble to this house, and I don't want you to be the first.' She gazed fondly at Tilly. 'I know you are a good girl, love, but you have a wild side to you which is fine in a lad, but in a girl can mean trouble. Just you take care, that's all.' She kissed Tilly on the cheek. 'I'm off to bed. Don't be too late – you have to be up in the morning.'

When she was alone, Tilly thought of her mother's words. Ethel certainly would not be impressed if she went to London with Eddie Chapman. But deep down she knew that she hadn't seen the last of the man and the knowledge made her heart beat a little faster.

David Strickland walked up the gangway of the *Aquitania* and made his way to his quarters. He poured himself a whisky and soda from the tray of drinks on the small cabinet, lit a cigarette and sat in a chair. He drew deeply on the cigarette and slowly blew a circle with the smoke. Normally, after his leave, he was restless and anxious to sail, but this time he felt differently. This time he regretted the fact that he would be sailing away from Southampton and the girl he'd met.

There had been women in his life before, of course. They had all been like ships that passed in the night, but Tilly Thompson was different. He already knew that she was the young woman he wanted to spend the rest of his life with. To be the mother of his children – but not yet. Tilly was still young; she needed time to grow up a little. What was it about her that made the difference, he asked himself? Her spirit of adventure, certainly. Her lack of scepticism, her innocence? The way the corners of her mouth turned up when she was amused. The feel of her in his arms, the scent of her. The way she had returned his kisses, her trust in him – and her vulnerability. That indeed was charming but also a worry. He couldn't get Eddie Chapman out of his mind. God, he hoped she kept away from him! Tilly was in no way equipped to handle a man like that. But at least she had promised not to return to the club, so there should be no reason for them to meet again, and for that he was thankful.

Looking at his watch he rose from his chair, put out the cigarette, finished the whisky, undressed, took a quick shower and climbed into bed, knowing his steward would wake him in the morning.

The following day, when the *Aquitania*'s funnels announced loudly that she was due to sail, Tilly listened to the throaty roar and tried to imagine David, deep in the bowels of the vessel, surrounded by the ship's engines; but that world was foreign to her and she couldn't picture the scene. All she could think of was the time when he would return and take her into his arms again. He was what both her mother and brother would consider a good marriage prospect, and they would be right. When she was with him she felt secure; there was something very solid about him. That made him sound dull, but he was never that. She found talking to him fascinating. He had seen so much in his travels, met so many people. She envied him.

Life was so much easier for a man, she mused as she tidied the clothes in Madam Leone's. They were free to follow their dreams, whereas a woman was supposed to marry and bring up a family. She wanted so much more. Eddie Chapman had a different view. He thought a woman should be spoilt. She liked that. How nice it would be to have a man who felt she was something to be treasured. How romantic that sounded, she thought.

A client walked into the shop, and Tilly was brought back to reality.

The following morning Hilda Williams was sitting in for her sons, collecting the takings from the brasses who had been working the previous night. She was waiting for a new girl to appear. Elsie had only been with them a couple of weeks, but Hilda was sure she was cheating the twins and had quietly been watching her, without telling her sons. No chit of a girl was going to pull the wool over her eyes!

Elsie, a bouncy blonde, knocked on the door of the front room and walked in, plonked herself down on the chair in front of the desk, grinned cheekily at Hilda as she opened her handbag and withdrew some crumpled notes, and handed them over.

'It was a good night, Ma,' she said.

Hilda glared at her and said, 'You will call me Mrs Williams.'

The grin disappeared. 'Well, I'm sorry I'm sure.'

Hilda counted out the money and looked up and held out her hand.

Elsie frowned. 'What's that for?'

'The rest of the money you earned last night.'

'What the bloody hell are you talking about?' the girl blustered.

Taking a cigarette out of a packet, Hilda lit it, drew in the nicotine and blew out the smoke, her gaze never leaving Elsie's face.

'Now you listen to me, you scheming little bitch. You work for my boys, not for yourself.' As the girl opened her mouth to protest, Hilda snapped, 'Shut your face! I've had my suspicions about you from the first. I've been in this business for years and frankly I would never have employed you in the first place.'

'Now you look here—' Elsie began.

'No, *you* look!' She turned the list appertaining to the girl and ticked them off. 'Seven o'clock, Jim, eight, Burt, nine thirty Derek and ten Mr A.'

'And that's what I've done! There's the money,' Elsie protested.

'True . . . but what about the one at six o'clock and the two at eleven?'

Elsie paled. 'I don't know what you're talking about.'

'Course you do.' Hilda rose from the chair behind the desk and walked round it until she stood in front of the girl, who leaned back in her chair to try to get away from the menacing figure in front of her.

Pushing aside some papers on the desk, Hilda revealed a small but deadly sharp kitchen knife. Picking it up, she said, 'If I cut you, you won't look so pretty, will you?'

'You crazy old woman!' Elsie screamed.

'Ah, but I'm not, and I'm on to your game.

Open your bag and give me the rest of the money.'

With trembling fingers, Elsie tried to undo the clasp of her handbag.

'For Christ's sake, give it here,' snapped Hilda. Undoing the clasp, she emptied the contents of the bag on the desk. Brushing aside the cigarettes, matches, condoms, and purse, she picked up and counted the loose notes. She looked at the girl and shook her head.

'You made the biggest mistake of your life trying to take me for a fool, girl.'

'What are you going to do?'

Taking a pound note and a ten shilling one, Hilda gave them to Elsie.

'This is all you're getting for trying to cheat my boys. I will be telling them about you.'

'Please don't do that, missus,' the girl begged. 'I'll never do it again, I promise.'

'You won't get the chance, my girl, because you ain't working for us any more. If I were you, I'd buy a ticket out of Southampton, because if my twins see you around you won't be fit enough to work for anyone. Now bugger off!'

The girl fled. But once she was far enough away to feel safe, she leaned against a wall to catch her breath. 'You miserable old cow,' she muttered. 'Think you're bloody clever, don't you? Well, I'll pay you back if it's the last thing I do!'

CHAPTER EIGHT

Joe Thompson gently pulled on his horse's reins. 'Steady, boy, here we are. Whoa there.' Clarence stopped and tossed his heavy mane.

The drayman knocked on the door of the Blue Pelican club and waited.

The barman opened the door. Seeing the Watneys Brewery cart waiting, loaded with beer barrels, he said, 'Hang on. I'll go down to the cellar and open up.'

Joe put a feed bag over the horse's head, then set up the dual iron runner which enabled him to run the barrels down on to the pavement. Before long the barman pushed up the cast iron opening to the cellar in the pavement and climbed out. He counted the barrels, which were deftly delivered, and signed the delivery note.

'Got a bucket here,' said Joe. 'Would you fill it with water to give old Clarence a drink, please, mate?'

Muttering under his breath, the barman disappeared and returned shortly with the requested water.

As he took it Joe said, 'No drink for me then?'

'We're not running a bloody charity, you know,' snapped the barman. He dropped the cellar top down, stamped on it to make sure it was closed, and walked back into the club.

'Miserable bugger,' Joe muttered. Most of his customers gave him a half-pint of beer or a cup of tea after his delivery, which was always gratefully received. Rolling and lifting the barrels, which were then run down another ramp into the cellar, was hard work.

Removing the feed bag from Clarence's nose, he held up the bucket for the animal to drink. As he stood waiting for the horse to quench his thirst, Joe studied the building in front of him.

'This 'ere place looks a bit posh, don't it, boy?' he said, addressing his remarks to his four-legged friend. 'My Tilly has been here with her mates, imagine that.' Placing the now half-empty bucket on the cart, he stroked the horse's long nose and nuzzled his neck. 'You and I prefer the open road, don't we, my beauty?'

Climbing on to the cart he picked up the reins, made a clicking noise with his mouth and moved off. His son Jago had told him he didn't like Tilly going to the club, but as far as he could tell the place seemed all right. The boy was worrying unnecessarily.

As he drove to his next destination, Joe pondered over his children. Both his older girls were married and settled, Jago was doing well in the butcher's shop, and young Tilly seemed content with her job. He smiled softly, knowing her penchant for fashion. Well, she certainly looked the goods when she went out. It was time she thought of settling down. Perhaps the young man she was seeing would be the one? He hoped so. He seemed a nice enough chap; a bit older than Tilly, but that was no bad thing. She needed someone she could look up to and who could influence her, because she did have some wild ideas. Still, she was young yet. She'd get over it.

A car backfired and Clarence neighed and became unsettled. Joe tightened the reins. 'It's all right, my beauty,' he crooned softly. How he hated these newfangled motors. What's wrong with real horse power, he wanted to know? He worried that if they became really popular, his firm might use them instead of horse-drawn vehicles. But he was quite sure in his heart that that day was a long way off.

When his working day was finished, Joe settled Clarence in his stable and walked home to find Tilly making a pot of tea.

'I could kill for a cuppa,' he told her. 'It's been

a busy day. Hey, I went to the Blue Pelican club with a delivery. Nice-looking spot, I thought.'

She stopped pouring the tea for a moment. 'I like it, Dad, but Jago doesn't seem keen. Well, not on me being there.'

'I can't imagine why. It looked fine to me.'

She didn't enlighten him. She was feeling a bit down if the truth were known. Now that David had sailed, she was restless. She'd been out with her friends to the pictures, but she longed for a bit of excitement and had decided to ask her employer for the following Wednesday morning off. She would take up the invitation for a trip to London with Eddie Chapman.

Madam Leone wasn't too pleased when Tilly approached her, asking for time off, but Tilly made the excuse that she needed to visit her sick grandmother in Bournemouth. She was so convincing that her employer agreed, adding, 'Do not let this become a habit, Miss Thompson!'

The following day during her lunch time Tilly made her way to the nearest telephone box and, taking Eddie's card from her pocket, with a pounding heart put her money in the slot and dialled his number.

'The Blue Pelican club,' a strange voice answered.

'Can I speak to Mr Chapman, please?'

'Who shall I say is calling?'

'Miss Tilly Thompson.' She kept taking deep breaths as she waited, trying to keep calm.

'Tilly! How lovely to hear from you.'

'Hello, Mr Chapman. I have decided to accept your invitation for that trip to London,' she said breathlessly. She heard him chuckle softly.

'Have you? Well, that's absolutely fine. Did you manage to get the morning off?'

'I did, next week.'

'Splendid. I'll find out about the trains and get in touch, all right?'

'That'll be fine,' she said. 'Goodbye.'

'Goodbye, Tilly.'

As she replaced the receiver she suddenly thought, how will he let me know? My God! He surely wouldn't come to her house, would he? That would really put the cat among the pigeons . . . but no, he didn't know where she lived and she prayed that he wouldn't find out!

As she walked back to the dress shop she almost wished she hadn't made the call at all.

Her fears were cast aside when just before closing time Eddie Chapman entered Madam Leone's. As soon as she saw him, Tilly walked towards him, before her employer could.

'Tilly, the train I want to catch leaves Southampton at nine thirty. Do you want me to pick you up?

'No, no, I'll meet you outside the main entrance to the station on the Commercial Road side, if that's all right with you?'

'I'll look forward to it,' he said. 'We will have a great day, I promise.'

She was grateful that he didn't linger, but now she had made the arrangements, inside she was all a flutter. She had promised David she wouldn't go to the club, so in one way she hadn't broken her word, but in her heart she was aware that he had really wanted to keep her and Eddie apart. She was filled with guilt, but at the same time thrilled by the idea of a trip to London. This was the wild side of her that worried her mother, she knew, but no harm could come of it, surely. It was just a day out in London, after all. But deep down she knew she was playing with fire.

During the following days, Tilly fought with her conscience and the need to ring Eddie Chapman and cancel the arrangement, but she couldn't bring herself to do so because she wanted to visit the metropolis so much.

On Sunday afternoon when she and Beth walked in the park she was still on edge.

'Whatever is wrong with you today?' Beth asked. 'You're like a tight spring ready to jump.'

Tilly couldn't keep her secret any longer. 'I'm

going to London next Wednesday with Eddie Chapman.'

'You what?'

Tilly explained the situation. 'He said he knew the city well and I do so want to go.' There was a look of defiance in her eyes as she gazed across at the shocked expression of her friend.

'Blimey! Your Jago would have a fit!'

'I know.'

'And what about David?'

Tilly's fiery nature flared. 'And what about David? We're not engaged or anything! We're just good friends.'

Taking a powder compact from her bag and checking her face in the mirror, Beth said, 'I bet he'll take you to somewhere fabulous to eat.'

'Do you think so?' asked Tilly eagerly. 'I hadn't thought of that.'

'You'd better be dressed for the occasion in case he does. By the way, does your mother know?'

Tilly looked askance. 'Are you mad? Of course not. I'll leave as if I'm going to work, and if you don't mind, I'll tell her I'm meeting you after-wards.'

'All right, but there will be a charge for such a favour.'

'A charge . . . whatever do you mean?' demanded Tilly.

'That you tell me all about your day!'

Laughing, Tilly said, 'I'll tell you everything, I promise.'

Eddie Chapman sat at his desk smiling softly to himself. So the girl had made the move he had hoped for without any further pressure from him, which was fine. How nervous she had sounded on the telephone and when he'd visited her place of employment. Nevertheless, she was still coming. She had a lot of spirit and he liked that in a woman.

There was something about young Tilly that he found both exciting and endearing . . . and very desirable! Perhaps it was her youth – her innocence. He would have to handle her carefully. He didn't want to spook her, because he fully intended to further their relationship. Chuckling to himself, he took a cigar from a box on his desk and cut off the end, then lit it. Yes indeed, he would certainly give her a good time. Next Wednesday held great promise. He rose from his desk, laughing to himself as he made for the door.

CHAPTER NINE

Tilly dressed carefully for her trip to London. She had to be careful not to arouse her mother's suspicions, so she wore a black skirt, a white blouse, a smart tailored light jacket and a cloche hat.

'Goodbye, Mum,' she called as she left the house. 'Don't forget I'm seeing Beth later so I'll be late home.'

She quickly closed the door before she could be questioned, her heart pounding as she made her way to the railway station, her mind full of questions. Was she being foolish? Would Eddie Chapman take advantage of the situation? If he did, what would she do?

She saw him standing outside the station, waiting. He smiled as he saw her approach.

'Hello, Tilly, you're in good time. I like a woman who is punctual,' he said.

Tilly thought he looked very smart and very sophisticated in his light grey suit, white shirt and striped tie.

'Come along,' he said, taking her arm. 'I've bought the tickets and the train is due in about ten minutes.'

As they waited for the train, Tilly tried to ignore the nervous tension that had gripped her, tightening every muscle in her body, it seemed.

'Where are we going when we get to London?' she asked.

'I have arranged for a car to pick us up at Waterloo station and take us to Buckingham Palace and the Houses of Parliament; then I thought we could go to Harrods for lunch, after which we can look round the store, knowing how much you want to see the place.' He smiled slowly. 'I have yet to meet a woman who doesn't like to shop.'

'That sounds wonderful,' she said, wondering at the same time how many women he had known.

The train drew into the station. Eddie took her by the arm and led her to a first-class carriage. 'We may as well travel in comfort,' he said as he opened the door for her.

She sat back in the comfortable seat, feeling very special. Eddie Chapman certainly knew how to entertain a lady, she mused, and wondered more than ever what the day ahead held for her.

Eddie was good company and a good conversationalist. They covered a wide range of subjects, ending with Tilly's frustration at being unable to do so many things that a man was able to do, simply because she was a woman.

'Such as what?' asked Eddie, barely hiding his amusement.

'I want to see the world!' she exclaimed. 'Men can get on a train and push off to any destination they want. They can go to sea. People listen to their opinions. Women are not supposed to have any. A woman is expected to marry and have children and that is their only role in life.'

'Florence Nightingale would disagree with you, and the suffragette movement certainly would,' he remarked. 'And women do travel, you know.'

'Only if they have money. There isn't much chance of me being able to afford to do that.'

Chuckling, he said, 'You will have to make sure you marry a rich man. Then you could.'

'I couldn't marry anyone just for their money!' She was outraged. 'That would be dishonest.'

Eddie was highly amused. 'Tilly Thompson, you really are a breath of fresh air. I can see that today is going to be very entertaining.'

As he spoke, the train pulled into Waterloo station.

They alighted from the carriage, then walked through the barrier and out of the station to where Eddie could see the car he had ordered waiting.

He helped Tilly into the back, then spoke to the driver.

'Buckingham Palace,' he said, 'but don't drive too fast, as I have a young lady with me who wants to see the sights.'

'Right, sir,' the driver said.

Eddie pointed out various places of interest on their journey after they crossed Westminster Bridge. 'There's Horse Guards Parade . . . here's Westminster Abbey.' They stopped the car for a moment outside the palace, and Tilly jumped out of the vehicle to run over to the railings.

'It's very big,' she said with a note of awe in her voice.

'The Union Jack is flying,' said Eddie, 'so the king is in residence.'

Tilly waved enthusiastically. 'Just in case he's looking out of the window,' she explained, to Eddie's amusement.

Back in the car, as they drove up The Mall, he pointed out Clarence House, St James's Palace and, to Tilly's great delight, mounted horse guards heading for the palace. They passed Hyde Park and Kensington Gardens on their way to Harrods.

Tilly was thrilled with the sights and sounds of the capital: the buzz of the place, the shops, the fashions of the smart ladies walking along the streets, the motorised vehicles. Southampton was not without the latter, of course, but here in London there were more, which added to her excitement.

Eventually they pulled up outside Harrods. Looking at the splendid displays in the huge windows, Tilly held her breath, unable to truly believe she was here.

Eddie Chapman sat and watched the animated expressions on her face as she gazed out of the window of the car. He was delighted that the day was being so enjoyed; it gave him a good feeling to be able to give this very unusual young girl such an exciting time.

The driver opened the door of the car and they both got out. Eddie dismissed him, saying, 'I will call you later. We are going to be here for some time.'

The driver grinned and, looking at Tilly who was now standing in front of a window full of the latest fashions, said, 'I am sure you will be, sir.'

As Eddie came and stood beside her Tilly said, 'I thought at Madam Leone's we sold high fashion, but these dresses are amazing.'

'Come along,' said Eddie. 'We'll have a look round before we have lunch, and then we can look some more afterwards.'

Tilly was in her element as they went from one department to another. The jewellery department took her breath away. With a deep sigh, she said, 'How wonderful to be able to afford such beautiful things.'

'Money isn't everything,' Eddie remarked.

She cast him a disdainful glance and said, 'Only people with money would say something like that. Try asking someone who is poor!'

Eventually they made their way to one of the restaurants and looked at the luncheon menu. Tilly considered the mouth-watering dishes on offer and was unable to make a decision as there was so much to choose from.

'Would you like me to order for you?' Eddie asked, seeing her confusion.

With a look of relief she said, 'Oh, would you?'

They started with hors d'oeuvres followed by chateaubriand, which was carved at the table, much to Tilly's delight, and finished with a delicious raspberry soufflé. Eddie made sure to choose a good bottle of wine to accompany it. Tilly looked round at the other elegant diners, taking in every detail of their clothes. How exciting it must be to live in this city, she thought.

Afterwards, they sat drinking coffee and chatting.

'I am too full to move,' Tilly said with an enormous grin. 'Thank you, Mr Chapman, that was a wonderful meal.'

'I'm glad you enjoyed it . . . and please call me

Eddie. Mr Chapman makes me feel like an old man.'

'You're hardly that!' she said, laughing.

'I'm happy to hear you say so,' he said. He summoned the waiter and settled the bill, then looked at Tilly. 'Are you ready for more window shopping?'

'Are you sure you want to? Haven't you had enough?'

'Gracious no. I love to see the look on your face when you see something you really like. Come on.' He held out his hand.

Shyly she took it and they left the restaurant. Eddie led her purposefully to a department selling cocktail gowns and began to look among the dresses on the rails. Eventually he took one out and held it up for her inspection. 'What do you think of this?'

Tilly let out a gasp. 'Oh, Eddie, it's absolutely exquisite!' The soft floating voile was shaded in hints of autumn from burnt orange through light browns and gold to soft lemon, and lined with pale coffee-coloured satin.

'Try it on,' he urged.

She looked shocked. 'I couldn't possibly do that.'

'Of course you can,' he said. 'I would like to see what you look like in it. Please, Tilly – just for me.'

How could she refuse? Besides, she desperately wanted to.

As she looked at her reflection in the mirrors of the dressing room, she couldn't believe how lovely she looked. The dress made her feel so glamorous, so grown up – so womanly. She drew back the curtain and stepped outside to face her escort.

He stared at her for what seemed an age.

'I don't know when I have seen a young woman look so beautiful,' he said as he gazed at her intently.

She smoothed the skirt and twirled around, saying, 'It is beautiful, isn't it? But I had better take it off now, otherwise I might be tempted to take flight wearing it.'

Inside the changing room she stood looking once again at her reflection and with great reluctance removed the dress. Putting on her own clothes she looked away, unable to bear the comparison. She hung the dress back on the hanger and emerged from the cubicle.

Eddie Chapman took the dress from her and, handing it to the assistant, said, 'Thank you, we'll take it. Please put it in a box for me, will you?'

Tilly couldn't believe what she was hearing. 'What are you doing?' she asked with a shocked expression as the assistant took it away.

'We are going to the Ritz hotel this evening and

95

I wanted you to have something special to wear. After all, today is a special occasion. I think you will need a pair of shoes to go with it, don't you?'

She was speechless. Then, looking down at her patent black shoes, she had to agree with him. They were quite unsuitable. However, she wasn't comfortable.

'Mr Chapman – Eddie – I really can't let you do this.'

He moved closer and his smoky brown eyes gazed into hers. 'Tilly, please let me. You have no idea how much pleasure today has given me – and I want to dance with you again. That's all there is to it, I promise. It will just complete what has been a perfect day.'

The intensity of his gaze was mesmerising and she heard herself agreeing. 'But where will I get changed?'

'When we get to the Ritz, you can go into the ladies' powder room and change there. Leave your other clothes with the cloakroom assistant.'

They moved off to a shoe department where he purchased a pair of satin shoes in the same shade as the lining of the dress.

'These should do, don't you think, Tilly?'

She was impressed with his choice and just nodded, lost for words.

Eddie found a phone booth and called for his

car to pick them up outside the store. Once they were seated inside the vehicle, he instructed the driver to take them for a drive around the city. He pointed out the Tower of London. 'We don't have time today to visit it, so we will have to come another day,' he told Tilly. 'You must see the crown jewels – they'll take your breath away.'

His remark was not lost on her. He was talking about coming to London again. She didn't know whether to be pleased or worried.

They passed lots of other sights – Piccadilly, the statue of Eros, Bond Street, Oxford Street, Park Lane – until eventually they stopped outside the Ritz hotel.

The driver opened the door and helped Tilly out of the car, handing her the boxes containing her dress and her shoes.

Eddie paid the driver and dismissed him. Turning to Tilly, he said, 'When we are ready to leave, we'll get a cab to take us to the station.' Holding her arm, he led her to the entrance to the hotel.

Tilly smiled at the uniformed doorman who held the door for her. 'Thank you,' she said.

Once inside, Eddie showed her where the ladies' room was and then where he would be waiting. With beating heart, Tilly walked into the palatial rest room. The opulence of it took her breath away.

The lady behind the counter asked, 'Can I be of service, madam?'

'I want to change my clothes,' Tilly told her.

Coming round the counter to her the woman said, 'Come this way,' and led her to a small private room. 'You can change here, madam. Then give me your clothes and I will take care of them. Will you be changing back into them?'

Tilly suddenly realised she couldn't walk into her house wearing her new finery. It would cause questions to be asked. She turned to the woman.

'Yes, I will. I have a train journey later.'

Once inside the room, she changed her clothes. To her surprise, inside the box she discovered a jewelled band which matched the dress and was to be worn round the forehead, in the latest fashion. Once dressed, Tilly combed her hair, set the band in place, put on her new shoes, folded her day clothes and placed them inside the box. She twirled in front of the mirror. Could this really be her?

As she handed the box to the cloakroom attendant the woman looked at her and smiled. 'You look wonderful, madam, if I might say so?'

With a happy smile Tilly said, 'Thank you so much. You certainly may say so!' Then she stepped out of the room and walked towards Eddie, who was sitting in a plush chair with two cocktails in front of him.

Getting to his feet, he said, 'You look amazing. Here, sit with me for a moment and have a drink.'

'What is it?' she asked as she sat down.

'A champagne cocktail.'

She took a sip. 'It's full of bubbles,' she said, 'but I do like it.'

'Have you enjoyed your day so far, Tilly?'

'Oh, yes. It's been wonderful. You have been so kind I don't know how to thank you.'

'That's easy,' he said softly. 'Come and dance with me.'

They carried their drinks into the ballroom where a band was playing. A waiter led them to a table for two. Eddie had a quick word with the man, who nodded and left. When the band finished playing their number, they struck up a tango.

Holding out his hand, Eddie said, 'Shall we?'

Feeling like the queen of Sheba in her new gown, Tilly rose from her seat and walked on to the floor and into his arms, where she became lost to the music and to him.

CHAPTER TEN

It was a wonderful evening. They danced, ate a light meal – as they were only peckish after such a sumptuous lunch – laughed and had fun. By now, Tilly was completely relaxed in Eddie Chapman's company. He was a great companion, she discovered, and funny too, which took her by surprise.

At last he looked at his watch and said, 'I think it is time to leave.'

Tilly was surprised at the lateness of the hour. Feeling like Cinderella, she returned to the cloak-room, changed her clothes and joined Eddie in the foyer. He didn't comment on the change, but took her arm and led her outside where the doorman called a cab for them.

Once on board the train, the excitement over-came her and Tilly felt her eyes closing.

Seeing his companion fast asleep, Eddie put an arm round her and made her comfortable. He gazed at her features – so composed, so innocent . . . so beautiful – and he longed to make love to her. Yet there was something so trusting about this beautiful, fiery, wonderful girl, he felt almost guilty about his lustful feelings. Still, he longed to take her into his arms and love her.

Just before the train entered Southampton station, Tilly stirred. Although half asleep, she realised that Eddie's arm was round her. Looking up, she saw his face but inches away.

Eddie tipped up her chin and kissed her softly on the mouth. 'Wake up, Sleeping Beauty. We're almost home.'

Still a little dazed, she sat up. 'I'm so sorry,' she said. 'How rude of me to fall asleep.'

'That's perfectly all right,' he said as the train stopped. 'You've had a busy day. I'd better get you home.'

They got into a taxi outside the station and Tilly asked him to drop her at the corner of her street. She didn't dare let him take her to the door; it would cause too many questions if she were seen.

When they arrived at their destination, Eddie helped her out with her packages and kissed her again, so thoroughly as to leave her breathless.

'Thank you, Tilly Thompson, for one of the most enjoyable days I've had for a very long time. I can't wait for our next outing.'

She watched him climb back into the vehicle, still stunned by his kiss. Then, walking to her house, she was relieved to see it in darkness. She quietly unlocked the door, closing it carefully behind her so as not to disturb anyone, and crept up the stairs to her bedroom.

Opening the wardrobe door, she hid the box containing her new finery. There it would have to stay until she could think of an excuse to produce it.

As she undressed, she went over the day's events, reliving the sights and sounds of the city, the many departments in Harrods, the food at lunchtime . . . and the evening at the Ritz hotel. The feel of Eddie's arms around her as they danced . . . and his kiss as they parted. Why did this man fascinate her so? He behaved like a perfect gentleman, she felt safe in his company, and yet . . . there was a frisson of excitement about being with him, of dancing with danger.

She climbed into bed and snuggled under the bedclothes. He had suggested they return to London another time to visit the Tower of London and see the crown jewels. She saw no reason to refuse, but . . . if she continued to see him, would he demand more of her than a goodnight kiss? He was not a young boy but a man of the world. She might be an innocent in such matters, but she was sensible enough to know that she was playing with fire. With a deep sigh, she turned over and was soon asleep.

Whilst Tilly was dreaming about the sights of London, Ken Williams was cavorting in the bedroom of Queenie, the barmaid from the Horse and Groom.

As he lay back against the pillows Ken, wiping the sweat from his brow, said, 'Bloody hell, Queenie girl, you know how to wear a man out, I'll say that for you!'

Flicking her long hair back she laughed and said, 'What's the matter, love, getting too old for a good fuck are you?'

'Cheeky bitch! No I bloody well am not, but I wouldn't mind a cup of tea and a smoke while I gets me breath back.'

Pulling a silk dressing gown around her voluptuous figure, Queenie rose from the bed, throwing a packet of cigarettes at him.

'Here, light one of these whilst I put the kettle on.'

Eventually he pulled a towel round his waist and followed her into the kitchen where he sat and watched her, noting how the fine material clung to her curves.

'My, but you are a fine figure of womanhood,'

he said, playfully slapping her backside as she passed him.

By the way,' she said as she made the tea, 'you know you were thinking of opening up a gambling club? Well, I heard about a place up for rent in Oxford Street that might suit.'

He grimaced. 'That Eddie Chapman turned our Charlie and me down. We had hoped he'd come in with us.'

'Aw, go on, you don't need him or anybody else. You and Charlie should do it on your own.'

'I don't know if we'd get a licence,' he said. 'We aren't very popular with the old bill. Not that they can prove anything against us – we're very careful.'

'Bloody hell! What sort of attitude is that? If you don't try you won't know, will you?'

He grinned up at her. 'You are quite a girl, you know. Of course you're right. I'll have a word with Charlie tomorrow.' He drank from his cup.

Queenie loosened her dressing gown and sat astride his knee. Facing him, she drew his head down between her full breasts. 'Well, are you man enough for another tussle?'

He raked her nipple with his teeth and slipped his hand between her legs. 'Let's find out, shall we?'

* * *

Eddie Chapman had also heard about the property in Oxford Street. He called the letting agency and asked to look round the building. He had toyed with the idea of opening a legally run gambling club but had put it to the back of his mind until he was told about this place. It sounded ideal, and he was never a man to miss an opportunity.

He walked around the rooms, his mind working overtime. They were all on one floor: one large room, big enough for a bar and space for tables and chairs, and two others large enough for roulette tables and blackjack. The small room could be used for poker, a very popular card game with the punters. He would have to have work done on the lavatories and decorate throughout, but he was pleased with what he saw. It would be perfect for what he had in mind . . . if he could get a licence. He would have to make enquiries. A visit to the local police force would be a wise move before he made any definite plans about the building.

Thanking the estate agent, he walked back to the Blue Pelican and rang to make an appointment to see someone at the police station about the possibility of getting a licence.

Tilly had been walking on air since her trip to London and could hardly wait to see Beth to tell her all about it. The girls met after work on Friday.

Tilly gave her a blow-by-blow account of her day, but when she got to the part where Eddie Chapman bought her the cocktail dress, Beth interrupted.

'He bought you a dress? Blimey!'

'And a pair of satin shoes to match,' Tilly told her with a delighted grin.

Her friend looked concerned. 'Was it wise to let him do that?'

Tilly felt as if someone had just pricked her balloon. 'Whatever do you mean?' she demanded.

'Now don't get mad!' exclaimed Beth. 'But men don't buy those kinds of things unless they want something in return.'

'I don't know what you're getting at,' Tilly protested. 'All the time we were together he was a perfect gentleman.'

'Did you dance together?'

'Yes we did, but that hardly constitutes a crime, does it?'

'Did he kiss you?'

Hesitating, Tilly said, 'Well, he did as a matter of fact. Twice.'

'Ha! There you are then, that's just for starters. Has he asked to see you again?'

'Not exactly . . . but he did say we would have to see the Tower of London another time.'

'There you go!' said Beth triumphantly. 'This is

only the beginning. You continue to see Eddie Chapman and before you know where you are he'll want to take you to bed.'

'Don't be so disgusting! What a dreadful thing to say. Whatever has got into you?'

Beth raised her eyebrows and stared at her. 'Look, Tilly Thompson, you are my best friend and I don't want to see you end up in trouble. If you can't see what the man is up to I can! If you want to play with fire I can't stop you, but don't say I didn't warn you.'

Tilly just glared at her.

'You're nineteen, he must be at least twenty-seven, far too old to be content with holding hands and a few kisses. I bet he's had several women before now,' Beth continued.

Her hackles now raised, Tilly snapped, 'So what? What on earth has that got to do with me?'

Shaking her head, Beth said, 'You don't want to listen because you know I'm speaking the truth. Just be careful, Tilly, that's all I'll say.' She looked at her watch. 'I must fly. I promised Mum I wouldn't be late. I'll see you tomorrow.'

Left alone, Tilly ambled homewards deep in thought. Beth was only thinking of her interests, she knew that. She also knew that her friend had only put into words what had been going though her own mind, although she would never have admitted such a thing. But she had enjoyed Eddie's company. It had been an exciting day and she knew that she couldn't wait to go back to London with him. But should she refuse?

On Monday morning, a letter arrived in the morning post addressed to Tilly just as she was leaving for work. Not recognising the writing, she stuffed it in her pocket until she took a coffee break.

To her great surprise she saw it was from Eddie Chapman. He was inviting her to go to Salisbury Races with him!

Dear Tilly,

I have a horse running during the race meeting at Salisbury on Wednesday next, and I wondered if you would care to come with me. I could pick you up from work at one o'clock, and we could catch a train. We would miss the first race but that isn't a problem. Give me a call if you are free.

Regards,
Eddie

Tilly was thrilled. She had never been to a race meeting in her life, and judging by the letter there certainly was no question of a hidden agenda here.

It was almost businesslike. He'd even signed it *Regards*. That would surely satisfy even the sceptical Beth.

At lunchtime, she went to a nearby telephone box and rang the club. She felt her heart beat a little faster when eventually she heard his voice.

'You received my letter safely then?'

'How did you find out my address?' she asked.

She heard him chuckle. 'It isn't hard when you know where to look,' he told her. 'So are you free on Wednesday?'

'Yes, I am,' she said.

'I'll be outside the shop with a taxi waiting,' he told her.

As she walked back to Madam Leone's she was filled with excitement. But she decided that this time, she would keep her meeting with the club owner to herself.

CHAPTER ELEVEN

Eddie Chapman was pleased with himself. The meeting with the police chief had been amicable and he had been told that as far as the local force were concerned, they couldn't see any reason for not granting a licence for the gambling club, should he apply in the near future.

'So far, Mr Chapman, you have run your present premises well and without trouble, but I have to say one thing,' said the officer.

'What is that?'

'It has been brought to my attention that the Williams brothers have paid a couple of visits to the Blue Pelican and this does give us some cause for concern.'

'No need for that,' said Eddie. 'They put a business proposition to me which I refused. They are not the sort of people with whom I want to have any dealings on any level, so I can assure you that is not a problem, Superintendent. Any gambling club owned by me will be run strictly by the letter of the law.'

'In that case, Mr Chapman, go ahead with your application.'

The two men shook hands. As Eddie walked out of the police station he wore a smile of satisfaction. He would get in touch with the estate agents on his return to the club and start negotiations for the property.

Later in the day the two Williams brothers talked over their plans for opening a club.

'Queenie said we don't need another partner and when you think about it she's right,' said Ken. 'It was good of her to tell me about the place in Oxford Street. I walked by it yesterday on the way home and it's in an ideal spot.'

Looking at his watch, Charlie said, 'The estate agents will be closing now so we'll call first thing in the morning and go and take a look round before we make a decision. Besides, I have a date. I want to go home and get changed.'

'Who is it this time?' asked his brother.

'A nice young lad I met in a bar last night. Blond hair, blue eyes and eyelashes any woman would envy. Besides, he's relatively inexperienced, so he's pliable, just how I like them. Nathan, he's called, known as Nat.'

With a sly look his brother said, 'Be careful. Gnats can have a nasty bite.'

With a broad grin, Charlie said, 'Maybe I'll like that!'

Getting out of his chair, Ken said, 'You just take care, that's all. I'll see you in the morning.

In a scruffy flat in the Northam area, Nat Summers sat drinking a cup of tea with his sister Elsie, who was getting ready for work. As she put on her lipstick she turned and looked at her brother.

'Where are you off to this evening, all tarted up?'

'I'm off on a heavy date with a bloke I met last night. I should be all right – he's got plenty of money according to my sources.'

'And who might this man be?'

'Charlie Williams.'

The girl looked startled. 'Not one of the Williams twins?'

'Yes, that's right.'

She sat beside her brother. 'Now you listen to me, Nathan, you keep away from them. They are bloody dangerous – *and* that old bitch of a mother they have. I worked for them for a while. The old cow tried to drive me out of Southampton.'

He cast a knowing glance at her. 'Now why would she do that? Were you creaming off the top again?'

'Well, I did have a few punters of my own on the side.'

'When will you learn? This isn't the first time you've been caught pulling that stunt, is it?'

'So what if it isn't? They don't have to lie on their backs and earn their money. We brasses take all the risks.'

'As far as I see it, then it was your own fault and I'm going to get all I can from this geezer.'

'Then you are no better . . . but for God's sake don't tell that bastard I'm your sister or I will be in deep shit. I'm hoping they think I've left the town.'

Putting out his cigarette, he said, 'All right. I don't want you queering my pitch anyway.'

'Bad choice of words, dear boy!' She kissed him on the cheek and left the flat.

Nat walked over to the mirror above the fireplace and combed his hair and straightened his tie. Then, picking up his jacket, he put it on. He carefully folded a white handkerchief and placed it in his breast pocket before preening in front of the mirror again.

'You are a good-looking bitch,' he said and grinned at his reflection. Charlie Williams had been completely fooled by him. The old man thought he was naive and pliable, which was exactly the impression he had wanted to give, but he would screw every last penny out of the old guy before he'd finished with him. Then it would be time to move on to pastures new.

*　*　*

The *Aquitania* had docked in New York and when David Strickland came off duty he showered and changed. Walking down the gangway he hailed a waiting cab and asked the driver to take him to Broadway, where he sat in a restaurant and ate lunch. Whilst eating he pondered over the problem of what to buy as a gift for Tilly. He wanted something unusual, to match her personality.

Leaving the restaurant he walked along the street that was at the hub of the busy city, looking in all the shop windows along the way. He stopped in front of a boutique and gazed at an emerald green satin evening jacket. Down the front and sleeves it was richly embroidered with flowers, picked out in warm coloured silks and decorated with small seed pearls. It was exquisite, and the colouring would suit Tilly's auburn hair wonderfully. Opening the door he entered the shop.

He had no idea of Tilly's size but one of the female assistants looked about the same build and he asked her to try it on.

'You can change it, sir, if it isn't right,' he was told.

When he explained that he was a member of the crew of the *Aquitania*, and would be taking it home, she said it made no difference. 'You can return it on your next visit.' He was relieved, as the jacket was expensive.

'Thank you, I'll take it,' he told her.

He then shopped for himself, buying underwear and shirts, before seeing a lady's silver filigree bangle, to be worn above the elbow in the latest style. He bought that too and had it gift-wrapped.

Feeling tired after his shopping, David walked into the bar of an hotel and settled down with a glass of beer to recoup his energy before going to see a film. It was his way of relaxing after a busy trip.

As he sipped his drink he wondered what Tilly was doing. He missed her company and her amusing small talk. She made him laugh and he wished she were here now so he could show her New York. How she would enjoy herself here, he mused. Before going to the cinema, he bought her a book of photographs of the city. At least this way he could show her what New York looked like.

The following morning, the chief engineer sent for him.

'Sit down, David. I have a proposition to put to you. I don't want to influence you in any way, but I think this a great opportunity.'

'What do you mean, the property has already been let?' Charlie Williams asked into the mouthpiece of the telephone. Looking across at his twin, he shrugged in surprise. 'When did that happen?' He listened for a moment, growing more furious by the second. Then he slammed the receiver down.

'The property was let yesterday . . . and do you know who's got it?'

Ken shook his head.

'That bastard Chapman! He's pulled a flanker!'

'Hardly,' said Ken. 'He didn't know we were interested too, did he?'

'Suppose not,' Charlie conceded reluctantly, 'but what a bloody coincidence!' Shaking his head, he said, 'He's really getting too big for his boots – sly git!'

Knowing his brother's temper, Ken tried to calm him. 'Now don't go getting riled; he's a businessman like we are. We were just a bit slow off the mark, that's all.'

'Well I'll be very interested to see what he makes of the place. It will need some doing up, I expect. We'll just keep a watchful eye and see how he makes out.'

'He's pretty shrewd – I'm sure he'll make it look good. He has the finances according to the rumours I've heard.'

'So how did he make his money, tell me that?'

'I don't know and frankly I don't care! Now come on, we've got a lot of paperwork to get through.'

Charlie let the matter drop for the time being,

but as usual when he held a grudge it gnawed away at him, and now he wanted to learn more about bloody Eddie Chapman. He would start making a few discreet enquiries. After all, everyone had secrets, and now he wondered what Chapman's were. He wasn't a nob so his money wasn't inherited, so how had he made enough to start his business? Besides, it was always useful to learn as much as possible about the opposition.

Seeing the thoughtful expression on his brother's face Ken interrupted his ruminations. 'How did you make out with your young man the other night?

With a broad grin, Charlie said, 'What a bloody joy he was! Beautiful body, clean, nice tight arse . . . and willing. We had a great time and I'll be seeing him again later this week. I might even buy him something to show him how pleased I am with him.'

'Now don't go spoiling a good thing. Keep him lean and keep him keen is my advice.'

'Since when have I ever listened to you, you old bugger?'

Ken laughed. It was true. In business they bounced ideas off each other, both appreciative of the other's input, but in private matters it was a different kettle of fish. Both men went their own way.

'Just watch yourself, that's all,' said Ken as he got to his feet. 'I'm going to see if Mum's all right.'

'Give her my love and tell her I'll call in later in the week.'

Hilda Williams was doing her laundry in the kitchen, rubbing the sheets against a washboard when Ken arrived.

'Hello, love. Everything all right?' she asked.

He looked at her red hands and said, 'For God's sake, why don't you send them sheets to the laundry? We can afford it.'

'They don't wash them as clean as I do,' she replied, pushing the sheets down into the hot soapy water to soak. 'I'll rinse them in a minute, put them through the mangle and hang them to dry outside. They smell so much better dried in the fresh air.'

Ken knew better than to argue and followed his mother into the living room where a kettle sat on the hob of the shiny blackleaded stove.

'Did you ever catch up with that bitch of a whore I told you about?'

'No,' he said, 'She's probably scarpered to another town by now.'

'Cheeky mare!' Hilda exclaimed. 'Trying to take us for a fool. Well, I told her right enough.'

Her son laughed and said, 'I'm sure you scared the shit out of her, Ma. She won't dare stay around.'

Making a pot of tea, the old girl asked, 'How's things, then?'

'Charlie is really pissed off because we had our eye on a property in Oxford Street, but it's taken.'

'What did you want it for, anyway?'

'We was going to open a gaming club.'

She stared at him. 'Don't be bloody daft! The filth would never grant you two a licence for that.'

'They have never been able to pin anything on us. They would dearly love to charge us with living off immoral earnings, but we've got that covered.'

'They aren't silly, son. They will be watching your every move, so take care . . . and forget about any gaming club, because it ain't going to happen!'

As he sipped his tea, Ken thought the old girl was probably right, but it had been a nice idea at the time and although he didn't say anything to his twin, it stuck in his craw that Eddie Chapman had rented the property under their noses . . . and if he decided to go into that business, there was little doubt that he would be successful in obtaining the necessary licence. He could cope with the disappointment, but Charlie was a different matter. He hoped he wasn't going to have trouble with his brother over it.

CHAPTER TWELVE

The following Wednesday lunchtime found an excited Tilly sitting once again on a train with Eddie Chapman. Another new adventure. She listened as Eddie told her about the races.

'It's over the sticks,' he explained, 'which for me is much more interesting. Flat racing is fine, but not so exciting for the spectator.'

'Do the horses fall sometimes?' she asked.

'Oh, yes, quite frequently, but most of the time the animals are fine, although the jockeys might take a nasty tumble. Jockeys have many broken bones during their careers. It's all part of the job.'

'Which race is your horse in?'

'The four thirty.'

'What's its name?'

'Rufus the Red, named after King Rufus who was shot in the eye when he was out hunting in the New Forest . . . you've heard of the Rufus Stone which marks the spot, I expect?'

She looked at him in amazement. 'Yes, of course I have.'

'Then why do you look surprised that I know about it? It's local history, after all.'

'I suppose it is, I just didn't imagine you to be the sort of man who would be interested in such things.'

He started laughing and said, 'I'm not quite sure what sort of man you think I am, Tilly.'

Grinning at him, her eyes twinkling with mischief, she said, 'To be honest, I haven't made up my mind yet, but you are certainly full of surprises.'

His gaze met hers and he said, 'I like the idea of being a man of mystery.'

She became a little flustered by the intensity of his gaze and turned away. Looking at the passing countryside, she said nothing more.

When they arrived at the racecourse, Eddie ushered her upstairs into a private box, a comfortable room with an assortment of drinks and glasses on the side, a bottle of champagne on ice and a large silver platter of delicious-looking sandwiches with various fillings. Through glass doors, steps led down to outside seats which overlooked the racecourse and the winning post.

Leading her through the doors, Eddie said, 'I had sandwiches made rather than a proper lunch so we can sit here and watch the races.'

As he spoke a waiter appeared with a small table on which he laid out plates and the sandwiches. 'I'm Jack, your waiter for the day. Shall I open the champagne, sir?' he asked.

'Please,' said Eddie. He handed a race card to Tilly and showed her how to use it, explaining about the list of runners and jockeys in each race, their past records and other information about them. He then handed her twenty pounds in notes.

'What's this for?' she asked, taken aback by the gesture.

'That is your mad money,' he explained, 'for you to make bets on the horses.'

'I can't take this,' she said, filled with embarrassment.

'Of course you can. It's all part of the day. Now don't be difficult – you're here to enjoy yourself. Please don't spoil it for me.'

'All right. If I win I'll pay you back.'

'Fine. Now, choose a horse and put some money on it.'

'How do I do that?'

'We can ask Jack to take our stakes – that's the money – to the tote, which is just down the stairs.'

Tilly looked at the names of the runners in the next race. Knowing absolutely nothing about the trainers or jockeys, she chose a horse because it had a name she liked.

'I fancy Persuasive Lady,' she said.

With a frown, Eddie said, 'It's an outsider and I have to tell you it doesn't have much of a chance.'

'It's the only name I like,' she said decisively.

'In that case, you must back it. I fancy the favourite, although it isn't much of a price.' He beckoned to the waiter.

He wrote his own bet out on a betting slip, then wrote one for Tilly.

'Do you want to back it to win?' he asked.

Not understanding what was the alternative and not wanting to appear ignorant of such things, Tilly said, 'Of course!'

There were four races left to run, so she decided to place five pounds on the horse. It sounded a great deal of money, but she didn't know any other way to decide. Five pounds a race would use up the stake money that Eddie had insisted she have.

The runners rode past them on the way to the start and when Eddie pointed out her horse Tilly was pleased with her choice. Surreptitiously, she crossed her fingers for luck.

The race began and as the horses raced round the track, almost out of sight as they climbed a slope in the distance, Tilly watched through Eddie's binoculars until they came into view along the final furlong, heading towards the winning post. She heard the commentator getting more and more excited as he positioned the leaders for the punters. All she could hear was the name of her horse.

'Persuasive Lady is catching up to the favourite, Jasper's Lad, she's gaining . . . can this rank outsider do it?'

Tilly was on her feet yelling her horse's name at the top of her voice. 'Come on, Lady, you can do it!'

There was a flurry of horseflesh as they passed the winning post. She turned to look at Eddie, unsure of the result.

'Persuasive Lady wins! Jasper's Lad a close second . . .'

Tilly didn't hear the rest. She flung her arms round Eddie's neck. 'I won! I won!' she cried.

Picking her up and swinging her round, he kissed her and said, 'You did! Congratulations!'

She suddenly became aware of what she'd done and extricated herself from his hold. 'I'm so sorry. I was completely carried away with the excitement of it all.'

Laughing, Eddie said, 'Come now, don't be embarrassed. I've done that to a complete stranger before now . . . and another man at that!' Which dispelled any discomfort Tilly was feeling.

Clapping her hands, she said, 'Oh, Eddie, wasn't that exciting?'

'Indeed it was. You beat my horse by a short head. You've won a lot of money, young lady.'

With wide eyes she asked, 'Have I?'

'Indeed you have. That horse was fifty to one. You have over two hundred and fifty pounds coming back.'

She put her hand over her mouth to smother the scream of delight which was rising in her throat. 'Honestly?'

'Honestly. Beginner's luck is what we call it. Perhaps you'd better pick out my runners for me.'

'Oh, I couldn't! What if they lost? That would be dreadful.'

With a broad grin on his face Eddie said, 'Here, we should toast your success,' and he handed her a glass of champagne. 'And you had better eat some sandwiches. Winning and champagne is heady stuff. You need something inside you.'

Before the four-thirty race, Eddie took Tilly to the parade ring, where the horses were being walked around. As an owner he was allowed into the inner circle where he introduced her to Jeremy Frampton, the trainer. After the introductions the two men walked to the side out of earshot.

'What sort of chance has Rufus got?' Eddie asked.

'A reasonable one. The opposition is good but he's worth an each way bet.'

This time Rufus was being run legally, without any enhancing drugs. As Jeremy had pointed out in a previous telephone chat, 'He's up to the field of runners and we must be very careful.'

Eddie and Tilly returned to the box to watch the race, and he suggested she back the horse each way instead of to win. 'Put two pounds each way, as the field is pretty good.'

It was good advice as the horse came in third.

The last race was over, the sandwiches were eaten and the champagne bottles empty. Tilly insisted that she pay back the twenty pounds to Eddie.

'I don't know what I would have done if I had lost it all,' she told him. 'That would have been terrible. How would I have ever been able to repay you?'

'You didn't have to, Tilly . . . but had you felt really bad about it, I would have had to think of a way. That might have been interesting.'

Was he teasing, she wondered, but when she saw his expression she didn't think he was. She shivered slightly. What would he have decided?

Seated on the train for the return journey, Tilly pored over the race card, which now made more sense to her. She had loved the whole experience and couldn't wait to go to another race meeting now she knew what to do. In her handbag she still had almost two hundred pounds after losing some on the following races and repaying her stake money to Eddie. It was a small fortune. How on earth was she going to tell her family about it? Suddenly, she realised that there was no way that she could. Jago would blow his top if he were told she'd spent the afternoon at the races with Eddie Chapman, and David wouldn't be pleased either. Oh, dear – she hated secrets and this sudden feeling of guilt. And there was the beautiful dress still hidden in the back of her wardrobe!

Seeing her look of consternation, Eddie asked, 'What's the matter?'

'Nothing,' she replied quickly. How could she tell him the truth, especially as he had given her such a wonderful day out? 'I've had one of the best days of my life,' she said. 'Thank you so much, Eddie.'

'I'm pleased you had such a good time,' he said. 'I do hope there will be more, but for the next few weeks I'm going to be tied up as I'm opening a new business which will keep me up to my eyes in work. But after that, if you are free, we'll do something else.'

Tilly didn't like to question him about the new business and in one way was relieved that he wouldn't be available, because it would give her time to decide whether she should really stop seeing him in the future. She knew that she should listen to those who warned her about him, but he was so interesting to be with. Apart from kissing her, he'd been a perfect gentleman, so where did he get his reputation from?

She hid her winnings inside the box with her dress at the back of the wardrobe. She would have loved to give some of it to her mother to help out with the household expenses, but there was no way she could do so without an explanation, other than saying a client had tipped her and bringing home the odd joint of meat now and again. David would be home soon and much as she was looking forward to seeing him, she still felt guilty about breaking the spirit of the promise she had made to him. They had become such good friends that she really didn't want to displease him.

She wasn't the only person dealing with their conscience. Her mother's employer, Gerald Bradbury, was struggling with his. After the visitation from Charlie Williams in his office, Gerald had abstained from booking any of the prostitutes for ten days, but after that his sexual frustration wore down his reserve and he went to spend an evening of physical gratification with one of the Williamses' girls in a hotel on the outskirts of

Southampton. But although she was more than accommodating, he was fighting with the desire to hurt her as they had sex. Knowing the trouble he'd had before when he let his sadistic feelings overtake him, he managed to keep control until she was paid and had left him alone.

He fought off his longings for another week, then he drove around one of the renowned red light districts of the town, looking at the girls standing waiting for punters. He couldn't bring himself to stop, and filled with frustration he drove slowly on until he saw a girl standing alone, out of sight of the others. He slowed to a stop and wound down the window of his car and waited.

The young blonde strolled up to him. 'Looking for business, darling?' she asked.

He liked her; she was perky and pretty.

'Yes, I am,' he said. 'Get in.'

Once she was seated beside him in his Ford, he drove towards the common, a large acreage of land with trees, lakes and plenty of shrubs affording lots of cover for such a meeting.

'What's your name?' he asked.

'Elsie. What's yours?'

'You don't need to know,' he said as he parked the car deep in a small wooded area. 'Let's get into the back,' he said, opening his door.

CHAPTER THIRTEEN

The *Aquitania* docked at midday, announcing her arrival with the deep throaty roar of her funnels. When he came off duty, David Strickland showered and changed. His steward had carefully packed all his clothes for him and as he sat down to have his lunch, he thanked the man who had looked after him during the previous months.

'Thanks for taking such good care of me, Harry,' he said. 'I'll really miss you.'

'And I'll miss you too, sir. How long will you be working ashore, do you know?'

Shaking his head, David said, 'Not really. I said I would do it for six months and then decide whether to return to sea or stay longer.' He smiled at his steward. 'You know us old seadogs, unless we can feel the deck moving beneath our feet, it doesn't seem right.'

Clearing the plates from the small table, Harry said, 'I couldn't go ashore, not until I retire. I'd drive my old woman mad. It's bad enough when

I'm on leave – after a week ashore I get restless. My wife, Lizzy, sends me off to the pub out of the way.'

Rising from his seat, David put on his jacket and handed Harry a sealed envelope. 'Here, buy your wife something.'

'Thanks very much sir. I'd like to say it's been a pleasure to look after you. I'll help you carry your bags off the ship.'

As they walked down the gangway, David had mixed emotions, and asked himself if he had made the right decision. It was too late anyway, he thought, and at least he would now have more time to see Tilly. He couldn't wait to give her his news.

When Tilly finished work for the day and left Madam Leone's, she was very surprised to see the young engineer waiting for her.

'David! How lovely to see you.'

He took her into his arms in a warm embrace and kissed her softly. 'Can we go to Lyons and have some tea?' he asked. 'I have some news to tell you.'

She agreed, curious to know what it was. It came as a big surprise when, once they had ordered tea and cakes and settled down, he told her of his move.

'I'm going to be working ashore for the next six months, teaching trainee engineers, so I'll be around.'

'Oh, David, that's wonderful!' And indeed she was pleased, but she couldn't help thinking that it would make life difficult if she wanted to see Eddie Chapman again.

Eddie Chapman was walking around his new premises with the foreman, deciding on the alterations that were required.

'If we knock this wall down here it will give me another sizeable room. Will that cause any problems?' he asked.

'Not really,' said the man. 'This is a load-bearing wall, but we can put a joist in, so that will be fine.'

'Good, then that's what we'll do.'

Walking around the rest of the place, Eddie was very pleased with the work. The walls had all been stripped of the old wallpaper, replastered to make them even, and rehung with new paper. It was ivory in colour, but heavily flocked, which made the rooms look opulent. Graceful chandeliers would hang from the ceilings and rich gold velvet drapes at the windows. It was going to look expensive and classy and bring in the men with money to burn – and make him wealthy. All he would have to do was keep his nose clean with the law and rake in the money! What could be better? Absolutely nothing, he thought, as he took a large cigar from his top pocket and lit it. Nothing could stand in his way.

Hearing footsteps on the bare boards behind him, Eddie turned, expecting to see the foreman; but someone else was walking towards him. Someone he'd not seen for several years and whom he had hoped never to see again.

'Hello, Eddie,' said the newcomer. 'You're looking well.'

Ethel Thompson cleared the remains of the breakfast things from the dining table. Gerald Bradbury glared at her.

'Get me another pot of tea and tell Cook the last one was like water. Undrinkable. And hurry up.'

Carrying the tray to the kitchen Ethel delivered her message.

'Cheeky bugger!' exclaimed the cook. 'I made it same as always. What's got into the man?'

'I don't know,' said Ethel. 'He's been acting strangely these past few days. I heard him having a hell of a row with Mrs Bradbury the other evening. I had to clear up a broken glass the next morning.'

'Well, she's enough to annoy any man,' Cook grumbled. 'Toffee-nosed madam, making out she's better than she is. And she's a lazy bitch.' Cook nudged Ethel. 'I bet she's bloody hopeless in bed!'

'What a thing to say!' exclaimed Ethel, but she grinned at her companion just the same.

Speaking in low tones, Cook confided, 'I heard tell that the old man has other women on the side.'

'Really?'

'And I heard he ain't too choosy, if you know what I mean!'

Ethel was shocked. 'You don't mean . . . ?'

'Indeed I do. I have a friend who's a chambermaid at a hotel on the outskirts, and she swears he goes there with different women, quite regular like.'

'Who'd have thought it of him with all his airs and graces?'

'Well, duck, there's none so queer as folks, as they say. Here, take this pot of tea to the randy old sod.'

Ethel walked into the breakfast room and placed the tray on the table. 'Will there be anything else?' she asked.

Gerald Bradbury didn't answer and when Ethel looked at him she saw he was gazing into space, deep in thought, a frown creasing his brow. He seemed oblivious of her presence, so she left the room, wondering just what was on his mind that seemed so serious.

Bradbury's hands shook as he poured a cup of tea. Taking a handkerchief from his pocket, he wiped the perspiration from his forehead. He had to get a grip on himself, he knew that. How he behaved now and in the future was of the utmost importance. He must maintain his position above all else or he would be ruined. Straightening his back, he let out a deep breath. He was a strong character, feared by many in his own profession for his ability; he just had to keep his equilibrium and it would see him through. He rose from his chair, went into his study, picked up his weighty briefcase and left the house.

Later that evening, Jago Thompson was sitting at the bar of the Red Lion in the high street. He liked the pub with its Tudor origins and its minstrels' gallery, he was intrigued by its history. It was said that it was used as a courtroom for the trial of the nobles who plotted against King Henry V. The present day clientele were usually of a decent class, so he was surprised to see Charlie Williams enter the bar, accompanied by a young man.

Jago didn't like Charlie. He'd sometimes met the twins when he'd been playing poker at one of their private card parties, but Charlie was a twisted man in Jago's eyes. Not only for his preference for pretty, young men, but also in his manner. He'd seen him deal with punters down on their luck in a card school. Charlie loved to taunt such players, and one day, Jago was certain, someone would pay him back.

He watched as the young man was given money to go to the bar for the drinks. He also saw the lad pocket the change, which was not handed over when he returned with the drinks to the table. It seemed obvious to Jago that this young chap was lining his pockets, which amused him. Served Charlie right.

Sipping his gin and tonic, Charlie looked at Nat Summers and asked, 'Whatever is the matter with you tonight? You've got a face on you like a dried prune.'

Young Nat couldn't tell him the truth. His sister hadn't been home for two days and he was so worried about her, he'd reported her missing to the police. But he didn't want to talk to Charlie about Elsie so he just said, 'I've got a headache, that's all.'

'Well, I hope it's better before we go home. I have plans for later!'

Playing Charlie's sex games was not what Nat wanted, especially tonight, but he wanted to touch Charlie for money so he would have to play along. Nat had learned quickly that before sex Charlie was always generous. After was too late. Once the man had satisfied his sexual urges he didn't want to know about anything until next time. So Nat smiled provocatively at his lover.

'Have I ever denied you anything?'

'No, and you'd better not,' Charlie said threateningly.

Fucking bastard! Nat thought. When I've had enough money from you, you ugly old sod, I'll be off and you won't see me for dust.

At that moment, the bar door opened and Tilly walked in with David Strickland. Jago rose to his feet and beckoned them over to his table.

'Hello, David,' he said. 'When did you dock?'

'Today. Can I get you a drink?'

'Thanks; half a bitter will do nicely. Here, Tilly, sit beside me.' As David went to the bar he turned to his sister. 'You must be a happy girl with your boyfriend home again?'

'He's going to be ashore for the next six months,' she told him. 'He's going to instruct trainee engineers,' she said proudly.

Jago grimaced. 'He must be pretty bright then.' He leaned closer to Tilly. 'You couldn't do much better than this chap, you know. Nice bloke, good job.'

'Oh, for goodness' sake,' she snapped, 'will you

stop trying to marry me off! There's a million things I want to do before I settle down.'

David's return stopped further conversation between brother and sister. Just then the bar door opened, and when Eddie Chapman entered with his blonde lady Tilly was rendered absolutely speechless.

Jago saw the stricken look on the face of his sister and turned to see who had come in. 'Well, I see the owner of the Blue Pelican is still with the same woman,' he said.

'What do you mean?' asked Tilly, curiosity overcoming her feelings.

'They've been keeping company for several months now. Some say she's his mistress, but it's only speculation. No one seems to know very much about the man at all, which in itself is a bit strange, I think. Men of mystery usually have some secret to hide.'

Tilly turned away so that her back was towards the couple. She couldn't bear to see Eddie with someone else after he'd kissed *her*. Although their time spent together had been free and easy, without any demands from Eddie, she felt a thread of jealousy creeping through her veins, and as soon as she could she suggested to David that they go somewhere else.

'Do you feel like dancing?' she asked him.

'There's a dance on at the Pier. I would love to go.'

'That's just fine with me,' he said, so saying goodbye to Jago they left the Red Lion and walked along the esplanade to the Royal Pier, where they deposited Tilly's coat at the cloakroom and took to the floor.

'It's so good to hold you again,' whispered David, his head against hers as they danced the slow foxtrot. 'I've missed you so much, Tilly.'

She couldn't help feeling a sense of guilt, because she couldn't say the same. She'd been so caught up in her conflicting feelings about Eddie that David's absence had passed almost unnoticed, although she had been pleased to receive a letter from him a couple of days before his return.

'How was New York?' she asked.

'Busy. I've brought you something home I hope you'll like.'

'Really?' She smiled up at him. 'That was nice of you.'

'I have to get settled in my new quarters and see what hours I'll be teaching, but I would love to see you on Sunday, if that's all right?'

'Why don't you come and have a meal with us?' she suggested. 'We eat just after two o'clock as Dad and Jago like to go for a couple of pints at the pub. After, we can go for a walk.'

'Thanks, I'd love to. Your father can tell me about Clarence.' He grinned at her. 'And I can tell him about my dog.'

'Now don't tease,' she said, 'Dad is very proud of old Clarence.'

'And so he should be.'

As they sat out the next dance he asked, 'So, what have you been doing whilst I've been away?'

'Not a great deal,' she lied. 'Life has been very dull.'

'Well, we'll certainly have to change that whilst I'm home. I'll have the weekends free, so we'll be able to do things whilst the weather is still good.'

'That'll be nice,' she said, but her private thoughts betrayed her. It was Eddie Chapman she wanted to see. She knew without a doubt that when he was free he would get in touch with her and ask her out – and she would go.

CHAPTER FOURTEEN

Eddie Chapman had caught a glimpse of Tilly in the bar of the Red Lion, and had seen her turn away. He would have liked to speak to her but he had a lot on his mind, and as time passed he could not relax. Finishing his drink, he turned to Greta and said, 'Sorry, love, but I need to get back to the club. I'll take you home, but I can't stay, I'm afraid – I've got a lot of paperwork to get through.' This wasn't entirely true, but he needed to be alone to think over the problem that had presented itself.

Walking into the club a short while later, he made straight for his office – and solitude. Lighting a cigar, he relived the scene that had taken place in his new building where he'd been faced with his past when Frank Graves had walked up to him.

'Hello, Eddie. You're looking well,' he'd said.

They had first met whilst Chapman was still living in Woolwich. They had both been in their late teens, playing snooker in the local working men's club. Both had been good at the game and a friendly rivalry had developed. They had a lot in common, both coming from working-class families, both ambitious to get on, both scraping around earning a living.

Eddie's father was a locksmith and had shown Eddie, as a boy, the intricacies of various locks and how to open them without a key, trying to teach him how to solve the problem should he ever find himself locked out of a building. He also taught him to open safes. It became a game between them, his father setting him a task, himself overcoming the obstacle. He became an expert.

As Eddie grew up, he found he was good at selling and would buy stock cheaply and sell it on the street for a profit, saving as much as he could towards opening his own business.

Frank, who worked for a delivery service, had teased him.

'By the time you save enough to open a business, you'll be an old man,' he said. 'What you need is a pile of money to give you a start.'

Eddie had laughed. 'And where will I ever get that?'

'I know,' Frank said, scratching his chin.

Intrigued, Eddie said, 'Go on, I'm listening.'

'Just think about it. You're a whizz at opening

locks – you should put that talent to good use.'

'Yes, and probably land in jail. I know you only too well.' Frank was never shy of bending the rules to suit his purposes, and Eddie was aware of that.

'It would be a one-off job,' Frank insisted. 'I know of a place that keeps its wages in a safe on a Thursday evening to pay its employees the next day. It's worth a few grand. We could share the cash and go our own way, after which we would keep our noses clean. We don't have police records so no fingerprints, no history. If we're careful we should be able to get away with it. Just think, Eddie, it would give you the start you need.'

'And what if we were caught?'

Shrugging, Frank said, 'It's a risk, but think of the prospects if we pull it off.' Getting to his feet he said, 'Think about it. I'll be back at the snooker hall in a couple of days; let me know your answer then.'

Eddie had gone home and thought of nothing else. He had decided to turn Frank down, but changed his mind when an empty property came on to the market. The temptation was just too great. He wanted to open a small club and the property was perfect. Then he planned to open a bigger one when he'd made enough money. It would be the start he craved.

Two days later they met again.

'Well?' said Frank as they sat at a table in a quiet corner. 'Have you thought about my idea?'

'Yes, but I would need to know more. How are we to set about it?'

There was a gleam of triumph in Frank's eyes as he laid out his plan.

It all sounded feasible, and Eddie had to admit Frank had been very thorough in his preparation. There was only one main problem and that was the night watchman. Eddie voiced his concerns.

'The man on patrol worries me,' he said.

'I've watched the building for weeks on end,' Frank told him. 'He works to a timetable. He's got a hut alongside the building where he makes cups of tea. He drinks so much he can't be far away from the lavatory for too long; I think he's got a problem with his waterworks, to be honest. We will have an hour to open the safe. Can you do it?'

'Depends on the make.'

'Right, I'll find out. It so happens that one of the places I deliver to made it, so I'll ask a few questions.'

Eddie looked sharply at him. 'Be careful.'

'Don't you worry; I'm not about to put it all at risk, am I? Just one thing more.'

'What's that?'

'When we do the job, if anything does go wrong

144

and one of us is caught, he stays shtum. No grassing each other up. Not that it will, but it's best to plan ahead.'

Eddie gave this considerable thought. 'All right,' he said. 'Let's shake on it.'

A few days later, Frank supplied Eddie with the name of the make of the safe. It was one he knew well and had worked on with his father. A feeling of excitement, an anticipation of success, raced through him. The adrenalin began to pump. The two men decided to make their move the following week.

'Keep an eye on the night watchman,' Eddie urged. 'We don't want him to go sick and someone else take his place, do we?'

'I'd already thought of that,' Frank said.

The night of the heist drew nearer. Both men were on edge, waiting. Eddie kept going over the mechanism of the safe in his mind, trying to recall everything his father had taught him. The two men still played snooker, trying to keep their behaviour as natural as possible, to allay any suspicion should questions be asked, until the Thursday night arrived.

They left the snooker club at ten o'clock and separated outside.

'I'll see you on the corner near the building at

two,' said Frank. 'Keep hidden by the bushes, out of sight. I'll come and find you. Be careful not to smoke in case someone sees the light from your match.'

Four hours later, Eddie crept out of the house, made his way to the appointed destination and pushed his way into the bushes opposite their target to wait. A short time later, Frank joined him and handed him a pair of gloves.

'You need to wear these all the time.'

'How the hell can I open a lock wearing gloves?' demanded Eddie.

'Well, make sure you wipe away any finger-prints,' said Frank. 'Got a handkerchief?'

'Of course I have.'

'Then use that and burn it afterwards. Come on, we need to open the padlock on the back gate to get inside,' he said. 'It's just an everyday lock, nothing complicated.'

So it turned out to be, and Eddie opened it very quickly. The two men entered the yard, carefully closing the gate behind them, and made their way to the back of the building. The door was unlocked as the night watchman was inside at the far end of the building. The two men hid inside until he passed by their hiding place and out of the building to his hut on the site.

Once inside the office, Eddie flexed his fingers

and set about opening the safe under the light of a torch held by his mate. He thanked God that he'd remembered all his father had taught him, and after twenty minutes he turned the handle and opened the safe. Inside were bundles of notes of different denominations, neatly stacked, ready for the taking.

The two men filled two large bags with the money, closed the safe door, wiped away all fingerprints and walked to the door of the office, opening it and peering along the corridor to see if it was empty. It was.

They quickly and quietly made their way to the outside, unlocking the outer door from the inside. There was no sign of the night watchman. Running as fast as they could, they let themselves out of the back gate, replaced the lock to allay any suspicion on the part of a passing copper, and walked away.

Frank was euphoric. 'We bloody did it!' he cried.

'Keep your voice down,' Eddie snapped.

'Sorry,' Frank quickly apologised, 'but it went so bloody smoothly.'

'Well, don't get any fancy ideas,' Eddie said. 'This was a one-off. From now on we keep our noses clean.'

'Look, you take the money home with you and stash it away. Split it down the middle and I'll meet you tomorrow night at the snooker hall around eight o'clock and you can give me what's mine.' He slapped Eddie on the back. 'There you are, my friend, you have the stash you need to get you started.'

'Now listen,' Eddie said. 'We will have to be very careful and not go spending lots of money, otherwise people will wonder where it came from and before you know it we'll be behind bars.'

'Don't you worry about me; I'm off to the big city. No one knows me in London. I can make a new life for myself.'

The two men shook hands.

'See you tomorrow then,' said Eddie and made his way home, letting himself into his parents' house and creeping stealthily up to his bedroom. Only then did he relax. Opening the bags, he stared at the contents, unable to believe the luck they had had that night. He started to count the money and stacked each bundle in their separate denominations. There was five thousand pounds in total!

He wiped the sweat from his forehead. Two and a half thousand pounds each. It was a fortune! He found he was trembling, and he quickly shared the money between the two bags, putting his on the top of his wardrobe, pushed well back, out of sight.

Lying on the bed, one hand behind his head, he

began to plan. He would tell his father he was able to pay the first month's rent on the vacant premises out of his savings, then he would start by selling his goods from the shop instead of the street. A little later when the fuss – and there would be one when the robbery was discovered – had died down, he could start in a small way and gradually build up.

He undressed and climbed into bed, but his brain was working overtime, and it was some time before he fell asleep from sheer exhaustion. The next day he worked as usual, went home for a meal, parcelled up Frank's share of the money in brown paper and walked towards the snooker club to meet his friend.

Eight o'clock passed and Frank hadn't arrived. Eddie ordered another pint of beer, and waited.

The barman looked over some time later and spoke to him. 'Not playing snooker tonight then, Eddie?'

'No, I'm waiting for Frank, but it looks as if he's stood me up. Perhaps he's met a girl some place.'

The barman stared at him. 'Haven't you heard the news then?'

'What news?'

'Frank's been arrested.'

'He what?'

'Yeah, earlier this evening. It appears he'd been drinking all day and got into a fight at the Lord Nelson. He glassed a sailor. Poor sod's in a bad way in hospital. Your mate will go down for GBH at least.'

Eddie drank up and staggered out of the bar, stunned by the news. Would Frank keep shtum about the robbery? It had nothing to do with the attack on the sailor, although Eddie guessed Frank had foolishly been celebrating . . . but what now?

As he walked home, clutching the parcel of money, he wondered what to do. It would not be wise to go and visit his friend, he decided. He would just have to wait and see what happened.

The next few weeks were a nightmare for Eddie. He kept expecting to be accosted by the police and asked to accompany them to the station. His nerves were stretched to breaking point.

His father and mother noticed the change in him, but when they questioned him he made various excuses. He was tired, he had a bad head, a cold coming. He tried very hard not to let his nervousness show at home, but he wasn't sleeping.

Weeks passed and no one came calling at the Chapmans' house, and eventually Frank's case came up before the court. Eddie didn't dare go, but he bought the local paper and read about it.

Frank was sent down for seven years. The sailor had recovered but his injuries had been severe and the judge told Frank he was lucky not to be facing a murder charge.

Now, many years later, Eddie Chapman sat in the office of the Blue Pelican club in Southampton, wondering just how Frank Graves had traced him. He wanted his share of the money, of course, which was only fair, and Eddie had promised to let him have it the following day.

Years inside His Majesty's prison and hard times had changed Frank, though. He was now an embittered man who made Eddie nervous. He had looked around the new building with envy.

'You've done all right for yourself whilst I was inside,' he told Eddie, 'whereas I have nothing but bad memories.'

'Why on earth did you go on a bender?' Eddie asked him.

With a wry grin, Frank said, 'I was celebrating of course. We'd pulled off a bloody great job. How much was it in all?'

'Five grand.'

'Bloody hell! Then I'm a rich bugger, right?'

'Yes,' said Eddie. 'What are you going to do with it?'

'Listen, mate, I've been banged up for a bloody

long time, so I'm going to live it up. All the women I want, plenty of decent food and drink. I've got a lot of catching up to do and I intend to make up for all those lost years.'

There was a note of desperation in his voice that Eddie didn't want to hear. Looking sternly at his friend, he warned him, 'You be careful. Don't waste this money; remember it was going to give us both a stake in life. Be sensible with it. Used the right way it will set up a future for you.' Then he added, 'There's no more where that came from, Frank, so don't piss it all up a wall and come back for more.'

Frank's mouth tightened. 'Don't tell me what to do, Eddie. I've had people telling me what to do for years and I'm sick of it!'

Eddie tried to pacify him. 'I'm only trying to give you some sound advice, that's all.'

'Well, thanks, but I don't need it. I'll come round to your club at eleven o'clock tomorrow morning, collect my money and then I'm off.'

The following morning, Eddie Chapman went to his bank and drew some money to add to the amount he had in his safe. He put it all in a small case and waited for Frank Graves to arrive.

Graves was very punctual. As the clock in the bar struck eleven, Frank walked in through the door, and looked around.

'Very nice,' he said. 'I'll hand it to you, Eddie; you *have* made a new life for yourself. Congratulations.'

Eddie handed him the case. 'There's two and a half grand in there,' he said.

Glaring at Eddie, Frank said, 'What about the interest?'

'What interest?'

'You've had the use of the money for seven bloody years, my friend. That will have earned a lot of interest, so where's mine?'

Eddie felt the anger rise but controlled it. He went to the office safe and, opening it, took out five hundred pounds and handed it to the other man. 'That's it! Now we're even. Your pot is empty.'

Taking the cash and picking up the case, Frank grinned at him. 'Thanks. Just tell me one thing. Did you move down here hoping I wouldn't find you?'

'Not at all. It was just a progression, that's all. I thought Southampton, a seaport town, not as sophisticated and frantic as London – not as much competition – was a good move, that's all. How did you find me?'

'One of the cons who came into the prison a couple of years ago was talking about this place, and he happened to mention your name. If he hadn't, you would have had the money all to yourself. Now that wouldn't have been at all fair, would it?'

There was a look of menace on Graves's face that Eddie didn't like, but he made no further comment. He held out his hand to the other man.

'Good luck, Frank. I hope you find what you're looking for, but don't come back.'

Laughing, Graves took his hand. 'You always did call a spade a spade,' he said. Holding up his case he said, 'With this in here, my life will begin again.' He turned away and swiftly left the club.

As Eddie watched him go he was filled with unease. He was certain that that was not the last he would see of Frank Graves and it worried him.

CHAPTER FIFTEEN

The next three weeks passed without incident. Tilly spent time with David, whom she introduced to her friends. They sometimes went out as a crowd, at other times on their own. It was midsummer, with hot days and balmy evenings. The couple walked, talked and, borrowing Jago's bicycle, rode out of the town centre to quieter places.

'Do you miss being at sea?' Tilly asked David one evening as they sat on a bench on the esplanade, overlooking the water.

'I would be lying if I said no. I'm enjoying teaching and being able to spend time with you, but yes I do. Life at sea is like living in a different world, Tilly. I can't expect you to understand, but apart from the work there is a certain camaraderie among seafarers; you live and work in confined spaces, after all. I do miss the feel of the sea beneath the ship, the sway – the movement when you're in your bunk which somehow lulls you to sleep – the atmosphere as you walk the decks.

There is nothing quite so beautiful as a night sky full of stars and the ocean lit by moonlight.'

As she listened she could hear the nostalgia in his voice, a yearning almost, and she realised that however long he was going to be ashore teaching, the sea would draw him back eventually. For some reason it made her sad. Anyone married to such a man, she concluded, would only ever be a part of his life. The sea would be a formidable mistress, and she supposed that if you were married to a seafarer, you would have to be prepared to share him.

Gazing at him as he looked out over the water, Tilly wondered if David was the man for her. She really liked him, admired him even. Because he was older and well travelled, he could talk to her about many things which enthralled her . . . but the excitement she felt when she was with Eddie Chapman wasn't there. She tried to analyse the reason. Was it because Eddie had a dubious reputation? David was reliable and solid. That sounded dull, but he was far from that . . . so what was it?

'A penny for them.'

She came back to the present. Looking at David, she said, 'Oh, they're worth much more than that.'

He studied her face and putting an arm round her asked, 'Do you think you could ever consider being the wife of a seafarer?'

Tilly was startled. Had he read her mind? Was he being serious or was this just a hypothetical question? Thinking for a moment, she said, 'I suppose if you really loved a man, it wouldn't matter what he did for a living, would it?'

He hesitated and Tilly wondered for one moment if he was about to propose to her. God, she hoped not! What would she say?

'No, I suppose it wouldn't,' was all he said, and she breathed a sigh of relief.

As she climbed into bed that night she was pleased that David hadn't asked her to marry him. It wasn't that she didn't want to get married, eventually, but for now she wanted to do other things, and she wasn't entirely sure with whom.

On Monday, Southampton was buzzing. On the previous day, a man walking with his dog on the common had found a body. It made headlines in the local paper and everyone was talking about it.

For young Nat Summers it was particularly bad news. He was convinced it was the body of his missing sister. The police had called on him with an article of clothing for him to identify. He remembered the sick feeling in the pit of his stomach when he saw the blouse. He had rushed from the room to the bathroom and thrown up.

The policeman had explained, as gently as he

could, that the body was partially decomposed, but it was a female and they would know more after an autopsy. Seeing the young man's obvious distress, the officer asked, 'Do you have anyone you can call to be with you?'

He shook his head. 'No, but I'll be fine.' It would be useless getting in touch with their parents. Both he and Elsie had escaped their home life in their early teens, unable to continue to live with a drunken father and a belligerent mother. There would be no sympathy or comfort there.

'We will have to talk to you again,' he was told.

'Can I make you a cup of tea?' asked the constable.

But Nat just wanted to be alone. Rising to his feet he led the man to the door and thanked him.

'I'm sorry to be the bearer of such news, son,' the policeman said, placing a hand on the young man's shoulder.

Alone at last, Nat lit a cigarette and walked into Elsie's bedroom, where he sat on the bed. Although he'd often warned her to be careful, he'd never really believed that she would come to a sticky end. Not Elsie. She was one tough young woman who had always been able to look after herself.

He gazed round the room and saw on the dressing table a framed picture of the two of them taken earlier that year at a fair on the common, and thought how sad it was. They'd had such a great day there. Riding in the bumper cars, going on the swings until he'd pulled them so high, Elsie had begged him to stop before they swung over the top. And now it was on the same common her body had been found. Clutching the picture to his breast, he wept for her – and for himself.

Gerald Bradbury sat down with his family to dinner and sipped from his wine glass as he waited for his soup to be served. He glanced at the local paper on the sideboard and saw the headline. BODY FOUND ON SOUTHAMPTON COMMON.

The wine glass shattered as it landed on the floor. 'Gerald!'

The sharp voice of his wife pulled him together. 'Sorry,' he said. 'It slipped from my hand.'

Simon picked up the paper. 'I wonder who this poor girl is?' he remarked. 'They say that the results of an autopsy will tell the officials how she died. Must be a bit of a grisly job as the body has been lying about for weeks, apparently.'

'For God's sake, Simon, we are about to eat!' his father exclaimed.

'Are you all right, Gerald?' asked his wife. 'You've gone quite pale.'

He rose from his chair and threw his napkin down. 'I've just lost my appetite,' he snapped and glared at his son as he stomped out of the room.

'For goodness' sake, Simon, this wasn't the time,' his mother admonished him.

'Sorry,' he said.

Gerald went into his study and, closing the door behind him, poured himself a stiff measure of brandy. His hands were shaking. Taking a large sip of the alcohol, he found he was sweating profusely and mopped his brow with a handkerchief.

It had all been a terrible accident. He'd got carried away and the girl had protested that he was hurting her. It had only excited him more, especially when she started to struggle, but when she started to scream he'd put his hands round her neck to silence her. Before he realised it, her body had gone limp and he saw that she had stopped breathing. He remembered shaking her vigorously, trying to make her breathe, but to no avail. Then he had panicked and carried her body deep into the trees and bushes, covering her with scrub. He should have realised it was only a matter of time before the body was discovered . . . and now it had been.

Holding his head in his hands he tried to think. No one had seen him pick her up and drive away. There was no way that the police would trace her to him. From now on, though, he would have to stop using prostitutes – and that included the Williamses' girls. He presumed that the Williams twins would keep their clients' names confidential to reduce the risk of being up in court for living off immoral earnings, so if he was careful he should be in the clear. He finished his drink and tried to concentrate on the business papers before him.

Eddie Chapman looked around his new premises with a satisfied smile. It was all coming together now. The interior was finished and he had ordered the furnishings. The bar was being stocked and the staff chosen. Opening day was in two weeks' time and he could hardly wait. Now he felt he could take a day off to celebrate and immediately thought of Tilly. Where could they go?

There was a sale of horses at Ascot racecourse coming up and Jeremy Frampton had called him to say there were a few promising animals on offer. Tilly had so enjoyed her day at the races, he was sure she would enjoy this experience. He would get in touch with her.

As Tilly left Madam Leone's that afternoon, Eddie Chapman was sitting in his car outside waiting for her. He tooted his horn and beckoned her over.

'Tomorrow I have to go to a sale of racehorses at Ascot. Would you like to come?'

There was a look of disappointment on her face as she said, 'I'd love to, but I have to work.'

'Ring the shop in the morning and say you're unwell,' he suggested. 'Come on, Tilly, live a little!'

And so the following morning she sat beside Eddie in the passenger seat of his car as they sped through the countryside, filled with excitement at yet another adventure with this charismatic man.

'How's your new business coming along?' she asked.

'Grand. It will be opening in two weeks' time. I do hope you'll be there on opening night,' he said. 'I'll send you an invitation.'

Her heart sank. How on earth could she go? She could hardly ask David to take her, or Jago, and she certainly couldn't go alone.

'That's very kind of you,' she said, 'but I don't think I can come.'

'Whyever not? You'll be my guest; I'll take care of you.'

'I'll have to think about it,' was all she could say.

The sale was very exciting for Tilly, who had never been to one before. Jeremy Frampton had taken them to look at the magnificent animals on offer. He was telling Eddie about the ones he liked, quoting their pedigree in a language that was foreign to Tilly. She didn't understand who had sired whom or why this horse was out of something or other. It didn't detract from the interest, though.

The two men had decided to bid on two of the horses, so they stood around the showing ring and waited.

Tilly was amazed at the prices being offered and Eddie explained that the price was always in guineas. It was traditional. Then one of their choices was led into the ring – a handsome chestnut stallion who tossed his mane and snorted, prancing as he did so. Tilly thought he was beautiful and said so.

Jeremy Frampton said, 'You have a good eye, my dear. He has great potential.'

Tilly listened to the auctioneer, calling for bids and peering round the ring, making sure that he didn't miss the lift of a hand or the flick of an eyebrow as the buyers made their bids. But the price went too high and Jeremy dropped out of the bidding.

Then a horse was led in with an almost blue-black coat. It walked round the ring with such grace that Tilly drew a breath.

'Just look at him,' she said. 'Now that's a winner if ever I saw one!' So entranced was she watching the horse that the bidding was over before she realised it.

'Who bought him?' she asked.

'I did,' said Eddie.

'But that wasn't the one you were waiting for,' she said with some surprise.

'I know, but you're right, he looks every inch a winner.'

She looked at him aghast. 'You bought him on my say-so?'

He nodded.

'But what if I'm wrong? How awful that would be. He's worth a lot of money, isn't he?'

'Indeed he is.'

'Oh, dear. I wished I hadn't said anything.'

Jeremy looked at her. Seeing her obvious distress, he said, 'Don't take on so, Tilly. You're right, that horse *is* a winner. I'll put money on it, and if we hadn't thought so, Eddie wouldn't have bought it. Come on, let's go and celebrate.'

They went to the bar and drank champagne.

Jeremy couldn't stay long as he and his head lad had to see the animal safely into the horsebox and off to the stables. Eddie suggested he and Tilly leave the racecourse and have some lunch nearby.

'Let's go to Windsor,' he suggested.

'Will we see the castle?' Tilly asked eagerly.

'Why not?'

Eddie acted as a guide and parked the car near Windsor Castle. They looked at the ramparts and the tower, which was recognisable anywhere. Tilly stood and stared in awe.

'You can just imagine Elizabeth the First riding in a carriage through these gates, can't you?'

Eddie looked at the shining eyes of his companion, delighted and amused at her enthusiasm. Tilly's company gave him so much pleasure; it was like seeing the world through fresh eyes instead of his jaded ones. Jaded and sceptical, due to the life he led and his distrust of people.

'You are a pure romantic,' he told her. 'Come on, let's go and eat.'

They sat outside, eating their meal overlooking the Thames and watching the pleasure boats taking passengers along the river. Seeing the look on Tilly's face Eddie asked, 'Would you like to take a trip too?'

'Could we?'

'It's too late to go all the way up the river to Hampton Court, but we can take a shorter one. Come on, one is due to leave soon.'

They sat on the top deck, open at the sides and covered by a canopy, as the boat made its lazy journey. Tilly took delight in the surrounding countryside and the swans that glided by. She was thrilled at the sight of a family of ducks with their ducklings.

'Oh, Eddie, do look! They're so pretty.'

Taking her hand in his he said, 'And so are you.'

She flushed at the compliment.

'Once my club is up and running,' he said, 'we're going to have lots of good times together, that's if you want to?'

She looked at him and without hesitation she said, 'I do want to.'

He clasped her hand more tightly and asked, 'Are you quite sure about that, Tilly?'

'Quite, quite sure,' she said, returning his gaze.

'Good,' he said, and, raising her hand to his lips, he kissed it.

She wanted to smooth his hair as he bent forward, to touch him. She didn't care what anyone said about this man, she wanted to be with him, even though she knew she was making a lot of trouble for herself with Jago . . . and David.

Jago she wasn't so worried about, but David was another matter. He was so nice and she really liked him. What on earth would he have to say? She argued that they were just friends after all, but that wasn't really true. Their relationship had grown since he had been home and deep down she knew that he felt they had a future together. But she wanted to live for now. At nineteen she still had a few years to enjoy herself. And she wanted to spend more time with Eddie Chapman.

CHAPTER SIXTEEN

The police investigation into the murder on the common continued. The post-mortem results showed that the girl had been strangled. Dental records proved beyond doubt that the body was that of Elsie Summers. Her brother Nat had been called into the local police station to help the police with their inquiries.

Detective Inspector Ridgeway sent for a cup of coffee for the young man and passed him a cigarette.

'I know this is difficult for you, Mr Summers, but I have to ask you some questions. We want to find out who was responsible for the death of your sister.'

'I understand,' said Nat. 'I want the bastard found too!'

'I'm sure you do. Now your sister, Elsie, earned her money from prostitution, right?'

'Yes, she did.'

'Did she work for anyone else?'

'She didn't have a pimp, if that's what you mean. When she was killed, she was working alone.'

'Before that?'

Nat hesitated. 'She did belong to an escort agency.'

The detective looked up sharply. 'Did she work for the Williams brothers by any chance?'

Nodding, Nat said, 'Yes, but not for long.'

'And why was that?'

The young man thought for a moment before answering, knowing that if he gave them the information they wanted, his relationship with Charlie Williams was finished and that maybe his own life would be in danger.

Sensing his reluctance, the detective said, 'Any information you give us will be strictly confidential.'

'Well, Elsie was taking extra punters on the side and pocketing the takings. Old Ma Williams found out and fired her.'

Sitting back in his seat the detective asked, 'How do the Williamses work? They don't have a house for their girls.'

'No,' said Nat, 'but they use various hotels in and around Southampton.'

'Do you know which ones they are?'

'Yes, I do.'

Whilst Nat was helping the police, Charlie and Ken Williams were together, talking about Elsie Summers. Although her name had not yet been made public knowledge, one of their informants within the police force had told them the identity of the corpse. It wasn't long before Charlie realised that she was related to his young lover.

'We could be in the shit here, Ken. If that young bleeder spills the beans, we could be in serious trouble.'

'Then it's up to you to see that he doesn't. I suggest you pay him a visit and make sure he keeps his mouth shut!'

'And if he doesn't?'

Ken glared at his brother. 'Do I really have to spell it out to you?'

Charlie looked perturbed and said, 'We have to tread very carefully here. So far we have beaten the law, but if Nat goes missing . . . After all, we've been seen together. If he disappears, they'll come straight to me.'

'Then you'll have to make sure that your hands are clean. Look, Charlie, I don't care how you do it, but keep his mouth shut!'

Tilly Thompson was facing problems of her own. Having decided that she would be seeing more of Eddie Chapman, she knew that she would incur the wrath of her brother, Jago. And then there was David, whom she was seeing that evening.

Being a basically honest person, she didn't want to keep her friendship with the club owner a secret for ever, and she felt it was better that David heard about it from her than from any other source, but she was dreading having to tell him. There was no one she could confide in to advise her. Beth had already expressed reservations about her relationship with Eddie and her parents were occupied with their own lives and scarcely intervened in hers. But how was she to bring the subject up in conversation with David?

They met later that evening and went for a drink at the Red Lion at Holy Rood. As they sat at a table in the bar, David gave her the perfect opportunity.

'I rang the shop yesterday,' he told her, 'and the manageress said you were unwell. Are you feeling better?'

Tilly could feel her heart pounding. Taking a deep breath, she said, 'I was fine, but I had an opportunity to go somewhere exciting so I rang in and told them I was poorly.'

He looked surprised. 'You did? What was so exciting that you had to tell such a lie?'

She sensed his disapproval, but staring him in the eye said, 'I went to a horse sale at Ascot.'

'You did what?' He didn't give her chance to reply before asking, 'Who did you go with?'

'Eddie Chapman.'

For a moment, David was speechless. His look of dismay turned to one of anger. 'You promised me you wouldn't go near the man.'

Tilly felt dreadful. She saw the anger in his eyes, but she also knew that she had hurt him.

'I am sorry I broke my promise, David, really I am, but it was a chance of a lifetime. I have never been to Ascot or a horse sale.'

He studied her face, trying to understand her reasoning. He failed.

'Will you be seeing Chapman again?'

'I expect so.' As she said the words, she knew that she was ruining what they had between them.

He gazed at her and said, 'Look, Tilly. I'm older than you and I've been around. I can understand how you could be enamoured with such a man – he's sophisticated, his world seems exciting to you, and you're easily impressed – but please, I beg you, don't be foolish and continue down this road.'

His remarks only made her angry. 'What on earth do you mean, easily impressed? I'm not a fool. Of course his life seems exciting – because it is! Don't you understand me at all? I want to see as much as I can of life. I don't want to die an old woman, not having lived!'

'And you think that Eddie Chapman is the answer to your prayers?'

'Don't be ridiculous! I just want to have a bit of fun, that's all.'

'Is that how he sees it . . . just a bit of fun?'

'What are you driving at?'

'For God's sake, Tilly, Eddie Chapman is not a young teenager out for a hoot, he's a man of the world.' He gazed at her with an earnest expression. 'He won't be content just to hold your hand and give you a goodnight kiss. You continue to see him and believe me, he'll want a lot more than that!'

She didn't know what to say, because deep down she thought he was probably telling her the truth, and although the words gave her a frisson of fear they also excited her. The danger of such a relationship made the adrenalin pulse through her. She looked at David, but couldn't find the words to allay his fears.

He waited in vain for her to change her mind. Finally he picked up his glass, emptied the contents and said, 'I'd better take you home.'

She found her voice at last. 'David, I'm really sorry.'

'So am I, Tilly, so am I.'

They walked home in silence. At the door of her house, he took her by the shoulders and said, 'I think you're making a dreadful mistake. When you realise it, give me a call.' He kissed her on the forehead and walked away. Tilly put her key in the lock and entered the house.

Joe Thompson looked up from his armchair. 'You're home early.'

'Hello, Dad. Yes, the evening didn't pan out very well.'

'Had a row with your boyfriend?' he asked, seeing how down she looked.

'Something like that.'

'Ah well, my girl, true love never does run smoothly.'

Sitting down opposite her father, she said, 'Why is life so difficult sometimes?'

He chuckled. 'It's all part of growing up, of making decisions, choosing paths. It's all character-building stuff.'

'What if you make the wrong decision?'

'Then you learn by your mistakes. We've all made them, but in the end, if you're made of the right stuff, it will sort itself.'

She looked fondly at her father. 'You're quite a wise old man.'

'Not so much of the old, missy! How about making us a cup of tea?'

As she rose from her chair she asked, 'Is Mum working this evening?'

'Yes. The Bradburys are giving a dinner party.'

A dinner party was the last thing that Gerald Bradbury wanted, but the arrangement had been long standing, so he tried his best to be the perfect host. One of his guests was the chief constable, an old friend.

After dinner when the men were alone, drinking port and smoking cigars, the case of Elsie Summers came up. Her name was now public knowledge and had been widely read in the local and national press.

'It won't be long until we find the perpetrator,' said the chief constable.

'Do you have any evidence, then?' asked Gerald, his heart pumping madly as he waited for an answer.

'It's all a matter of time,' he was told. 'There is always someone somewhere who has seen something. We're busy questioning the other prostitutes.'

Another guest who was a solicitor like Gerald said scathingly, 'Any man who pays a harlot for sex must be mad!'

Gerald Bradbury's shirt collar suddenly felt too tight and he tried to ease it.

'There will always be those who will,' said the policeman, 'and there will always be those who go too far – and that's when the trouble starts.'

In the kitchen Ethel Thompson and the cook were also talking about the murder on the common.

'These girls put themselves in danger every time they takes a punter,' said Cook.

'It's no way to earn a living,' Ethel said.

'In some cases it's the only way some of those poor bitches can survive,' Cook declared. 'I feel sorry for them. The blame is on the men who pay them for sex. If there were no randy buggers about, there would be no need for the women!' She lowered her voice. 'I wonder if she was one of his?' She inclined her head towards the stairs leading to the dining room.

Ethel looked shocked. 'You don't mean that?'

'I bloody well do. He may put on his airs and graces but I told you what I heard about him going to hotels.'

'I know, but I still find it hard to believe. Do you think his wife knows?'

With a shrug Cook said, 'I doubt she gives a toss. Come on, best get these dishes cleared.'

In the red light district of Southampton, the police were questioning several women on the streets, asking for any information about the night of the murder, no matter how insignificant.

One of them said, 'Well, I did see a car driving past very slowly. It was certainly a punter, but he didn't stop. He drove further down the road, and I do believe that's where the girl who was murdered was, but I can't be sure.'

'Can you describe the car?'

'Yes I can, because I was hoping he was going to stop by me,' she said.

'So you saw the driver too?'

'It was a bit dark but I saw enough of him.'

The policeman took out his notebook and started to write.

CHAPTER SEVENTEEN

Nat Summers thought he would go to his local for a drink. He hated sitting around the empty house alone, knowing that Elsie wouldn't ever come home again. Putting on his jacket he walked to the front door and opened it. Charlie Williams stood there, his hand outstretched as he reached for the knocker.

'Well, young Nat, there you are.' And he pushed by him and walked into the room.

The young man felt as if his legs were turning to jelly, as he had no choice but to follow Williams. His heart was racing as he looked at Charlie, waiting to see what he had to say.

'Where were you off to, then?' Williams asked.

'Down to the pub for a quiet drink. What do you want?'

'That's no way to talk to me, lovely lad.' He caressed the boy's cheek.

Nat fought with the impulse to turn away, but he knew that he was in great danger and one wrong move could be very costly.

'I'm sorry to hear about your sister,' Charlie said, staring hard at him, waiting for some reaction.

Nat decided to play it straight and see what happened. 'Thanks,' he said.

'It must have been a terrible shock when you heard,' Williams continued. 'I suppose the police questioned you?'

There was no point in lying. 'Yes. I had to identify a piece of her clothing. I really don't want to talk about it, Charlie. It's far too painful.'

'But I'm afraid we must talk about it. Did you tell the filth that Elsie worked for us?'

'No, of course not! Do you take me for a fool?'

Charlie grabbed him by the throat and squeezed gently. 'I do hope you are telling me the truth, because if not, you leave me no choice.'

Nat froze, but managed to nod his head in response and to his relief Charlie released his hold.

'Of course I didn't tell them,' Nat lied. 'It didn't have anything to do with her murder . . . did it?' he asked bravely.

Charlie Williams admired his spirit. 'No it didn't. We had nothing to do with Elsie's death. We both thought she'd left the town.' He sat on the shabby settee, took out a cigar and lit it. 'Will you be seeing the filth again?' he asked casually.

'Not as far as I know. I've identified her clothing,

they now know the body is Elsie, what more can I do?' Nat stood nervously waiting for the next question.

Patting the seat beside him, Charlie said, 'Come and sit with me.'

Seeing the predatory look in the man's eyes, Nat knew what he wanted and it made him feel sick. This was his home, the home he had shared with his sister; it was not the place to satisfy Charlie's sexual needs. The very thought was obscene.

'Not tonight, Charlie,' he said. 'For Christ's sake, my sister is dead! How can you even think of it?'

'She wasn't *my* sister, so why should I care!'

'You bastard!' Nat yelled at him. 'She was mine and I loved her. Now get out of my house!'

Before he knew what was happening, Nat had been hurled across the room by one blow from Charlie, who continued to rain punches on him until he was almost unconscious. Then he raped him.

Getting to his feet, Charlie Williams did up his flies and stood over the bruised and inert body of the young boy. He gave Nat one final, vicious kick.

'Let that be a lesson to you, sonny. Nobody ever refuses a Williams. Any more trouble from you and I'll finish the job . . . do I make myself clear?'

Barely able to move, Nat managed to nod.

With a malicious smile, Charlie said, 'Well, no one will want you looking like that, but I'll come calling when you're better.'

Nat heard the front door slam and tried to move. He screamed with pain and thought he was going to die. Within seconds he lost consciousness.

The following day the hospital notified the local police station that a young man named Nathaniel Summers had been found by a neighbour, who had called an ambulance as the boy was in a bad way, and was now in the South Hants Hospital. He was in the emergency ward and was asking to speak to a detective.

Detective Inspector Ridgeway, who had interviewed him after his sister's body had been identified, left the station immediately.

When Ridgeway was shown into the ward and led to the curtained bed, he blanched when he saw the state of its occupant. Pulling up a chair, he gazed at the bandaged and bruised face.

'Who did this to you, son?' he asked.

Between swollen lips, Nat managed to whisper, 'It was Charlie Williams. He's going to kill me if he finds out I've talked to you.'

Ridgeway pulled his chair closer. 'I'll put you under police guard whilst you're in here, and when you're well enough to be moved I'll stash you away in a safe house, but if I do that you'll have to help me put the Williams brothers away. That means you going into court and being a witness. Are you prepared to do that?'

'As long as you keep him away, I will. The bastard all but did for me, and then he raped me.'

Ridgeway cursed under his breath. 'Don't you worry, son. I swear I'll put the buggers away, with your help. I can get them for living off immoral earnings and Charlie for GBH. Now you rest. In half an hour I'll have you moved to a private room with a copper on the door.'

Eddie Chapman walked around the Ace of Clubs, the name for his new business, checking everything. The rooms were now complete, curtained, carpeted and furnished, and he was delighted with the result. It looked classy and expensive. One room had three roulette tables, another held tables for blackjack, and the third was filled with round tables for those who preferred playing poker.

The bar was well stocked with wines, spirits and beer on tap for those who preferred it. Cooked food was not on the menu as Eddie hadn't wanted to use space for a dining room, but there was a choice of sandwiches to be had for those who needed something to eat as they played.

The staff, all male, were to wear black trousers,

white shirts, ties and smart striped waistcoats. Eddie had decided that he didn't want the distraction of females on the staff, but he was quite willing for the punters to bring female companions with them should they wish to do so.

He was fully expecting a visit from the Williams brothers when he opened the club. Curiosity alone would bring them there. He also knew that they would not be pleased with what they saw, which might cause him some trouble, but he was prepared for that. He'd hired two doormen to sort out any problems which might occur. He knew for a fact that some losers didn't take their run of bad luck well, and if they were fuelled with alcohol it could make for a difficult situation. He needed to prove to the law that everything was under control from the very beginning.

He had sent out invitations to some of the town's most important businessmen, hoping to bring in a classy clientele. He had sent one such invitation to the chief constable, hoping he would come and see the place for himself. He had also sent one to Tilly Thompson, on the back of which he had written, *Please do come. I want you to be a part of my life and enjoy my success. You will be my personal guest. Eddie.*

As he mailed the invites he knew that there was just one more thing he had to do before another day passed, bringing the opening nearer. He climbed into his car and drove to the Polygon area, parked in front of a small block of apartments and made his way to the first floor, and knocked on the door of number three.

Greta Harper, his mistress, opened the door. When she saw him she smiled warmly.

'Hello, Eddie, darling. What a lovely surprise. Come inside.'

He followed her into the comfortable and elegant living room and sat in an armchair.

'To what do I owe this unexpected pleasure?' she asked.

He came straight to the point. 'I'm sorry, Greta. You won't like what I have to say, but I thought it only fair to tell you to your face.'

Her expression changed from one of happiness to one of consternation. 'What on earth are you talking about?'

'I'm talking about our relationship. It's over, I'm afraid.'

She looked completely shaken. 'What do you mean, it's over?'

'Just that. We've had good times together but I won't be seeing you again. It's over.'

She stormed at him. 'How dare you come here and say such a thing and cast me aside like an old shoe? Have you no respect for me at all?'

'Of course I have, otherwise I wouldn't be here. But things have changed.'

'Changed? Changed for whom, might I ask?'

'For me,' he said calmly. 'I have different plans now and I'm sorry, my dear, but you have no part in them.'

'You bastard!' She flew across the space between them, hand raised ready to strike him.

Eddie was prepared for such an outburst and caught her wrist in an iron grip. 'Now don't be foolish, Greta. I never made you any promises, did I?'

She just glared at him, too full of anger to reply.

'Did I?' he repeated loudly.

Pulling her hand from his grip, she held her wrist and rubbed it. 'No, Eddie, you didn't, but that doesn't mean you can treat me like this.'

'Oh, come now. I've treated you well. I've bought you clothes and jewellery, taken you to places you would never have been to without me. We've had a good time together. Try to remember that.'

'Don't use that condescending tone with me!' she snapped. 'We had good times and you were generous, but believe me, you were treated well too. My time was yours – my body was yours. I earned whatever you gave me!'

He chuckled softly. 'I would never have put it

quite like that. I prefer to think that we were good together, but now things have changed for me.'

She looked scathingly at him. 'It's that girl we saw in the bar that time, the one you danced with, isn't it?'

'What if it is?'

With a mocking laugh she said, 'She won't be woman enough for you, Eddie. She's an infant! Good God, she can't be more than eighteen, nineteen. What are you now . . . a cradle-snatcher?'

She saw the anger in his eyes. 'My life has nothing more to do with you,' he said. And taking some money from inside his coat he put it on the coffee table in front of him. 'Here,' he said. 'Take yourself on holiday somewhere, on me.'

Greta picked up the notes and threw them in his face. They fluttered to the ground around him.

'Don't you treat me like a whore,' she screamed. 'I'm better than that.'

Ignoring the fallen notes he said, 'I wasn't – and you are,' and he walked to the door. Turning, he said, 'I'm sorry, Greta. Goodbye. Take care of yourself.' As he closed the door there was an almighty crash against it from the inside. He smiled and walked down the stairs.

Tilly opened the envelope addressed to her the following morning, as she sat at the table eating her toast for breakfast. When she read the contents, she quickly put the invitation card back in its envelope and pushed it into her pocket before her parents could see. But Ethel had already noticed.

'What's that then?'

'Just a party invite from a friend,' Tilly answered.

'That's nice. When is it for?'

'Next week.'

'I hope you've got something nice to wear, love?'

Oh, I have, thought Tilly. I'll wear the dress that Eddie bought me in London. She had decided that she would go after all. How could she refuse when he had asked her especially to be there? If she was going to be seeing Eddie, it might as well start with the opening of his club. David knew of her feelings and Jago had better get used to the idea too.

She already had the matching shoes but with some of her race winnings, still hidden away, she would buy an evening bag to go with the outfit. She would pop out during her lunch break and see what she could find. Suddenly she felt the adrenalin flow. This would be the start of an exciting life if the past outings were anything to go by. If she couldn't do the things that rich people could, like travelling the world, at least she could enjoy Eddie Chapman's version of it, which was a hell of a lot more exciting than hers.

CHAPTER EIGHTEEN

The opening night of the Ace of Clubs arrived. Eddie had called Tilly at her place of work to make sure she was going.

'I want you there,' he told her. 'You will come, won't you?'

'Yes, I will,' she said.

'I'll send a taxi for you at eight o'clock,' he said and hung up.

As Tilly prepared for the evening, she took out the dress that Eddie had bought her in London. She had put it on a hanger in the morning, whilst she was alone in the house, and steamed it with a kettle to take out the creases, not wanting to iron it in front of her parents. She didn't want them to see it until she was ready to leave. There would be too many awkward questions, which she wanted to avoid if possible.

Putting the dress over her head, she did it up and preened in front of the mirror. It was truly beautiful and she felt special wearing it. She had managed to buy an evening bag in a coffee shade which matched both the material and the shoes.

Looking at her wristwatch she saw she had fifteen minutes before the taxi came, so she quickly brushed her hair, powdered her nose, applied a light coating of mascara, and put on some lipstick. Her heart was pounding with excitement and nerves.

Her timing was perfect as she swept down the stairs, said goodnight to her parents and was out of the door before they could make any comment.

'Bloody hell,' said Joe to his wife, 'was that our Tilly in that creation?'

'Yes,' said Ethel, 'she's off to a party somewhere. I've never seen that dress before. I expect she bought it at Madam Leone's.'

'I don't know much about women's clobber but I would say that made a dent in her wages.'

'She's probably paying it off weekly,' said Ethel, and returned to her knitting.

The taxi arrived in front of the club, but when Tilly tried to pay the driver he said, 'It's all right, miss, Mr Chapman has seen to it.'

Taking a deep breath, Tilly walked through the double doors. The room was already full of people. She saw quite a few notable businessmen she recognised from seeing their photographs in the local paper, and in his uniform was Southampton's chief constable. The bar looked inviting, the barman waiting to serve customers who, after their free glass of champagne, would be paying for their drinks.

As she hesitated, she saw Eddie making his way towards her, wreathed in smiles.

'Tilly!' he said and kissed her cheek. 'You look absolutely stunning. Come with me and meet some of my guests.' He took a glass of champagne from a tray held by a waiter and handed it to her.

Time seemed to pass by in a haze for Tilly. Eddie introduced her to several people. 'This is Miss Tilly Thompson, a friend of mine,' he told them. They all treated her with great deference, which made her feel important, and she revelled in it.

Eddie took her on a tour of inspection and she marvelled at the elegance of the decorations. 'Who chose the drapes and furnishings?' she asked him.

'I did. Do you like them?'

'You have great taste, Eddie,' she said. 'It all looks classy and very expensive.'

Laughing, he said, 'That's because it is. I am so pleased it shows.'

Shortly afterwards, he said, 'You'll have to excuse me for a moment, but I have to officially announce we're ready for business.'

He stood looking handsome and resplendent in

his dinner jacket and, tapping the side of his glass to get the attention of his guests, he spoke.

'Ladies and gentlemen, the gaming rooms and the bar are now open for business. Thank you all for coming here this evening. Please, enjoy yourselves.' As he made his way back towards her he was waylaid by several people and stopped to talk to them.

Tilly stood and watched, sipping from her glass, until suddenly someone beside her said, 'What on earth are you doing here?' It was her brother Jago.

Smiling at him, she said, 'I might have known you would be here. I know you like a flutter but I expect you're going to play poker, aren't you?'

'This is no place for you!' he exclaimed.

'She's here as my guest.' Eddie appeared beside her.

Jago looked at the club owner in disbelief.

'I can assure you, your sister will be quite safe in my keeping.'

Tilly held her breath.

Eddie smiled at Jago and said, 'I've heard you're quite a poker player. I do hope you have a good evening.' There was a note of steel in his voice as he stood in front of Jago, daring him to make a scene. Defying him to do so.

Looking from one to the other, Jago decided that this was not the time or place to air his views.

He could talk to Tilly when they both were in the privacy of their home. Looking at his sister, he said, 'You just be careful.' And he walked towards the card room.

'Your brother doesn't approve of me,' Eddie remarked with an enigmatic smile, 'but he'll get used to the idea of us being together in time.'

'I'm not so sure about that,' she admitted.

'Come on,' Eddie said. 'Let's go and watch the punters playing roulette and see if we have any serious gamblers among them.'

Tilly was intrigued watching the players place their chips and the croupiers spin the wheel. The whole scene, the atmosphere, the language of the croupiers, fascinated her. The exchange of the chips – of both the losers and the winners. There was such an air of festivity, which she found enthralling.

'I want to play!' she said.

'I don't think that's such a good idea,' said Eddie.

'I still have money from my winnings at the racecourse,' she told him. 'I've brought some with me.'

He turned her towards him and said, 'Look, Tilly. Gambling can be fun, but it can get a hold of you and before you know where you are you are playing with money you can't afford to lose. I've seem many men ruined by gambling.'

'I wouldn't be so stupid,' she insisted. 'I've

brought a small amount with me and if I lose it, that's fine. When it's gone, it's gone.'

'All right,' he said, relenting, 'but first let me tell you about the game and its rules so you know what you're doing.'

For the next fifteen minutes, Tilly was instructed thoroughly, until she was ready to play.

'I'll stand with you,' said Eddie, 'but as the owner I can't play myself. Anyway, I'd rather do my gambling at the racecourse.'

Tilly exchanged her money for some chips and stood at a table ready to play.

As she did so, Eddie glanced up and saw the Williams twins in the doorway. He excused himself. 'Look, I have to go. Will you be all right on your own?'

'Of course,' said Tilly and laughed. 'What will you do if I break the bank?'

'I'd bar you from ever coming in here again!' And he left her at the table.

Walking over to Charlie and Ken, he said, 'Good evening, gentlemen. Can I buy you both a drink?'

'Bloody right!' said Charlie belligerently.

'Thanks,' said Ken. 'Nice place. Congratulations.'

The three men walked to the bar. The brothers ordered gin and tonic; Eddie asked for plain tonic water, with ice and lemon.

'On the wagon?' asked Ken.

'I never drink when I work,' Eddie told him. 'I always like to have a clear head.'

'Very wise,' Ken said and sipped his drink. 'Cheers!'

Charlie, however, was still sulking that Eddie Chapman had stolen a march over them by managing to get the premises they had wanted and opening the club. The fact that he and his brother would probably never have been granted a licence was forgotten.

'S'pose you think you're mighty clever to have this place?'

With a frown, Eddie said, 'That's got nothing to do with it. I saw an opportunity when this place came up for rent. It was all a matter of timing, and if you can't accept that, Charlie, then I'm sorry.'

Ken quickly intervened. 'That's what business is all about,' he said. 'Well, drink up, Charlie, we have our own business to look after.'

Somewhat reluctantly Charlie downed the contents of his glass.

'Thanks for the drink,' said Ken. 'I'm sure the place will do well.'

Eddie watched them leave with some relief. Ken didn't worry him but his brother did. Charlie was a dangerous individual who would have to be watched. He would instruct his doormen to let him know if the man came anywhere near the premises in the future.

He turned to walk back to Tilly, but as he did so he saw Frank Graves enter, dressed neatly in a dark suit. Eddie cursed under his breath and walked over.

'I thought I told you not to come back?'

'How could I miss such an important occasion? After all, I did have a hand in making this possible. Without my stake to add to yours, you wouldn't have been able to start to build your business world.'

Glowering at him, Eddie said, 'Don't get any funny ideas, Frank.'

Looking around, Frank said, 'It would be only fair for you to offer me a partnership in this place.'

Eddie burst out laughing. 'You must be joking!'

'No, not at all. I think I earned it.'

'You earned nothing that's mine, let's get that clear, my friend. I gave you your share. What have you done with it? Drunk it already?'

'No, not all of it. I've been living the high life, making up for lost time. But it was expensive.'

Eddie curbed the fury that was rising inside him. He knew that this man was going to be a problem, but no one was going to spoil what he had, certainly not Frank Graves. Gripping him by the arm, Eddie led him outside and said to his doormen, 'This man is not welcome here. Escort him away. There's no need to rough him up . . . unless he returns.' Glaring at his former friend, he said quietly, 'If you come anywhere near me or mine again, you will give me no choice but to deal with you. Don't push me or you'll be very sorry.' Turning on his heel, he walked back into the club.

The chief constable was just about to leave. He held out his hand to Eddie. 'Congratulations, Mr Chapman. The club is attractive and well run. I'll be keeping an eye on it, you understand.'

'Thank you, sir. Do by all means, but I can assure you you'll get no problems from me.'

'I do hope so,' he said, 'because it would be a pity to have to close you down.'

At last Eddie was able to return to find Tilly. She was having a great time, as he saw for himself by the pile of chips sitting in front of her.

'I can see you are having beginner's luck again,' he said, putting an arm round her.

'Oh, Eddie, this is such fun,' she said.

'Perhaps it's time to stop and cash your chips whilst you're ahead,' he suggested.

'Do you really think so?'

He could tell she didn't want to. 'It's up to you.'

'Just another couple of spins of the wheel?' she wheedled.

'Very well,' he replied, 'but beware that you don't lose it all.'

The next two turns didn't go Tilly's way and she lost money. Gathering her remaining chips she said, 'You've spoiled my run of luck, so now I'll stop.'

'Now that's a sign of a good gambler,' he said. 'Knowing when to stop is really important. Come on, we'll cash in your chips.'

Tilly was delighted with her winnings.

'Save them until we go to the races next time,' Eddie said, highly amused at her enthusiasm.

'Are we going again?'

'If you'd like to.'

'Oh, I would really. We had such a great day last time.'

'We'll have many more great days,' he said, pulling her towards him and kissing her on the mouth.

Jago, emerging from his game, looked at his sister in Eddie Chapman's arms and was horrified. What on earth had she got herself mixed up with, and where was David? Why wasn't she with him? There were a lot of questions he would be asking her when they got home.

It was late when the club eventually closed. As the last customer left the building, Eddie lifted Tilly up and swung her round and kissed her soundly.

'What a great night!' he said, with a broad grin.

'It was so much fun,' she said, 'but I'm so tired.'

'I'll get you some coffee, then after I see to the staff I'll take you home.'

'You don't have to,' she protested. 'I can go by taxi.'

Tipping her chin, he gazed into her eyes and said, 'I told your brother you would be safe with me and that means seeing you to your doorstep.'

He beckoned to a waiter and asked him to make a pot of coffee for both of them. Then he ordered a drink for each of the staff to thank them.

As they sat drinking their coffee, Eddie turned to Tilly.

'I'm so very pleased you were here with me this evening. It's essential to have someone special to share your successes with.'

She was deeply touched. 'I was happy to be here,' she said. 'It was *so* exciting. You really do live an interesting life. You are so lucky, because so many people don't.'

'You like excitement, don't you, Tilly?'

'I do! I don't want to die without having lived a bit. Does that sound awful?'

'Not at all. It sounds like a person with a spirit which should be cherished.' And drawing her into his arms, he lowered his mouth to hers, exploring

197

it with his tongue until he made her senses swim and her legs go weak.

When he eventually released her he said huskily, 'I'd better take you home. You are a dangerous young woman, you know.'

'I am?' she whispered.

'Oh, yes. A man could very easily fall in love with you, Miss Thompson, and that is dangerous.'

She didn't know what to say. Eddie Chapman thought *she* was dangerous – now that was a great surprise!

And when he took her home and kissed her again, she looked at him, smiled softly and said, 'Be careful, I'm dangerous. You said so yourself!'

He chuckled and said, 'So I did. But you are also funny and delightful company. I'll see you again very soon.'

Tilly was still smiling as she walked into her living room, where she found her brother Jago waiting for her.

CHAPTER NINETEEN

'What the hell do you think you're playing at, Tilly?' he asked before she even had time to close the door.

Her hackles rose. 'I'm going out with Eddie Chapman, that's what I'm doing,' she defiantly replied, 'which is none of your business.'

'And what's happened to David Strickland?'

'We broke up. I told him about Eddie, so that was the end of our friendship.'

'I just don't understand you at all! David was such a nice decent man and you gave him the shove to go out with Chapman. You must be losing your marbles!'

She threw down her handbag on the table in anger. 'Now you listen to me,' she said, glaring at Jago. 'You are not my keeper. I am old enough to make my own decisions and choose how to live my own life without your interference, so leave me alone!'

He tried a different tack. 'You are my youngest

sister and I feel responsible for you. Chapman is too old for you, Tilly. He's a man with a certain reputation. If you continue to see him you will be the talk of the town.'

Her eyes flashed as she said, 'Is that what worries you, what people will think?'

'No, of course not. What I do worry about is what sort of reputation you will have if you continue to be seen with him. And what about his mistress?'

'What makes you so sure he has a mistress?'

'Oh, come on! Greta Harper has been going out with him for quite a time. They don't just hold hands, you know.'

For a moment, Tilly was thrown. She had been so carried away by the charisma of Eddie Chapman, and his charm, that she had pushed to the back of her mind the blonde she had seen him with.

'Well I don't know anything about her. Eddie is great company and we have fun together.'

Jago began to reason in a more gentle fashion. 'Just suppose he has dumped her. She won't like that, and I would say she was a vengeful person. She wouldn't take that laying down. A scorned woman is not a pretty thing, Tilly.'

She sat beside him and tried to make him understand. 'Look, Jago, Eddie is a perfect gentleman all the time; he takes me to places I would never see without him. It's a different world, one that is thrilling and exciting. Is it so wrong of me to want to enjoy those things?'

'Of course not! I'm all for everyone living life to the full, but it can be dangerous for a woman to visit the fleshpots of life. You have so much more to lose than a man.'

Suddenly weary of the conversation, she stood up. 'I'm tired, Jago. I've had a wonderful time this evening and nothing you say will change my mind. Try to be happy for me instead.' Picking up her handbag, she made her way upstairs and to bed.

Jago stayed in his chair, gazing into the dying embers of the stove. Tilly was determined, and when she decided about anything she became stubborn. He wondered if David could change her mind, and resolved to get in touch with him the next day. He could ring up the place where he was teaching and arrange to meet him for a drink and a chat.

Two evenings later, the two men sat in the lounge bar of Jago's local pub and talked.

'I'm sorry that you and Tilly broke up,' her brother said.

David shrugged. 'There wasn't much I could do about it. She's mesmerised by Eddie Chapman. To

Tilly, he's exciting and mysterious and therefore very attractive.'

'I really thought that eventually you would be my brother-in-law,' Jago told him.

With a rueful smile David said, 'It was my hope too. I know that Tilly needs to spread her wings before she settles down. She's a spirited young woman who longs for excitement and adventure. I was prepared to wait, but she has made a choice. Chapman can provide what she's looking for – she thinks.'

Jago shook his head. 'I'm worried about her, David. If she's not careful, she'll find herself in a situation she can't handle.' He sipped his beer and added, 'Chapman is a man of the world and Tilly, though adventurous, is an innocent – and not at all streetwise.'

'I agree with you a hundred per cent, but we've all had to learn by experience, and Tilly now will have to do the same.' Leaning forward, he said, 'Neither of us can live her life for her, Jago . . . she wouldn't let us, anyway.' He sighed. 'All we can do is wait and be ready to pick up the pieces if necessary.'

With a surprised look, Jago asked, 'Are you prepared to do that even though she's dumped you?'

David chuckled. 'You could have put it a bit

more kindly, but yes. I love Tilly, you see. If I have to wait for her to come to her senses, then I will.'

'I'm not sure she deserves such loyalty,' remarked her brother.

'Don't be so hard on her; she's feeling her feet, that's all. Don't tell me you didn't do the same at her age?'

Jago had to laugh. 'Yes, I suppose I did. You tend to forget though, don't you? I remember once . . .' And the two men spent the rest of the evening swapping tales of their youthful misadventures.

The police inquiry into the murder of Elsie Summers was gathering pace. Her brother Nat had been moved from hospital and placed in a safe house with police protection. He'd given the detectives dealing with the case a list of hotels which the Williams twins had designated for business, and these were under constant surveillance, the names of the prostitutes working there noted. Evidence collected from other prostitutes on the streets was being scrutinised for clues. The car was giving them a problem. They did not have the licence number so were unable to trace it to the owner.

Gerald Bradbury was a bundle of nerves as each day passed, waiting for the knock on the door that would herald a policeman standing there with a warrant for his arrest. He was becoming impossible to live with. Over dinner one night an almighty row erupted. Ethel Thompson was there and witnessed most of it.

It all started with an innocuous remark from Simon which his father jumped on, and escalated into a full-blooded row with young Simon storming out of the room. Dorothy Bradbury glared at her husband. 'I suppose you're happy now!' she snapped. 'The poor boy can't breathe in this house without you jumping down his throat.'

'Mind your own business!'

Throwing down her napkin, Dorothy looked across the table at her husband. 'What the hell is wrong with you? You have been like a bear with a sore head for too long and I'm sick of it. What's the matter, Gerald? Haven't you been able to satisfy yourself with your other women lately?'

He choked on his food and Ethel froze to the spot. Surely they hadn't forgotten she was there? But such was the anger being exchanged between the couple that nothing else seemed to register.

'I don't know what you're talking about,' he blustered.

'You know full well what I mean. You hardly come near me normally, but just lately you've become insufferable with your demands!'

Ethel, now horribly embarrassed, coughed to remind them of her presence.

Gerald looked up. 'Get out!' he snapped.

Ethel hurriedly left the room but stood outside listening. This was too good to miss! She heard Mrs Bradbury speak.

'There's no need to be so rude to the staff. I don't suppose you speak to your women like that?'

Now Gerald Bradbury was so enraged that he threw caution to the winds.

'No. I don't need to. My women, as you call them, are only too happy to satisfy my every need, unlike my own wife.'

Ethel heard the sound of a chair being pushed back as Mrs Bradbury rose to her feet. 'Then I suggest you move into the spare room. I no longer wish to share my bed with you.'

'As there was never much joy between the sheets with you, my dear, I'll happily do so.'

Ethel heard her mistress's footsteps heading for the door and rushed away before she was discovered. She entered the kitchen and quickly shut the door behind her, and Cook looked up.

'What's the matter?' she asked. 'You look all flushed.'

'Well,' said Ethel, 'you'll never believe what I just heard.' She repeated the conversation that had taken place in the dining room.

'Bloody hell!' Cook exclaimed. 'Imagine the missus standing up to him like that. I never knew she had it in her! Still, a woman can only take so much. If my old man wandered, I'd take a carving knife to him. Wouldn't you do the same?'

'The only other person my Joe has any love for, apart from his kids, is Clarence his horse, so I've no worries.'

Cook thought this was highly amusing and her laughter echoed around the large kitchen. After a few minutes, however, she became thoughtful.

'What is it?' asked Ethel.

'You don't suppose he had anything to do with that poor girl found on the common, do you?'

'Good gracious, no! Mr Bradbury may like his women, but I can't imagine him to be a violent man.'

As the following weeks passed by, Tilly was having the time of her life. Eddie Chapman persuaded her to take a week of her holiday, thus enabling her to be free to go out with him during the day. He took her racing, and to the Tower of London where she was overwhelmed by the crown jewels, glistening in their display cases. He wined and dined her at the best hotels in London, Bournemouth and Southampton. They became a couple – and people talked!

She was very aware that in the best restaurants in Southampton, whenever they entered, they were the centre of attention from the other diners. And when she went to the Blue Pelican some evenings and they danced, she saw heads bent and gossip exchanged between people who watched their every move.

Tilly couldn't have cared less. She was having fun. Eddie and she seemed to share a similar sense of humour, he was interesting to talk to and he treated her like something precious. He was always solicitous towards her . . . and he made her knees feel weak when he kissed her. Which he did with growing ardour each time they parted. It thrilled her to be held in his arms, but it also unsettled her. He was so obviously more experienced than she was and she wondered how long he would be satisfied with just a kiss. Would he demand more from her? If he did . . . would she be strong enough to refuse him? Such was his fascination that she thought she probably wouldn't.

Eddie's new club was doing well. The punters were satisfied that it was being run legally and that the tables were true, without any loaded dice, and they spent their money freely.

The Williams twins watched from afar, seething with jealousy. Charlie was vitriolic about Chapman.

'Every time I see that bastard, I want to put his lights out!' he told his brother.

Ken tried to calm him. 'So the man is a success. Let it be – there's nothing we can do about it. We're doing all right with our own business.'

'The private poker parties have dropped off,' Charlie snapped. 'Our punters now go to the Ace of Clubs. He's screwing up our trade.'

Which was true. No longer were people prepared to pay to join their private gambling parties. Why should they? They paid their membership at Eddie's club and enjoyed their games without the need to hide away from the law . . . and the atmosphere was so much more professional. This didn't set well with Charlie, who took it all personally and vowed that somehow or other he would get back at Eddie Chapman one way or another.

Greta Harper was another who was unhappy with the good-looking club owner. She had heard the gossip about Eddie's new woman. They had been seen together in the places where he used to go with her. She wondered if he'd taken the new girl to bed yet. She was very young and probably inexperienced, so she figured he would take it easy at first, but she knew that eventually their relationship would end up in the bedroom, and the thought made her furious.

There was to be a gala night held at the Blue Pelican and she intended to be there, with an escort of her own. It was time someone put the young girl straight, and who better than she?

CHAPTER TWENTY

Ethel Thompson sat reading the local paper. When she turned the page, she was brought up short by a picture of her daughter laughing up at a man. She read the caption beneath. *Eddie Chapman, successful owner of the Blue Pelican club and the Ace of Clubs, with his attractive girlfriend, Miss Tilly Thompson.* The article went on to describe Chapman as an entrepreneur who had come to Southampton to set up his businesses, and was someone to watch for the future. It also wrote about the forthcoming gala evening to be held at the Blue Pelican club.

Letting out a deep sigh, Ethel frowned and shook her head. Tilly's wild streak was taking her into a different world and it wasn't one that thrilled Ethel. She decided it was time to have a talk with her daughter.

When Tilly arrived home after work late that afternoon it was to find her mother sitting alone in the living room, waiting for her.

Tilly walked over to her and kissed her cheek. 'Hello, Mum. My feet are killing me,' she said, sitting down and kicking off her shoes. 'We had such a busy day today.'

Ethel didn't answer but pushed the paper over towards her daughter, the picture uppermost. Tilly looked at it, then at her mother.

'Who is this man and what were you doing with him?' Ethel asked.

Taking a deep breath, Tilly said defiantly, 'Well, if you read the article, you'll know who he is!'

'Don't you use that tone of voice with me, young lady! I thought you were going out with that nice engineer until I saw your picture with this man, who I might say looks far too old for you.'

'Eddie *is* older than me, but I can't see what difference that makes.'

'It says here,' Ethel picked up the paper, 'that you're his girlfriend. Is that true?'

Tilly rose from the chair and took the large brown teapot off the stove. Pouring herself a cup, she said, 'Yes, we're going out together. David and I were really only good friends. We broke up some time ago.'

'Because of him?' Ethel pointed to the picture.

'Yes,' Tilly said sharply, sitting down.

'I did warn you some time ago about behaving

yourself and not bringing trouble to this house, didn't I?'

With her green eyes flashing with anger, Tilly said, 'I am not bringing trouble, so you don't have to worry about the neighbours, Mother. Eddie Chapman is a lovely man and we have a great time together.'

'No doubt frequenting these clubs of his.'

'Good God, Mother, it's all perfectly innocent. The clubs are perfectly decent – our Jago goes there, but the way you're talking you'd think they were brothels!'

Her mother looked shocked. 'I don't know what's got into you, speaking to me like that.'

Tilly got up from the table. 'What about the way you are speaking to me? You are making judgements about me when I've done nothing wrong! I'm having a good time, enjoying myself, that's all, but the way you're going on you'd think I'd committed a dreadful sin.' And she walked upstairs to her bedroom, slamming the door behind her.

Ethel pursed her lips and thought that there was a certain amount of truth in Tilly's words. She wasn't really doing anything wrong, but her choice of escort seemed inadvisable to her mother's mind. However, having voiced her concerns, there was little else she could do.

* * *

The night of the gala evening arrived. All around the town, people were getting ready, many with their own agenda: Tilly, in her innocence, filled with excitement; Greta, accompanied by a new male escort and vengeance in her heart; the Williams brothers, jealous and resentful . . . and David Strickland.

Tilly was wearing a plain black beaded dress, and the emerald embroidered jacket that David had bought for her in New York. She'd only worn it once before, when David had taken her out to dinner before they split up, but it looked wonderful over the black dress, and she wanted to make an impression tonight of all nights. Eddie had told her that this evening was important to him and his business and she didn't want to let him down.

When she arrived at the club, there were already several people there, but as soon as she walked through the door, Eddie rushed over to her.

'Hello, darling. You look wonderful.' He kissed her on the cheek.

Cameras flashed, which startled her.

Grinning, Eddie said, 'I've made sure the local papers are here to record this evening.'

Oh dear, she thought, more photographs for Mother to see. But she smiled at the photographer none the less.

The guests were greeted by waiters offering

champagne. A long table was set out with a tasty finger buffet. After the first drink, the clients bought their own from the bar. The small band was playing soft music in the background. The club had a very festive air about it and Eddie, the perfect host, worked the room with Tilly, greeting everyone, seeing they were well cared for.

About an hour later, Tilly looked up and saw David Strickland enter the club with a beautiful young girl on his arm. She was shaken to the core, and stunned into silence mid-sentence.

'What's the matter?' Eddie asked.

Shaking her head, she said, 'Nothing. I just lost track of what I was saying, that's all.' She turned away.

She and Eddie sat at a table with his bank manager and his wife. The men talked business and the two women made small talk, but all the while Tilly was aware of David, taking his guest to the table and choosing food for her, bending over her solicitously and eventually guiding her to a table near their own. And then Jago arrived with a young lady and joined them.

Tilly was trying to concentrate on her conversation with the bank manager's wife, but when David and his lady took to the floor and danced together she couldn't take her eyes off them. She was unaware that Eddie had stopped talking to his guest and was looking at her. He followed her stricken gaze and saw David on the dance floor.

'Come on, darling, let's dance,' he said.

'Not just now.'

But Eddie ignored her refusal. Taking her firmly by the arm, he led her on to the floor and held her close, staring into her eyes as they danced.

'Your old boyfriend has moved on, Tilly, just as you have,' he said. 'I can't imagine that you are having any regrets . . . are you?'

'No, of course not!' she said quickly. 'I was just surprised to see him, that's all.'

She felt him stiffen for a moment as he looked over to the entrance. As they turned round the corner of the floor, she saw that the blonde woman she'd seen with Eddie in the past had arrived with a male escort.

'They're all coming out of the woodwork tonight,' she said with a wry smile.

He squeezed her gently and smiled down at her. 'Never mind, darling. We're together and that's all that counts, isn't it?'

She looked at him with affection and said, 'Absolutely!'

Later on in the evening, when Eddie had been called away to speak to someone, Tilly was sitting alone when David came over to the table.

'May I?' he asked, pointing to the empty chair beside her.

'Of course,' she said. What else could she say?

'You look wonderful this evening,' he said. 'That jacket really suits you.'

'Thank you. And how are you?'

'Fine.' He looked round and said, 'Chapman is doing well. I saw your picture in the paper. Tell me, Tilly, are you happy?'

'Deliriously! I'm having the time of my life.' There was a note of defiance in her voice, which she regretted as soon as she had spoken. 'I *am* pleased to see you, David. How are things with you and the students?'

'Oh, you know – some are great, some are lazy and some are useless and I've had to let them go.' He gazed steadily at her. 'It's never easy to let go,' he added.

She knew he wasn't talking about the students, and she was filled with guilt, but before she could say anything Eddie returned and sat down.

He smiled across at David. 'I do hope you and your young lady are having a good time?'

Rising to his feet, David smiled and said, 'Thank you, we are. This is a nice place; you deserve to do well.' He looked at Tilly and said, 'It's lovely to see you, and you look stunning. I knew that jacket would look good on you.' He walked away.

'Jacket? What's he talking about?' demanded Eddie.

'David bought this jacket for me in New York when we were seeing each other.'

'The man has good taste,' he said, but he didn't look pleased.

'Excuse me,' said Tilly, feeling the need for some breathing space, 'but I must go to the ladies' room.'

She closed the door behind her and walked over to one of the washbasins. Running the cold tap and cupping cold water in her hands, she bent over and bathed her face.

'Things getting too hot for you in there?'

Startled, Tilly opened her eyes and saw Greta Harper standing looking at her. Her heart sank and she could hear Jago's words echoing in her ears. 'A scorned woman is not a pretty thing.'

'Hello,' said Tilly, patting her face dry. 'It was getting warm with so many people.'

'Let's not beat about the bush,' said Greta. 'You know who I am. I'm just here to tell you not to get too cosy with Eddie. You're just a passing fancy. Eddie is used to a real woman, not some young teenager!'

'What makes you think that because I am *so* much younger than you I am not a real woman? I probably have more stamina, after all!'

As Greta, flushed with anger, made to reply, Tilly interrupted, 'Never mind the age difference. Let us *not* forget we are both ladies,' and she swept out of the room. She felt exhilarated, having got the better of the woman, but none the less embarrassed by the confrontation.

When she joined Eddie at their table he noticed her flushed face. 'Is everything all right?'

'Yes, why shouldn't it be?'

He didn't pursue the subject but he did notice that Greta came out of the ladies shortly after and guessed that she had said something to Tilly. He determined to put his ex in her place before the evening came to an end.

Jago appeared at his sister's side and, looking at Eddie, said, 'I'm sure you won't mind if I dance with this young lady?'

'Of course not.' He got to his feet as she rose to take the floor with her brother.

Still bristling from her encounter with Greta, Tilly waited until they had danced away from her escort and then said, 'I hope you are not out to make trouble for me tonight, our Jago!'

'I wouldn't dream of it; not here, anyway.' He gazed at her and said softly, 'I'm just concerned for you, that's all.'

Realising that his concern for her was genuine and without rancour, she said, 'I'm fine, honestly.

Really, Jago, I'm having so much fun and I'm really happy.'

'I saw David talking to you earlier,' he said.

'Yes, we had a chat. I was pleased to see him – he's a nice chap.'

'I don't think you know just how nice . . .' he began.

'Let's just dance,' she said sharply; then grinning at him she added, 'For an old man you're doing quite well.'

He laughed at her and said 'You cheeky monkey!' The old camaraderie was back and Tilly was relieved. But when Jago led her back to the table and Eddie, he held her chair for her then looked at Chapman. 'You take good care of my sister, or you'll have me to deal with!'

'Jago!' Tilly cried.

But Eddie put his hand over hers and said, 'Don't be cross. Your brother is right to try to protect you.' He smiled at Jago and said, 'Have no fear, she's in very safe hands.'

Her brother nodded and walked back to his table.

The Williams twins' entry into the club had not gone unnoticed by the owner. He said to Tilly, 'Will you excuse me? I have to see some people.'

'Of course, go on. I'll be fine.'

The brothers, resplendent in evening dress, were

standing by the bar, drinks in their hands, when Eddie approached them.

'Good evening, gentlemen,' he said.

'You've got a good crowd in tonight,' Ken remarked, looking round.

'Making a bloody mint, aren't you?' snapped Charlie.

'I am sure your business is a success too,' said Eddie. 'Let's drink to that, shall we?' He ordered his usual tonic water with lemon and ice. Holding up the glass he said, 'To both our successes!'

Ken drank readily, Charlie reluctantly.

'I have to go and look after my guests,' Eddie said, setting down his glass. 'Enjoy your evening.'

He walked to the door where he had a quiet word with the doormen. 'Keep an eye on the Williams boys,' he said. 'I don't want any trouble tonight of all nights.'

Whilst the party at the Blue Pelican was in full swing, at the Horse and Groom in the Ditches Queenie the barmaid was flirting with a new customer.

'Well, handsome, where have you been all my life? What can I get you?'

'Pint of bitter, please,' the man answered with a grin.

Putting the pint glass in front of him she said,

'There you are, darlin', best bitter in town. You new around here?'

'Yes, came down from the smoke for the weekend. Thought I'd have a change of scene, change of air, you know.'

'Change of woman?' she asked provocatively.

'You don't waste any time, do you?' He laughed. 'Well, maybe I am ready for a change . . . are you offering?'

'Are you asking?'

'Yeah, why not? What time do you finish?'

'I can be out of here just after closing time if I've a mind to,' she said.

'You got your own place?'

'Good enough one for the likes of you,' she said. 'What's your name?'

'Frank – Frank Graves.'

CHAPTER TWENTY-ONE

Shortly after closing time, Queenie left the Horse and Groom with Frank Graves and walked to her flat nearby.

To Frank's surprise it was tastefully furnished. The living room had a three-piece suite in soft shades of beige and brown, with brighter cushions to lift it. His surprise must have been obvious because Queenie grinned at him.

'What did you expect, something brash and flash?'

'Yes, I suppose I did,' he admitted.

'Never jump to conclusions,' she said as she walked to the kitchen and put the kettle on. 'I'm always hungry when I get home. Fancy some scrambled eggs?'

'Sounds good to me,' he answered. He stood in the doorway watching her as she bustled around, preparing the eggs, putting bread ready to toast.

Pointing, she said, 'There are cups, saucers and

plates in that cupboard. Get them and put them on the table, will you?'

A few minutes later, they sat down to eat.

'So, tell me about yourself,' she said.

'Oh, I'm not very interesting.'

She cast a knowing look in his direction. 'I'm a bloody good judge of character and I'm sure you have led quite a life, one way and another.'

Frank chuckled. 'You are quite a lady.'

Queenie burst out laughing. 'That's the last thing I am. So, Frank, you're a stranger in town, is that it?'

'Not exactly. I've been here before to visit an old friend.'

'Anyone I might know?'

'Maybe – he seems to be pretty well known. I'm talking about Eddie Chapman.'

Queenie's interest was immediately caught. 'Tell me more,' she said.

The last guests at the Blue Pelican had left. The tables were cleared, the glasses washed up and put away. When the club was back to its pristine condition, the staff were dismissed and Eddie took Tilly upstairs to his apartment where he made them some coffee.

They sat together on the settee, and he put his arm round her and kissed her.

'What was that for?'

'For being at my side tonight, for being a perfect hostess – and for being you.'

'What do you mean, being me? I can hardly be anyone else!'

'And I thank God for that, darling Tilly. Most people came here tonight for a reason. The bank manager to see that his investment was paying off, the Williams brothers to see how well I was doing, hoping I would fail, your brother to see you were being treated right by me . . . and Greta to cause trouble. I'm not too sure why your ex-boyfriend came, though, are you?'

'No. Just to have an enjoyable evening, I expect. After all, why shouldn't he?'

'You're probably right.' He sipped his coffee, then looking at Tilly he said, 'I would really like it if you were free to spend more time with me. Your job puts too many restrictions on your time.'

'I know, but I have to earn a living.'

'You could work for me.'

Tilly was more than a little surprised by the suggestion. 'Doing what?'

'Being my assistant. I would pay you well.'

'But that would change everything!' With a look of consternation she said, 'I don't think that would work at all.'

'Why ever not?'

'Because our relationship would be on a different level. You'd be my boss; I would have to treat you differently.

He was highly amused. 'What rubbish! You would be free to come out with me, which is the whole idea.'

Tilly's anger surprised him.

'In other words there is no real job; you would be paying for my company. It would be like being a kept woman! No thank you, Eddie.'

He tried to reason with her. 'Not at all. There are lots of things we could do together, but with you working in the dress shop it curtails any outings other than on your half-day and at weekends.' He drew her closer to him and said softly, 'I want you to be an important part of my life, darling.' He cupped her face with his hand. 'Doesn't that mean anything to you?'

'I thought I *was* an important part already.'

'You are, you are! But I want more.'

Seeing the determined look in his eyes, Tilly's heart sank. What was he suggesting, she wondered?

Staring into his eyes, she said, 'You're not suggesting marriage, I'm sure?'

Her candour threw him and he hesitated.

'No, I thought not! What are you suggesting, Eddie? That you want me to be your mistress? Is that what you have in mind?'

He caressed her cheek. 'Would that be a problem for you? We could have some wonderful times together.'

'And *if* I agreed, would you cast me aside after a while the way you did Greta?'

He chuckled softly. 'She got to you tonight, didn't she?'

'Yes, we exchanged a few words.'

Letting out a sigh he said, 'Come on, darling, I'll take you home. It's been a long night; let's not end it quarrelling.' He stood up and taking her hand drew her to her feet. Gathering her into his arms, he kissed her passionately. When he eventually released his hold he said, 'All relationships change, Tilly darling. They either progress – or they end. You have to decide where you want ours to go.'

As he left her outside her house, Eddie kissed her again. 'I'll be in touch,' he said.

The house was in darkness; the family was in bed. Tilly was grateful for the solitude. She made herself a cup of cocoa and sat by the dying embers of the fire.

Well, she thought, it was bound to happen at some time. She had known that a man like Eddie Chapman wouldn't be content for ever with a caress and a kiss. She had been playing with fire and she knew it, but now he had put his cards on the table and she had to make a decision. She tried to analyse her feelings. Was she attracted to him? Certainly! Did she like being with him? Of course. He was exciting, interesting and great fun. Was she in love with him? She pondered over this for a long time. She didn't know. Would she like him as a lover? There was no doubt – if she were honest – that when he held her and kissed her, she was aware of sexual longing. It was exciting and at the same time disturbing. She had to battle to control herself – and her wanton thoughts had surprised her. She had often tried to imagine being bedded and made love to by this charismatic man. Oh, yes, she could certainly see Eddie as her lover. But what of her future then? Marriage was not on his agenda, she was sure of that. If she agreed, she surely *would* be the talk of the town. Could she cope with such notoriety? Would her family?

Her mind in a whirl, she put down her cup and went to bed. She'd think about it all tomorrow.

As he drove home, Eddie went over all the events of this evening. It had been a great success. His bank manager had been pleased; the chief constable had congratulated him. He had taken Greta aside without Tilly's knowledge. He smiled to himself as he thought of Greta's outrage at seeing him with his new companion.

'You'll soon get tired of the "little girl",' she had said. 'I know you too well, Eddie. To her at the moment you seem to be some sort of knight in shining armour, but wait until she gets to know you better and learns of your other tricky deals. Her balloon will be burst and she'll go scuttling back to her mother!'

He had gripped her wrist. 'You must learn when to keep your mouth shut, Greta my dear. It would be very unwise to cross me. You know me well enough to know I mean what I say.'

Snatching her hand free, she had glared at him and walked away.

Eddie's mouth tightened as he thought about their exchange. She didn't know enough to be a real threat to him, but a little knowledge was a dangerous thing. He'd have to be very careful in future.

He wondered just what Tilly's response to his proposition would be. She was a darling girl, she made him laugh and he loved her honesty and her enthusiasm for life, but he wanted more from her. He wanted to take her to his bed, to make a real woman of her. He had been patient enough. He was a man with needs, after all. Celibacy wasn't his style.

*　　*　　*

The following morning Eddie received a call from Jeremy Frampton, who wanted him to visit him at the stables.

'Goodwood is coming up soon,' Jeremy said, 'I reckon we could make a killing in the future with Rufus and I need to see you about it. It's Sunday, so can you come up this afternoon?'

'Yes, I can get away. I'll be there about two o'clock.'

Eddie immediately sent a messenger to Tilly's house. *I'm going to see Rufus and Jeremy at the stables. I'll pick you up at twelve thirty.*

As she read the note, Tilly thought this must be an unexpected meeting as he hadn't mentioned it last night. Would he press her for an answer about their relationship? She hoped not, as she had been unable to reach a decision. In fact, she had put it to the back of her mind, knowing the implications.

Tilly heard the sound of the car engine outside and looked at the clock. As always, Eddie was punctual. She said goodbye to her parents and left the house.

During the drive to Newmarket, Eddie didn't allude to his earlier proposition but made conversation about Jeremy.

'He has several horses in his yard that he trains

for other owners,' he told her. 'He's been in the business for years and really knows his stuff. He wants to run Rufus at Goodwood shortly. You'll like the racecourse – it's smaller than Ascot and much prettier.'

'I'm invited to the meeting then?'

He cast a glance in her direction and said, 'I fully expect you to be there, Tilly.'

His tone implied that no excuse would be acceptable and Tilly wondered just what her employer would say if she asked for the day off. What if she refused? Which, of course, was exactly the point Eddie had been making the previous evening.

Eddie drove the car into a long drive. At the end was a large farmhouse-type building, and beside and behind it were the stables.

As they stepped out of the car and walked towards the stables, Tilly was surprised at the size of the yard. There must have been at least thirty individual stalls. Horses' heads peered over some of them; some of the horses were being saddled by grooms. In the distance she could see a circular track with four horses being ridden out by the stable lads. It was a hive of activity.

Eddie walked over to the stall where Rufus was stabled and stroked his nose. He produced a carrot from his pocket and gave it to the horse.

Tilly stroked the dark mane and neck of the

animal. Looking up at Eddie, she said, 'He really is a beauty, isn't he?'

'I think so. You're a handsome devil, aren't you?' he said as he stroked him.

Jeremy Frampton joined them. His trousers were tucked into wellington boots and he was wearing a flat corduroy cap. He smiled at Tilly.

'Your shoes will be ruined in this mud,' he said, pointing to the ground. 'The horses bring it back from the track.' He went into the tack room and came back with a pair of boots. 'Here, put these on. They're the smallest I can find, and at least they'll save your shoes.'

'Thanks,' said Tilly, and changed into them.

'Why don't you have a walk round while I talk to Jeremy?' Eddie suggested.

She left them to chat and went to make the acquaintance of some of the other horses. Jeremy and Eddie disappeared inside the tack room.

After wandering around the stalls for a while, Tilly walked back towards the tack room and paused outside, not wanting to interrupt the two men. She could hear them chatting, and was puzzled by what she heard.

'What do you mean, you don't want to run him to win?'

'Well,' explained Jeremy, 'last time out he came third so his price won't be much, but if he loses again here, then at the next meeting the odds will be better and we can make a killing.'

'You're not going to dope him, are you?'

'No, no. The jockey who is booked to ride him has huge gambling debts; he'll follow my instructions as to how to ride him for a fee, no questions asked.'

'You're going to ask him to pull the horse?' Eddie sounded doubtful.

'Right! Don't look so worried; the jockey's an old hand. No one will suspect, I give you my word.'

Tilly held her breath as she listened and waited to hear Eddie's answer.

'You're sure?'

'I swear,' Jeremy promised.

'All right, but make sure nothing goes wrong. Come on, let's go and find Tilly.'

Hearing this, she flew along to another stall, so that when the two men emerged she was in conversation with one of the grooms.

'There you are,' Eddie said. 'Shall we go?'

'All right, but I must change into my shoes,' she said, putting out one foot to show the boots she was wearing.

'I'll get them for you.' Jeremy went into the tack room and came out with her shoes.

She held on to Eddie's arm and changed her

footwear. Handing back the boots she said, 'Thanks, Jeremy.'

With a grin he said, 'They're not quite your style, Tilly my dear, but here we leave style behind, I'm afraid.'

'I'm very grateful,' she told him.

He waved to them as they drove away.

'The meeting at Goodwood is on August the tenth, so tomorrow ask your employer for the day off,' Eddie told her.

'What if she refuses?' asked Tilly with some trepidation.

'Let's wait and see, shall we?'

The following morning, Madam Leone flatly refused to let Tilly have the day off.

'No, Tilly. I can't keep giving you time off. First it was a Wednesday morning, then a week's holiday at a most inconvenient time . . . and now this. You must make up your mind if you want to work for me or not!'

Leaving the shop at closing time, she found a phone box and rang the Blue Pelican. When she told Eddie her news, to her relief he just said, 'All right, leave it with me.'

What on earth did that mean, she wondered?

She found out at the weekend.

*　　*　　*

After a couple of days, Madam Leone's attitude towards her changed, becoming almost deferential, which puzzled Tilly. She couldn't make it out, but at the end of Saturday when it was near to closing time Eddie Chapman entered the shop.

Tilly walked over to him. 'What on earth are you doing here?'

Madam Leone came out from her office, wearing her coat. She handed the shop keys to Eddie and said, 'Here you are, Mr Chapman.'

Tilly looked from one to the other.

Eddie shook Madam by the hand and thanked her. He held the front door open for her, then closing it turned to Tilly.

'What on earth is going on?' she demanded.

Holding up the keys he said, 'Madam Leone's is now yours, my darling.'

'What? What are you talking about? Stop playing stupid games!'

Laughing, he picked her up and swung her round. 'This is no game, Tilly. I bought Madam Leone out. The business is yours.'

She was shocked and speechless.

Leading her to a small sofa in the corner, he sat her down and settled beside her. 'It's simple really. Now you are free to come out with me whenever you like.'

She couldn't believe what she was hearing. 'This

shop is mine to run, is that what you're saying?'

'Exactly!'

'Then however can I be free? I'll be needed here all the time.'

'No, I've seen to that. I've hired a manageress with plenty of experience. You can hire an assistant yourself, to help her. Then there won't be a problem. You can come and go as you please.'

Her fury was like a tornado.

Getting to her feet, she stormed at him. 'You did all this without consulting me? You say the business is now mine, but *you* hired a manageress.'

'But you can hire an assistant.'

'How very kind of you!'

Eddie looked angry. 'I thought you would be pleased.'

'Well you thought wrong! I wouldn't work for you at your club; now I have to work for you here. How dare you take over my life like that!'

Getting to his feet, he said, 'You won't be working for me, Tilly.' He handed her a contract. 'If you read this you will see that the business is in your name, not mine.'

She took the papers from him and read the contents slowly. Then looking at him she asked, 'Why would you do this for me?'

'Because I think you're very special.'

'But what happens if we fall out and part?'

He gathered her in his arms. 'O ye of little faith,' he said softly, 'should such a terrible thing happen, the business is yours with my love. It will give you independence, a start in life. We all need one, you know.'

Shaking her head she said, 'I don't understand you at all.'

He chuckled. 'I am a man of mystery, remember? The more time we spend together, the more you'll understand.' Tipping her chin upwards, he covered her mouth with his.

Tilly felt her senses reel, and she returned his kisses with equal ardour.

'Oh, Eddie,' she murmured, 'life with you is full of surprises.'

'Does that mean you will be staying around?'

She knew that her answer would be significant. He was asking whether she would commit to a more serious relationship. A physical one.

'Yes, it does,' she whispered.

CHAPTER TWENTY-TWO

There had been a breakthrough in the investigation into the murder of Elsie Summers. One of the local prostitutes had told the police about a punter who had turned violent with her.

'I'd had him before and he'd been fine,' she told the two detectives, 'but one night he went mad. He hit me. The more I begged him to stop, the worse he became.'

'How did you get him to stop?'

'I reminded him that if he were found out, his reputation would suffer.'

The detective looked up and asked, 'What reputation? What did you mean?'

'Well, love, he's a solicitor and well thought of.'

The two men looked at each other, then turning to the girl one of them asked, 'Do you know this man's name?'

'Of course I do. He was one of my regulars until he turned nasty.'

'So who is he?'

'Mr Gerald Bradbury.'

'Bloody hell!' one of the men exclaimed. Then, looking at his companion, he said, 'He drives a car, doesn't he?'

'Yes, but I don't know what kind. Let's find out.' Turning to the girl he said, 'Thanks, miss, you've been a great help. Don't leave Southampton; we may need to question you again.'

'Where the hell would I go? I live here.'

After showing the prostitute out of the building, the two detectives also left and made their way to the offices of Gerald Bradbury to check on his car, which was parked outside. It matched the description given by the previous witness.

They walked to the offices of the local paper and had a print made of a picture of Gerald Bradbury, taken by a reporter at a local business luncheon. Armed with this they went in search of the woman who had originally described the vehicle and said she had noticed the driver. They eventually caught up with her in a dockside pub. Taking her to one side, they showed her the picture.

'Is this the man you saw in the car the night that Elsie Summers was murdered?'

She gazed at it for a moment. 'I can't be absolutely sure, but it looks like him.'

'Would you be willing to take part in an identity parade?'

With a worried look she asked, 'What would I have to do?'

One of the men explained. 'You would be standing behind a glass screen. A line of men would stand on the other side and you would have to see if you could recognise the man you saw in the car. It's a one-way mirror, so he wouldn't be able to see you.' As the girl hesitated the detective said, 'Think of poor Elsie. That could have been you if you had climbed into that car.'

She nodded slowly. 'To think I was disappointed when he drove on. Christ! It doesn't bear thinking about, does it?'

'Precisely!'

Two hours later, armed with a search warrant, the two detectives walked into Bradbury's office unannounced.

'What the hell are you doing, marching into my office like this?'

'Gerald Percival Bradbury,' said one, 'we have a search warrant and we would like you to accompany us to the station to help us with our inquiries.'

The colour drained from his face. 'Inquiries about what?'

'The murder of Miss Elsie Summers.'

The solicitor was stunned. He had lived in fear of discovery, but as the weeks had passed he had begun to relax, pushing the incident to the back of his mind. Now his greatest fear was staring him in the face.

Rising from his seat, he buttoned his jacket with trembling fingers and walked from his office with the two men. Pausing beside his secretary's desk, he said, 'Cancel all my appointments until further notice.'

Seeing the stricken look on his face she asked, 'Is everything all right, sir?'

'Yes. Just call my house, will you, and tell my wife I'll be in touch.'

Outside, as he climbed into the police car, Gerald saw that his own vehicle was being towed away.

In the afternoon, Bradbury was made to stand in line with other men in an identification parade. The prostitute standing on the other side of the mirror looked carefully along the line of men, then pointed out Gerald Bradbury as the driver of the car she had seen on the night of the murder.

The Williams brothers soon heard about Bradbury's being questioned through a contact in the police station.

'Do you think it has anything to do with his being one of our punters?' asked Charlie.

'God, I hope not! What has that young boyfriend of yours had to say lately?'

'I haven't seen the little bleeder. He disappeared from the hospital and I can't find any trace of him.'

Running his fingers through his thinning hair, Ken said, 'I hope that this is about one of Bradbury's clients. Mind you, he wouldn't want it known he was one of ours, no way. He'd be finished if that got out. In any case, how would the police know? We've chosen our hotels carefully and he always went to one out of town. I shouldn't worry; after all, as a solicitor you have to deal with lots of dodgy people. Come on, I'll buy you a pint. Let's go to the Horse and Groom and see Queenie.'

When they walked into the public bar, Queenie rushed over to where they were standing.

'Hey, boys, I met a geezer the other night who has an axe to grind with Eddie Chapman,' she told them.

In fact Frank Graves had told Queenie very little, only that he and Eddie had known each other way back and that Frank was here to collect a debt. He was no fool. The fewer people to know about his background the better as far as he was concerned. But he was out for all he could squeeze from his old partner in crime and as he walked into the Blue Pelican that morning he was determined to collect.

Eddie saw him enter the premises, and seeing the look on the other man's face he took him to his office, out of earshot of his staff.

Lighting a cigar, Eddie looked at Frank and said, 'What do you want this time, as if I didn't know!'

'Well, Eddie, I've been thinking. The police would give a lot to discover who stole the payroll from that place in Woolwich.'

Eddie Chapman laughed. 'You aren't serious? That was years ago.'

'What difference would that make?'

'You haven't thought this through, my friend. If you were to tell the police, you would have to implicate yourself and I don't think you'd relish more time spent behind bars.'

'I could say I heard about it from someone!'

'Sounds a bit weak, don't you think? They'd see through you in a minute. Besides, how could they prove anything against me? There was no proof, no fingerprints . . . and I don't have a police record.' Leaning forward to remove his cigar ash he said, 'Unlike you, Frank, I was very careful. I didn't splash my money around. I waited a very long time before I used any. By then I had a nice little legitimate business going, buying and selling.'

Graves started to curse under his breath.

'Go ahead, my friend, go to the police; it would

be your word against mine. And whereas I am an honest citizen, you have been inside. They would probably send you down again with your record, thinking it was you who stole the money. Yes, do it! With you inside I would be spared your constant demands.' Getting to his feet, Eddie said, 'This is the last time you enter my club. You are barred, do you understand? Come again, I'll have you removed physically. Now get out!'

Left alone, Eddie sat thinking. Graves was going to continue to be a problem, he could see that. The man was like a dog with a bone. He would have to be dealt with because who knew when he might spill the beans to someone, either in temper or during a drunken night out. Eddie just couldn't take the chance on having his future ruined by such an embittered man. After all, he'd done right by him. He'd paid over Frank's half of the money with interest. It wasn't his fault if he'd wasted it. He puffed on his cigar, deep in thought, then picked up the telephone.

At the police station, Gerald Bradbury was sweating. He refused to answer any questions until there was a solicitor present, and when one of his associates arrived they were allowed time together before facing the detectives in the interview room.

Steven Durrington looked at his old friend as he asked, 'Are you in real trouble here, Gerald?'

With shoulders slumped and a hand held to his head, he said, 'I think I might well be.'

'But this inquiry is about the murder of a prostitute!'

'I know.'

'I've been told that they are examining your car. Might they find anything that would prove damning to you?'

Gerald shrugged. 'I really don't know. Maybe.'

'I take it that you knew this woman?'

The other man nodded.

'Were you a client of hers on that night?'

'I'm afraid so.' Gerald took a handkerchief from his pocket to wipe the sweat from his brow. 'Have you got a cigarette on you?'

Durrington took out a packet of Players and a lighter and laid them on the table.

'Gerald, did you kill Elsie Summers?'

'It was an accident!' he cried.

'Keep your voice down,' urged the other man. 'You had better tell me what happened.'

Bradbury told him about picking up the girl and taking her to the common, and how when she wouldn't comply with his wishes and he'd tried to force her she'd tried to scream.

'I was scared someone would hear her,' he said,

his voice trembling. 'I put a hand round her throat to stop her . . . and she stopped breathing!'

'What did you do then?'

'I carried her into some bushes and covered her with twigs and bits of shrubbery. I panicked!'

Steven Durrington scratched the top of his head. 'Christ, Gerald!'

'What am I going to do?'

'We can put forward a plea of manslaughter. It wasn't premeditated.'

Bradbury's face was ashen. 'Is there no other way out?'

'They are going to ask you if you knew the woman, and you can't lie. Where did you go before you picked her up?'

With a guilt-ridden look Gerald told him. 'I drove around St Denys looking for someone but I didn't fancy any of the women standing around, so I was going to drive home when along the road away from the others I saw this girl on her own.'

'I don't see that you have a leg to stand on. Any of those girls in St Denys could have seen the car, and maybe you.'

'I was part of an identification parade this afternoon,' he said. Putting both hands to his head, he began to sob. 'I'm ruined. I can't go to prison. I'll never be able to stand it.'

The two men spoke at length, and when they were eventually taken into the interview room Steven Durrington said, 'My client would like to make a statement.'

There was pandemonium in the Bradbury household that afternoon when a uniformed police sergeant and a woman constable arrived at the residence and asked to speak to Mrs Bradbury.

Ethel took them into the front parlour, where Mrs Bradbury was reading.

Listening outside, Ethel couldn't hear exactly what was said, but she heard a cry of anguish from her mistress and hurried away to tell Cook.

'Maybe the old man has copped it in an accident,' she suggested, 'or maybe he's had a heart attack? But the missus sounded deeply distressed.'

'Ooh,' said Cook. 'If so, she'll tell us all in good time.'

But Mrs Bradbury wasn't forthcoming. When the two officers left she rang for Ethel and said, 'Mr Bradbury won't be home this evening for dinner, tell Cook, and I'm not hungry. Just bring me a tray of tea, please.'

The two women in the kitchen pondered over all this as they prepared the tea.

'What did she look like?' asked Cook. 'Was she upset?'

Thinking for a moment, Ethel said, 'Well, no, not really. She looked more angry really. She was a bit cold like when she spoke to me.'

'Maybe the old bugger has left her for one of his fancy women!'

'Then why would the police come round? It don't make sense.'

But when the local paper came out that evening, the headline told its own story. LOCAL SOLICITOR CHARGED WITH MURDER.

CHAPTER TWENTY-THREE

When Ken and Charlie Williams read the head-line in the local paper, they panicked.

'Oh, my God!' exclaimed Charlie. 'What do we do if, when he's questioned, he tells them about meeting the girls in a hotel? We'll be done for!'

'We'll just deny all knowledge. The girls are hired as escorts as far as we know, and that's that.'

'So what if they question any of the girls and they split on us?'

Charlie thought about this for a while, then came to a decision.

'We'll get Ma to have the girls in and talk to them. Threaten them if they grass us up. Let's face it, she's enough to frighten anyone.'

That night in the front room of the Williams house-hold, Ma Williams held court. Sitting around her were all the girls who worked for the Williams brothers.

'Right,' she began, 'you have all read the papers, I expect?'

They all started talking at once.

'Shut up and listen!' Ma cried. Silence prevailed. 'The police are going to be questioning you all over this case. Bloody Elsie Summers, she was trouble enough when she was alive.'

'That's a bit harsh,' said one of the girls. 'The poor little bleeder's dead!'

'I'm well aware of that,' Ma Williams snapped, 'and if we're not very careful we'll all be out of work because of it.'

There was a murmur of discontent among the girls.

'Now, this is how it works. Should you be questioned, you on no account tell the filth that we knew about you having sex in the hotels with your punters. As far as my boys were aware, they just hired you out as escorts. What you did after that wasn't our business. Got it?'

'Then we'll be fined for prostitution!' complained one.

'Well, it wouldn't be the first time, duck, would it? You dump us in the shit, you won't get no more good bookings and you'll be back walking the streets . . . if you're in a fit state, that is!'

'You threatening us, Mrs Williams?' asked one stroppy girl.

'Bloody right I am. You do right by us, you got no worries. Do I make myself clear?'

They murmured their assent, if reluctantly. Once outside they all decided to go to the nearest pub for a drink.

Settled at a table in the shabby smoke-filled room, they discussed their future with the Williams brothers.

'Well, I don't fancy having my face cut,' said one, 'and that's what that old bitch did to one of her girls who crossed her when she ran a brothel.'

'It's all very well for them,' said another, 'but we won't be getting any bookings from them while this murder is being sorted. Them twins won't take the chance, will they? So we'll be back on the streets anyway!'

'What are we gonna say if the filth asks us about the hotels?' asked another.

Picking up her glass of beer, the ringleader said, 'That's up to each and every one of us to decide. To be honest, I don't know what I'm going to do.'

At the Bradbury house, Cook and Ethel were stunned by the news of their employer's arrest. They sat in the kitchen drinking tea and discussing the matter.

'You did wonder if Mr Bradbury had anything to do with that girl they found,' said Ethel.

'I know I did, but I didn't really believe it. I

wonder what will happen now? Will the missus stay here, do you think?'

Sipping her tea, Ethel said, 'Would you? I mean, think of all her airs and graces . . . she won't be invited out anywhere now, and who would accept an invitation from her? Such a scandal!'

'We could both be out of a job, have you thought about that?'

With a horrified look, Ethel said, 'Lordy, no! That would be a bit rough. You with your skills could get another job soon enough, but me, well, I don't know.'

Getting to her feet, Cook said, 'Well, I shouldn't worry just yet. Whatever the missus decides will take time, so we should be all right for a bit. Did she say anything to you this morning when you took up her breakfast?'

'No. She was just as snooty as ever.'

'You've got to hand it to her,' Cook said, 'that took some doing. She must be aware that everyone knows what's happened. His business will be down the pan too, won't it?'

With an indignant snort Ethel said, 'There you are, that's what happens when a man can't keep his trousers shut. Randy bugger!'

In her bedroom, Dorothy Bradbury was pacing the floor in despair. What would become of her?

She would be ostracised by her friends. How could she walk outside where everyone knew her and her husband and hold her head high? It wasn't fair! It was Gerald who had brought disgrace to her and her family. Poor Simon had been distraught when he heard the news. He too would suffer taunts from many of his associates. If he was lucky a few real friends would stick by him, but she didn't have that luxury. The women she knew wouldn't want her – they'd already made that clear, since none of them had as much as called her on the telephone. Fortunately she had accounts at all the main stores and a certain amount of money of her own, but she had no idea of her husband's financial position. His bank balance ought to be healthy in his capacity as a man of the law . . . that was a laugh! She supposed she ought to visit him – but why should she? He had *murdered* that girl. She half believed him capable of doing it, but hated to face up to the fact of the matter. The father of her son had killed someone – a prostitute at that. Oh, the shame of it! Picking up a scent bottle, she threw it across the room in anger.

'You filthy bastard!' she cried. Gerald with his constant sexual needs had put them in this situation and she hated him!

* * *

Tilly Thompson was at the dress shop, interviewing girls for the position of sales assistant. The manageress Eddie had hired seemed to know her job. They had been through the stock and the order book together. The woman had suggested they have an end of season sale, to move the summer fashions so they could renew the stock ready for the winter. They had dressed the window together, advertising the sale with several outfits marked down to entice the customers into the shop. Tilly had to admit, it did look very attractive.

Eddie had told her he would finance any orders until she was on her feet when she could pay him back. Once she had got over the shock of his buying the shop, she was excited and pleased, but she had kept the news to herself. Her parents and brother wouldn't have approved, she was sure. Especially Jago! He would be wondering what the catch was.

She could hear him now. 'And what does Chapman want in return?'

She already knew what he wanted. He was talking of going to London soon, of seeing a show and staying overnight. Tilly was aware that she would be expected to share his room. The thought of being in bed with him was both worrying and exciting. She knew nothing about sex. It was never discussed in her house, and her friend Beth was as innocent of such things as she was. She longed to share her news about the shop with Beth, but since she couldn't possibly tell her that she was soon to lose her virginity, she dared not.

She was suddenly filled with a longing to see her friend and have one of those days where they laughed together, shared their thoughts and feelings and just had a good time. Since she had been going out with Eddie she'd not had a chance to see the crowd they belonged to, and she missed that too.

She also wondered what had happened to David. Was he still going out with the girl he had brought to the club? She really missed him, she realised to her surprise. He was so easy to be with. He had never made any demands on her, unlike Eddie. Their relationship had been built on friendship and it had always been free and easy.

Straightening some clothes on a display, she thought that had she not started going out with Eddie, she wouldn't now be the proud owner of this prestigious business. But was the price going to be too high?

It was Jago who discovered his sister's new position when Madam Leone herself came into the butcher's shop one afternoon.

He smiled at her, knowing who she was. 'You taking the day off today?' he enquired.

'No, indeed I'm not,' she said. 'I've retired. I am now a lady of leisure.'

Thinking of his sister's job, he asked, 'What's happening to the shop, then?'

She looked somewhat puzzled. 'Your sister owns it now.'

'Don't be daft. She hasn't got that kind of money.'

'No, but Mr Chapman has. He bought me out and gave it to her.'

'You must be mistaken!'

'Young man, I know what I'm talking about. The contract is made out in her name.' Smiling, she said, 'She's done very well for herself.' After choosing some meat from the display in the window, she paid for it and left the shop.

Jago was stunned by the news. Tilly had said nothing to their parents, he was certain, otherwise they would have told him. He frowned as he thought about it. When did any man show such generosity to a woman without getting something in return? What on earth was his sister thinking of?

That evening, Jago waited until Tilly had eaten then threw her coat at her and said, 'Come on down to the pub. I want to talk to you.'

She was about to refuse, as she was very tired,

but then she saw the look on his face. 'Won't be long, Mum,' she called as they left the house.

Jago said nothing at all until they were seated, away from the other customers, with a couple of halves of beer in front of them.

'What is this all about, our Jago?' she demanded.

'Your previous employer came into the butcher's shop today,' he said, and Tilly knew her secret was out.

'And so?' she enquired.

'Well, it would seem that you are now a woman of property. Congratulations! What a pity you didn't share the good news with Mum, Dad and me.' He stared at her and added, 'Unless you had something to hide.'

'I'm not hiding anything! It was all so unexpected. It only happened last Saturday as we were closing, and since then I've been busy getting the stock sorted with my manageress.'

He raised his eyebrows in surprise. 'A manageress? I thought you would have been the manageress, since it's your shop.'

'Are you trying to tell me how to run my business?' She was furious.

He studied her thoughtfully for a moment and then said, 'No, of course not, but what I don't understand is why Eddie Chapman would do such a thing for you . . . unless there are conditions?'

'He just wants me to have more free time to spend with him, that's all!'

'It's a bloody expensive way of doing that, isn't it?'

'That's why I have another woman to run it. It will leave me free to do what he wants.'

'And what does he really want, Tilly? Tell me that!'

She felt her cheeks flush. 'None of this is your damned business, Jago. Now get off my back and leave me alone!' She got to her feet and walked out.

A few moments later, David Strickland entered the bar. Seeing Jago sitting on his own, he went over to him.

'I wondered if you would be here,' he said. 'Can I get you a drink?'

'Thanks, half a bitter. I'm glad you came in. I'm in need of good advice.'

'That sounds ominous,' David said, and he walked to the bar. Waiting to be served, he looked around. There was something very comforting about an English pub, he thought. The atmosphere was friendly and companionable, so that even if you were alone it was like being among friends. However, looking across at Jago, he thought it seemed wasted on him tonight and wondered just what was troubling him, because something certainly was.

Taking the drinks over, David sat down beside his friend and asked, 'What's the problem?'

With a frown, Jago told him, 'It's Tilly. That man has bought her a business.'

'What business? What man?'

'Eddie Chapman has bought out the owner of Madam Leone's and given it to Tilly.'

'Are you sure about that? I mean, why would he do such a thing?'

'My sentiments exactly!' Jago told him the whole story. 'Then when I tackled her about it in here, she stormed out, just before you came in.'

Lighting a cigarette, David sat thinking. 'Of course, it's a great opportunity for her.'

'Are you out of your senses? What does he want in return? Answer me that!'

The two men sat discussing the matter, both concerned that Tilly was in a situation that neither of them felt happy about.

'Oh, he's so smooth, that man,' said Jago. 'Let's face it, to a young girl like my sister, he must seem like a film star. Look at his way of life . . . that's enough to impress most women.'

'I don't see that we can do anything about it,' David said.

'She won't listen to me, but she might if you had a word. You once told me that you loved her.'

'I did say that and I'm still in love with her, but she has to make up her own mind as to what she wants. Sadly, it seems she's done so.'

Jago glared at his friend. 'If I was in love with a girl, I'd bloody well fight for her! The waiting game is not for me. This man could destroy her!'

Shaking his head, David said, 'She's got too much spirit to let him do that . . . but she could get badly hurt in the process. Maybe I'll go and see her. Remind her I'm still around.'

'I wish you would,' Jago said. 'I'd feel a lot easier in my mind.'

Just before closing time the following day, Tilly was surprised to see David Strickland walk into the shop. She smiled and walked towards him.

'Good afternoon, sir. Are you looking for a gown for your girlfriend, perhaps?'

With a puzzled look he said, 'I don't have a girlfriend.'

'But what about the young lady you took to the Blue Pelican club?'

With a chuckle he said, 'That was the sister of another tutor who had planned an evening with her brother, but he'd had to cancel at the last minute . . . so I came to the rescue.'

Unaccountably, Tilly felt her spirits lighten at this news. 'Then what can I do for you?'

'I thought we could go for a drink to celebrate your new position.' At the look of surprise on Tilly's face he added, 'I saw Jago yesterday and he told me. Congratulations. I think it definitely needs to be celebrated, don't you?'

Although she didn't really want to answer questions about the shop, she dearly wanted to spend a little time with David, so she agreed.

They walked across the park to the Polygon hotel and settled in the intimate cocktail bar, where David ordered two champagne cocktails. He gazed at her with affection. 'Congratulations!' They clinked glasses and he said, 'You're looking really well, Tilly.'

'Thank you, so are you. Are you keeping busy?'

'Yes, I am. We're holding exams soon so there's a lot of work to be covered.'

'Would you rather be at sea?'

He frowned for a moment before replying. 'Yes, I suppose I would, but then my being ashore hasn't worked out quite as I had planned.'

'What do you mean?'

He leaned back in his chair. 'One reason for taking the post was so that I could spend more time with you, but of course it didn't happen that way.'

'Oh, David, I'm so sorry. I feel I've let you down.'

'Darling Tilly, it's not your fault that things didn't work out the way I planned, but I must confess I do miss you. I miss the conversations, the laughs, your enthusiasm and curiosity. You have a way of creeping under a man's skin, you know.'

She was at a loss for words.

'I worry about you,' continued David. 'I know that Chapman is exciting and attractive and can fulfil a lot of your dreams, but I can't imagine that marriage enters into his plans. I'm worried that in the end you'll get hurt. I wouldn't like to see that happen.'

As she gazed at the concerned expression on David's face Tilly's emotions were torn. He was right about Eddie and marriage, and as she looked at him she found that she still had strong feelings towards this man sitting opposite her. How could she not love him? He was attractive, masculine, wise, kind and compassionate and an interesting companion. Everything a girl looked for in a man . . . and yet, Eddie Chapman had that certain something which drew her to him, like a moth to a flame.

'I don't know what to say, David. You're very special to me, I really mean that, but . . .'

He slowly shook his head. 'He really has a hold over you, Tilly, and if I'm honest I envy him that. I just hope that the novelty of it all will wear off, but I hope it won't take too long because I may not be around when it does.'

Tears brimmed Tilly's eyes. 'I don't really deserve such kindness,' she said.

'Kindness doesn't come into it. At this moment I want to hit him into next weekend.'

She was taken aback; David had never shown any sign of aggression.

'One day, Tilly, you'll understand.' He looked at his watch. 'I'm so sorry, but I have an appointment with my head of department. I'll walk you to the tram.'

As they waited for one to come along, David tucked her arm through his. 'Please be very careful, Tilly. Don't let the cost of your business cloud your common sense.'

'What on earth do you mean?'

'No real gift should ever have to be repaid in any way, otherwise it's only a bribe – or worse, a type of emotional blackmail.'

The tram arrived before she could answer.

David kissed her softly on the lips and said, 'Remember, I'm around for just a little while, and then I'm out of your life altogether.'

As the tram moved away, Tilly pondered on his words. Was she being bribed? The shop had been bought without her knowledge and handed to her. Was it a bribe or emotional blackmail? Probably both, if she were honest. David would have been too clever to take such bait, but for her it was a chance in a lifetime, and she knew she wasn't as strong as he was. And now the die was cast!

CHAPTER TWENTY-FOUR

Ethel Thompson was in a state. Not only was her job in jeopardy, but also her son had just told her about Tilly's now owning the gown shop where she'd worked . . . and that it was a gift from this Eddie Chapman she'd heard so much about. She tried to recall what she'd heard about the man round the dinner table at her employer's house, weeks before the trouble. As far as she could recall, it had been good. But to buy a business for her daughter – that was something else! What had that girl got herself involved in now? She would have it out with her tonight when she came home.

Tilly was totally unprepared for the onslaught that greeted her when she walked through the front door at the end of her working day.

Ethel had spent her time getting worked up about the consequences of such a transaction and she let fly with all her pent-up emotions as soon as she saw her daughter.

'I knew that one day you'd bring trouble to this house, you with your wild ways! It was bad enough coping with the scrapes you got into at school, but now . . . well, I don't know what to say!'

Tilly realised that Jago had spilled the beans about Madam Leone's. Looking at her mother, she said, 'It seems to me that you have plenty to say!'

Ethel was incensed. 'How dare you speak to me like that?'

Tilly's hackles rose as she faced the maternal wrath.

'As always, Mother, you have jumped to your own conclusions. Wouldn't it have been better to ask me about this instead of accusing me of something as you usually do? I imagine my bloody brother has been spreading gossip about me, and I'm assuming he told you about the shop?'

Sitting in a chair by the fire, Ethel defiantly crossed her arms and said, 'Yes he did and I'm wondering just why the information didn't come from you?' She glared at her daughter. 'I would have thought you would have been pleased to share such news with your family . . . unless you have something to hide.'

'There is no secret here,' Tilly cried. 'I've been very busy as this was such a surprise, that's all.'

'You just didn't get round to it, is that it?'

The sarcasm in Ethel's voice didn't escape Tilly. Letting out a sigh, she said, 'If you like.'

'Well, I'm listening. Perhaps you'll get round to it now.'

Taking off her coat, Tilly sat at the table and tried to explain about having time to spend with Eddie, but as she unfolded the tale she knew that it sounded weak and unconvincing.

Unfolding her arms, her mother said, 'Well I must say, this Mr Chapman is very generous. Wouldn't it have been cheaper just to suggest you be his mistress?'

Tilly was shocked. 'What on earth are *you* suggesting?'

'Oh, come along! You're a bright girl. No man does this out of the goodness of his heart. What are the conditions?'

Her mother's quick grasp of the situation left Tilly speechless.

Seeing her consternation, Ethel said, 'I've been around a lot longer than you, my dear, and I probably understand more about life that you give me credit for.' She stood up and moved the large brown kettle on to the hot plate of the fire, and then put some tea into the pot. 'This man is taken with you, that's obvious, and you with him. After all, he's taken you to places you've only dreamed about, but don't be blinded by it all, Tilly. He'll want his pound of flesh.' Gazing at her daughter, she wanted to shake some sense into her, but knowing how headstrong Tilly was she just spoke quietly, now that her anger was cooling. 'You're old enough to be responsible for your actions.' Shaking her head, she added, 'Don't let him use you. You're worth so much more than that.'

Her mother's insight had staggered Tilly and she didn't know what to say.

Ethel poured them both a cup of tea. Sitting down at the table opposite her daughter, she said, 'You'll go your own way, of that I'm in no doubt, but be very careful. Men are, by nature, predators. It goes back to the days when we lived in caves, but in this day and age we no longer need to be dragged around by the hair, just you remember that!'

Tilly looked at her with growing respect. 'You are full of surprises, Mum.'

'Your father learned that years ago. Just remember what I said, that's all.'

As she was cashing up on Saturday evening in the shop, Tilly received a call from Eddie.

'Rufus is running at Goodwood next week,' he told her without preamble. 'He's in the three-thirty race, so we'll catch a train in the morning, have some lunch and I thought we could stay over. It's a pretty part of the country; we can spend Sunday in Chichester and take a train home in the evening.'

Tilly found his dictatorial tone annoying and remembering her mother's words said, 'Saturday is our busiest day, Eddie. I'm not sure I can get away.'

His voice took on a steely edge. 'That is what you have a manageress and an assistant for, darling. I'll check on the times of the trains and I'll see you tonight at the Blue Pelican.' With that, he hung up on her.

She pursed her lips and continued with her task. She knew she was being unreasonable, but it galled her that he had told her what to do without asking if she wanted to accompany him. Had he done so she would have agreed without hesitation, even though she knew it would mean sharing a room with him. He had made his intentions quite clear on that score. Well, she would definitely have something to say to him later at the club.

When she eventually arrived at the Blue Pelican, Eddie greeted her warmly.

'Hello, darling,' he said, kissing her cheek. 'You look good enough to eat. Here, sit down.' He led her to a table. 'I'll get you a drink.' He called a waiter over.

After ordering, he glanced at her and said, 'You look very angry. Who has upset you? Was it a difficult customer?'

'As a matter of fact you did!' she retorted, her green eyes flashing.

'Me?' He looked astonished. 'How on earth did I do that?'

'When you rang me earlier and gave me my *orders* for Goodwood! You sounded just like my father, talking to me when I was a small child.'

He burst out laughing. 'Sorry, darling, I didn't mean to but I was trying to sort out a delivery that was late and I was rushed.' He cupped her chin in his hand. 'And believe me, as far as you are concerned, the last thing I feel is fatherly.'

What could she say? It would have been churlish to pursue the matter further. In any case, Eddie was called away to take a phone call, so no further conversation was possible for the moment.

Tilly was surprised when David Strickland and a stranger entered the club. David saw her immediately and came over to her table.

'Hello, Tilly. I wondered if I would see you. I'd like to introduce you to Bruce Talbot, another tutor at the college. We needed a drink after a strenuous day and he'd heard about the Blue Pelican . . . so here we are.'

Tilly shook the man by the hand.

'Can I get you a drink?' asked David.

'No thanks, I already have one.' As David went to the bar she turned to Bruce and said, 'Why don't you both join me? Eddie looks as if he is going to be tied up for a while.' She had seen him waylaid as soon as he put down the receiver.

'Thanks, I will,' said Talbot. Looking around, he said, 'Nice place. I've heard nothing but good things about it.'

Smiling, she said, 'Eddie Chapman, the owner, will be pleased to hear that.'

David returned with two glasses of beer and sat beside Tilly. The two men started telling her some hilarious tales about the young men they had been instructing, and Tilly found herself really enjoying their company. For her it was like old times with David when they had chatted and laughed and been at ease with each other.

Half an hour later, Eddie came over to the table and Tilly introduced Talbot to him, explaining who he was and how much he liked the Blue Pelican.

'Bruce said he'd heard nothing but good things about the place.'

Eddie smiled at the man and said, 'That's what I like to hear. We do our best.' Turning to Tilly, he said, 'Look, darling, I'm sorry, but I have to talk to someone in the office. It's a business matter that won't wait, I'm afraid.'

David looked up and with a slow smile said, 'Please don't worry; we'll look after Tilly for you. She's in safe hands with us.'

Eddie's smile didn't reach his eyes, but he was his usual charming self. 'I'm sure she is.' He excused himself and promised to make his absence as short as possible.

The band stared to play, as they usually did at this time of the evening. Hearing the strains of a waltz, David turned to Tilly and held out his hand. 'Shall we?'

She rose from her seat and walked to the floor with him. As he took her into his arms, her nostrils caught the scent of his cologne; it felt very comforting and familiar. They danced without speaking until the last chord was played. As Tilly made to leave the floor, David held her closer.

'What's the rush?' he asked.

The next tune started, and they continued to dance.

'This feels so good,' he said softly.

'What does?'

'Holding you close to me after so long. You, my darling Tilly, have left a great void in my life. I'm not sure I'll ever be able to forgive you.'

'Please, David, don't talk like that. It only makes everything more difficult.'

Gazing into her eyes, he said, 'I love you, you

271

little goose, you must know that, and we belong together. You with me – not you and Mr Smooth.'

'David! If you don't stop this nonsense, I'll walk off the floor and leave you standing.'

'All right, but let me just say one thing more . . . with me you would spend the rest of your life as the wife of a man who would love you until your teeth drop out and your leg falls off and not care a toss!'

She started to chuckle. 'You are a complete fool, David Strickland.'

'But you know I speak the truth, Tilly Thompson, and one day you'll remember my words.'

They walked back to the table grinning at each other, which did not escape the notice of Eddie Chapman, who had been watching them from the top of the stairs. His jaw tightened as he walked slowly down. But as he approached the table, his usual smile greeted the three of them. Sitting down, he apologised for his absence and offered to buy the men a drink, but David quickly declined.

'That's very nice of you, but we have to go.' Bruce was about to argue, but David kicked him under the table, then got up from his seat and looked at Tilly.

'It was good to see you again. Come on, Bruce, we need food inside us to build us up for tomorrow's students.

Once outside, Bruce complained about being rushed.

'Sorry, old chap; I just can't stand to see Tilly with that man. Come on.'

Bruce wasn't a fool. 'You think a lot of her, don't you?'

'I'm in love with her and I'm hoping she will soon come to her senses, but I'm getting very impatient with the waiting!'

Inside the club, Eddie took Tilly's hand and kissed the palm. 'Sorry I was away so long. I can't wait for next weekend so we can spend more time together. You'll see, my darling, we'll have a wonderful time.'

Tilly wondered if he would be saying the same if all her teeth had fallen out and a leg had dropped off. She very much doubted it.

CHAPTER TWENTY-FIVE

Within the depths of the main police station in Southampton, the case against Gerald Bradbury was being studied. The detectives involved had been busy gathering statements from all the prostitutes who worked the red light area, plus those who had previously worked for the Williams brothers and had been forced to join them during the inquiries, after the twins had suspended their escort service. It had caused hardship among their girls, which in turn had stirred up great resentment, causing several to happily help the police with vital information.

'We'll soon be able to bring the Williamses in for living off immoral earnings,' remarked one of the detectives with obvious glee. 'I've been after those two buggers for years.'

The girls had supplied the police with details of the hotels used for prostitution and many of the clients' names. When they had been visited and questioned in turn, it had caused dismay and panic among those who were married. The men who were fortunate enough to open the door to the detectives themselves had been able to keep the nature of the visit away from their wives with whispered explanations of going down to the police station to give a statement, but others had been caught out when their wives had received the detectives in their absence. The fallout had been enormous.

As one detective said, 'The divorce courts will be having a heyday very soon.'

Charlie and Ken Williams were a bundle of nerves, wondering if the girls they had employed would keep their mouths shut, but old Ma Williams was more astute.

'A few of them are bound to split on you,' she warned. 'There's been no business for them in the comfort of an hotel, some have gone back on the streets to earn a crust, and they won't thank you for that, you may be sure. You two should make yourselves scarce. Shove off somewhere.'

'Like where?' asked Charlie.

'As far away as possible. Take a ferry to France.'

'France!' Charlie was appalled. 'That's full of Froggies wearing black berets and stinking of garlic.'

'So? You'll smell worse than garlic in a bleeding prison cell, my son. It's your choice.'

Ken, the wiser of the two, agreed with his mother. 'She's right,' he told his brother. 'I don't want to go down for a stretch. We could go down to Marseille; it's a seaport. Maybe we can get a few girls there to work for us . . . and the weather's better.'

'Best make up your mind damned quick,' said Ma. 'I don't reckon you've any time to waste.'

The twins decided to take her advice.

'All right, Ma,' Charlie conceded, 'we'll pack our cases tonight and take a ferry tomorrow. We can get to Cherbourg and go from there.'

But the following morning, as they were about to board the ferry, they were both arrested.

The week passed quickly for Tilly, as the shop was busy. Most of the sale goods had been cleared and the new winter stock had been ordered, which had excited her, as she had been able to choose for herself the type of clothes that would be on offer. She had a good eye for fashion, which was shared by her manageress. One or two items were seriously expensive, but Tilly felt confident that they would sell to those in the town whose husbands were members of the higher echelons in the business world. She had added a few pieces of knitwear, copied from Coco Chanel, who was so popular with women in London, and also selected a few pricey but exclusive fashionable hats, a thing never before sold in the shop.

As she remarked to Grace, the manageress, 'Women will be able to complete an outfit now. We have frocks, costumes, cocktail dresses, coats – and the hats. The gloves and shoes they can buy elsewhere.'

As the days progressed she became more and more nervous about the coming weekend. The idea of getting undressed was the first problem. Would there be a bathroom where she could do so in private? Would she have to do it in front of him? And then there was the bed – and all it entailed. Would having sex hurt? What would her mother say when she told her she'd be away for the weekend? No longer could she make excuses and say she was staying at Beth's house.

Eddie too had been very busy during the week overseeing both the Blue Pelican and the Ace of Clubs, so they hadn't met, only spoken over the telephone when he rang her at the shop at the end of each day. And now it was Friday evening.

Just as she was cashing up, the shop door opened and Eddie walked in.

'Hello, darling,' he said as he kissed her. 'I can't wait for tomorrow to have you all to myself. I've not had a moment to breathe this week.'

'Yes, I've been busy too,' said Tilly, whose

fingers were trembling as she put the cash into a bag ready to deposit in the overnight safe at the bank.

Taking the bag from her hand, he drew her close to him and kissed her longingly. She pulled away.

'Eddie! Someone might come in and see us.'

'Does that really matter?'

'Yes it does,' she persisted. 'It's not good for business – it's unprofessional.'

With a look of amusement he said, 'Gracious, I do hope that owning a business isn't going to change you.'

'Don't be silly.'

He walked to the door. 'Are you coming to the club tonight?'

'No,' she said, 'I want to wash my hair and pack.'

'Fine. I'll pick you up at your house in a taxi at ten o'clock in the morning.'

She was about to tell him that she would meet him at the station, but he had gone. Now her mother would know for certain with whom she would be spending the weekend. Oh, why was life so complicated?

It was with some trepidation that Tilly, carrying her suitcase, walked downstairs the following morning, but to her relief the kitchen was quiet and empty. Ethel was working, as were the men of the house. She quickly scribbled a note saying she would be away overnight and would be home on Sunday evening. Hearing a car toot outside she let herself out of the house and into the waiting taxi.

Eddie squeezed her hand as she sat beside him. 'Hello, darling. It looks as if the weather will be good today so the track will be firm, which is just how Rufus likes it.'

'Good,' she said. 'Has he got a strong chance of winning?'

'Indeed he has, and the price should be reasonable.'

Tilly remembered the conversation between Eddie and his trainer about building the price by having the jockey pull the horse the last time it ran.

'We'll have to keep our fingers crossed, then.'

From Goodwood station a taxi took them to the racetrack. Once there, Eddie led her to the stables where Jeremy Frampton was busy with the head lad. He greeted them warmly.

'Today we clean up,' he said with a broad grin. 'I hope you've already laid your bets with a bookie?' he said, looking at Eddie.

'I have, and I'll put more on with the tote and the bookmakers here at the track. I only hope you're right because I've laid out a lot of money on this race.'

'Me too,' said Frampton. 'I'm banking on this race to solve all my financial problems.' He rubbed the horse's nose, fed him a small carrot and said, 'You won't let us down, will you, Rufus?'

The animal chewed on the carrot and threw his head back, shaking his mane as if to agree. They all laughed.

'There you are, what did I tell you?' Frampton said.

Taking Tilly's arm, Eddie said, 'Right then, I'll see you in the winners' enclosure after the race. Tilly and I are going to get a bite to eat.'

As was his habit, Eddie had a private box where they were served with soup and a hearty steak, followed by fresh strawberries and cream and washed down with pink champagne.

As they waited for the coffee, Eddie took Tilly's hand in his. 'This will be a weekend to remember,' he said, smiling softly at her.

She looked into his eyes, shining with happy anticipation, saw the smile on the full lips that spoke of passion, and wondered if the memory of the weekend would be momentous or something to regret. The chemistry was still there between them, the fascination, the excitement, but the expectation was fraught with worry. Eddie

Chapman was a man of experience, whereas she had none. Would he be disappointed? Would she?

As the first race was called, they went outside, taking their coffee with them, choosing the horses they would lay bets on, sending the waiter to the tote with their betting slips, teasing each other when one won and not the other. But before the three-thirty race in which Rufus was to run, Eddie gave Tilly a hundred pounds and instructed her to lay half at the tote and the other at a bookie's. He would do the same and they would meet back in the box.

She found it exciting to be walking and queuing among the punters for a change. After placing her bet at the tote, she walked outside and carefully strolled along the stands of the bookies, listening to their spiel, checking the prices they were offering against Rufus the Red. They were all very similar, she found, but one of the bookies was offering twelve to one against the others' ten. She handed over fifty pounds for a win and slowly made her way back to the box, watching the tic-tac men feverishly signalling to their own particular bookies who would quickly rub out one price against a horse and replace it with another.

Once back in the box, she handed the two tickets to Eddie and they sat down to watch the race. As the horses passed the box on the way to the start, Rufus looked ready, prancing, his ears pricked, tossing his head, snorting with anticipation.

Eddie stood up and watched the jockey ride him along the course. 'He looks fit and ready,' he said.

They both watched through binoculars as the race began in the distance, and listened to the commentary. Rufus was lying towards the back of the runners as they made their way along a stretch and up a hill.

'He's near the back,' Tilly remarked with some concern.

'It's a long race,' Eddie explained. 'It's too early for him to make his move, but he has a great finish. You watch, the jockey will start to bring him up soon.'

Hardly daring to breathe, Tilly watched closely. As predicted, the horse began to gain pace and slowly pass one horse after another, coming through on the inside.

Without realising it, Tilly began to yell. 'Come on Rufus!'

The horse was now in third position and gaining rapidly as they approached the final furlong.

'Come on Rufus!' Eddie too was shouting out now, and the crowd below them were yelling in a frenzy as the horses neared the winning post.

Rufus was neck and neck with the leading horse,

and still gaining, when all of a sudden it was as if he stumbled and lost his momentum. By the time he'd recovered, two horses had passed the finish line in front of him.

Eddie plumped down in his seat, his face white.

'What on earth happened?' asked Tilly, who was equally shocked. 'That race was his!'

'I don't know, but I'm going to bloody well find out!' Eddie snapped. 'Come on.' He strode angrily from the box.

He passed the winners' enclosure and made his way to Rufus, standing and sweating in front of the sign which designated the third place. Jeremy Frampton was putting a blanket over him as they approached. He looked drawn and ill.

'What happened?' demanded Eddie, grabbing the jockey's arm.

'I don't know, Mr Chapman. We had the race all but won when something startled him. I was looking ahead so I didn't see anything. I'm sorry, sir.' He walked off towards the weighing room.

With pursed lips Eddie walked over to Frampton. 'Have you an explanation?'

The man was speechless and just shook his head.

'I've lost a packet today!' stormed Eddie.

'I'm sorry about that,' said Jeremy. 'I've probably lost my livelihood. Unless some miracle occurs, I'm about to become bankrupt.'

But so incensed was Eddie that he just walked off in a temper.

Seeing the distress on the trainer's face, Tilly put her hand on his arm. 'I do hope you find a way out of your predicament,' she said softly.

Frampton just nodded his thanks.

Tilly made her way back to the box, where Eddie was drinking a brandy, still fuming.

'It wasn't anyone's fault,' she ventured. 'It was just unfortunate.'

'A bloody disaster I would call it.'

'You might have had a kind word for poor Jeremy. He's facing ruin.'

'It won't be the first time!'

'But it could be the last,' she snapped at him. 'I didn't realise you could be so heartless!'

He stopped pacing and faced her. 'Frampton was a fool,' he said. 'If he was in financial difficulties, the last thing he should have done was put all his available money on a horse race. He of all people should know there is no such thing on a racetrack as a certainty. That was sheer idiocy. I've told you before, never spend more money on a meeting than you can afford to lose.'

'But you bet very heavily today.'

'I did, and I expected to win, but even so I still only lost what I could afford to if the unexpected happened. Not enough to ruin my life.'

'Are you always so calculating?' She faced him, defiance and anger written all over her face.

'Always.'

'So where do I fit into your calculations?'

He rubbed his eyes wearily and said, 'This is not the time for such questions, Tilly.'

'On the contrary, I think it is the perfect time.'

Sighing deeply, he sat down and asked the waiter for some more coffee. She waited.

'Very well,' he said eventually. 'You were not among any of my calculations, Tilly darling. You appeared out of the blue. In fact my life was ticking along nicely until you walked into my club that night with your young friends.'

She was pleased at his unexpected response, but asked, 'Are you sorry that I did?'

He stared into her eyes; his serious expression was like a magnet as she looked back at him, holding his gaze. 'In some ways, I suppose I am.'

She was startled.

'You see, you have completely disrupted the plans I had made. I had the next few years care-fully mapped out, then you arrived on the scene.'

'How on earth could I upset your plans?'

'Not my business plans,' he explained, 'but my personal life. That you certainly have.'

'I suppose you mean Greta?'

'No, I don't mean Greta. That would have run

its course in time. I mean the way I think of you, of being with you. Taking you to places and seeing the delight written all over your face. Your innocence.'

She raised her eyebrows at him. 'My innocence? How strange you should say that when you plan to take it away from me.'

He gazed at her with affection. Taking her by the hand, he chuckled and said, 'Your sense of humour is also one of my greatest pleasures. Oh, Tilly darling, you are a great joy in my life, and that was unexpected. I don't know quite where it's going to lead us, but I'm intrigued by the possibilities.' Leaning forward, he kissed her. 'Come along, let's go down to the stables and see if Jeremy is still around.'

'I only hope the poor dear isn't hanging from a rafter,' she said wryly.

'Now you just behave,' he said. 'I need to find out just how much financial trouble he's in.'

CHAPTER TWENTY-SIX

Whilst the day at Goodwood was causing problems, they were nothing to those facing the Williams brothers, who had been separated after their arrest and were being interviewed in different rooms at Southampton police station.

Detective Inspector Ridgeway, facing Charlie Williams, could scarcely hide his satisfaction as he fired the first question.

'How long did you think you could fool the police with your game?'

'Don't know what you're talking about,' Charlie muttered morosely.

'The so-called escort service, where you provided the women, is what I mean, as you well know.'

Charlie sneered at the man. 'There's nothing illegal about that.'

'Absolutely! But when the women meet the men in hotels for paid sex and hand over the money to you, then you are living off immoral earnings, and that, my friend, is punishable by law.'

'What them girls did with the men at the end of the evening has got nothing to do with me or my brother,' he protested. 'I never took any money other than a booking fee.'

'You're lying!'

'Prove it!' Charlie challenged.

With a slow smile the detective said, 'Believe me, I intend to.'

He sounded so confident that Williams began to feel nervous. He remained silent, staring at the man.

'Gerald Bradbury was one of your clients, wasn't he?'

Charlie denied it emphatically.

'But we have witnesses to prove it. Oh, Charlie boy, we have got you and your brother by the short and curlies this time. This time you will be sent down for a nice long stretch. I can't wait to see you both in court!'

'I want my solicitor!' cried Charlie. 'I'm not talking to you without him so get stuffed!'

The detective rose from his seat and told the two policemen standing at the door to take the prisoner back to his cell. He shot a mocking look at Charlie and said, 'You had best get used to it, because you'll be spending quite a time in one.'

Charlie jumped to his feet, sending his chair flying, and was restrained by the policemen as he hurled abuse at the retreating figure of the detective.

In a different room, Ken Williams was facing similar questions. But he, being the more restrained of the two, refused to say anything at all in the absence of his solicitor. He just sat and listened to the accusations with a blank expression. The only time his eyes showed a flicker of interest was when one of the detectives mentioned his mother's involvement.

'Well, we all know about Ma Williams,' he said.

'Mrs Williams to you!' snapped Ken.

'All right, Mrs Williams. She's got a crime sheet as long as my arm. She's probably the brains behind the whole shebang.' As Ken was about to protest the detective said, 'We know that Elsie Summers once worked for your so-called "escort agency", and that your mother fired her for creaming off the top with a few private punters.'

Ken was visibly shaken. How the hell did they know that? Certainly not from Elsie herself, before she died. It only took him a moment to realise that her brother, Nat, probably knew and had squealed to the cops. Little bleeder! No wonder he disappeared . . . maybe with police protection. But that would be hearsay, not strong enough for a court case . . . so he had to surmise that some of the girls had given evidence against them. If he was right, they were in deep trouble. He cursed the fact that they hadn't scarpered to France earlier!

Ma Williams was also brought to the station and questioned. The detectives who led the interrogation got nothing from the old girl apart from a mouthful of abuse. After a while, they let her free on police bail.

As one of them said, 'Christ! She's a tough old bird, but in the end we can probably get her for aiding and abetting. We'll have to see.'

It was about this time that Dorothy Bradbury decided to visit her husband in gaol. She hated the very idea of being seen in such a dreadful place as Winchester prison, where Gerald was being held pending his trial, but she was worried about money and how she would be able to cope with living expenses once he was sentenced.

She sat among an assortment of people in the waiting room, some men, but mostly women, some with small children, fretful at being kept waiting. She looked around with disdain. How common they all were.

'What's your hubby in for, love?' enquired the woman beside her.

Dorothy froze. Then with a superior look she said, 'Murder!'

'Bloody hell!' exclaimed the woman, and shut up.

They were all eventually shuffled into a large room with tables set around. Seeing the others taking a seat at any one, she followed suit . . . and waited. At last the prisoners were let in through a door at one end, their warders positioning themselves at intervals around the walls, ever watchful. Dorothy's gaze never left the door until she saw her husband enter. She was shocked when he appeared.

Gerald was dressed as usual in a suit, as those on remand were able to wear their own clothes. It wasn't the mode of dress that surprised her, but the droop of the shoulders, the hangdog look. This man with whom she'd spent so many years, with his pompous, arrogant ways, who had treated her to the sharp end of his tongue for most of that time, suddenly appeared pathetic.

She straightened her back as he walked slowly towards her. Was that a look of fear in his eyes? Good gracious, she did believe it was. And why not? He was here because he'd killed a common prostitute! And now he had to face his wife. She began to enjoy the situation.

Gerald sat opposite her and with some hesitancy he said, 'Hello, Dorothy, my dear. It's good of you to come.'

Glaring at him, she spoke. 'It is not a place I would ever have thought I would have to tolerate, but there are matters that must be sorted. Financial matters.'

'Of course, of course,' he said. With a beseeching look, he added, 'Dorothy, I can't tell you how sorry I am.'

'I don't want to discuss it,' she snapped. 'You have bought shame and misery on me and Simon, as well as on your profession. I just want you to make financial arrangements with your banker or solicitor, or whoever. My life is ruined socially, as you can imagine, so I want to sell the house and move away.'

He looked down and his shoulders sagged even more. With a deep sigh he said, 'I'll see that you are amply provided for, you and Simon.' Then he lifted his gaze. 'It would perhaps be better if you divorced me, in the circumstances.'

'I have already seen my solicitor,' she said coldly. Leaning forward, she hissed, 'You filthy, dirty bastard! You deserve all you get!'

Gerald Bradbury watched as his wife left the room, her whole body bristling with outrage. He had no regrets about losing her – they had never been really happy – but he was sorry for Simon. A weak boy to his mind, but nevertheless a decent chap. He hoped he would be able to get on with his life in the future, whereas the future for him looked very bleak indeed. How he regretted the madness that had led to his incarceration. But had his wife been the wife she should have been, he would never have had to look elsewhere. He knew in his heart he wasn't being entirely fair, but laying the blame at her door helped to soothe his conscience. He thought nothing of the life that he had taken.

The lunchtime trade in the Horse and Groom was quiet, so Queenie the barmaid was pleased to see Frank Graves walk into the public bar. But she was concerned when she saw his pale countenance.

'Hello, stranger. Where have you been these past weeks?'

'In hospital,' he told her.

'What was wrong?'

'I was beaten up by a couple of thugs one night.'

'Do you know who they were?' she asked, a frown creasing her brow.

'No, I don't,' he lied. 'They took my wallet and my watch, the bastards! They dislocated my shoulder and broke a couple of my ribs, and I had concussion. I was lucky – it could have been worse.'

'I really don't know what's happening these days. The police are never there when you need them.'

Frank knew the place where he'd been attacked

had been carefully chosen and he was equally certain that the thugs had been sent by Eddie Chapman to keep him quiet and teach him a lesson. He'd suffered worse than that in prison where, with hardliners on all sides, fights had often broken out. But he would pay Eddie back for this. He was a patient man; he could wait.

Queenie was polishing glasses. Looking up at him, she asked, 'You got somewhere to stay, Frank?'

Shaking his head, he said, 'No, not yet. When I've had a pint I'll look for a cheap B and B somewhere.'

'You can always doss down at my place whilst you look if you like.'

A smile creased the corners of his mouth. 'I'm not feeling very strong at the moment, Queenie.'

'That's all right, love. I'll be gentle with you.'

He laughed at the mischievous look in her eyes. 'You'll have to be. My ribs still hurt.'

'After your drink, go to the café down the street and get some fish and chips inside you. I'll meet you there when we close.'

And he did, thankful that he wouldn't have to wander the streets looking for a bed. He liked Queenie. Apart from being very accommodating between the sheets she had a heart as big as her bosom.

* * *

294

Whilst Frank Graves's plans were settled for the time being, Eddie Chapman was talking to Jeremy Frampton, trying to sort out his financial troubles. The two men were deep in conversation beside the stable where Rufus was being prepared for the trip home. Tilly was stroking the horse's nose, talking to the head lad.

'Pity about today's race,' she said.

He agreed. 'Bloody great pity, miss. He had the bleeding race in his pocket. It wasn't the jockey's fault; something spooked old Rufus. We'll never know what. Never mind, he should do well when he races again.'

She watched as Rufus was safely stowed in his horsebox. Eddie and Jeremy were still talking, so she stayed put. Eventually Eddie patted Jeremy on the shoulder and with a smile shook hands with the trainer, then walked towards her.

'You look pleased with yourself,' said Tilly.

'I am. I've just bought into Jeremy's yard. So his losses are covered and I own seventy-five per cent of the property.'

She looked astounded. 'What do you know about training horses?'

Putting a hand though her arm, he walked her away. 'Absolutely nothing. Jeremy will stay on as trainer. Nothing changes except I am the new owner and will have complete control over all costs and outgoings. I'll soon have it back on its feet, you'll see. Come on, let's go back to the hotel and celebrate.'

They took a taxi from the course and soon arrived at the hotel, where Eddie ordered some champagne to be sent up to their room. Then, turning to Tilly, he took her hand and led her away. Her heart was thumping as they climbed the stairs.

The bedroom was large. Big enough for the double bed, chests of drawers and a wardrobe. There were also two comfortable armchairs and a coffee table in front of the fireplace.

As they took off their coats, there was knock on the door. Eddie let the waiter put the champagne in an ice bucket on the table, then tipped the man and showed him out, closing the door firmly behind him. Letting out a deep sigh, he said, 'At last we're alone.' He took off his jacket and hung it in the wardrobe, and did the same with Tilly's. Then he opened the champagne and filled two glasses, handing one to her before loosening his tie.

'Here, darling. Let's drink to the winners' enclosure and all our horses that will be there some day.'

'I'm pleased that today hasn't put you off racing,' she said.

'Never! Racing is the sport of kings. I love it. I've always wanted to own a horse and I've accomplished that, and now I own a racing stable. That was something I hadn't thought of.'

'Not in your calculations?' she asked archly.

'Touché!' He laughed. 'But as I told you, darling, sometimes things just happen . . . like you walking into my life, and now this! How lucky can a man get? Come here.' Putting down his glass, he led Tilly to one of the armchairs, sat down, and pulled her on to his knee.

Removing the glass from her hand, he placed it on the floor. Then he drew her closer and kissed her, slowly, deliberately and passionately.

Tilly felt all the tension leave her body as she responded, her senses swimming as Eddie continued his practised, gentle assault on her mouth. He undid the buttons on her dress and slipped his hand inside, caressing her breast, running his thumb over her pert nipple. Then, picking her up, he carried her to the bed.

Swiftly he removed her dress, slipped off her underwear, then kissed her eyes, her neck and her breasts, caressing her thighs until Tilly thought she would faint with all the sensations her body was feeling.

He softly told her how beautiful she was, how they were going to have many good times together, how he cherished her and would take care of her always. She scarcely heard his words, so carried away was she under his expert fingers. No longer was she suffering with nerves; they were swept away by the awakening of her senses, her own passion.

Eventually they lay side by side, exhausted and sated. She gazed at him with wonderment, hardly able to believe that she was no longer a virgin, that she had lain with a man who had just made wonderful love to her. Her body, however, knew the reality.

Eddie smiled softly at her and kissed her gently. 'You are so beautiful,' he said.

She couldn't find any words, but just nestled into him, their naked bodies entwined, and fell fast asleep.

When she woke, it was to find herself still in the arms of her lover, who was awake and looking at her with great affection.

'What time is it?' she asked.

'Almost nine o'clock. Are you hungry?'

Realising that she was, she nodded.

'Then you'd better get dressed or the dining room will be closed,' Eddie said as he slipped out of bed and made for the bathroom.

She watched his naked figure. His shoulders

were powerful, his body well covered, but without surplus fat. She gazed at the long muscular legs that had been wrapped around her. She bathed in the memory of their lovemaking. Eddie's experience had taken her to a different sphere. She had known what it was to experience sexual longings and to give rein to them. His sensuous mouth had explored her body until she was led through sensations she had never even dreamed about. And yet, although she was mesmerised by him, excited by him and caught up by his powerful charisma, she knew that she wasn't in love with him. It was an extraordinary revelation.

CHAPTER TWENTY-SEVEN

The following morning, Eddie made tender love to Tilly again, then later had breakfast sent up to the room before they left to explore Chichester and its cathedral, stopping for lunch before catching a train back to Southampton.

Ethel Thompson was on the front doorstep, chatting with her neighbour, when the taxi pulled up outside. Both women saw Eddie kiss Tilly goodbye. The driver opened the cab door for her, handing her her small overnight case.

'Hello, Mum,' Tilly said as she entered the house.

'Well, I can see that your Tilly is doing all right for herself,' the neighbour remarked with a smirk. 'I saw her picture in the paper with that man at his nightclub. She always seemed a nice girl. Who'd have thought it?'

'Thought what?' Ethel challenged her. 'My Tilly is *still* a nice girl!' Turning on her heel she went inside, slamming the door behind her. Once in the living room she glared at her daughter.

Joe was sitting reading the paper, unaware of all that had been going on, as Ethel and Jago hadn't told him anything about Tilly's new man or her new business.

'Hello, love. Where have you been, then?'

'I was at a race meeting at Goodwood and stayed overnight.'

'I like a bit of racing myself,' he said. 'Used to go with my dad when I was younger; I like a flutter. Did you win any money?'

'Not much,' she told him.

'Humph!' from Ethel. 'Just how much did you lose, I wonder?'

Tilly felt the colour rise in her neck and face. She picked up her case and escaped to the privacy of her bedroom, knowing that her mother had correctly assessed the situation. But as she put her clothes away, she told herself she was old enough to make her own decisions. After all, she was the proud owner of her own business now, thanks to Eddie Chapman.

The following lunchtime, Beth entered the shop and grinned at Tilly.

'Hello, stranger.'

'Beth! How lovely to see you. How are you?'

'Fine. I've missed you, and when I heard that you were the new owner of this establishment I had to come and see you.'

'How did you hear about it?'

Beth looked somewhat uncomfortable. 'Well, Tilly, you are the subject of a certain amount of gossip around the town. These things do get about, you know.'

'I suppose you mean me and Eddie?'

Beth just shrugged her shoulders, and after a moment said, 'The pictures in the local rag didn't exactly help you keep things quiet.'

'I suppose not. Look, have you time for coffee and a sandwich?'

'Yes,' said Beth, 'this is my hour off. Let's go and catch up with everything.'

Tilly told her manageress she would be away for a short while, and the two girls set off arm in arm for the nearest café, where they settled for a chat.

'How are the rest of the gang?' asked Tilly.

'All much the same,' said her friend. 'We still go off for picnics on our bikes sometimes. We miss you, Tilly, but of course you're living a different life now. Do you ever see anything of David Strickland?'

'He came into the club one evening and then called in to the shop and took me for a drink to celebrate when Jago told him I was the new owner.'

'That was nice of him,' Beth remarked. 'You

know, I really liked him. I thought the two of you would make it together for life.'

Looking down at her hands, Tilly said quietly, 'So did he.'

Gazing intently at her friend, Beth asked, 'Are you really happy, Tilly? Has it all been worth it?'

'I'm having a great time,' she said somewhat defensively.

'Are you in love with Eddie Chapman?'

Tilly hesitated before answering. 'He's exciting and interesting. We have a marvellous time together. He's great fun to be with, you know.'

'You didn't answer my question,' Beth persisted.

Tilly looked at her and said, 'I know. I admire him tremendously, but no, I'm not in love with him.'

Beth looked shocked. 'Then what are you doing with him, ruining your reputation?'

'I don't give a damn what other people think!'

'You never did! But why persist if you don't love the man?'

'Don't you see, my life is exciting. We do all sorts of things, like trips to London, the races. I'm not rotting away in a backwater.'

'Well, I hope it is all worth it in the end.' Looking at her watch, Beth said, 'I'd better make tracks. Do keep in touch. Try to make time to spend with your old friends – you may need them in the future.' She squeezed Tilly's hand. 'Take care,' she said, and left.

Tilly sat drinking her coffee, brooding over the conversation. She was well aware of the gossip spreading about her. She had ignored the stares from others when she and Eddie were together out of sheer bravado and stubbornness. It was inevitable with Eddie's high profile. Now that he was so closely involved with Jeremy's racing stables, she was more than a little anxious, wondering if between the two of them they would run the yard properly. It had obviously been losing money: would they be tempted to recoup the losses by illegal means? If so, she wouldn't want to be part of it. Eddie wasn't averse to changing the odds, she'd seen that for herself, but just how far would he go? That was her concern.

Suddenly full of doubts and confused thoughts, she returned to the shop and told Grace to lock up herself at closing time; she was taking the rest of the day off. She walked home and got her bicycle out of the shed, and rode it to her favourite place, the shore.

She leaned the bike against a tree and removed her stockings to paddle in the waves. Picking up a pebble she practised skimming, delighted that she could still do it.

'Well done!'

She turned to see who had spoken and was surprised to see David Strickland standing behind her. He picked up two more pebbles and handed her one.

'I bet I can beat you!' he challenged her.

Laughing together, they tried to outdo one another until, weary, Tilly gave in.

'All right, you win. What on earth are you doing here?'

'I finished early,' he told her, 'and I often come here. Sometimes I bring a book to read. This is where we first met, if you remember.'

'Of course I remember,' she said softly. 'How could I forget?'

Gazing into her eyes he said, 'I think you've forgotten about me completely, darling Tilly.'

'No, David, I haven't.'

'What brought you here today?' he asked. 'I would have thought you would be busy in the shop.'

'I just needed to be on my own, to do some thinking, that's all.'

He led her to an upturned boat and perched beside her on the keel. 'Can I help in any way?'

Shaking her head she said, 'I'm afraid not. This is something I have to sort out for myself.'

'Does it have anything to do with Eddie Chapman?'

'Yes, I suppose it does.'

'He isn't treating you badly, I hope?' he asked, full of concern.

'No, no, it's nothing like that. I can't explain, so please don't ask. Let's talk about you. What's happening in your life these days?'

'Sadly, very little. I'll soon be coming to the end of my stint ashore, then I too will have to make a decision.'

'About what?'

'Returning to sea. Teaching was only meant to be a temporary thing, but they've asked me to stay on.'

'Would you be happy to do that?'

'Not as things stand at the moment, and you know what I mean. If we were still together we would talk about it and then we would decide what we wanted.'

'I don't think you would be happy ashore permanently even if we were still together,' she said firmly. 'You're a seaman, David, and I've lived among seafarers in the port long enough to know that.'

He laughed. 'You're probably right. Being on board is in the blood, but being away is more tolerable if a man knows he has a woman to come home to.'

'Please, David, don't,' she said, getting to her feet.

He got up and stood beside her. 'Why not?' he demanded. 'You're not in love with Eddie Chapman. You're just blinded by his lifestyle, his charisma. He won't offer you a stable future. Not like me!' Taking her roughly into his arms, he said, 'How much longer will it be until you see him for the man he really is? Stop being an idiot. I can't bear to watch you being used, especially when I know that deep down it's me you love!' Pulling her close, he crushed her lips with his.

At first Tilly resisted, but gradually she responded and kissed him back.

As he released his hold he said, 'You couldn't kiss me like that unless you really loved me.'

Tears brimmed her eyes and she pushed him away, ran to her bicycle and rode off.

David stood silently and watched her.

CHAPTER TWENTY-EIGHT

Eddie Chapman was in the office at the racing stables, studying the books with Jeremy Frampton, who was turning the pages and explaining the contents. Eddie was horrified at the results.

'We have to find a way to cut the running costs,' he said. He went through all the outgoings, questioning everything. Then he turned to the list of incoming monies, which were the fees charged to the owners of the horses stabled for training.

'Thank Christ something looks healthy,' he said. 'I need to take these books home and study them more closely. I'll return them in a few days and we'll talk again.'

As he climbed into his car, Eddie knew that a firm hand was required at the financial helm of the yard. Frampton was an excellent trainer but it was patently obvious to Eddie that he was useless at the business side of things. He had agreed to cover the debts in return for seventy-five per cent of the business, but what the yard needed was a cash injection – and soon!

His own businesses were doing well, thank heavens, he mused. The new Ace of Clubs was ticking over nicely and the profits were growing each week. Men were coming from surrounding areas to pit their wits and money against the tables. How foolish! Eddie smiled to himself at the stupidity of gamblers, chasing a fortune. The tables always won and that meant he was banking good money daily.

The Blue Pelican continued to be busy, especially at the weekends. The Williams boys were safely out of the way so were no longer a threat. Ken was all right, but Eddie had been concerned about Charlie's twisted nature. With a frown he thought about Frank Graves. He knew that the man had been hospitalised after the beating he'd taken at Eddie's instructions, but his presence still niggled away at the back of his mind. With Graves still around, he would never feel absolutely secure.

Tilly was feeling somewhat insecure also. Her unexpected meeting with David Strickland had shaken her to her foundations. She had been happy with Eddie, even though she realised that she wasn't truly in love with him, for she did feel a

309

deep affection for him, and her admiration for him knew no bounds. But when David had taken her in his arms, she had known that he was the one she really loved. It had come as a great shock.

Being so young, she didn't know what to do. Life with Eddie Chapman was full of exciting moments, and these were heady experiences for one so unworldly with a passion for adventure. She admitted to herself that she wasn't yet ready to give them up to settle down. Good gracious, she had her whole life in front of her and she wanted to fly!

At the Winchester Assizes, the first day of Gerald Bradbury's trial had arrived. The courtroom was full. The jury were already settled and the judge had just taken his seat. The case had caught the interest not only of the local press but of the nationals as well. At the back of the court sat young Nat Summers, pale-faced and rigid, his gaze fixed on the back of Gerald Bradbury's head. With the Williams brothers under arrest, it was deemed safe for Nat to come out of hiding.

The case for the prosecution was strong. Prostitutes called to give evidence had been promised immunity in return for their services to the crown. With nothing to lose, they had all been more than willing to appear. The two barristers made their opening speeches, and the first witness was called.

At the Bradbury house, Dorothy Bradbury busied herself sorting her clothes and packing precious pieces ready to move, pushing the court case to the back of her mind.

Downstairs Cook and Ethel were sitting having a quiet cup of tea, talking about the trial and the scandal, and the gossip it had evoked.

'It's poor Simon I feel sorry for,' Cook remarked. 'Since his father was arrested he's been so quiet, and his mother isn't any comfort to the poor lad. He came down to the kitchen early this morning and my heart bled for him.'

'Did he say anything to you?' Ethel asked.

'He looked at me and asked how his father could have done such a thing. I didn't know what to say to him. I just told him that everyone has a dark side. I asked him how his friends had reacted.'

'What did he say?'

'That some were being very kind, but others . . . well, he didn't say any more.'

Pouring another cup of tea, Ethel offered her opinion. 'Although it means we are out of a job, I think the best thing the missus could do is to move away and start again. She's filing for divorce, did you know that?'

Nodding, Cook said she did know. 'I don't blame her at all. If I was her I would change my name by deed poll when the divorce came through, then she'd have a clean sheet, so to speak. She should be all right for money, I would have thought. I wonder where she'll go?'

'If I were in her shoes, I'd put a lot of miles between me and Southampton. Have you done anything about getting another job yet?'

'I've put a few feelers out,' Cook told her, 'but I won't go until I have to – not for her sake,' she tipped her head towards the door, 'but for Simon's. He needs to feel he has someone who cares about him.'

With a smile of affection Ethel said, 'You would have made a good mother. Do you ever regret not getting married?'

'I almost did,' the other woman said, 'but my lad was killed on the Somme and I never fancied any other man. I certainly wouldn't have put up with the likes of the master, nasty bully. He made young Simon's life hell and I'll never forgive him for that.'

The two women washed up the cups and got on with their work, lost in their own thoughts. Ethel was wondering if she would be able to get another job locally. She knew quite a few influential people, having served them when they had come to dinner, and she thought she might stand a good chance if she approached one or two. But like Cook, she would hang on until Mrs Bradbury upped sticks for another address. Not that she would miss her, but much as she disliked the woman she did feel some pity for her. Since the arrest of her husband, not one member of her social circle had contacted her. She was completely ostracised by Southampton society, of which before, through her husband, she had been a prominent member. How the mighty had fallen!

In the courtroom one of the prostitutes was standing in the witness box, being questioned by the counsel for the prosecution.

'In your own words will you please tell the court what you observed on the night in question.'

'Well, my lord,' she said, looking at the judge, 'I was walking up and down waiting for punters when I see this bloke in a car driving slowly past staring at the girls. He looked as if he had a few bob so I steps forward and smiles at him, but he drives on.'

'Do you see the driver of the vehicle in this room?' asked the barrister.

'Yes, sir. That's him over there sitting in the dock.'

'Are you absolutely sure – remember you are on oath?'

'I'm certain, sir. That's him all right, no doubt about it.'

'No further questions, my lord,' said the barrister and sat down.

The defence tried to shake the girl's testimony with his questioning, but she refused to be moved.

'I suggest this is a case of mistaken identity,' counsel said.

'Suggest all you like, dearie, you wasn't there, I was – and that's him sitting there as large as life!'

Another woman was called and made her way to the stand and took the oath.

'Do you recognise the man sitting in the dock?'

'I do. It's Mr Gerald Bradbury.'

'How do you know the accused?'

'He was one of my regular punters.'

'Explain to the court what you mean by that, please.'

'Once a week, usually on a Thursday night, we would have an appointment at a hotel at Netley, where he would pay me to have sex with him.'

'Why a hotel at Netley, not Southampton?'

'Well, sir, he's well known, and he thought he wouldn't be recognised out of town.'

'Did he ever show any signs of violence towards you?'

'Not to begin with. Normally he didn't talk much, just got on with it, but one night, the last time I saw him, he scared the living daylights out of me. He started getting rough, and then he began thumping me around. The more I got scared the more he seemed to like it.' She glared across at the prisoner.

'What did you do to stop him?'

'I told him we was in a hotel and I'd scream if he didn't stop, and I told him if I did people would come running and his reputation would certainly suffer, 'cause I'd tell them who he was. That's when he stopped.' She looked at the judge. 'My face was so swollen and bruised I couldn't work for a week!' she told him, flushed with indignation.

'So you were out of pocket,' the barrister suggested.

'Not exactly. When I told my boss and he saw the state I was in, he gave me a fiver to tide me over.'

'Your boss? I don't understand?'

'I work for the Williams brothers. They book the appointments, we pay the money over to them and then they pay us a percentage . . . for our services,' she said coyly.

'Did the Williams brothers know you were meeting the men for sex?'

'Of course they did. That's what we was booked for. What did you think, that we was sitting having a chat?'

There was laughter round the room.

In the back of the courtroom, Detective Inspector Ridgeway grinned at his associate. 'We've got them now!'

'I told the twins never to book me with him again. They said they wouldn't and to leave it with them, and it wouldn't happen again.' She looked down for a moment then back at the solicitor and said, 'But of course it did, didn't it? Poor Elsie . . . she was a nice kid.'

'We don't know what happened yet, miss. That's what we are here to discover.'

The case continued late into the afternoon when it was adjourned until the following morning.

Back at the police station, Detective Inspector Ridgeway and his team were jubilant. 'We have the Williams twins bang to rights now,' he said. 'It's an open and shut case when it comes to court. And about bloody time too! Come on, let's go to the pub. I'll buy you all a pint.'

Hilda Williams had also been in court. Her heart sank when she listened to the damning evidence, knowing that her two boys would be going down for a stretch when their case was brought before the court.

As she trudged wearily to the station, she thought she too would probably end up in the dock for aiding and abetting. Well, she was too bloody old to do a runner; besides, the boys would need her to keep their spirits up when she visited them. They would not be happy when she put them in the picture about what had happened in court. But there was nothing to be gained by telling them lies. Better for them to prepare themselves mentally for their incarceration. She would tell them to be hard men when they were inside; it was the only way to survive. She knew that from experience.

She stopped at a pub close to the police station for a drink to try to drown her sorrows. Fortunately she and the boys had money stashed away, which would tide them over for a bit. She'd make sure the police never discovered it. When the boys did come out of prison they would be unable to continue with the escort business. They'd have to find another way to make money.

As she sipped her beer she felt deeply depressed . . . and old.

CHAPTER TWENTY-NINE

During the next few days, Eddie Chapman
pored over the accounts from Frampton's yard,
making phone calls to suppliers of hay and
feed, getting a better price, cutting costs wherever he could until he had done all that was
possible to tighten the financial reins. He was
secretly thrilled at being in a position to be an
integral part of the racing world. He had always
loved visiting racecourses, and when he had
bought his first horse it had thrilled him even
more when he, as an owner, walked into the
parade ring and mixed with other owners and
trainers as they gave their instructions to their
respective jockeys. And now his personal
standing would be even higher.

However, he knew that there was a desperate
need for a big cash injection to allow him to improve
the yard; make it a place where he could invite
more prestigious owners to move their animals.

Eddie had always been ambitious and had the

drive and ability to cash in on the right opportunity at the right time. He had a nose for a good buy and he knew that this was another wonderful chance. Yes, he could afford to subsidise the yard to a certain degree, but it would need more than his money to build the business into the one he envisaged.

He voiced his thoughts when next he met Jeremy Frampton.

'I know what you mean,' said the trainer, 'but at the moment we don't have a horse that could win big money.' He paused. 'Of course, there are always other ways.'

'What are you talking about?'

'Let's take a walk and I'll tell you,' said Frampton. 'There are too many people about here.'

The two men strolled away from the stable yard.

Frank Graves, now fully recovered, had got himself a job in the docks as a welder, a skill he had learned when he was in prison. He was still living in Queenie's flat. It had originally been meant to be for just a couple of nights until he found other accommodation, but he was still there a week later. They got on so well together that one night, after the bar closed, Queenie made a suggestion.

'Why don't you stick around for a bit? I've got used to you being here.'

He was both pleased and surprised. 'Do you really mean it?'

Laughing, she said, 'Have you ever heard me say anything I don't mean?'

'No. Quite the opposite, if I was honest.'

'Of course now you have a job and can pay your way that makes a difference,' she stated firmly. 'I have never kept a man in my life and I don't bloody well intend to start now.

Although he was content with his job and the woman who willingly shared her bed with him, his feeling of envy and resentment towards Eddie Chapman had not diminished at all. He would take a walk every evening when Queenie was working and watch the comings and goings at the Blue Pelican, where Eddie seemed to spend most of his time.

He had read of Chapman's purchase of a racing stable, an event which had been well publicised in the local paper, orchestrated by the man himself, building his public persona. It had only added to the fuel which kept the flames of hatred burning inside Graves. But he would wait until the opportunity to get even presented itself. That was another thing that prison had taught him . . . patience.

During the two weeks that followed, Tilly spent more time away from the shop than in it. Eddie, full of his plans for the stables, took her to various racecourses, spreading the word to other owners, talking to them, getting known. He was good at selling ideas and some of his targets had showed an interest in his plans, which pleased him immeasurably.

Tilly, however, was filled with foreboding, knowing that he and Frampton were not above using illegal means to win races, but of course she was unable to voice her suspicions.

Eddie was still a considerate lover, spoiling her with small expensive gifts that she didn't really want, but when she said as much he just looked at her, mystified.

'I always look after what is mine, darling,' he said. 'I love spoiling you.'

She bristled at his words. 'I am not yours! Nobody owns me,' she told him.

He just laughed at her. 'I love it when you're angry: your eyes flash and your nostrils flare. It's very sexy.'

How could you argue with such a man? But she was finding his possessiveness smothering. She felt she was losing her freedom, the thing she most valued. Eventually, she determinedly turned down his next invitation.

'What do you mean you don't want to come with me?' he demanded.

'I want time for myself,' she argued. 'You make claim to my every minute. I can't breathe – I need some time alone.'

He was not pleased. 'I don't understand you at all. I bought the shop for you so you would be free to come with me whenever I wanted.'

'That's the trouble, Eddie. It's all about what *you* want. What about what I want?'

'But I thought you enjoyed being with me. You used to be excited when I took you to places.'

Not wanting to appear selfish, she tried to explain. 'I was, and to a certain extent I still am, but ever since you bought into the racing stable you've become so single-minded. I can understand – I know you want to make it work, but I really don't need to be with you when you're going round trying to drum up business. I want to spend some time, at least, trying to build up my own.'

When he tried to argue with her she was insistent. 'Please understand. I love the shop, I have new ideas, which I want to implement, but I can't if I'm with you all the time. At least give me credit for being business-minded.'

'Very well,' he said tersely, 'but there will be times when I need you with me, and then I won't take no for an answer!'

* * *

Gerald Bradbury's trial was drawing to a close. He had insisted on going into the witness box himself, against the wishes of his barrister, saying he wanted to be able to explain what had happened; certain he would be able to convince the jury that it was all a terrible mistake.

The prosecuting counsel had torn him to strips with his questioning, pointing out to the jury that not once had the defendant shown any remorse, which was indeed true. Bradbury, being the arrogant man he was, was so bent on showing he was a worthy citizen who just happened to have fallen by the wayside that he had completely dismissed young Elsie, calling her a woman of the streets and almost deeming her unworthy of his attention.

The prosecution had built up a watertight case, leaving counsel for the defence little room for manoeuvre. He could only bring in eminent personages to state that Bradbury was a good man, much admired in his profession. But as he sat down he knew that his client would be serving a long sentence. It was merely a case of waiting to see how long.

The judge summed up the case for the jury.

'Gerald Bradbury may be a man of distinction, as various witnesses for the defence have testified, but nevertheless this man, by his own admission, took the life of young Elsie Summers. Then, realising what he had done, he tried to cover his crime by hiding the body. If you think this deed was premeditated, you have no choice but to find the defendant guilty of murder. If you think that it was an accident and the defendant panicked, then the verdict will be one of manslaughter.'

The jury left to reach their conclusion and the court was cleared.

Bradbury sat in a small room with his barrister. 'I'm not going to get away with this, am I?' Gerald asked, his voice trembling, his hands shaking as he lit a cigarette.

'I'm afraid not,' the barrister said. 'But your previous good name may save you a bit of time inside.'

Bradbury put his head to his hands. 'Prison! I don't know if I can face it.'

The barrister remained silent. There were no words that could comfort his client.

The jury were unable to come to a unanimous verdict and so the case was carried over until the following day. Gerald Bradbury was taken back to his cell to wait.

But the following morning when the warder opened the cell door, he found Bradbury dead. He had torn strips from his sheet to make a rope, and tied one end to the bars of the window and the other round his neck.

Ethel Thompson opened the door of the Bradbury house to a police officer, who asked to speak to Mrs Bradbury. She took him into the study and called her mistress.

The police officer didn't stay for long. Ten minutes later, Ethel let him out, then knocked on the door of the study and walked in.

'Is there anything you'll be wanting, madam?' she asked.

Dorothy Bradbury looked up at her and without expression said, 'A pot of tea, please. I have a funeral to arrange.'

'Pardon, madam?' said Ethel, somewhat puzzled.

'Mr Bradbury is dead. He hanged himself in his cell this morning, as if he hadn't brought enough shame to this house! He should have faced his punishment like a man, but I suppose that was too much to ask. If you see Simon before I do when he comes home, please say nothing but send him to me. Do you understand?'

'Of course, madam,' said Ethel, and hurried off to the kitchen to report the latest happenings to Cook.

After relating to her exactly what Dorothy Bradbury had said, she looked at Cook and remarked, 'I've never seen a woman so cold as she was when she told me her husband was dead. She was furious with him; there wasn't a shred of pity in her whole body. Honestly!'

'Ah, well, Ethel, who knows how we would react if we was in her shoes. He not only took the life of that poor girl, but he's ruined Simon's and hers. She has to leave the town where she's spent her whole life because of him. I don't think I'd have much sympathy either.'

'I suppose you're right. It just seemed a bit harsh to me. It's the boy I'm worried about. What a lot of baggage he will have to carry for the rest of his life. Imagine if he meets a young lady he wants to marry in the future . . . he'll have to tell her about all this. What if she thinks "like father like son"?'

'Surely no one could think that of the lovely lad!' Cook was appalled at the thought. 'You just have to look at him to know what a lovely nature he has.'

'Let's hope you're right,' said Ethel as she turned away to lay the tray for tea.

CHAPTER THIRTY

Joe Thompson was making another delivery to the Blue Pelican club. Once the barrels of beer had been unloaded and signed for, he put a feed bag over Clarence's head, smoothing his nose for a minute. Then, climbing on to his cart, he lit a cigarette and inhaled the smoke, enjoying the taste of the nicotine.

He sat with his own thoughts while Clarence chewed his way through the oats in the bag. His family must think he was a simpleton, he mused. Neither his wife nor his son ever discussed Tilly's affair with this club's owner in front of him. Good God, he read enough about them in the local paper. He had also heard the gossip going round about his daughter. Tilly was a lovely girl and he was proud of her, but like any father he was beginning to worry about her association with a man who was so much older and more sophisticated than she was. He also knew about the purchase of the gown shop. It only added to his concern.

As he sat ruminating over all this, he saw Eddie Chapman walking along the street, heading for the club. Joe climbed down and waited.

'Good morning, Mr Chapman,' he said as Eddie walked towards the front door. 'Could I have a word?'

Looking somewhat puzzled, Eddie paused. 'A word about what?'

'My daughter. Tilly.'

Eddie was taken by surprise. He looked at the delivery cart, then at the man standing in front of him in his working clothes, but when he looked into Joe's eyes he recognised the same stubbornness he'd seen in Tilly's.

'Of course. Come in. We'll go up to my office.' Looking back at Clarence, he asked, 'Will he be all right?'

'He's fine,' Joe assured him.

The two men climbed the stairs to the office, where Eddie invited Joe to take a seat. 'What can I do for you?' he asked.

'I want to know what your intentions are towards my daughter.'

Eddie attempted to hide a smile. 'I'm not sure what you mean,' he said.

'I would have thought my meaning was pretty clear. My Tilly is a strong-minded girl, always was from a small child, but I've read about the two of you in the paper, heard the gossip around the town. My girl's reputation is in shreds, which she doesn't seem to mind, I have to say, and I just wonder what it is that makes her cock a snook at society. Perhaps you can explain.'

For once Eddie was lost for words. He greatly admired the man's loyalty to his daughter, but what could he say?

'Well, Mr Thompson, I'm sorry if you're worried about Tilly. I can assure you that I mean her no harm. I am extremely fond of her. She's a delightful girl, and I enjoy her company.'

Joe stared long and hard at the man sitting opposite him. 'Don't take me for a fool, Chapman; I think that you enjoy rather more than her company!'

Under such scrutiny, Eddie felt uncomfortable.

'Are you planning to marry my girl in the future?'

'You don't beat about the bush, do you, Mr Thompson?'

'Never believed in it,' Joe stated, 'and I would appreciate an honest answer.'

Eddie took him at his word. 'Marriage to anyone is not part of my plans for some considerable time.'

'I thought not,' Joe said. 'How old are you, son?'

No one had called Eddie son for many a year.

He felt as if he was up before his headmaster being admonished for some misdemeanour.

'I'm twenty-five,' he said eventually.

'And my girl is nineteen. Now marriage to an older man is one thing, but to be used by such a person is sacrilege. You are taking up the time in her life when she should be learning about the world, building her character, and meeting young men who may fall in love with her and eventually walk her down the aisle. She was going out with a lovely man, an engineer – did you know that?'

'Yes, I've met him. But may I say, Mr Thompson, it was Tilly's choice to continue with our relationship. I didn't pressure her in any way.'

'Of course you did!' Joe's eyes flashed with anger. 'You showed an impressionable young girl a life she had only read about. You used that to get what you wanted. And then you bought her a business! Now she's obligated to you. That by my standards is devious.'

'I did that so that she would have more free time to spend with me,' Eddie explained.

'You did that so she couldn't be free of you if she wanted to be.'

'What exactly do you want from me?'

'I want you to leave my Tilly alone to get on with her life. To be young and free to go out with people her own age . . . to grow up.'

'Tilly is free to leave me whenever she wants, Mr Thompson. As you so rightly say, she has a mind of her own, and when she makes a decision no one will change her mind. Until then, I don't see anything I want to alter. She's happy – isn't that the most important thing?'

'Ah well, you see, there's the rub. It's like a child at Christmas, thrilled with a new toy, but eventually the novelty wears off and it prefers the box the gift came in. When the novelty of you and your ways wears off, Tilly will come to her senses. I'll just have to wait for that moment.' Joe rose to his feet and, glaring at Eddie, he pointed his finger at him. 'You harm my girl . . . I'll have you!' And he walked out of the room.

Eddie got to his feet and poured himself a drink from the tray beside the desk. Nobody had spoken to him like that in years; it was a little unnerving to say the least. Taking a sip of his drink, he smiled slowly to himself. He had to hand it to the old man, he was a fiery old devil. He now knew from whom Tilly inherited her spirit. He frowned, remembering how she had refused to go with him to a race meeting. Was the novelty of being with him wearing off?

Tilly was indeed happy, but it was because her shop was doing good business. The new winter stock she had ordered had arrived and was selling well. She had sold several expensive coats and hats to wealthy women, who greatly admired the cut of the clothes. As one remarked, 'It is so nice that I can buy such style in Southampton instead of having to go up to London.' The woman had also purchased an evening gown to wear at a ball to be given by the local Chamber of Commerce.

One or two clients had come to the shop out of curiosity to see for themselves the young lady who was the talk of the town. Tilly had charmed them and sold them some merchandise. They left thinking she was a lovely girl and secretly admiring her courage for standing up to public opinion.

One afternoon, David Strickland rang the shop and invited Tilly to have dinner with him. Much as she wanted to go, she hesitated until he told her that he might be leaving soon.

'What do you mean, leaving?'

'I've applied to return to my ship,' he told her. 'I'm waiting for an answer.'

She knew that she couldn't bear to let him leave without seeing him and agreed to meet him later at the Tivoli restaurant.

She dressed with care that evening, choosing a long black skirt and plain white blouse to wear beneath the emerald green embroidered jacket he had bought for her in New York.

When she walked downstairs, her father looked up from his paper.

'My, but you're a sight for sore eyes, love. Going somewhere nice?'

'I'm meeting David for dinner,' she told him. 'He may be going back to sea.'

'Give him my regards. Nice chap; I liked him,' he said with a certain amount of satisfaction. When Tilly had left the house he wondered if perhaps the novelty of her relationship with Eddie Chapman was waning at last. God, he hoped so.

David was waiting outside the restaurant when Tilly arrived. He kissed her on the cheek and said, 'You look lovely, but then you always do. I've booked a table. Shall we go in? We can have a drink at the bar whilst we wait.'

Once the drinks had been ordered, David asked, 'How's the business going?'

She was enthusiastic in her reply. 'Absolutely great! I've had some new winter stock in and it's flying off the rails.'

'I passed by the other day and looked in the window. I thought the models were wearing some stunning outfits.'

'Thanks,' she said. 'I'm really enjoying myself being a businesswoman.'

'I do believe you're growing up at last,' he teased.

'Before we know it, you'll have a chain of stores around the town.'

'I've a long way to go before that ever happens.' With a broad grin she added, 'But what a great idea!'

The restaurant manager came over to tell them their table was ready.

When the soup had been served, Tilly looked across at David and with a frown asked the dreaded question. 'When do you go away?'

'I'm not sure until I hear from the company. Another week and then I should know.'

'Are you pleased to be going back to sea?'

He tilted his head to one side and answered her. 'If I'm really honest, yes I am. This break has been interesting, but I need the deck of a ship beneath my feet, to feel the swell of the waves, breathe in the smell of the sea.' Laughing, he said, 'I'm just an old seadog at heart.'

'But that is where you are happiest, so you should go back.'

'And you, Tilly, tell me honestly, are you doing what makes you really happy?'

The waiter appeared to take away their soup plates and top up their wine glasses. When he walked off, David prompted her. 'Tilly?'

'I'm happy when I'm in the shop. When a client walks out of the door with one of my garments, it thrills me.'

'And otherwise?'

She shrugged. 'Oh, I don't know. I was, but somehow I don't seem to have any time to call my own.'

'What do you mean?'

'Eddie likes me to be with him. We've been going racing quite a bit lately now he's bought into a racing stable. I love racing, but it isn't my life. It seems to be his at the moment.'

'Then don't go.'

'He doesn't like it when I refuse.'

The look of dejection on her face, the sadness of her voice, made David long to take her into his arms and comfort her. 'He doesn't own you, Tilly darling. You're free to go where you please and when.'

'But I owe him so much! After all, he bought the shop for me.'

'Yes, that was a clever move on his part.'

'Whatever do you mean?'

Leaning across the table, he took both her hands in his. 'Can't you see? Once you had accepted his gift, you were in his pocket for ever. He calls the shots and you feel you have to go running.'

Knowing that David was right didn't make her feel any better. She didn't dare tell him her concerns about illegally run races. He would be horrified.

'Yes, I suppose you're right,' she conceded. 'He's not unkind to me, David, I wouldn't like you to think that.'

'You could always say you didn't want the shop and give it back.'

'But I love the shop!' Her eyes grew wide at his suggestion. 'I don't want to give it up.'

'Then he's got you just where he wants you.'

She sipped her wine as the waiter appeared with the main course. 'Anyway, let's not talk about Eddie any more,' she said. 'Tell me about your students and that other tutor friend of yours.' And so the subject was changed.

After the meal, David walked her home through the park. The evenings were closing in and the signs of autumn were all around. Shrubs had shed their blooms, summer bedding was dying back and the leaves would soon be turning colour.

They sat on a bench and looked around at the neatly mown grass.

'You won't get this kind of view at sea,' Tilly teased.

'True. But you haven't stood at a ship's rail and watched mountainous waves breaking, or a storm raging in the distance. Or even seen calm ocean, looking like a millpond, with dolphins swimming alongside the ship. It's different, yet beautiful in its own way.' He turned towards her and tipped up her chin. 'But I'm looking at the most beautiful view of all right now.' He leaned forward and kissed her, at first gently, but as she responded he gathered her into his arms, held her closely and kissed her with unbridled passion.

'Oh, Tilly darling, when are you going to come to your senses? I can't bear to think of you with Chapman. He doesn't deserve you.' And he kissed her again.

When eventually they moved apart Tilly said, 'Oh, David, you are making things so difficult for me.'

Caressing her cheek he said softly, 'Am I, darling? I'm so pleased.'

'What am I going to do?' There was a plaintive note in her voice, like a child looking for guidance.

'Only you can decide that, Tilly. All I can do is tell you that I still love you. But you have to make the final choice.'

'But you'll soon be going away.'

'Perhaps it's as well that I am, then I won't be around to cloud the issue.'

'But I don't want you to leave.'

He held her by her shoulders and stared into her eyes. 'Even if we were married I would have to go away. My life isn't ashore, I've proved that to myself, so you'll have to take that into consideration.'

'If you went cruising, you'd be away for even longer.'

'That's true, but it's all part of the life I live. Being married to a seafarer can be lonely for the wife, but you could work if you wanted to. Maybe open another business, one that is really your own. I wouldn't stop you.'

'I don't have the money to do that.'

He smiled at her. 'There are such things as bank loans, you know. I could stand as your guarantor.'

'Would you really do that for me, after the way I've treated you?'

'In a flash. But of course you will have to give up Eddie Chapman. Come on, I'll walk you home.'

Outside her house, David took her into his arms. 'I'll let you know when I'm due to leave. But then you will have to give me an answer, darling Tilly. I have a life to live too.'

'You're giving me an ultimatum?'

'Yes, I suppose you could put it like that. But you don't seem to understand, you can't keep me hanging on for ever. It isn't fair.'

Snuggling into him she said, 'I know, I do know.'

He kissed her goodnight. 'I'll be in touch. Just remember that I love you.'

Tilly watched him walk away, wanting to run after him, to feel his strong arms around her, keeping her safe. With a deep sigh, she took out her key and opened the door.

Joe was drinking a cup of cocoa before going to bed. He had purposely stayed up after his wife had retired in the hope of seeing Tilly when she returned.

'Hello, love,' he said, noting the thoughtful expression on her face. 'Have a nice time?'

'Yes, thanks, Dad.'

'Want a cup of cocoa?'

'That would be lovely,' she said, remembering how she and her father had often shared moments like this when she was small.

They sat on either side of the dying embers of the fire in silence for a while, until Joe spoke.

'What's on your mind, Tilly? You look as if you've lost a pound and found a sixpence.'

'I have to make a big decision, Dad, and it's a bit of a worry.'

Puffing on a cigarette he asked, 'Do you know what you want to do?'

'Yes, but I don't know how to do it, that's the problem.'

He was thoughtful for a moment and then he said, 'Well, love, I've always found it best in life, when faced with something unpleasant, never to beat about the bush. Come straight to the point is the best way. That's if you have the courage.'

'That's sound advice,' she said. 'Thanks.'

'Anything your old dad can do to help?'

She shook her head.

'Then I suggest you get a good night's sleep, so you'll have a clear head to think in the morning.' He rose from his chair and kissed the top of her head. 'Goodnight, Tilly love.'

'Goodnight, Dad, and thanks.'

Tilly sat alone, wondering how she was going to approach Eddie, and when, now knowing she wanted to be with David . . . and what was she going to do about the shop?

CHAPTER THIRTY-ONE

Unbeknown to either Tilly or David, Greta Harper had been in the bar at the Tivoli with friends, and had observed the two of them together. She'd seen David lean across the table and take Tilly's hands in his whilst he talked earnestly to her. Greta was thrilled. Could it be that the young madam was two-timing Eddie Chapman? He wouldn't like that if he knew. It would give her the greatest pleasure to be the one to tell him.

When Eddie answered the phone the following morning, it was to hear a familiar voice.

'Hello, darling. How are you?'

'What do you want, Greta?' he asked abruptly.

'Now, Eddie darling, that's no way to talk to someone who has your best interests at heart.'

'What on earth are you talking about?'

'Did you know that your little girl is still seeing her engineer?'

There was silence for a moment. 'What do you mean?'

'Well, I happened to be in the bar at the Tivoli last night and whom did I see in the dining room but young Tilly with her so-called ex-boyfriend. They looked very cosy to me, darling.'

'I'm not her keeper,' he protested. 'She's free to see whom she likes.'

'Oh, come along, Eddie, we both know that's not true. You are much too possessive for that. When you think that someone belongs to you, it's keep off the grass to all and sundry. I just thought you should know. I wouldn't like to see you of all people taken for a fool.'

He slammed down the receiver. Greta wouldn't make up a story like that, so what on earth did Tilly think she was doing? He would have words with her later and get to the bottom of this.

A call from Jeremy Frampton put his plans on hold. He wanted to meet at Winchester. He had something he wanted to discuss, and it had to be immediately.

Eddie left instructions with his manager at the Blue Pelican and took a taxi to the station.

Frampton was waiting for him in a quiet corner of the lounge bar of the White Horse inn. He

342

shook Eddie by the hand and said, 'I think I have the answer to our cash flow problem.

Intrigued, Eddie said, 'I'm listening.'

'I have a couple of my own horses in the yard, as you know. One of them hasn't any great form, but if we were to put in a ringer we could make a packet between us.'

'What exactly do you mean?'

'We can buy another horse I know of, with form, which looks just like Night and Day. They're as alike as two peas in a pod, even to the white flash down the nose. Both eight-year-old geldings. We run Flying Flynn under Night and Day's name. The odds will be in our favour, so we lay bets around the bookies days before the race, then on the course the day of the race. We'll clean up!'

'If the ringer has form why would the owner sell him?'

'The trainer is due to retire and is selling off a few of his assets. I got to hear about it yesterday. If we want him we have to move today.'

'How much?'

'A hundred and fifty guineas. It's a lot, I know, but we'll get it back in spades.'

'And what are the odds of our being found out?'

'Small, I would say, if we did it just the once. Then later we can run the ringer under his own name. He'll do well, I guarantee it!'

Sitting back in his chair, Eddie thought carefully. There was always a risk when doing anything unlawful, but he had such plans for the yard, with owners of repute who were interested. If they could just pull this off, he would be in a position to carry out such plans. He thought back to the chance he took with Frank Graves all those years ago. It was a one-off that had paid handsomely. This was too good an opportunity to miss.

'All right, let's do it,' he said.

Jeremy Frampton shook his hand. 'Good decision, Eddie. We won't look back after this, I promise.'

'We only do it the once!' Eddie emphasised. 'Never push your luck, that much I've learned in life.'

'Absolutely. I'll make the arrangements then. You'll have to give me a cheque for the purchase, though, as you know I don't have that kind of cash.'

Eddie made out the cheque and handed it over. 'When do we run the horse?'

'In ten days' time at Doncaster. You'll be there of course?'

'Damn right I will. I want to be in the winners' enclosure.'

Frampton grinned at him. 'There's nothing like it, my friend. Right, I'll be on my way. I'll be in touch.'

Eddie sat with another drink, pondering over the plans that he would soon be able to instigate. With a winner he would be on his way up, yet again. He would make sure that Tilly was with him on the great occasion. This time he would not take no for an answer.

On the train to Doncaster, Jeremy Frampton sorted out his plan of action. He would stable Flying Flynn elsewhere and on the day of the race he would load Night and Day at his stable as normal, then drive to Flying Flynn's stable and swap the horses. That way only he and his head lad would know what was going on. The lad was reliable; he'd helped out before and was happy to earn some extra money, which bought his silence. After all, he wouldn't want to be caught with his fingers in the till either. They could swap the horses again after the race. Eventually he could sell Night and Day and quietly move the other into his stable under its own name. He gleefully rubbed his hands together. It was a great plan.

In Southampton, the two Williams brothers were waiting to appear in court charged with living off immoral earnings. Several prostitutes had made statements and were willing to give evidence. They had nothing to lose, having been given an amnesty for the time being. Those who had worked for the twins would be back on the streets anyway after the case. No more bookings in comfortable hotels for them: the police had seen to that, warning the managers of the hotels in question that they could lose their licences if they allowed rooms to be used for prostitution. They had all denied any knowledge of such goings on, of course, but although the police had doubts about a few of them, without definite proof of their complicity they had to make do with severe warnings.

Ma Williams had visited both her sons, trying to comfort them in her own inimitable way.

'Now you remember, don't take no truck from no one! Any sign of weakness on your part and your life will be hell. Remember your reputation as hard men. The other cons will know about you, but there are always those who will test you. There's always one bugger who thinks he runs the place; he'll come at you for sure. Just be ready at all times.'

'What will we do when we come out?' Charlie had asked. 'We can't run the brasses any more.'

'I've got money stashed away. We'll start another kind of business. I'll think of something, don't you worry about that. You just keep your eyes peeled inside. And you be extra careful, Charlie. Keep yourself to yourself. There will be plenty of boys wanting to be your pet. They can use that to trap you if you aren't careful.'

'What do you mean, Ma?'

'There will be some who want you hurt. Some pretty boy will lure you to some place and before you know it a gang'll set upon you. I've seen it all before.'

'How did you manage inside?'

'I was the biggest bitch there!' she said triumphantly. 'No one crossed me and got away with it. You must do the same.'

He laughed. 'What, be the biggest bitch there? I can do that all right.'

'This isn't funny!' she snapped.

His grin faded. 'Don't you think I know that? I'm dreading it.'

'Sure you are, son, but nobody must ever know that. At least you'll be able to keep an eye on each other, inside.'

But when the case came up a few days later, the boys were each sent down for five years, Charlie to Winchester prison and Ken to Lewes. Ma Williams was furious. She would have to make separate journeys to see her boys.

The local force was jubilant at having incarcerated the twins after so long.

Detective Inspector Ridgeway was especially pleased. 'Those two bastards have got away with murder for far too long. It's a pity it was a real killing that was the catalyst for it all, though.' He looked round at his men. 'Anyone know what Mrs Bradbury is doing these days?'

'Her place is up for sale, sir,' said one.

Cook and Ethel were working out their notice. Dorothy Bradbury had found a buyer easily; after all, the house was among the finest in the town. She and Simon were moving down to Devon the following week.

'Seems that the missus used to go there as a child,' Cook explained. 'Poor Simon won't know a soul.'

'That's just as well, surely,' Ethel said. 'After all, they want to make a clean start. They certainly won't want people to know about their old man and the murder.'

'And him hanging himself!' added Cook. 'It was all in the national newspapers, not just the local ones. Here!' She moved closer. 'I heard her with her solicitor making arrangements to change their names by deed poll.'

'Very wise of her,' said Ethel. 'That's just what I would have done. So, have you got another post?'

'Yes I have. I'm going to be cooking for Mr Bradbury's business partner. He approached me yesterday.'

'Blimey! I hope he isn't into prostitutes too.'

'No, not him. He's not all that fit, I've heard. A good tumble would probably kill him!'

They both laughed at the thought. 'What about his wife, what's she like?'

'Seems a nice woman. Good manners, polite, talked to me in a friendly way, not like her upstairs. What about you?'

'I spoke to Mrs Bentley, the banker's wife. I heard her maid was leaving, so I start there next week.'

'Well then, we too will have a fresh beginning. Let's hope it works out for all of us. For all I think the missus is a bit of a bitch, I can't help feeling sorry for her.'

'Me too,' Ethel agreed. 'Maybe this awful business will make her a bit more human.'

'You're joking! She's so strait-laced she doesn't need to wear corsets!'

Upstairs, Dorothy Bradbury was putting the finishing touches to her packing. She sat in the chair by the bedroom window and looked out on the tree-lined avenue. Tears welled in her eyes. Letting out a deep sigh, she slowly shook her head. To think things had ended like this. Although her relationship with her husband had not been a happy one, she had loved the social side of her life, the position she held in the higher echelon of society. All gone, thanks to the disgrace that had been spread across the pages of the newspapers. It had been a bitter pill to swallow.

At least she was financially secure. In Gerald's will he had left a decent legacy to Simon and everything else to her. It was the only kind thing he had ever done for his son. It would take time for probate to be settled but she had enough ready cash for the move to Devon. She had bought a fine house in Dartmouth. She wanted to live by the sea, and Dartmouth was so pretty.

Simon thought he might like to travel, and when his money was released he would be free to do so. She didn't mind being alone; after all, she'd felt pretty much so when Gerald was alive. No, she would start again, building a social life – really living, feeling free. She had changed their names by deed poll, choosing her maiden name, Hardcastle. It had a certain ring to it, she thought. A touch of class. Yes, she was ready to begin again . . . and no man would ever again spoil her life.

CHAPTER THIRTY-TWO

Tilly was keeping busy at Madam Leone's, filling her every moment with rearranging the stock, dressing the window and dusting the shelves. Anything to stop her worrying about having to tell Eddie that their relationship was over. She wasn't at all sure how he would react and she would have to pick her moment carefully. It was something that needed a lot of thought. She couldn't just blurt it out when she saw him. Besides, she felt guilty about it; after all it wasn't as if he had treated her badly. Quite the contrary: he had been generous to a fault, had given her a good time, widened her experience ... and of course there was the business he'd bought for her. He had said that if ever they were to part, she was to keep it, as everyone should have a start in life. That was very magnanimous of him, but would he still feel that way when she told him of her intentions? In many ways she felt she was letting him down. She *was* fond of him, but she wasn't in love with him. It was David who had eventually stolen her heart.

As she straightened the gown on the model in the window, she recalled the earnest expression on David's face when he told her that he loved her. How amazing was that? After all, he was aware that she had been having an affair with Eddie. She was lucky that despite that he still wanted her. How many men would feel the same? And she did wonder whether, if they were to marry and had a row, he would throw the fact in her face. Could he really put it behind him?

One person who would be delighted if she left Eddie was Jago. He'd had little to say on the subject of late. As he visited the gambling club quite often she supposed that he had accepted that his sister was going out with the owner. Had he really disliked the idea, he wouldn't go near the place. Her mouth twitched at the corners. Jago would have found that really difficult, she thought, knowing how much he liked a flutter at the tables. And winning would have been all the sweeter for knowing that it was Eddie Chapman's money he was putting in his wallet.

At that moment, the telephone rang, disrupting her thoughts. Grace came to the back of the window. 'Mr Chapman for you,' she said.

With a sinking heart, Tilly walked to the phone

and picked up the receiver. 'Hello, Eddie. What can I do for you?' she asked.

'I would like you to come to the Blue Pelican tonight,' he told her. 'I need to talk to you.'

She thought he sounded angry and wondered why. 'Very well,' she said, 'I'll be there at about seven o'clock.' As she replaced the receiver, she noticed her hands were trembling. Was tonight going to be the time to tell him of her decision? She felt her heart beat a little faster at the thought. What was it her father had said? Never beat about the bush, come straight out with it. But was that the best way when it came to dealing with Eddie? If only David were here to give her strength and support. But this was something she had to do herself.

She dressed with care that evening, telling herself that if she felt she looked good, it would give her added confidence to face the ordeal in front of her. She had chosen a dress from the shop, one from her new stock of cocktail frocks. It was in lightweight pale green velvet trimmed with black bugle beads, and with it she wore a long necklace of jet beads with matching earrings and long black silk gloves. Looking at her reflection in the mirror, she thought she looked very sophisticated, and older than her nineteen years. Next month was her birthday, when she would leave her teens behind. Twenty sounded very grown up, she thought. Well, she *had* grown up these past few months. Eddie Chapman had seen to that.

When she walked into the club there weren't many people about. Usually, they didn't start arriving in numbers until around eight o'clock. She saw Eddie talking to the barman and went over to him.

'Hello, Eddie.'

He turned to look at her. 'You look stunning. Is that one of your new models?'

'Yes. Do you like it?'

'I do. It's very stylish.' But there was a certain coldness in his voice which she didn't understand. 'Let's go up to my office,' he said, and walked towards the stairs.

She followed in his wake, wondering what it was he wanted to talk to her about. Probably something to do with the stables, she thought wryly. He talked of nothing else these days. But when they settled in the office, his first question surprised her.

'What were you doing in the Tivoli the other evening with Strickland?'

Taken aback, she hesitated for a moment. Was this a heaven-sent opportunity to tell him their relationship was over?

'He invited me out to dinner as he will soon be leaving,' she said.

There was a look of relief on his face. 'What do you mean, leaving?'

'He's going back to sea. His teaching appointment is almost finished and he's applied to return to his ship. I wanted to see him before he left.'

Eddie was now all smiles. 'Oh well, that explains it.'

'I didn't think I needed to explain my movements to you,' she retorted angrily.

'Of course you don't, darling. Don't be silly.'

'Then why did you feel you had to question me? And anyway, how did you know?'

'Someone told me. I just wondered why you were there with him, that's all. When does he leave?'

'I don't know; he's waiting to hear. He said he'd get in touch when he knew.'

His smile faded. 'Why would he bother to do that?' His eyes narrowed as he waited for her reply.

Taking a deep breath, Tilly thought of her father's words. Here was the perfect opening and she wouldn't beat about the bush. But just as she opened her mouth to tell him, the phone rang.

'Excuse me,' Eddie said as he picked up the receiver. He listened for a minute and said, 'Just a moment, Jeremy.' Looking at Tilly, he said,

'You'll have to forgive me, but this is business. Go downstairs and get yourself a drink. I'll be down shortly.' And the moment was lost.

But knowing it was the trainer on the line, Tilly only pulled the door to. She stood outside and listened to Eddie as he talked to Frampton. She could only hear one side of the conversation, but what she did hear chilled her.

'So he's ready to go then?' After a pause, 'And you are absolutely sure no one will be able to recognise him when he's exchanged for Night and Day?' And then, 'Good. I'll start laying small bets here in Southampton. What do you think the price will be? . . . That's fantastic! We'll clean up and then we can really go to town on the new plans for the yard. I'll see you in Doncaster.'

As he put down the receiver, Tilly fled. She couldn't believe what she'd heard. Through her brother's love of gambling, and his tales of racing, she knew that they were talking about a ringer. She remembered Jago telling her about an old scandal years ago when the Derby winner had been a ringer. It had caused no end of trouble in the racing world at the time.

When Eddie came to the bar to join her he was full of himself. He ordered a bottle of champagne, telling Tilly he had a sure winner running at Doncaster and that she was to go with him.

'You can be with me in the winners' enclosure. I want you to see me pick up the trophy.' He put his arm round her and kissed her cheek. 'Darling, we are going to be training really prestigious horses in the future as I implement the plans I have for the yard.'

He was so thrilled, how could she ruin it for him now by telling him of her own plans? And she couldn't possibly let him know she had overheard his conversation with Jeremy Frampton. That was dangerous knowledge.

Strangely enough, the next two hours were enjoyable. Eddie regaled her with his view of the future at the racing stables, and she admired his ability to envisage what changes could be advantageous. He had an extraordinary talent for business, which was why he was so successful, but knowing that the money he was hoping to raise for the venture was to be gained by illegal means was of great concern to her. What if he and Frampton were found out? He would surely lose the licences to run his successful clubs – he could be sent to prison! All his hard work would be for nothing. She longed to beg him not to go through with it, but of course that was impossible without confessing to having overheard his conversation with Jeremy.

Tilly watched his expression as he talked of his

plans. He was animated, excited and still exuding the fatal charm that had won her over when first they had met. She gazed fondly at him. After all, he had enriched her life, had cared for her in his own way . . . had spoilt her and had been a thoughtful and exciting lover. She really owed him a great deal and it broke her heart to know the risk he was taking.

'It all sounds wonderful,' she said as he waited for her opinion. 'And you are absolutely sure this is what you want to do?'

'Absolutely!' His eyes shone with excitement. He took her hand in his. 'Darling Tilly, we are going to have such a good life. We will travel round the country to all the race meetings. I intend to make a name for myself in racing circles and you will be there to share the glory with me.'

What could she say? She would have to go along with him until after Doncaster. Once that was over, then she would tell him about David. She felt she owed him that much. After all, it was only a matter of days. She could wait until then.

CHAPTER THIRTY-THREE

Frank Graves had been drinking all morning. He and Queenie had rowed the previous evening and he'd spent an uncomfortable night sleeping on the sofa, waking in a foul mood so late that he decided not to go to work. He had consequently done the rounds of the pubs before foolishly staggering into the Horse and Groom, where Queenie flatly refused to serve him and told him he could take his gear and move out of her flat.

In the next pub he visited, he sat morosely in a corner and picked up a copy of the local paper, in which he saw yet another article singing the praises of Eddie Chapman, who had made a donation to a children's home.

'Fucking Chapman!' he muttered. 'Look at the smarmy bastard, standing next to the mayor as if he had no skeletons in his cupboard. It's about time people knew the sort of man he really was.' He downed the last of his pint in a gulp, and stood up. Somewhat unsteady on his feet, he made his way to the door.

Eddie was standing outside his club talking to Detective Inspector John Ridgeway about the forthcoming police ball. He had just promised to supply some bottles of champagne for the raffle.

'Thanks,' said Ridgeway. 'It will be much appreciated. We have a good selection of prizes, thanks to the generosity of the local tradespeople. You will be coming yourself, won't you?'

'I wouldn't miss it for the world,' Eddie said. He shook Ridgeway's hand and turned to walk inside, so he didn't see Frank come round the corner . . . but he heard his voice.

'Eddie Chapman, you jumped-up bastard, I want a word with you. People should know about you and how you got your money!'

Eddie cursed under his breath as he saw that Ridgeway had stopped and was turning back as Frank approached. Glancing at the detective, Eddie said, 'Don't worry about it, I can handle him.'

But when Graves pulled a knife from his pocket and lunged at Chapman, who was able to dodge so that the weapon only ripped the sleeve of the jacket he was wearing and nicked his arm, the policeman stepped forward. 'No, Mr Chapman, this is now police business.'

It didn't take much to unarm Graves; he was too drunk to put up any defence.

'You're under arrest,' said Ridgeway, and read him his rights.

'Never mind arresting me, officer.' Graves pointed to Eddie. 'That's the bugger you should arrest. Do you know he knocked off a place in Woolwich and broke into their safe? That's where the bloody money to start his business came from.'

'I don't know what he's talking about!' Eddie exclaimed. 'The man's drunk.'

The detective cuffed Graves and bundled him into his car. 'I'm taking him to the station,' he said, and climbed into the driving seat.

Eddie watched him drive away, furious at the turn of events, cursing the fact that he hadn't removed Graves permanently instead of just having him beaten to teach him a lesson. The police would certainly listen to what the man had to say and would no doubt call him in for questioning; they would have to. Well, they had no proof. He had been very careful, not spending the stolen money for a long time – and then doing so slowly, as if his business was getting off the ground. There had been no fingerprints, he had made sure of that. He would just have to brazen it out.

*   *   *

When Ridgeway arrived at the police station with his charge, Graves was put in a cell and left to sober up. He immediately fell asleep on the wooden bench, covered with a blanket. When he woke he would be given a cup of coffee and then taken into an interview room to be questioned. Ridgeway was very curious about the statement made by Graves earlier and was determined to get to the bottom of the accusation.

Two days later, Eddie took a call from Ridgeway asking him to go to the station and help them with their inquiries. He readily agreed to do so – to have made a fuss would have been most unwise – but he did ask why.

'This man Graves has made some damning accusations against you, Mr Chapman, and of course we have to follow it up. I don't suppose it will take very long.'

'I'll be there in half an hour,' said Eddie. He sat at his desk going over in his mind what he was going to say, and when he had a clear picture of what that would be he walked out of the club.

John Ridgeway and another officer sat on one side of the table in the interview room and Eddie Chapman sat facing them, looking relaxed and interested.

'Now, Inspector, what's this all about?'

'Graves says that you were friends when you both lived in Woolwich. Is that true?'

'Yes, when we were both eighteen. We liked a game of snooker and used to play in a snooker hall most evenings, but that's all. We didn't socialise other than that.'

'What did you do for a living?'

'To begin with I had a stall where I sold all sorts of different goods to the public, then a shop became vacant and I rented it. It gave me more space for showing extra goods and at least if it rained outside it didn't matter, which suited me and my customers.'

'Graves insists that you knocked over a company together and stole the contents of the safe.'

'But that's ridiculous!'

'Your father was a locksmith, is that right?'

'Yes,' said Eddie. 'He had a small shop.'

'Did he pass on his skills to you?'

Chapman laughed. 'He did try, hoping that I would carry on the business for him, but I wasn't interested, Inspector. I was always more ambitious than my father. I didn't have the dexterity to begin with, or the interest.'

'You eventually opened your shop as a club, is that right?'

'True. I worked hard, saving my money until I

could afford to furnish it with second-hand stuff, then applied for a licence . . . and that's how I began. It took time, Inspector; this wasn't done overnight. I ran my shop for a year before opening the club.'

'So you deny having anything to do with this robbery?'

'Emphatically. The last I heard of Graves, until he turned up in Southampton a few months ago, was the evening I went to meet him at the snooker hall as usual and he didn't show. The barman told me he had been arrested for glassing someone in a public house when he was drunk.'

'So how could you afford to open up in Southampton, Mr Chapman?' asked Ridgeway, trying a different tack.

'I sold my club in Woolwich. It was doing well, so I got a good price for it. I wanted to better myself and moved here. A seaport town has good prospects. Seafarers have always got money to spend, and Southampton was thriving. I took my business plan to the bank and they liked what they saw. My life is an open book, Inspector. I worked hard to get where I am.'

'Have you any idea why Graves should make these accusations?'

'Jealousy, I suspect. I've done well and he hasn't. That doesn't sit well with him; he made that quite clear when first he came to visit me.'

'Was that when you gave him the money?'

'What money?'

'He says you gave him his half of the take from the robbery which you'd kept because he went to gaol before you could share the money stolen from the safe.'

Eddie laughed. 'He said he was broke. I gave him fifty quid and sent him on his way. I felt sorry for him, he'd had a tough time, but that was all. I told him not to come back for any more.'

'Why did you say that?'

'Because I was certain that he would ask me again for a handout. I'm not running a charity for a man who won't try to earn his own living. I've had to graft too hard for mine.'

Ridgeway looked across the table at him. 'Thank you for coming in, Mr Chapman, and for answering our questions. That's all for now. If I need anything else, I'll be in touch.'

Eddie got to his feet. 'That's all right. I'm only too pleased to be of help.'

The two policemen sat talking together after Chapman had left.

'What do you think, guv? Sounded reasonable to me.'

Ridgeway frowned. 'It was reasonable all right. Mr Chapman is a very smooth character – a little too smooth for my liking. There's something about

365

that man that niggles at me. Oh, he's charming and shrewd, but there's something going on behind those eyes of his when he's talking to you that just doesn't ring true.' He sat scratching his chin, deep in thought. 'I think we should take a trip to Woolwich, don't you?'

Eddie walked back to the club. He needed time to go over the last half-hour. The questions asked, the answers he had given. He came to the conclusion that it had gone well for him. Unlike Frank, he'd thought through his plans for the money. The police could check his story all they liked, but they would find that he'd been truthful with them. He had been patient with his ill-gotten gains, resisting the urge to splash out. It hadn't been easy, sitting on a small fortune. If only Frank Graves had been as cautious! The timing of all this couldn't have been worse, with the race at Doncaster coming up so soon, but Jeremy Frampton had assured him that he had everything covered. He hoped to God he was right.

He tried to put himself in Ridgeway's position. He would certainly check all the details he'd been given and Ridgeway was thorough, he was sure of that. Well, if he did so, it would take time, and by then the race with the ringer would be over.

He smiled softly as he thought that by trying to

implicate him Frank had put himself in the frame for the robbery. Maybe he would be sent down for it. That way the man would be out of his hair. In any case, he would be charged with assault with a deadly weapon, which should put him away for a while. Convinced that all would be well, Eddie returned to the club and his daily business, putting this morning's visit out of his mind.

CHAPTER THIRTY-FOUR

David Strickland was feeling very pleased with himself. He had just heard from the shipping company that he would be returning to his old ship, the *Aquitania*, after his teaching course was finished. He was delighted that he wasn't being moved to another ship, although he wouldn't have declined had that been the case. Crew members were often transferred between ships. He was just happy at the thought of returning to sea and passing the good news on to Tilly. He looked a little pensive. Had she come to a decision? Had she chosen to stay with Chapman or was she going to make her future with him? Well, there was only one way to find out. He would meet her when the shop closed and ask for her answer.

Tilly was about to lock up after closing when she saw David approaching. Seeing the determined look on his face, she guessed that he had heard from the shipping company and had come to ask for her decision. How could she make him understand that she had to wait a few days before telling Eddie that their affair was over? Unlocking the door, she beckoned to him.

When her staff had left and they were alone, she ushered him into the small room at the back of the changing rooms and made a pot of tea.

'How are you, David?'

'Well, thank you. I heard from the company today. I'm being sent back to the *Aquitania* when my teaching stint finishes.'

With obvious delight at the news, she said, 'That's wonderful. It's just what you hoped for – I'm so pleased for you.' She poured the tea, dreading his next question.

'I've come as promised to tell you my news; now I want to know what decision you have made about the future.' Taking a deep breath, he asked, 'Are you going to stay with Chapman or are you going to make me a very happy man?'

Gazing into his eyes, she said, 'It's you I want to be with, David.'

He pulled her gently towards him and kissed her softly. 'I can't tell you how much of a relief that is, darling. How did he take the news?'

She eased herself from his hold. 'I haven't told him yet.'

Frowning, David gave her a puzzled look. 'What

do you mean, you haven't told him – whyever not?'

'Please sit down, and I'll try to explain.' She sat opposite him. 'Eddie has a horse running at Doncaster in a few days' time. He's really excited because he's sure it's a winner and he can't wait to go into the winners' enclosure. He wants me to share the moment with him. I can't disappoint him as it means so much, and I feel I owe it to him to be there.'

David sat listening, a taut expression on his face. 'And when do you propose telling him that you're finished with him?'

'After the race, when he's had his moment of glory.' Seeing the grim expression on David's face, she pleaded, 'Please try to understand.'

'I am trying to,' he said coldly, 'but to be frank I'm finding it very difficult. What I can't accept is that having decided he wasn't to be your future, you didn't tell him straight away. You are being less than honest, don't you think?'

'What on earth do you mean?' She bristled with indignation.

'I assume you've seen him lately?'

'Yes. I was going to tell him the other day but he had to take a phone call just as I was about to.'

'How convenient!' His mouth narrowed into a tight line, and then he asked, 'Have you slept with him since we last spoke?'

'Convenient? It wasn't like that at all, it was just circumstances, the moment was lost. And no, of course I haven't slept with him!' It was true. Eddie had been so busy that he hadn't had time for any romantic interlude, for which Tilly had been more than grateful.

'Are you frightened of him, Tilly?'

'No, of course not! I have no reason to be.'

'How do you think he'll react when you do give him the bad news?'

Hesitating, she said, 'To be honest, I don't know.'

'Perhaps I should be there when you do.'

'Oh, no, David. I don't think that would be a good idea at all!' She felt sure Eddie would be incensed if that happened, and she wanted to handle this her way, making her announcement without acrimony, if possible. Truth to tell, she had no idea how Eddie was going to react and it did concern her, but she knew that if he saw David, waiting in the wings so to speak . . . well, it just wasn't right.

Getting out of his chair, David said, 'I'm really not happy about this, but I really don't have a choice, do I?'

Tilly rose from her seat and walked over to put her arms round him. 'Please, David, trust me. It's you I love. We have our whole future in front of us, I'm only asking you to wait a few days, that's all.'

He saw her expressive eyes pleading for his understanding, and holding her close to him he said, 'All right, but after the race it has to be over. Finally!'

'I promise. Now for goodness' sake kiss me!'

Which he did, very thoroughly.

As she watched David through the closed door, making his way to the tram stop, she wondered what he would have to say if he knew about the ringer. She hardly dared think about it. What if the duplicity was discovered on race day? What would happen to Eddie and Jeremy . . . would she be in trouble too just for being there with them? She wondered why Eddie had taken such a risk. He seemed financially secure: why did he want more? And more to the point, would he continue to break the law in the future? She now knew that he wasn't the man of high principles she had thought he was and she didn't want any part of it. It was time to bring their relationship to an end even if David hadn't been on the scene.

Jeremy Frampton was out on the gallops, watching his horses being exercised. Night and Day was running well, although not well enough to come anywhere in the race at Doncaster.

He had entered two other horses from the stables, which meant that the grooms would be travelling in the horsebox with them leaving him and the head lad, Larry, to go with Night and Day. Larry would lead the ringer round the paddock before the race. The jockey he'd booked was unable to ride out beforehand, so would not be aware of the change. The first time he would meet his mount would be at Doncaster. Jeremy had everything covered.

The starting price of Night and Day was twenty to one, even higher than he'd anticipated. He and Eddie had been carefully laying bets around several bookmakers so as not to cause the price to fall too much. On the day of the race, they would lay further bets on the course. Frampton rubbed his hands together in eager anticipation. This time they would both make a bundle!

Jago too had laid a few bets on the horse after Tilly had casually mentioned that she was off to Doncaster with Eddie Chapman, as the nightclub owner was expecting a good day. Jago was a bit puzzled by this, having studied the previous form of Night and Day, and under normal circumstances he wouldn't have put any money on it at all, but something urged him to do so. Eddie Chapman was a tricky chap and he wouldn't be so excited without reason.

*   *   *

Tilly was taken by surprise when Eddie told her they would be travelling to Doncaster the night before the race and staying in an hotel, thus ensuring that they could arrive at the course in good time. It meant she would be spending a night with him. No doubt he would wine and dine her before they retired, and would expect to make love to her. How could she let him? Especially when she was to tell him goodbye the next day. David would never forgive her if he knew. It was a dilemma.

Meanwhile, John Ridgeway and his sidekick had taken the train to London and then a bus to Woolwich, where the local police were being very helpful, showing them the reports on the robbery that Graves had told them about. Everything he'd told them checked out, even to the amount of money that was stolen. But then it had been reported in the local paper and Graves could have got the information from there and used it to implicate Chapman.

'It was a very neat job,' Ridgeway was told. 'The safe was picked by a professional. There was not a single fingerprint, other than those of the bank staff who had access to the safe.'

The two men also checked Eddie's story about his shop and the nightclub he'd opened on the same premises. Many of the shopkeepers from the area remembered Chapman.

'Hard-working lad,' they were told. 'He deserved to get on – he really was a grafter. Started with a barrow, moved into the shop. It took a while but then he opened the club.'

'Surely if he had the money he'd have spent it sooner to start his club,' said Ridgeway's partner.

'Unless he was very clever,' said Ridgeway. 'If he did it, we have absolutely no proof. Nor have we anything that puts Graves there.'

'But he admitted it.'

'Yes, I know, but how many times have people coughed for a murder they didn't commit? Without actual proof, it wouldn't stand up in court, but we do have him for assault with a deadly weapon. However, I will be keeping a closer eye on our Mr Chapman from now on. If he steps out of line, I'll have him.'

'You think he did it, don't you?'

'It's just a gut feeling but yes; I think that Graves is telling the truth. But, dammit, I can't prove it. Come on, we may as well go home.'

Friday found Eddie and Tilly on the train to Doncaster. She sat listening to him telling her about his horse and how they would be celebrating the next night. He was so thrilled at the prospect that she was worried. Should anything go wrong, he would be devastated.

'I'm so pleased you think Night and Day has a good chance, but you know that things happen. Remember when Rufus lost at Goodwood because he baulked at something?'

Taking her hand, he smiled. 'I know you mean well, darling, but I just have such a feeling about this horse. Of course the unexpected can always happen; we'll just have to keep our fingers crossed that he'll have a good race.' He leaned forward and kissed her softly. 'We will really celebrate. I feel I've neglected you of late; I've been so busy. Never mind, we have two nights together and I promise I'll make up for it.'

This was not what Tilly wanted to hear, and she wouldn't be spending two nights with Eddie, as tomorrow she would be returning to Southampton and David. It was just tonight she would have to cope with, and she had no idea what she was going to do. From the way Eddie gazed at her she knew he planned a night of passion and there was no way she could let that happen. That would really be dishonest.

When they arrived at Doncaster, they checked in to the hotel and followed the porter to their room. Eddie turned to her. 'I'm sorry, but I want to go to the racecourse and see that Night and Day has arrived safely. Do you mind?'

Breathing a sigh of relief she said, 'No, of course

not. I'll leave the unpacking and go for a stroll round the shops.'

He took out his wallet and made to give her some money, but she stopped him.

'I have money of my own. You forget I'm a businesswoman. I have my own cash.'

His eyes narrowed with displeasure for just a moment, but he was in a hurry to leave. Putting his wallet away he said, 'Very well. I like an independent woman, but not too much. You know I like to take care of you.' He kissed her cheek. 'I'll see you later.'

'Don't rush back,' she said. 'I'll be perfectly happy mooching about the shops.'

'Of course you will.' He smiled. 'I've never met a woman who isn't happy shopping.'

When she was alone, Tilly sat on the side of the bed. This was not going to be easy. She would have to find some excuse to keep Eddie at arm's length tonight and it would have to be believable.

Eddie Chapman arrived at the racecourse, paid off the taxi driver and made his way to the stables where the runners were being housed overnight. He walked along until he found Jeremy and the head lad, feeding the horse.

'Everything all right?' Eddie asked.

'Fine,' said Jeremy. 'Everything went smoothly.

The grooms are looking after my other runners, so Larry and I are looking after Night and Day.' He winked slyly.

Eddie stroked the animal, who snuffled as he ate the hay as if to say *Leave me alone, I'm eating*.

The two men walked outside and, lighting cigarettes, talked in low voices.

'I've laid several small bets around Southampton, at twenty to one,' said Eddie.

'I've done the same at home,' said the trainer. 'Tomorrow on the course, do the same with the bookies and the tote. But do it quickly as eventually the price must fall once they realise money is being spent on Night and Day.'

'Won't that cause concern with the officials?'

'If it does, what can they prove? Trainers make their money from backing their own horses and their friends are bound to bet on a horse they know. By tomorrow, this animal will be back in its stable and the real Night and Day in his. We'll run him a couple of times and then I'll sell him on and after a while bring Flying Flynn in under his real name.'

'Well, I'd best be off. I'll see you tomorrow before the race.' The men shook hands and Eddie left the trainer in search of a taxi to take him back to the hotel – and Tilly.

CHAPTER THIRTY-FIVE

During dinner that evening, Tilly discovered why Eddie needed more money as he told her of his plans to build up the stables, making them tempting to reputable owners with horses which would make the stud a name to be reckoned with.

'I want to put up state-of-the-art stables, clean up the yard, construct better gallops. Jeremy is an excellent trainer with a fine reputation, and will do well if everything else is in place for him to show new clients.'

Not if he's discovered running a ringer, Tilly thought, and again was appalled at how much Eddie was putting at risk.

'The clubs are doing well,' he continued. 'I have good managers so it will be easy for me to concentrate on racing.' He took her hand in his and kissed her fingers. 'We are going to live the high life, Tilly darling. Mixing with the best people. There is a lot of money to be made in racing, if you have the horses – and if you're smart.'

'But surely it's very expensive?'

Laughing, he said, 'Oh yes, but after tomorrow we will be able to put all my plans into action, and then we can sit back while the right owners come banging on our doors.'

Tilly thought, I know nothing about racing, but surely owners who have been with one trainer for some time are not going to leave them and move? It didn't make sense to her. It was the same with jockeys. She'd noticed, when reading her race card at various meetings, that the same jockeys often rode for the same trainers. But Eddie was so certain of himself, she didn't voice her concerns.

'Tomorrow at the racecourse, I'll give you some money to lay some bets for me,' he told her. 'I'll tell you how much to bet with the tote and how much to bet with the bookies. We want to get the money on Night and Day while the price is right.'

'What do you mean, while the price is right?'

'Because the more money is laid out the lower the price will fall,' he explained. 'So we will need to do it fairly quickly.'

Tilly wondered if that was wise. Wouldn't it give the authorities cause for concern? But she said nothing, not wanting Eddie to know she knew of his play. She couldn't wait for the race to be over, when she could leave and go back to Southampton and to David. Darling David who, despite every-thing, was waiting for her.

After the meal, which Tilly had purposely picked at, they drank their coffee leisurely, with a glass of brandy.

Eddie said, 'I think it's time for bed, don't you? We have a big day ahead of us.'

Tilly's heart sank.

They had dined at a restaurant near to the hotel, and when Eddie had paid the bill Tilly said casu-ally, 'Could we walk back to the hotel, do you think? I've not felt well this evening and I could do with some fresh air.'

He was immediately concerned. 'Was that why you didn't eat much?'

Nodding, she said, 'Yes, my stomach feels a little upset. I thought the brandy might settle it, but to be truthful I feel nauseous.'

'Come along then, darling. I don't want you to miss our big day tomorrow.' He ushered her outside.

When eventually they reached their room, Tilly rushed to the bathroom and put her finger down her throat to make herself sick. She stayed there for a while, cleaning her teeth and drinking water.

Eddie knocked on the door. 'Tilly, are you all right?'

She walked back into the bedroom.

Putting an arm round her, Eddie said, 'Poor darling, I had no idea. Come along, get undressed and into bed. I'll get a glass of water and put it beside you on the table.'

'I'm so sorry,' she said. 'Perhaps a good night's sleep will make me feel better.'

'Let's hope so. Now come along, I'll go and have a bath while you tuck yourself up.'

Breathing a sigh of relief, Tilly quickly undressed and slipped between the sheets. A little later, Eddie climbed into bed beside her and leaned over to kiss her cheek. 'This wasn't quite the night I planned,' he teased, 'but you try to sleep. I'll call you in the morning.

Turning her back on him, Tilly snuggled down, thanking her lucky stars that she had been able to convince him. But she wondered just what tomorrow would bring.

The next morning, Eddie sent for a tray of coffee and some dry toast as Tilly had said she was feeling a little better but still unwell, to allay any thought of lovemaking on his part.

It was a bright autumnal day with a breeze. Knowing how cold it could be on a racecourse, Tilly wore a light woollen dress with a long coat trimmed with fur. Pulling a cloche hat over her head, she felt sure she would be warm enough. As she said to Eddie, 'The last thing I need is to catch a chill.'

A taxi took them to the course. It was thronged with punters out for a good day's racing. The bookies were set up beside the course ready to take the money from people they hoped had backed losers.

Eddie and Tilly made their way to the stables first of all, to take a look at the supposed Night and Day and have a word with Jeremy Frampton.

'Everything all right?' asked Eddie anxiously.

With a broad grin, Jeremy said, 'Fine. The horse had a good night and is raring to go. I'll see you in the parade ring before the race.' The two men shook hands.

The horse was entered in the three o'clock race. Eddie gave Tilly two separate bundles of one hundred pounds and told her to put one with the bookies on Night and Day to win, and the other at the tote just before the race was run. Until then they made their way to the box that he had booked.

Both of them won a little money on the first two races and then they left to lay their bets.

'I'll see you in the parade ring,' he told her as they parted. 'Today, darling, we will clean up!'

It was with some trepidation that Tilly did as she was asked, wondering if by so doing she was as guilty as the men, knowing a ringer was being run. But what could she do, other than report what was going on to the Jockey Club? And she certainly couldn't bring herself to do that.

Eventually, clutching the betting stubs, she made her way to the paddock. She could see Eddie and Frampton in the centre as the horses were being paraded for the public to see, and choose which one they fancied.

As she joined them, Jeremy was giving the jockey his instructions.

'Don't rush him; keep a steady pace to begin with. Watch out for Jack the Lad, he wanders about a bit and could jump across your path, so you give him a wide berth. Let him have his head at the last two furlongs. He always keeps a bit in his tank if you don't push him in the early stages and he has a great finishing speed. Good luck.'

He gave the jockey a leg up and Larry led him out of the ring and on to the racecourse.

Eddie and Tilly returned to their box to watch the race.

Tilly's heart was beating as she watched through her binoculars while in the far distance the horses lined up at the start. Turning to look at Eddie, she saw a tic in his jaw and knew that he too was nervous and excited.

'They're off!' the crowd cried.

Tilly thought she would faint with excitement as she watched the race. Keeping to his instructions, the jockey held his mount in check, jumping cleanly, well away from the wandering Jack the Lad, until the final two furlongs when Night and Day gradually moved up the field, clearing each jump until he was in third place with the last three jumps ahead. He cleared the first one alongside the favourite, and pulled just ahead on the second. At the third and final jump, he was in the lead with the favourite close on his heels.

Tilly, Eddie and the crowd were cheering and yelling at the tops of their voices as Night and Day galloped to the winning post, finishing half a length in front.

Eddie threw his race card in the air, picked Tilly up and swung her round.

'We did it!' he cried and kissed her. 'Come along, darling. We are going to the winners' enclosure. The first time of many!'

They arrived in time to see Larry and Jeremy leading the horse in, Jeremy beaming all over his face.

As the jockey jumped down, Eddie pumped his hand. 'Well done, what a bloody fine race! Thank you.' Turning, he hugged Jeremy Frampton. 'We did it, we bloody well did it.'

The horse was unsaddled and the jockey went

to the weighing room after standing with Eddie, Jeremy and the winning horse for press photographs.

'The price dropped to three to one,' Jeremy told Eddie quietly. 'I hope you got your money on at a good price?'

'Oh, yes!' Eddie laughed. 'We can now carry on with our plans.'

Larry, having covered the horse with a blanket, was walking him round to calm him, patting his neck and talking to him. 'I'll get him back to the stables as quickly as possible,' Jeremy said quietly. 'We don't want anything to go wrong now, do we?'

'Absolutely not!' Eddie agreed.

Shortly afterwards Eddie, accompanied by Tilly, proudly stepped forward to accept the winner's trophy. He beamed from ear to ear as more photos were taken.

Clutching his trophy, Eddie put his arm round Tilly's shoulder and hugged her. 'Today has fulfilled a dream for me,' he told her gleefully. 'I'll just go and put this away safely and then I'll go and collect my winnings. You go and collect yours now. I'll see you back upstairs.'

Tilly joined the queue at the tote. As the man counted out a wad of notes, he grinned at her. 'You had a lucky race, miss. Good luck to you.'

She put the cash in her bag and made her way through the throng of people in front of the grandstand. Finding her bookie, she handed over the betting slip.

The bookie, his features weathered from years in the open, was grim as he counted out the money. He looked at Tilly and said, 'An unlikely winner. Did you have inside information, perhaps?'

'No. I liked the name,' she said quickly.

'Women!' he exclaimed as he handed over the money.

Tilly felt her cheeks redden with embarrassment. Thrusting the bundle of notes in her bag with the others, she walked hurriedly away.

She returned to the box where Eddie was waiting, pacing the room. Champagne was opened and the winnings put on the table.

'We have over four thousand pounds here,' he said, 'enough to pay for all my plans.' As he clinked glasses with Tilly he said, 'I was so very pleased you were here today. Success is wonderful, but not unless you can share it with someone special, and you are very special to me, Tilly darling.'

She didn't know what to say. Eddie was so thrilled and happy and she was going to spoil his special day. But before she could say anything, he put his glass down. Taking hers from her, he placed it on the table. Then, holding her hands in his, he gazed into her eyes. Leaning forward, he kissed her gently.

'I don't want to start my new venture without you. I want you beside me, always. Darling, will you make this day complete – will you marry me?'

CHAPTER THIRTY-SIX

Tilly could not believe that Eddie Chapman had just proposed to her. This urbane man, someone she had always felt was sufficient unto himself, able to do without others except when he wished otherwise, which would only ever be on a temporary basis. She was speechless.

Seeing her consternation, Eddie started to laugh.

'Gracious!' he said. 'I've never seen anyone look so shocked. Surely by now you must know how I feel about you?'

'But marriage?' she managed to answer. 'I didn't think that was in your future plans at all.'

He placed his hands on her shoulders and gazing into her eyes said softly, 'To be honest, darling, it wasn't . . . to begin with, but now it just seems so right. I do love you, Tilly. I've only just realised that. Me! Who always thought I could live without a permanent woman in my life.'

'Eddie, please stop!' she beseeched him, trying to

halt this declaration of his feelings, knowing that she was going to hurt him and not wanting to.

'No, you must listen to me,' he said.

'Eddie, I can't marry you!' It was not the way she wanted to tell him, but she couldn't let him continue.

He looked stunned. 'What do you mean?'

Tilly could feel her heart pounding. 'I'm so sorry, but I cannot marry you.'

He released his hold. 'Why ever not?'

'Because I'm in love with someone else.'

Coldly he said, 'What do you mean? You came with me yesterday, last night we shared a bed . . . and now you tell me you are in love with someone else.' His anger grew. 'What sort of game are you playing?'

'I am not playing games.' This was much harder than she had thought it would be. 'I didn't want to tell you before the race, knowing how much it meant to you.'

'So when were you going to allow me to share your feelings?' His tone was quiet – and deadly.

'After the race was over. Then I was going to tell you.' She tried to soften the blow and at the same time make him understand. 'I *am* very fond of you.'

He snorted with indignation.

'You have been such an influence – taught me

so much, spoiled me, shown me a wonderful way of life . . .'

'But obviously not wonderful enough to make you want to share it with me!' he interrupted. 'And who is this man with whom you are so in love . . . or need I ask?'

'David Strickland.'

'The engineer! So Greta was right about seeing you together. She said you looked very cosy.' He walked away, then turned back to her. 'That was some time ago,' he said accusingly, 'and yet you've stayed with me until today. Perhaps you can explain why?'

'David told me I had to choose between you both. He gave me time to make up my mind.'

'What took you so long?' His voice was like shafts of ice.

'I felt I owed you so much,' she said. 'You bought me a business, you treated me so well, I felt guilty about leaving you.'

'Oh, for God's sake! Are you saying you stayed with me out of duty? That really is an insult!'

'No! It's not like that at all,' she cried. 'I do have deep feelings for you, Eddie. Please believe that.'

He shook his head in disbelief. Picking up his glass of champagne he drank the contents and poured another. 'I'm pleased to hear that, because of course I can't let you go.'

'What do you mean?'

'This engineer can't give you the life that I can, and what's more I need you! You are an integral part of my plans. This was such a perfect day; I can't begin to forgive you for spoiling it. How could you do this to me, Tilly?'

'I came to support you because I *am* so fond of you – even though I knew you were running a ringer!'

'What?' His expression changed immediately. Now he was watchful and suspicious.

'I overheard your conversation on the telephone with Jeremy Frampton. I knew it wasn't Night and Day running today, but I still placed your bets for you. That makes me an accessory to a crime. I did that for *you*, Eddie. Now we're quits!'

'Quits, nothing! Have you told anyone else about this?'

'Of course not.'

He looked relieved. 'All the more reason for you to stay with me.'

'What on earth do you mean?'

'Well, darling, I can't have you running around out of my jurisdiction with such damning information. That wouldn't do at all.'

'I wouldn't tell anyone. Why would I? If I did, I would be in trouble with the law too.'

Pulling out a chair, he sat down and with an

enigmatic smile said, 'You know, you still are able to surprise me. You are devious, Tilly. I would never have believed it of you.'

'What do you mean, devious?'

'You decide to leave me for someone else, but you still carry on our affair. Let me make love to you, and enjoy it if my memory serves me right.'

His accusation angered her. 'We haven't made love since I decided. You've been too busy lately, so I haven't been devious.'

'Be honest, Tilly, had I not been busy, what would you have done? You said you wanted me to have my day of glory first, before you broke this news to me. You couldn't have been sick every time.'

'That's not fair!' she exclaimed.

He started laughing. 'You really are extraordinary to think you can get away with this. I'm sure your engineer would be furious to know we shared a bed last night.'

'But nothing happened!'

'You think he would believe that? Your naivety is one of your appealing traits, but believe me, no man would credit it – or accept it.'

She was lost for words. How could she tell David they had shared a room last night? He would be furious. There was a lot of truth in what Eddie had said.

Rising from his seat, Eddie walked over to her and took her in his arms. 'Forget those silly dreams. Together we are going to do great things – have a wonderful time.' He tilted her chin and kissed her slowly and thoroughly, working his magic as always, until she found herself responding, despite everything.

'You see,' he whispered, 'we are so good together. You wouldn't be content being the wife of a seafarer, darling. I know you too well. You crave excitement in your life and I give you that. If you lived an everyday existence, you'd be bored in a month.'

'That's not true!'

He gripped her tightly. 'It damned well is, however much you deny it, but no matter. You are staying with me. I won't let you go. Come on, I've had enough excitement for one day. Let's go back to the hotel, pick up our things and go home.'

Tilly felt it was the only thing to do for the moment. Once she was back in Southampton, she could sort everything out.

Jeremy Frampton and his head lad loaded their horse into the box and drove to Flying Flynn's stable, where they bedded him down and exchanged horses, taking the real Night and Day back to the yard where he was greeted by the staff with great excitement. His groom, who had been looking after the other mounts from the stable during the meeting, said to Frampton, 'I watched the race. I couldn't believe it when I saw him cross the finishing line. It was as if he was a different horse.' He stroked the animal's neck and talked lovingly to it.

Frampton was relieved that no one had been suspicious at the result. The fact that the yard had won a race was uppermost in their minds. He was delighted, because tomorrow he would collect his winnings from the betting shops nearby to add to the money he'd won at the track. Things were looking good.

Jago, too, was pleased with the result as he had a hefty bet on the horse at twenty to one and he was in the money, but he still couldn't understand how the horse had improved so much. He hadn't done particularly well at any previous meeting. He was deeply suspicious. And when Tilly walked into the house that evening, he said as much.

'I had a few quid on your boyfriend's horse at Doncaster,' he told her. 'I made a small bundle.'

Tilly became watchful. 'Good for you,' she said.

'I'm amazed,' said Jago. 'Night and Day hasn't had much form in his last few races.'

'Well, I don't understand such things,' she said. 'I'm tired, it's been a long day and I'm off to bed.'

But Jago knew his sister very well, and there was something on her mind.

'You all right, Tilly?' he asked.

She didn't look at him but picked up her case. 'Where's Mum and Dad?'

'Gone to the pub for a beer. I gave them a couple of quid out of my winnings. I'm just off to join them before closing time. Want to come along?'

'No thanks. See you tomorrow.'

In her room, she flung herself on the bed. What a mess she'd made of everything. If only she hadn't told Eddie about the race. She should have kept her knowledge about the ringer to herself. Now he would never let her go; he had made that quite clear. What was she going to say to David? He would be expecting her to have sorted everything and she was still involved with Eddie. What was she to do?

The following day was Sunday. Joe had gone to feed Clarence, Ethel was working and Jago was making a fresh pot of tea after he and Tilly had finished their breakfast when there was a knock at the door.

'I'll go,' said Jago.

Moments later, he returned with David Strickland in his wake.

Tilly felt her stomach tighten as David smiled at her and kissed her cheek. She knew he had come to see her, expecting good news.

The three of them sat chatting over their tea until David asked Tilly to go for a walk with him. 'It's a lovely morning,' he said. 'I thought a stroll down to the pier might be nice.'

There was no way she could escape the inevitable questions.

When they arrived at their destination, David paid their penny entrance and they strolled along the pier until he suggested they sit on one of the wooden benches beside the railings.

'We need to talk,' he said. Once settled, he put an arm along her shoulders and asked, 'How did things go with you and Eddie Chapman?'

She didn't know where to begin. 'Mmm . . . It was an exciting day,' she told him. 'Eddie's horse won the race. He was thrilled.'

He looked at her with impatience. 'And?'

'And after . . .' She hesitated.

'Oh, for God's sake, Tilly! Did you tell him you had finished with him or not?'

'Yes. Yes, I did.'

He looked relieved.

'But it was all very difficult,' she said.

Frowning, he asked, 'Why was it difficult?'

She took a deep breath. 'Because he had just asked me to marry him.'

'What?' He looked shocked and then angry. 'The bastard! And what did you say to him then?'

'I told him I couldn't marry him because I was in love with you.'

Breathing a sigh of relief, David leaned forward and kissed her cheek. 'Thank God for that. You had me worried for a minute. How did he take it?'

She felt the blood drain from her face. 'He said he wouldn't let me go,' she said in barely a whisper, 'and then we came home.'

'That reminds me,' David said. 'I rang the shop on Friday but they said you had left for Doncaster.'

'Yes. We went the day before the race to be at the course in good time for yesterday's racing.'

'So you stayed overnight?'

She just nodded, knowing that she was in trouble.

'Where did you stay?'

'In a hotel.'

He sat deep in thought for a moment, and then turning to her he said, 'But you didn't tell him about us until after the race, right?'

She didn't answer.

He held her by her chin, making her look at

him. 'Did you share a room with him?' he asked sternly. 'After all, if he didn't know about us, I assume that he would have booked a double room.'

'Yes . . . but nothing happened,' she added quickly.

He was enraged. 'Knowing that you were leaving him, you still shared his bed? How could you do that?'

'I pretended to be sick. He didn't touch me, I promise.'

His face was as if carved from stone. 'Are you saying he didn't hold you in his arms . . . even to comfort you?'

Tilly closed her eyes, trying to shut out the accusing look on David's face.

'Well did he?' he demanded

She was beside herself. 'What does it matter? He didn't make love to me!'

'How can you sit there and say that? Of course it bloody well matters! And I only have your word that nothing happened.'

Eddie was right, she thought. David didn't believe her. She was distraught.

'David, David, please believe me. I love you.'

'So much that you shared another man's bed!' He stood up. 'Well, it's now perfectly clear to me that we have no future together. I am really sorry, Tilly. I had such high hopes for us.'

'What are you saying?'

'You are obviously still infatuated with this man, and I'm wasting my time. I hope you'll both be very happy together.'

She watched him walk away, silent tears trickling down her cheeks.

CHAPTER THIRTY-SEVEN

Tilly sat for some time alone on the pier, steeped in misery, unaware of the hungry seagulls, calling as they swooped down looking for food, or the families strolling together, catching the last warmth of autumn. All she could think of was the fact that she had lost the man she loved. What a fool she had been. Eddie Chapman had fascinated her from their first meeting. Her infatuation for him had changed her life and cost her dearly. She had no one to blame but herself, her craving for excitement, wanting to live for the moment. What would happen to her now? David would return to his life at sea, and she supposed she would just go on. After all, she had her business to run: that would keep her occupied. Eddie at least said he needed her. But marriage? Well, that was a different thing. She gave a wry smile. It would at least silence the gossips!

Getting to her feet, she walked slowly to the end of the pier and looked out over the ships in the dock. Her heart ached when she thought that

David would soon be sailing away on one such liner and out of her life for ever. She couldn't blame him, not really. If the tables had been turned, how would she have felt? As for her future now, she really didn't have a choice. By laying out Eddie's money at the racecourse, she had become part of the conspiracy. What a fool she had been!

She wandered back towards the exit, gazing at the couples strolling arm in arm, now aware of the family groups, the playing children. She didn't know when she had felt more alone. She longed for someone to hold her, to comfort her. Eddie at least wanted her. Yes, she would go to him. He should still be at the flat above the club, probably dreaming of his plans for the stud.

As she walked, she persuaded herself that it wouldn't be such a bad existence. Eddie was good to her, and he had said he loved her, and at that moment she really needed to feel loved.

Arriving at the entrance to the club, she rang the bell and waited. Eventually she heard footsteps . . . and the door opened.

'Tilly, darling! This is a pleasant surprise. Come in.' Eddie Chapman stepped back. They walked up the stairs to his living room. 'Would you like some coffee?'

'Yes, thank you, I would.'

As he made the coffee, Eddie glanced over at

her and seeing her unusually sad expression said, 'You've seen the engineer then?'

'How do you know that?'

He carried two cups of steaming coffee over to the table and sat down. 'He didn't believe your story, did he?'

She shook her head. 'No, and don't you dare say I told you so!'

He rose from his chair and stooped down beside her. 'I wouldn't be so cruel.' Taking her hand in his, he kissed it and said, 'Never mind, darling, you'll be glad in the long run.'

She looked at him with eyes that pleaded for reassurance. 'Will I really? Do you promise?'

He stood up and pulled her into his arms. 'Oh, my poor Tilly.' He kissed the top of her forehead. 'You are so grown up sometimes and sometimes you are like a small child.' Cuddling her, he put her head on his shoulder, holding her even more closely as he tried to comfort her. 'You will learn that sometimes in life the thing we want most of all is often unobtainable.'

She felt the tears trickle down her cheek. Then, looking up at him, she asked, 'Will we really be happy together?'

'Of course we will!' he said, brushing aside her tears and kissing her gently. 'We are going to have a great time, you'll see.'

With a worried frown she said, 'Promise me that you will never again do anything unlawful, like Doncaster.'

She felt him stiffen. 'It was extremely unfortunate that you were a party to that, Tilly,' he said coldly, 'but you cannot make demands on me. No one makes decisions in my life but me.'

'I'm sorry,' she said firmly, 'but if you want me to be a part of your life, I have to know that nothing like that will ever happen again!'

'Hopefully, there won't be the need,' he said. 'Thanks to Doncaster, we have the finance we want.'

He hadn't said no, and that worried her.

'Come along,' he said, 'I'll take you out to lunch – we'll go and celebrate. We'll go to the Cowherds, and afterwards we'll walk by the lake and feed the ducks. We'll save some bread rolls and take them with us.'

Tilly knew that the subject was now closed and she would have to be satisfied that she had made her feelings on the matter very clear. She also knew that Eddie Chapman would do whatever was necessary to succeed, without recourse to her. Well so be it, but she wouldn't be rushed into marriage, and that was something where he would have to defer to her!

*   *   *

It was November and the roar from the funnels of the *Aquitania* signalled her departure. In the engine room, the noise from the turbines was deafening. Wiping the sweat from his forehead, David Strickland read the dials in front of him. At last the ship was on its way, leaving Southampton and Tilly Thompson behind. These past months had been a nightmare, ever since he had walked out of her life. He was just pleased to be back at sea. At least here he was in a world that he understood, where everything was ordered and busy, and there wasn't too much time to think.

But after dinner when he was off duty and walking the boat deck, wrapped up in his overcoat, collar up to keep out the chill wind, he couldn't keep the vision of Tilly out of his mind. He moved to a staircase to be sheltered from the wind and lit a cigarette. What would she be doing now, he wondered? Whatever it was it would be with Eddie Chapman! His mouth tightened in an angry line. That bloody man! He had ruined everything. He hoped to God he didn't ruin Tilly too.

He had been livid when he discovered that she had slept with Chapman. He still didn't understand how she could have, knowing that he loved her and vowing that she felt the same. How could he trust her after that?

The officer of the watch came along and joined him in his small haven.

'Cold night, sir. You all right?'

'Fine,' said David. 'Just had to get some fresh air, but I've had enough. I'm off to the comfort of my cabin.'

'Don't blame you,' said the man.

David rang for the night steward and asked for a tray of tea. He tried to read but couldn't concentrate, so he decided to turn in. After all, he was on an early watch in the morning. But dreams of Tilly with Chapman gave him a fitful night.

The past few months had been busy at the stud yard. New stables were being built and new gallops were being dug. Both Eddie and Jeremy Frampton watched their dream taking shape. Two runners trained by Frampton had won their races, which lifted the morale of the staff and helped the coffers. Night and Day had been run at a small meeting and had finishing seventh. But Jeremy was having trouble with Larry, his head lad, who had taken to the bottle. Larry had always liked a drink and Frampton had been aware of that, but until now it had never interfered with his work. Jeremy had warned him twice, and Larry had become belligerent and cocky.

In the tack room the two men faced each other. 'You can't fire me, boss. I know too much.'

Grabbing Larry by the front of his coat, Jeremy shoved him up against the wall. 'Don't you try to threaten me, you little tyke. You've made good money all the time you've worked for me and don't you forget it! Any more trouble from you and you'll be out on your ear, and then who will employ you?'

Glaring at his employer, Larry said nothing more. He straightened his coat and stomped out of the room.

Later that day, when Eddie Chapman called to check on progress, Jeremy told him of his problem. 'The little bugger has got too big for his boots.'

Eddie was immediately concerned. 'I don't like it,' he said. 'If he spills the beans over Doncaster then we're in deep trouble.'

'Don't you worry about him. He was too involved himself to do anything about it.'

But Eddie wasn't convinced. 'An angry drunk is a dangerous thing.'

'And a drunken lad is a danger to a yard! I won't have it. Unless he mends his ways, he'll have to go.'

Eddie didn't need to be told about dangerous drunks; he'd had enough of that with Frank Graves. The man had been sent down for eighteen months for attacking him, and the inquiries into the job in Woolwich had died a natural death through lack of evidence. But Larry was a different kettle of fish. Paying him off wouldn't work; he would come back again and again, milking them. An unfortunate accident would be the answer to their prayers, he mused. He was obsessed with his plans and nothing was going to spoil them. Nothing – and certainly not a little whippersnapper like Larry.

It was Tilly's twentieth birthday and Eddie planned a special treat for her. They went by train to London where he took her shopping, then to a show and finally to dinner at a fine hotel where he had booked a room for the night.

The dining room was palatial, with beautiful chandeliers, sumptuous furnishings and attentive staff. The food had been delicious. They were drinking their coffee and liqueurs when Eddie took from his pocket a long black velvet case and handed it to her. 'Happy birthday, darling.'

With a cry of delight, she opened it and gasped when she saw inside an exquisite emerald bracelet.

'Oh, Eddie, it's beautiful. Thank you so much.' She leaned forward and kissed him.

'Nothing is too good for my lady,' he said. 'Are you happy, Tilly?'

'But of course,' she said, somewhat puzzled by his question. 'Why do you ask?'

'Because I love you and I want to know that I make you as happy as you make me.'

She gazed at him with great affection. 'Of course you make me happy.' And it was true. He was generous, a wonderful lover, and usually considerate, although he still made demands on her time. But he was kind to her. She did love him in her own way, even if it wasn't like the love she felt for David Strickland, who still held first place in her heart.

'I am so glad you said that,' Eddie said, 'because I think it's time to put our relationship on a more formal basis.' He reached into his pocket again and placed a small box on the table, opened it and took out a diamond solitaire. Taking her left hand in his, he slipped the ring on her finger and smiling said, 'Now we are officially engaged.'

Tilly looked at the ring sparkling in the light. She didn't know what to say. She looked up at him and said, 'It's lovely . . . and so unexpected.'

'I'm not sure when we can have the wedding, darling. Things at the yard are taking up my time at the moment and I want us to go away, maybe to the south of France, for our honeymoon, but it will have to wait a while. Do you mind?'

'Of course not,' she quickly told him. Marriage

to Eddie wasn't something she was at all sure she wanted. But she couldn't tell him that. She had mostly recovered from the unhappiness caused by David's leaving her, and she was happy, to a degree, with Eddie, but she honestly couldn't see herself spending her future with him as his wife. It just didn't feel right. Ridiculous though it seemed, she could accept being his mistress, because there was a certain feeling of freedom attached to that. Her reputation was in shreds, but that didn't really worry her. What those close to her thought was the only thing that mattered and her family had now accepted her situation. Being a wife sounded so permanent. It didn't sit well with her at all.

When she arrived home the following evening and sat at the table to eat her supper with her family, Ethel was the first one to notice the ring.

'So he's going to make an honest woman of you at last, is he?'

'Thank you, Mother, for your congratulations,' Tilly said sarcastically.

Joe glowered at his wife. 'Ethel!' he admonished her. To Tilly he smiled and said, 'Congratulations, love. I hope you'll both be very happy. When's the wedding?'

'Don't know, Dad. Eddie is very busy at the moment, but there's no rush.'

'Will he be coming to ask me for your hand in marriage?'

Chuckling, Tilly said, 'I've no idea.'

'Well, he's had the rest, so he might as well have her hand too!' snapped her mother.

'That's enough, Ethel,' retorted her husband. He turned to Tilly. 'I'll be very proud to lead you down the aisle to the altar, my girl.'

Jago, who had been silent until now, asked, 'Is this really what you want, Tilly?'

'Whatever do you mean?'

'Are you in love with Eddie Chapman?'

'Well, I'm going to marry him, aren't I!'

'That's not what I asked,' persisted Jago. 'If David was to walk through the door now and make it up with you, would you still want to marry Chapman?'

Tilly could feel the tears welling in her eyes. 'You are a bastard, Jago, you really are!' She got up from the table and rushed up the stairs to her bedroom, slamming the door behind her.

'That wasn't very kind of you, son,' said Joe. 'After all, David isn't around, is he?'

'More's the pity,' Jago said. 'I'm off to the pub for a drink.'

Joe sat beside the fire, chewing on his pipe. He felt that his Tilly was making a mistake. He was certain she still had feelings for that nice young engineer. But he had no idea what had broken them up, and now the lad was away at sea. To his mind they made an ideal couple. Eddie Chapman was all right, he supposed, but he wasn't the man for Tilly. Alas, there was nothing he could do about it, but she was a strong-minded girl and she would sort herself out . . . at least he hoped she would.

CHAPTER THIRTY-EIGHT

Christmas was approaching and Tilly was doing great business with her selection of evening dresses, which were much in demand by the wives of important town dignitaries for the various dinners and dances to be held to celebrate the festive season.

She herself was in a quandary. Christmas had always been a family affair, but this year Eddie had told her they would be spending the holiday in a hotel in London. When she had protested and suggested he might like to stay in Southampton, visiting her family, and eating with them on Christmas day, he had declined very definitely.

'I'm not into family gatherings,' he told her. 'Good God, I don't even visit my parents. I send them a cheque to spend as they wish.'

'Well I'm not like that,' Tilly protested. 'Being with the family means a great deal to me, and frankly staying in a hotel surrounded by strangers is not *my* idea of Christmas.'

'But you'll be with me.'

She stared defiantly at him. 'But I won't be with my family. I'm sorry, Eddie, but I won't do it. I will be staying at home.'

'You seem to forget that you are my fiancée. We should be together.'

'And if you join me at home, we will be!' She would not be moved.

He was furious that she wouldn't fall in with his plans. 'But I want you with me,' he insisted.

'Then you will be disappointed. Remember, you once said to me that you can't have everything you want in life. This is important to me.'

'And what am I supposed to do?'

'The choice is yours. We can be together here or you can do whatever you wish.' And she walked away.

It was Christmas Eve and the atmosphere between Eddie and Tilly had been strained since her declaration. He expected her to change her mind, and she was adamant that she wouldn't. At the end of the day, she locked up the shop and walked home.

Through her business, Tilly was in a position, financially, to help her mother with buying the food for the holiday. This year they would eat really well, with lots of special treats.

'Will Eddie Chapman be joining us?' Ethel had asked.

'I don't think so, Mum. He wanted to spend Christmas in London at some hotel, but I didn't want to be away from you all. He doesn't do families, he said.'

Ethel raised her eyebrows. 'Families are the backbone of life,' she said. 'But then we don't know too much about his family life, do we?'

'No. He doesn't talk about his parents very much.'

'What a shame,' said Ethel. 'Well, he would have been made welcome, I'm sure you know that.'

Tilly hugged her mother. 'I know. Come on, I'll help you prepare the vegetables and then I've presents to wrap.'

Whilst they were peeling the potatoes, Jago walked in. 'I've brought a visitor,' he said, grinning broadly.

Tilly and Ethel stopped what they were doing and looked at the uniformed figure walking through the doorway.

'David!' Tilly felt the blood drain from her cheeks and she grabbed the kitchen sink to steady herself.

'Hello, Tilly, Mrs Thompson. Merry Christmas!'

Wiping her hands on her apron, Ethel walked over to him and shook hands. 'When did you get back?'

'Yesterday. The ship is in dry dock for six weeks. I met Jago in the local and he insisted I come round. I do hope you don't mind?'

'Of course not,' said Ethel. 'Sit down and I'll make us a cup of tea.'

'Never mind that,' said Jago. 'It's Christmas Eve – let's celebrate.' And he produced a bottle of Scotch. 'I'll just get some glasses.'

At that moment Joe walked in. 'David! What a surprise.' He pumped his hand. 'You're looking well, son.'

'He's just docked yesterday, Dad,' Jago informed him. 'He's home for six weeks whilst his ship has her bottom scraped.'

'Have you any plans for Christmas?' asked Joe.

'No, Mr Thompson, I've not had time to make any, and I have to be on watch some of the time.'

'Then you must spend it with us, mustn't he, Ethel?'

Tilly's heart sank. She was absolutely speechless. David Strickland was the last person she had expected to see and she couldn't quite comprehend the fact that he was standing before her . . . in her own home, and looking more handsome than ever.

'How are you, Tilly?' he asked quietly.

'Fine. I'm fine, thank you,' she stuttered.

'Would you mind very much if I accepted your parents' kind invitation?'

'Of course not. You're more than welcome, but please excuse me. I must get on with the potatoes.'

Her fingers were trembling as she picked up the knife and she put it down again in an effort to calm herself. She had been shocked to see David, but to hear his soft voice and to know that he was close by and not a million miles away on some ship was wonderful! She still loved him, she knew that. But how did he feel about her, and how would he react when he knew that she was engaged to be married to Eddie?

Never mind, she told herself, they would be together over Christmas and somehow that felt right. She would enjoy the moment and take what happiness she could from it before he went away again.

The men went off to the local for a drink together, leaving Tilly and her mother to continue with their preparations.

'David looks well,' said Ethel.

'Yes, he does.'

'Nice chap – I like him. I'm pleased we were able to invite him for Christmas. No one should be alone then . . . unless by choice, of course,' she said pointedly.

Tilly ignored the comment, and shortly after went to her room to wrap her presents.

The following morning, the family breakfasted together and exchanged gifts. It was a jolly occasion with much laughter and teasing, just as Christmas should be.

'Jago and I are meeting David in the local before dinner,' Joe said.

It was a Christmas ritual: the men off to the pub, which was open at lunch time only; the women cooking the meal, which was always served at three o'clock to give the men their time together.

Tilly was singing 'For Me and My Gal' softly to herself as she and her mother worked, laying the table, basting the large turkey, making the bread sauce, and watching that the steaming Christmas pudding didn't run out of water in the pan.

Eventually the front door opened. Tilly felt her heart flutter as they walked into the room, laughing together. She couldn't help but see just how well David fitted in with the family. She tried to picture Eddie in his place, but she knew it wouldn't have worked at all.

'Merry Christmas, ladies,' David said, smiling at them both. He held out two bottles of champagne. 'I thought you might like these,' he said to Ethel.

She was all aflutter. 'Champagne? How wonderful. How very posh.'

David opened the first bottle and filled the glasses Jago had brought out of the sideboard. 'I would like to propose a toast,' said David. 'To a happy Christmas – and may all our dreams come true.' He looked straight at Tilly as he spoke.

'May all our dreams come true,' she repeated, meeting his gaze.

The meal was a great success, The turkey was beautifully moist, the vegetables cooked to perfection, the potatoes nicely crisp, and after the Christmas pudding everyone was full to the brim. The conversation at the table had been interesting, with David telling them tales of his voyages: the butcher who had run berserk with a carving knife and had been locked away by the master-at-arms; the passengers and their strange demands. He took them into a different world, which seemed fascinating to the landlubbers.

After the dishes were cleared and taken to the kitchen David insisted on washing up. 'You two ladies have been busy all morning,' he said.

But Tilly said she would help him. 'Neither Jago nor Dad is capable of washing or drying dishes properly,' she told him, 'and you, Mum, you put your feet up.'

To her amusement, David tied one of her mother's aprons round his waist. Seeing her smile he said, 'Well, I don't want to get my trousers wet, do I? We seafarers are very useful in the home, you know.'

'So it would seem,' she said. 'You make sure you get all the grease off the plates.'

'Please, don't insult me.'

They both laughed. Tilly remembered how it used to be between them: there always was a lot of laughter. There wasn't much with Eddie.

'I'm really pleased to see you, David,' she said.

'And I you, Tilly. You haven't been far from my mind since we parted.'

'Really?' She didn't know when she had been so happy. 'I've often thought of you too.'

'I see that you're engaged now. When is the wedding?'

'I'm not at all sure there will be one,' she said quietly.

He turned to look at her. 'What do you mean?'

'I don't really want to be Mrs Eddie Chapman.'

David said nothing more until he had finished washing the dishes and wiping down the sink and the draining board. Then he said, 'Get your coat, Tilly, we're going for a walk. I think we need to talk.'

Joe and Ethel were settled in their comfortable chairs on either side of the stove, and Jago, curled up on the small settee, was already asleep when David and Tilly walked into the room.

'We're going to get some fresh air,' David said, and fetched their coats.

'Don't catch cold,' said Ethel as they left. Turning to her husband, she said, 'I wonder what's going on between those two?'

Joe smiled benignly. 'With a bit of luck, love, they'll be sorting themselves out. If ever I saw a couple that belong together it's those two.'

It was dark now, and there was a chill in the wind. David took Tilly by the arm and marched her along to the nearest small shop, where he pulled her into the doorway, giving them a modicum of shelter.

'Now explain to me why you don't want to be Mrs Chapman,' he demanded.

'Because I'm not in love with Eddie,' she said.

'Then why on earth did you agree to become engaged?'

'He took me by surprise. It was my birthday. I didn't see how I could get out of it.'

'I don't understand you at all sometimes, Tilly. You have such strength of character, but when it comes to Chapman you lose all reason. It doesn't make sense.'

'It's not as simple as that,' she protested.

'Has he got some hold over you?'

Tilly hesitated.

'That's it, isn't it?' He grabbed her by the shoulders and shook her. 'For God's sake tell me.'

'He ran a ringer at Doncaster a few months ago, and I knew because I overheard a telephone conversation about it. I even laid bets for him at the racecourse, which makes me an accessory. Then I stupidly told him I knew what he'd done.'

'No doubt he told you he couldn't let you go with such information.'

'That's about it.'

'Has he threatened you?' he asked angrily.

'No, not at all. I know you don't want to hear this, David, but Eddie loves me in his own way, and he treats me well.'

'And why wouldn't he? But if he really loved you, he'd let you go.'

'What am I going to do?'

'Oh, Tilly, Tilly, why do you always get yourself into so much trouble?'

Tears welled in her eyes and ran slowly down her cheeks. 'I don't mean to.'

Catching hold of her, David gently drew her into his arms. Tilting her chin upwards he gazed into her eyes and said, 'You really are not safe to be let loose, you know that, don't you?'

'I'm not that bad,' she protested, sniffing until he gave her his handkerchief.

'Here, blow into that. Were there ever any inquiries about the race result, from, say, the Jockey Club?'

'No. Not a word.'

'Then he got away with it. Is there a possibility that he will pull another flanker like this, do you know?'

'I asked him to promise me that he wouldn't.'

'And what did he say?'

Wiping her nose, she said, 'He said there shouldn't be any need, as he had made enough money to do up the stables.'

'What stables are we talking about?'

Tilly told him all about the yard and Eddie's grand plans for the future.

'He's an ambitious man,' David remarked. 'I can well see how it would worry him that you were in possession of information that could put paid to it all.'

'I wouldn't do that!' she exclaimed.

'But how could he be sure?' He thought for a moment and then said, 'Look, give me time to think about things. Tomorrow I'll come round and we'll try to sort out this dreadful mess.'

Tilly threw her arms round his neck.

'Oh, thank you, thank you,' she cried. 'I've been worried to death about the future.'

'Well, stop worrying,' he said, and then, 'I've been wanting to do this since first I walked into your house on Christmas Eve.' And he kissed her.

CHAPTER THIRTY-NINE

Eddie Chapman was not enjoying Christmas at all. He had cancelled the booking in the London hotel when Tilly had insisted she would be staying in Southampton with her family. Instead he had booked lunch for himself locally, which was for him a lonely affair, as the other diners were all *en famille*.

On Boxing Day, he drove to the stables in Newmarket, knowing that whatever the day, horses needed care and attention. At least there he would have some company.

Jeremy Frampton was surprised when Eddie drove into the yard. Walking over to the car he said, 'I didn't expect to see you over the holiday. I thought you and Tilly would be enjoying the high life.'

'She wanted to stay at home with her family,' Eddie explained, 'and that wasn't exactly my idea of fun. How's everything?'

'The builders are on holiday, of course, but

they'll be back at work tomorrow. We've finished mucking out and the horses have been fed, so come inside and have a drink. There's a skeleton staff on today and we're having a few beers and cold turkey sandwiches. You'll be more than welcome.'

A table had been set up in one of the barns used to house the hay for the horses. On the table was a barrel of beer and plates of sandwiches. Grooms were perched on bales of hay, chatting, eating and drinking. Larry, the head lad, was downing a fair consumption and getting more raucous with every glass.

Jeremy saw Eddie watching him. 'Yes, he's getting out of hand. I'm going to have to let him go, but I'll wait until after the holiday. I won't spoil his Christmas.'

Larry, whose glass was once again empty, clambered off the hay and walked over to the table. He was about to pour another beer when Eddie went up to him.

'Don't you think you've had enough?'

Through slightly bleary eyes, Larry looked up at him from his diminutive height. 'Hello, Mr Chapman. Merry Christmas.' He moved closer and with a wink said in a low voice, 'Building is going well. Good day's work that was at Doncaster.'

'I would advise you to go to your bed and sleep it off,' Eddie told him coldly.

'But I don't have to take your advice now, do I? After all, we're mates, you, the boss and I.' And filling his glass he returned unsteadily to the others.

Eddie fumed. This could not be allowed to carry on. Larry was now a liability and could really be a danger to his future. A loose tongue was not to be permitted.

He stayed in the barn talking to Jeremy and one or two of the girls employed at the yard until Jeremy brought the gathering to an end.

'Right! That's enough; we have a busy day tomorrow. Off you go. I'll see you in the morning and I want no hangovers!'

Eddie overheard Larry say that he was off for a walk to clear his head and invite another lad to join him.

'Not me,' the other lad said. 'I'm going to get my head down. You carry on.'

Larry set off out of the yard gates and down the country road.

Eddie walked back to the house with Jeremy, and after using his lavatory and having a quick chat said he would be on his way, as he too would have to work tomorrow.

He climbed into his car, started the engine, turned on the headlights and drove away. He was some way from the stables when in the beam from his lights he caught sight of Larry walking unsteadily ahead of him in the dark. Putting his foot on the accelerator, he increased his speed.

Larry half turned as he heard the sound of the engine behind him; then he was hurled into the air as the nearside wing caught him, landing unconscious in the stream running alongside the road.

Eddie drove on, his mouth in a grim line. That should shut the little bleeder up, he thought as he headed for home.

The following morning when Larry didn't show up for work, a furious Jeremy sent one of the lads to find him. But when he returned and said that Larry's bed hadn't been slept in, a search party was sent out to find him.

Jeremy insisted that they ride out at the same time. 'We might as well exercise the horses,' he said, 'then it won't be a complete waste of time!' And he stomped back to his office, cursing under his breath.

It wasn't long before one of the grooms came galloping back into the yard.

'You'd better send for an ambulance, boss. We found Larry badly injured in a ditch.'

'Is he alive?'

'Just about.'

Jeremy put through a call to Eddie and told him

what had happened. 'Did you see him when you left last night?'

'No,' Eddie lied. 'It was pitch black. I didn't see anything on the road. Is he going to pull through?'

'I really don't know. From what the others said, I would say it was doubtful.'

'We must just hope for the best then,' said Eddie, smiling to himself as he put the phone down.

Boxing Day in the Thompson household was a much happier affair. Tilly woke and jumped out of bed, quickly pulled her dressing gown around her and went downstairs to the kitchen, where she raked out the ashes from the blackleaded stove and, filling the coal scuttle, built up the fire.

Her father joined her. 'Morning, love. My word, you're up with the lark!'

She kissed him warmly on the cheek. 'It's a lovely day, isn't it?'

Glancing out of the window at the grey skies, Joe smiled to himself. When you're in love, he thought, every day seems filled with sunshine.

After the breakfast things were cleared away, Tilly helped her mother wash up and tidy round, then went upstairs to dress. David was coming round today! She couldn't wait to see him. The way he had kissed her yesterday told her without

428

the need for words that he still loved her. She was bursting with happiness.

She and Ethel prepared a cold buffet with left-over turkey, a variety of cheeses, pickled onions and bread. Later they would bake potatoes to have with it.

Tilly was on pins waiting for David to arrive. She made a pot of tea, plumped up cushions on the settee, and rearranged the ornaments on the mantelpiece until her father protested.

'For goodness' sake, girl, will you sit down. The lad will be here when he's ready!'

It was around noon when there was the sound of a knock. Before anyone else could move, Tilly was up and heading for the front door. She beamed when she saw David standing there.

'Hello, Tilly,' he said, kissing her on the cheek.

'What's it like out?' asked Joe.

'A bit chilly, but dry, thank goodness. I thought I might take Tilly out for a drink, if that's all right with you?'

'You go ahead,' said Ethel, 'but do come back for something to eat. We're having a cold buffet so it can be any time you like.'

'Thank you. You're very kind,' he said.

After the two of them had left the house, Joe turned to his wife and said, 'I reckon those two are sorted!'

'But she's engaged,' said Ethel.

'Not for much longer, if I haven't got my wires crossed,' Joe said with a satisfied smile. 'Didn't you notice? She wasn't wearing her engagement ring this morning.'

David and Tilly sat in the corner of the lounge bar in a nearby pub, sipping their drinks. He squeezed her hand.

'This is like old times,' he said.

'I've missed them so much,' Tilly confessed.

'Have you really? I mean truly?'

'More than you'll ever know. I've been a complete fool. I didn't mean to hurt you, David. I'm deeply sorry for that.'

'I do believe that you have finally grown up, Tilly Thompson.'

'It took a while,' she said with a wry grin.

'Are you sure that you have worked Eddie Chapman out of your system for good?'

'Oh, yes. He isn't the man I thought he was. I suppose I had him on a pedestal for some time. He swept me off my feet and I wasn't wise enough to see it – or him for what he really is. He isn't a really bad man, but he's ruthlessly ambitious and he won't let anything or anyone get in his way. I no longer want to be part of it.'

'Then we must get you out of it.'

'But how?'

'You have to tell him.' He could see the fear in her eyes and it worried him. 'What do you think he will do when he knows?'

'I don't honestly know.'

'Does it frighten you, Tilly?'

She nodded. 'You see, I'm part of his future plans. Part of the jigsaw. He wouldn't condone a missing piece. He likes things all neat and tidy.'

'Then I shall come with you when you see him.'

'I don't think that's a good idea at all. In fact it would probably make things worse.' She sighed. 'What a mess!'

Putting his arm round her, he said, 'Don't worry about it. You'll see, it will all work out for the best. When will you go to see him?'

'I have a lot to do in the shop tomorrow during the day, so I'll go to the Blue Pelican in the evening – early, before it gets busy.'

'Fine. Come on, let's go home. I'm getting hungry.'

The following evening, Eddie was sitting in his office going through his order forms when there was a knock on the door.

'Come in.' When he saw that it was Tilly, he put down his pen and asked, 'Well, did you have a happy Christmas in the bosom of your family?'

The sarcasm in his voice annoyed her. 'Yes, I had a wonderful time, being with the people I love. You should try it with your own family some time!'

'Oh my, we are touchy today. And what has rattled your cage?'

She faced him, eyes blazing, ready now for the task before her.

'You have, if you must know.' She opened her handbag and took out a small box. 'I am returning your ring, Eddie. I'm sorry, but I don't want to marry you.'

'Don't be ridiculous. You're just mad that I didn't want to be with you and yours over Christmas.'

'It isn't that at all. I don't want to be Mrs Chapman.'

'You don't have a choice, my dear,' he snapped.

'But I do. If you think I will ever give away your secret about Night and Day, rest assured I will not. Why implicate myself? I don't want to go to prison, so you're safe there, but I don't want to be a part of your life any more.'

He got out of his chair and came round the desk to face her. Tilly felt her heart racing with fear and her legs were shaking. What was he going to do now? But she didn't let him see she was afraid.

'You are ready to give up the life I can offer you? Why on earth would you want to do that?'

'Because she's going to marry me!'

They both spun round.

David Strickland walked into the room. 'Tilly is going to marry me, Chapman. That's why she's here today.'

Eddie looked at him. With a smirk, he said, 'Ah, the engineer.' He walked back to his chair behind the desk. 'And when did you show up?'

'Christmas Eve. And I'm going to be around for a while.' There was no doubt of the warning in his voice as he glared at the other man. 'I know all about your day at Doncaster. Tilly told me.'

Chapman's furious expression made Tilly fear the worst. What would happen now?

But David was relentless. 'I wouldn't want Tilly to suffer through your illegal dealings and so I shall remain silent, but you are to leave her alone from now on. You get on with your grandiose plans and let Tilly get on with her life. Without interference!'

Taking a cigar out of a box on his desk, Eddie lit it slowly and with great deliberation. After a moment or two, he smiled and spoke softly.

'One thing about playing poker,' he said, 'is knowing when to fold. It is a lesson I have taken into my life. So, Tilly darling, you are free to do as you wish. I will miss you, of course. My bed will feel very empty.' He glared at David as he said it, but David didn't take the bait. 'Keep the shop,' he added. 'It was a gift, after all.'

'Tilly will be signing it over to you,' David said firmly. 'She will be opening another.'

With a toss of his head, Eddie said, 'Please yourself.'

'I'm sorry,' said Tilly softly.

'So am I, darling.'

'Come along,' said David. Taking her by the arm, he led her out of the room, closing the door behind them.

Tilly all but collapsed against him, her legs giving way for a moment.

'Take a deep breath, Tilly,' he said. 'It's all over. Come along; you need a stiff brandy.'

'Oh, David, I was so pleased to see you.'

'I knew he would be awkward so I waited until you entered the club and then I listened outside his door, knowing I would have to step in at some stage.'

'I do love you,' she said.

'I'm glad to hear it. Now let's get out of here.'

Inside the office, Eddie Chapman was furious. The bloody engineer had won after all. He believed him when he said he would keep the secret of the fixed race: he seemed to be a man of his word. But he would really miss Tilly. He had grown to love her as much as he could love anyone. Still, the stables were now his main priority. He had fixed the head lad, so from now it should be plain sailing.

But, life sometimes conspires against you in unexpected ways, as Eddie was to discover.

CHAPTER FORTY

There was great happiness in the Thompson household when David and Tilly told the family that they were back together and would be getting married in the New Year.

'Bloody hell,' exclaimed Jago, 'you don't waste any time. Off with one and on to the next!' But she knew by the wide grin on his face that he was just teasing.

Joe hugged her and shook David by the hand. 'Welcome to the family, my son.'

Ethel kissed David on the cheek. 'I couldn't be more pleased.' And quietly to her daughter she said, 'You made the right choice this time. Be happy. He's a good man – look after him.'

Hugging Ethel, Tilly said, 'Oh, I will, I promise.'

'What will happen to the shop?' asked Jago, with his usual eye to business.

'Tilly will return the keys to Chapman,' said David, 'and we will be looking for premises for

her to open in her own name. It will give her something to do whilst I'm at sea.'

'Keep her out of trouble, you mean!' Jago said,
laughing heartily.

'That's all behind me now,' Tilly protested. 'I've
grown up.'

'About bloody time too,' he said, and then he
ducked as she threw a cushion at him.

The following morning, Tilly informed her
manageress and assistant of the forthcoming
changes. 'I would like you both to come with me
when I move,' she told them. Taking Grace aside
she said, 'I'll want time to spend with David when
he's home, and I can do that knowing you're here.'

'Thank you, Miss Thompson,' she said. 'I'm
sure that all your clients will follow you, with your
flair for fashion.'

'I just hope we can find the right place quickly,'
said Tilly. 'I want to get settled as soon as possible.'

David was already trawling the estate agents
with that in mind. As luck would have it, a suitable shop was soon to become vacant in East Street.
He took Tilly to see it and they both agreed it was
ideal.

'I need to pay Eddie back the money he invested
in the stock,' she told him.

'Well, sort it out as soon as possible and tell me

how much it is,' he said. 'We don't want to give him any excuse to call on you.'

Putting her arms round the man she loved, she said, 'I really don't deserve this after the way I treated you.'

'Don't give it another thought,' he said, his mouth crinkling at the corners. 'I'll find a way for you to pay me back.'

Kissing him, Tilly said, 'Oh, I do like the sound of that.'

Two weeks had passed since Larry Jackson had been admitted to hospital. His injuries had been severe. His right leg was broken, as were some of his ribs; his right shoulder was dislocated and his pelvis was fractured. The doctor told him he was lucky to be alive.

Now, although in great pain, with help he was able to sit up in bed. He hadn't been well enough to answer questions about his accident from the police, who had been informed, but they said they would return when he felt up to doing so.

This morning, after the nurse had given him his pills, he asked her to make a call to the Jockey Club on his behalf and ask for a representative to visit him in hospital, as soon as it could be arranged.

* * *

Ten days later, the Berkshire constabulary called at the stable where Flying Flynn was still housed, took photographs of the horse and questioned the owner and his staff. At the same time, police arrived at Jeremy Frampton's yard and took the trainer to the police station for questioning.

In Southampton, Detective Inspector John Ridgeway, liaising with the Berkshire police, called at the Blue Pelican club.

Eddie Chapman looked at the police officer in surprise when he was shown into his office, accompanied by his sergeant.

'Good morning, Inspector. What can I do for you?'

'I am arresting you on a charge of the attempted murder of Larry Jackson. Anything you say may be taken down and used in evidence against you.'

Chapman paled. 'What are you talking about?'

'Please, sir, come with us to the station. We would like to do this quietly and without fuss.'

Eddie saw the handcuffs in the sergeant's hands. 'Is that really necessary?' he asked. 'I'll come with you; I don't intend to do anything foolish. It's not my style.'

Nodding to the sergeant, Inspector Ridgeway said, 'Take him away.'

Putting on his jacket, Eddie Chapman looked round his office, wondering when, if ever, he would see it again. He had been convinced that Larry had died in hospital, but it seemed he had been mistaken.

Over the following weeks, the local and national papers were full of the case against Eddie Chapman and his partner, Jeremy Frampton. Larry Jackson had split on them both, giving the police all the details about the ringer they had run at Doncaster. He had told them where to find the replacement horse and how it had all been done to make a fortune for them all. But the most damning thing, as far as Chapman was concerned, was the fact that just before he was hit Larry had seen the colour of the car and guessed the identity of the driver.

The police in Southampton had traced the garage where Eddie had taken his car to have the damaged wing repaired.

'There *was* blood on it,' the mechanic told the police, 'but Mr Chapman told me he had hit a forest pony, so I didn't give it another thought.'

Reading the account of the case in the paper, Tilly was horrified to read about the charge of attempted murder, and fully expected the police to arrive at her house and arrest her. She couldn't tell her family of her involvement, but David knew and tried to calm her down.

'You may not be questioned at all,' he said. 'After all, you had no part in the actual operation.'

'But I laid some bets on the course, knowing what was happening!'

'Look, darling, as you well know, I have no time at all for Chapman, but I really doubt that he will implicate you.'

'Why would you think that?'

'He has his own code of conduct. Ambitious he might be, but the man isn't spiteful. He really was fond of you; what good would it do to bring you into it? After all, he's charged with attempted murder too. He wouldn't want you involved.'

'I can't believe he would deliberately run that man down. Eddie never showed that side of his character to me. I'm deeply shocked by it.'

'I can see how he would be driven to such measures. He was on his way to being someone in the racing world, which according to you he longed for. This man could have ruined it for him. He would do anything to stop him.'

'You never did trust him, did you?'

Shaking his head, David said, 'No. I always felt there was a dark side to his character. Sadly, I was right.'

The months that followed proved David's words to be true. Eddie Chapman managed to get a letter to

Tilly telling her that he wouldn't implicate her in any way. He thanked her for the happiness she had given him during their time together and – to her surprise – wished her luck with 'the engineer'. He asked her to try to not think too badly of him, but to remember, as he would, the good times they had spent together.

Although it was a relief to know that she was safe from the law, Tilly felt sad that a man who was basically a good person could have been so blinded by ambition that he committed such a terrible crime as to run someone down with his car. Eddie could have been a success without going beyond the law. If only he hadn't run that race, then none of this would have happened. It seemed such a pity. At least Larry Jackson would recover, and for that she was grateful.

It would be several months before Chapman and Frampton's case would be heard, and during that time normal life continued.

Tilly was now settled in her new gown shop, Madam Jolie, and her clients had faithfully followed her. There had been more talk about Tilly's past relationship with Eddie Chapman now that everyone knew he was awaiting trial, but as she was now engaged to her engineer her reputation was restored and the business thrived. David was back at sea, due to cross the Atlantic at regular intervals until his leave in August, when the wedding would take place.

Eventually the trial date was set. David was away at the time and Tilly decided to go to the Winchester Assizes on the opening day. Sitting in the public gallery, she saw Eddie brought up from the cells, and her heart ached for him, despite the terrible crime he had committed.

The two barristers made their opening speeches, laying out their cases, and the case was held over until the morning.

Driven by some unknown force, Tilly asked a solicitor if she could see Eddie, and was asked to wait.

Eventually she was led into a bare room containing a single table with a chair on either side. Five minutes later, she heard footsteps. Eddie, immaculately dressed as always, was led into the room by a uniformed warder, who stood back against the wall.

'What on earth are you doing here, Tilly?' Eddie said.

'I wanted to see you.'

Sitting down opposite her, he said, 'You shouldn't have come.' He looked pale and drawn and his usual spirit was lacking.

'Are you all right?'

He managed a smile. 'As well as can be expected under the circumstances, I suppose.'

'How could you do such a thing?'

His eyes clouded. 'It was a moment of madness. I just couldn't let one person ruin all my plans. But at least he's alive. I'm grateful for that.'

'I truly am sorry to see you here,' she said.

He saw the new engagement ring on her finger and taking her hand in his asked, 'Are you happy, darling? Is your engineer good to you?'

'Yes to both,' she said, but her heart was sad as she looked at him. She had no regrets about leaving him, but Eddie Chapman had taught her a lot and she was still fond of him.

'You've got two minutes,' said the officer.

'Tilly, darling, I don't want you to come here again. I want you to forget about me and get on with your life.'

'I'll never forget you,' she said, trying to blink away the tears.

'Time to go!'

Rising to his feet, Eddie leaned across the table and kissed Tilly softly on the lips. 'Have a good life, darling.' And he turned and went out through the door.

Walking back to the station, Tilly had to stop. Tears blinded her and she sat on a street bench and sobbed. It all seemed such a terrible waste.

444

She would do as Eddie asked and stay away. She couldn't face the court again, seeing him standing in the dock. It would break her heart.

When David docked, she told him of her visit to Winchester and the conversation she had had with Eddie Chapman. It upset her all over again. But David was very understanding.

'You were so young and vulnerable when you met him,' he said, 'and he had a profound effect on your life. But he made his choice and you made yours. He's right, you must get on with your life. Look to the future and leave the past behind.' Holding her close, he said, 'We will be deliriously happy and grow old and toothless together, with one leg apiece and surrounded by grandchildren.' And he kissed her gently, wiping away her tears.

It was a glorious August day for the wedding of Tilly and David. At St Michael's church, the groom, resplendent in his uniform, stood waiting for his bride to arrive. David's parents had come down from Liverpool and Tilly's two sisters and their families were also there. The old friends from earlier times all sat in their pews, waiting eagerly.

The organ rang out the opening bars of the Wedding March as the bride, dressed in ivory lace and a short matching veil held in place by a band of small rosebuds, with tea-coloured roses in her bouquet, walked down the aisle, proudly escorted by her father and followed by Beth in pale lemon, as bridesmaid.

As David stepped forward and took her hand, he whispered, 'You look beautiful.'

'And you look very handsome,' she replied, her eyes bright with happiness.

After the ceremony, the wedding party stood outside the church to have their photographs taken. There was much laughter and joshing as they were placed by the photographer, who was having a difficult time keeping order among such hilarity. But eventually it was over.

Joe, at the reins of his beloved Clarence, who was bedecked with gleaming horse brasses and ribbons, took them around the corner on a small brewer's dray to the Dolphin hotel, where the reception was being held.

After the splendid meal, David rose to his feet and tapped on his glass to get the attention of the guests.

'Ladies and gentlemen, friends and relations, thank you so much for being here today to share with me the luckiest day of my life. I am blessed to be able to call this beautiful creature beside me my wife. As many of my colleagues here today will testify, a seaman's life can be lonely, but the knowledge that when the ship docks he has a happy haven to go to makes it all worthwhile. My mother, who is here today, fully understands what I am saying. She and my father over there have survived such a marriage for twenty-eight years.'

There was a round of applause.

'Thank you, Joe and Ethel, my new in-laws, for having such a great family of which I am proud now to be a member. I would like you all to raise your glasses and join me in a toast to – love and marriage.'

They all rose from their seats and in unison said, 'To love and marriage.'

After the best man's speech, the reading of the telegrams and cards and the cutting of the cake, the band started to play and the bride and groom took to the floor.

'Hello, Mrs Strickland,' David said softly, gazing at his new bride with adoring eyes.

'Hello, my dearest husband. Oh, David, this has been such a wonderful day. And I'm so happy.'

'Of course you are. I'm a great catch,' he teased.

And they both started laughing. Tilly knew that whatever was ahead of them there would always be laughter in their life, and that would get them through the hard times as well as the good.

Whilst they were away, the long trial of Eddie Chapman ended. He was sent down for ten years for attempted murder and was to serve a further four for fraud. Jeremy Frampton was to serve five years and have his trainer's licence revoked

The Ace of Clubs was sold, as was the Blue Pelican club. The dreams and ambitions of Eddie Chapman lay in ruins, destroyed by a driving ambition to succeed – whatever the price.

But on honeymoon in the West Country, two people, very much in love, were starting out in life as a married couple. Their only ambition was to remain together, as the marriage service said, 'until death us do part'.

Just
for You

Just
for you

Just for You

Life on an Ocean Liner...
An exclusive interview with June Tate

Dancing Through the Jazz Age...
Songs and dances that moved a nation

Bright Young Things...
Fashion and flappers

A Snapshot of the World...
The 1920s

Just for You

June Tate spent several years working as a hair-dresser on the cruise ships the *Queen Mary* and the *Mauretania*, where she met many Hollywood film stars and VIPs. In this exclusive interview, June talks about this fascinating period of her life . . .

Just for You

An exclusive interview with June Tate

1) In your novel, TALK OF THE TOWN, your main character, Tilly Thompson, longs to travel the globe on an ocean liner. What made you decide to work on a cruise ship?

I desperately wanted to leave home and work in a different environment and, coming from a seafaring family with a love of travel, the Cunard Company seemed to be the answer. I applied for an interview and was extremely lucky, as I sailed on the *Queen Mary* two weeks later.

2) What was life like aboard the Queen Mary *and the* Mauretania?

Being a member of the crew, life was very restricted. There were rules laid down by the company. No fraternising with the passengers or crew, as dismissal was the price you paid. We did have parties though where these rules were broken, as far as other crew members were concerned. You just didn't get caught!

3) Where did you travel to and were you able to spend time exploring any exciting destinations on your days off?

Working on the *Queen Mary* took me to New York, which is a fascinating city where the shopping was wonderful! The *Mauretania* used to leave Southampton in December, returning in May, with New York as its home port. From there we would do several two-week cruises around the West Indies and a three-week cruise around the Mediterranean.

The hairdressers took it in turn to be on or off duty so were able to go ashore for a few hours and explore these fascinating places. So I have walked through the Acropolis in Athens, ridden a camel to the pyramids at Giza, seen the Sphinx, washed my hands in the river Jordan, been to the Mount of Olives and bathed on the golden sands of Jamaica and Barbados, and drunk rum punch in St Thomas in the Virgin Islands. These are just a few of the wonderful places I have visited during my time at sea.

4) Did you have regular customers visiting your hair salon on board the cruise ships, or was it a constant influx of new faces?

With each cruise we had an influx of new passengers. American women can be very demanding and would cause a scene at the drop of a hat. It could be very tiring mentally, as well as physically.

5) You met a lot of famous people whilst working on the ships. Who were you most excited about meeting?

There were many famous movie stars regularly travelling on the *Queen Mary*. Rosalind Russell was one. She swept into the beauty parlour with great presence. She was charming, as was Joan Fontaine, who was small and delicate with long blonde hair. Michael Wilding would pop into the beauty parlour looking for his wife, and I passed Judy Garland in the alleyway with her daughter Liza. Jeff Chandler rang the beauty parlour to speak to me as I had asked for a signed picture and I gave manicures to Zachary Scott and the then Maharaja of Baroda.

But the most exciting person I met was in a famous nightclub in New York called the Latin Quarter. There I was introduced to Errol Flynn, whose picture had adorned my bedroom walls. He held my hand for five minutes whilst he talked to me. I couldn't remember a word! But I don't think I ever really recovered from this!

6) What is your fondest memory of working on these ships?

I have many fond memories of those days: the Manhattan skyline as we sailed past the Statue of Liberty; walking around the decks at night staring at the stars; watching a storm at sea – but the sound from the *Queen Mary's* funnels when we were sailing used to give me goose bumps.

7) You must have met so many interesting people on the cruise ships and, as a hairdresser, heard many colourful stories. Have these inspired your writing?

A hairdresser gets to hear some very strange and interesting stories whilst the client is in the chair and I must confess to using some of these in my writing, under different names of course!

Just for You

Dancing Through the Jazz Age . . .

During the 1920s, Ragtime music developed into Jazz and young people in Britain rushed to dance halls and Jazz clubs as exciting new dances inflamed the hearts and minds of those only too ready for change. Afternoon tea dances were popular and, at night, dance palaces and nightclubs were the place to be. The crystal radio and the gramophone brought music from America to the ears and feet of the young flappers. They listened to Eddie Cantor and Blues singer Ruth Etting belt out her 'Ten Cents a Dance', which told the sad story of a nightclub girl. The music of George Gershwin and Irving Berlin also became very popular.

Meanwhile, in New York, musician Paul White-man was making a name for himself. His recording of 'Say it with Music' was a hit for five weeks with tremendous sales. It became so familiar that Britain's own Henry Hall used it as a signature tune. In the West End, Jack Buchanan was a popular star of Ivor Novello's musicals. He was suave and sophisticated, singing the popular 'And Her Mother Came Too'.

With this music came the famous dances of the Twenties. Perhaps the most popular of all was the Charleston, with origins in South Carolina and African-American styles. The Bunny Hop, the Black Bottom, the Rumba, the Samba and the Conga also swept through the dancehalls and music clubs around the country.

While America suffered prohibition, cocktail hour became popular in Britain with the young in high society, and nightclubs attracted the carefree and wealthy. Drinking cocktails was generally thought of as degenerate by the masses, but it didn't stop those bright young things in the West End. They dressed in their finery and met with friends to drink and dance the night away.

Just for You

Bright Young Things . . .

The Great War had placed women on the work front, taking jobs previously only held by men. It awakened a spirit of independence, initially frowned upon by a society that thought a woman's place was in the home. Women's fashion took a backseat during this time as the necessity of uniform and functional clothes took prominence. The Roaring Twenties, however, saw massive social and political change for women in Britain. Arguably the most pivotal of which was the vote for women, championed tirelessly by Emily Pankhurst and the Suffragette movement.

Until the Twenties high fashion had been the prerogative of the rich women of society, but the flappers changed all that. Rebelling against the pre-war rules of society, these hedonistic young girls abandoned the heavy, long, corseted dresses of the Victorian era in favour of a radical loose-fitting shift dress. This was cheaper to produce and easy to make with readily available and simple dress patterns. A fashionable flapper had short hair, either cut into a bob or the even shorter Eton Crop. It was the perfect hairstyle for the popular cloche hat, which was all the rage at the time. Some women also began to incorporate trousers into their wardrobe; American movie stars set the trend with wide-leg trousers, worn with smart jackets. Coats in the 1920s were often a wrap-around style, many with fur-trimmed shawl collars. The coat fastening was usually a huge button or big tab. T-bar shoes with buckles and bows also featured prominently at this time. This mannish style, instigated by designer Coco Chanel, saw chests flattened, waists disappearing and shoulders broadened.

Women often accessorised their outfits with long necklaces. Jet beads were in demand, as were feathers in the hair and bands of ribbon around the forehead. For those outgoing young women who dared to smoke in public, long cigarette holders were a fashion must-have.

Just for You

A Snapshot of the World . . . the 1920s

1920

- First commercial broadcast aired on radio
- Oxford University opens its degrees to women for the first time
- The British Broadcasting Corporation (BBC) is founded

1921

- Lie detector invented
- Insulin discovered
- The first edition of *Good Housekeeping* appears
- *Reader's Digest* published

1923

- The Duke of York and Lady Elizabeth Bowes-Lyon marry. The couple would have two children, one of whom, Elizabeth, would later

become Queen
- Wembley Stadium in London is built

1924
- First Olympic winter games
- The first Labour government comes into power in Britain

1925
- John Logie Baird invents the first working mechanical television
- Virginia Woolf's *Mrs Dalloway* is published
- F. Scott Fitzgerald publishes *The Great Gatsby*

1926
- English crime writer Dame Agatha Christie disappears (later located at a hotel)
- Elizabeth Windsor (later to become Queen Elizabeth II) is born
- The style guru, Coco Chanel, introduces her 'little black dress'
- Nineteen-year-old Gertrude Ederle swims the English Channel. Her time of 14 hours 31 minutes beats the record previously set by a man

1927
- Warner Brothers produces the first part-talkie, *The Jazz Singer*

1928

- The first all-talking movie, *Lights of New York*, comes out
- The Equal Franchise Act is passed, giving women equal voting rights with men; all women over the age of 21 can now vote in elections
- Amelia Earhart is the first woman to fly across the Atlantic as a passenger and log keeper
- Penicillin discovered

1929

- Many young women vote for the first time on 30 May. This has since been referred to as the Flapper Election

Just for You

Don't miss . . .

June Tate's other passionate and popular sagas.

Riches Of The Heart tells the heartrending story of Lily Pickford, cruelly abandoned by her father and forced into a life of vice on the streets of Southampton.

No One Promised Me Tomorrow will move you to tears as terrible circumstances separate a single mother from her beloved daughter.

For The Love Of A Soldier is a powerful and uplifting saga of a love that transcends the social boundaries of the 1940s.

Better Days evokes the glamour of the 1950s and New York. But when Gemma Barrett attracts a dangerous man, her world is turned upside down.

Nothing Is Forever will enthral you as Flora Ferguson must fight for her happiness when all she holds dear is at stake.

For Love Or Money is the story of talented young singer Connie Ryan, who must make a choice between fame and fortune, or lasting love.

Every Time You Say Goodbye shows a swinging Southampton in 1943, despite the war. But fun-loving Kitty Freeman must be careful what she wishes for . . .

To Be A Lady tells the gripping tale of Bryony Travis' dream of becoming part of high society to escape her criminal background.

When Somebody Loves You shows that people are not always what they seem, as Elsa Carter is drawn into a seedy underworld by a charming man.

To Be A Lady

June Tate

Big Dan Travis – second-hand car-dealer and first-rate gangster – has always tried to give his daughter Bryony everything: love and affection, a beautiful home in Southampton, a top-notch private education. Yet he can't give her what she really longs for – to be a lady.

Desperate to be a part of 1950s high society, Bryony spends hours poring over *Tatler* magazine, dreaming of ways to escape her father's shady world and join the sophisticated set. When she meets James Hargreaves, the handsome son of a wealthy barrister, Bryony is given the opportunity she's been yearning for and suddenly she's having the time of her life, dining at the Savoy and attending polo matches at Cowdray Park. But she's about to learn the aristocracy and her father's dangerous gangland friends aren't as different as she'd imagined . . .

Praise for June Tate's passionate and popular sagas:

'A page-turner for all saga lovers' Katie Fforde

'Her books are always guaranteed to touch the hearts of her readers' *Lancashire Evening Post*

'Excellent and gripping' *Sussex Life*

'Her debut book caused a stir among Cookson and Cox devotees, and they'll love this' *Peterborough Evening Telegraph*

978 0 7553 2111 7

headline

When Somebody Loves You

June Tate

It's 1936 and every morning Kingsland Market in Southampton is bustling with shoppers. Elsa Carter, a vivacious young woman, takes pride in her colourful fruit and veg stall and enjoys the friendly banter with the other traders – except for slippery Clive Forbes.

Oozing with charm, Clive is an expert salesman, but Elsa senses there's a darker side to him. Thank goodness she knows her fiancé Peter, a cub reporter on a local rag, is a man she can trust. When Peter is sent away to report on a smuggling ring, Elsa meets Jean-Paul, a devastatingly handsome Frenchman who's selling antiques through Clive's stall. Elsa suspects Jean-Paul's business with Clive may not be strictly above-board, but she finds herself drawn to him – and, to her horror, straight into the path of danger . . .

Praise for June Tate's passionate and popular sagas:

'A page-turner for all saga lovers' Katie Fforde

'Excellent and gripping' *Sussex Life*

'High hopes and heartache share top billing in this compulsive read' *Northern Echo*

978 0 7553 2966 3

headline

A Long Way Home

Victor Pemberton

'Can we come home yet, Mum?'

It's 1939 when Hannah and Louie Adams wave a tearful goodbye to their mother in North London and leave for the safety of the countryside. All too soon, however, the evacuees discover that life with their new guardians will be far from idyllic. When the homesick Louie is sent to another family, Hannah is devastated. And even her blossoming friendship with local lad Sam Beedle can't make up for the cruelty she suffers behind closed doors.

Hannah decides there is only one way out – she must walk back to her mother in Blitz-torn Islington. Thirty-six hours later, cold, weary and frightened, she arrives home to a shocking sight. Now Hannah must fight not only to survive the war, but also to stop a dangerous secret from destroying her family . . .

Praise for Victor Pemberton's hugely popular novels:

'History with a heart on its sleeve' *Northern Echo*

'Evokes nostalgic memories for those who knew pre-war London' *Historical Novels Review*

'A vivid story of a community surviving some of the darkest days in our history' *Bolton Evening News*

978 0 7553 3456 8

headline

When the Boys Come Home

Pamela Evans

As German bombs wreak havoc on West London, for Morgan's Dairy it's business as usual. But when owner Dai Morgan is killed in an air raid, his daughter Megan is determined to continue in her father's footsteps and she braves the streets to deliver the milk by horse and cart.

Megan finds comfort in the knowledge that her twin girls are tucked away in a Welsh village, but she worries about her husband, Will, abroad with his platoon. And when Will's best friend, Doug Reynolds, returns, wounded and disfigured, she doesn't hesitate to take the poor man in.

However, Doug is not the man she thinks he is. And when the boys come home, Megan has battle scars she can't allow Will to see . . .

Praise for Pamela Evans' much-loved sagas:

'An unforgettable tale of life during the war' *Our Time*

'A richly warm and human story of ordinary people doing their best to surrive as the Blitz ravages London' *Peterborough Evening Telegraph*

'This book touched me very, very much. It's lovely' *North Wales Chronicle*

978 0 7553 3057 7

headline